Maggy's Child

Maggy's Child

KAREN ROBARDS

Delacorte Press

Published by
Delacorte Press
Bantam Doubleday Dell Publishing Group, Inc.
1540 Broadway
New York, New York 10036

ISBN 0-385-31205-9

Manufactured in the United States of America
Published simultaneously in Canada

This book is dedicated to:

My newest nephew, Stuart Blake;
the three men in my life—
Doug, Peter and Chris; and Saint Jude

"*R*emember *Tia* Gloria saying that a body's sins always come home to roost? She was right: here I am."

The voice in her ear was husky, amused—and devastatingly familiar. For an instant it seemed to Maggy Forrest that the world stopped spinning on its axis. The solid oak of the bar against which she leaned, the infectious twang of live country music, the dark, smoky atmosphere of the nightclub itself all seemed to disappear.

Nothing was left in the whole world but Nick's voice in her ear.

One hand clenched around the cool brass bar rail as she turned slowly to face him. There was no mistake: Her mind was not playing tricks on her. On an instinctive level she had known it even before she turned around, before her conscious mind registered the thick crop of rough black curls and the broad-shouldered football player's physique.

"Nick."

He was as tall as she remembered, and as handsome, too. Sinfully handsome, she had always thought, though with his tough pugilist's face he shouldn't have been. His features were too rawly aggressive, his jaw and cheekbones too broad, his lips too thin for true masculine beauty. His nose still listed slightly to the left, the victim of one too many street fights in his teenage years. Above the crooked nose, his hazel-green eyes gleamed down at her. Heavy-lidded and usually seeming almost sleepy, they were the key to the devastating effect he had on the opposite sex, she had decided long ago. Nick had always looked as though he knew everything there was to know about women, and once Maggy had been no more immune than any other member of her gender to *that*.

"Hello, Magdalena."

Even the smile was unchanged, sexy and wicked and tender all at the same time. She'd once been the biggest fool in the world for that smile.

Ah, Nick. Twelve years seemed to vanish as she stared up at him. She forgot that he was thirty-two now and she herself was almost thirty as a rush of memories swamped her: Nick showing up with a bag of groceries when there was nothing left to eat in the tiny apartment she had shared with her father; Nick helping to drag her drunken father home when, time after time, he passed out on the street; Nick siphoning gas from a stranger's car so that she could drive to work in the old wreck he had managed to get running for her when she turned sixteen; Nick waiting up for her when she sneaked out at night, warning off the importunate males who were always sniffing around her. Nick always protecting her. He had been the one solid thing in her world as she had grown up. She had always, always, loved Nick best.

Nick. At the realization that it really was he standing there before her, pure involuntary joy shone out of Maggy's eyes and curved her lips into a smile. Then the reality of the situation hit her, and with it came an icy wave of horror: Nick was back. Her arms, which had lifted instinctively to hug him, dropped. Her smile wavered, then firmed again. But in its new incarnation it wasn't the same smile.

He had never in his life missed a trick, and he didn't now.

"Not glad to see me?" His smile widened, and took on a cat-with-a-mouse quality. "Why, Magdalena! You're hurting my feelings."

"Of course I'm glad to see you. It's been—ages." It was her social voice, the one that had been drummed into her by a vocal coach in the months after she married Lyle, and it made his eyes narrow.

"Twelve years. And to think you've managed to stay married to Lyle Forrest all that time. Wifey number three bats a home run! I hear you gave him a son."

Oh, God. Maggy felt as if a huge hand had closed around her chest, crushing it, keeping her from drawing air into her lungs. Grimly, she battled the sensation.

"We have a son, yes."

"I saw him."

"You *saw* him?" Maggy couldn't have felt more shocked if he had hit her over the head with a baseball bat.

"This afternoon. At Windermere. I came calling, but you weren't home."

She'd been at the hairdresser's. The hand crushing her chest tightened its grip as she thought of Nick at Windermere without her. With David—and maybe even Lyle.

"You came calling?" It was ludicrous, the way she kept parroting everything he said, but she couldn't seem to help it. She knew she was gaping at him, but she couldn't seem to help that either. She'd always known, somewhere deep in the recesses of her mind, that she would see Nick again. But she wasn't ready. Not now, not yet! He had caught her totally by surprise. Her defenses weren't in place.

"You wouldn't expect me to be in Louisville and not come calling, now would you?" His eyes mocked her. "With us being such old friends and all? The boy—David, is it?—looks just like you. You've done old Lyle proud."

"Yes. Yes, I'm—we're both, Lyle and I—we are very proud of David." Maternal affection warmed her for an instant as she thought of her eleven-year-old son. Like her, he was tall and slender, fine-boned, auburn-haired, chocolate-eyed, with dark winged brows and a wide, mobile mouth that at the moment sported a set of nearly invisible braces, about which he was wildly self-conscious. In tennis whites or golf clothes, he looked so absurdly patrician that it was hard to believe that he had sprung from her own far from patrician loins.

Of course, Lyle claimed all the credit for the way David had turned out.

"You've done well for yourself, Magdalena. I'll give you that." Nick's eyes ran over her. Maggy bethought herself of the nine-hundred-dollar black suede jeans she was wearing, of the real alligator belt and boots, of the ivory silk shirt, of the six-carat diamond on her finger, of the solid gold watch clasped around her wrist. The ensemble was deceptively simple to look at, but even without the jewelry it had cost more than she had once made in a year. When she'd been Magdalena Garcia. Before she'd married Lyle.

Of course, Nick had no way of knowing how expensive her clothes were, though he could hardly miss the ring, which sparkled with brilliant pinpoints of light even in the semidarkness. Maggy would have felt guilty at being caught by Nick with such material excess had the panic that now filled her left any room for a secondary emotion.

"What are you doing here?" That was the question. Maggy's hands clenched and her mouth went dry as she waited for the answer.

Nick smiled that devastating smile at her. "Guess."

Maggy's gaze locked with his, and her breathing stopped. The possibilities were endless—and endlessly terrifying.

"There you are. We've been looking everywhere." The light, sweet tones belonged to Lyle's niece, Sarah Bates, who, with her best pal, Buffy McDermott, was pushing through the crowd of people to join Maggy at the bar. Maggy glanced at her friends with a mixture of relief and fear. On the whole she was glad to have her tête-à-tête with Nick interrupted—but what would Sarah and Buffy make of Nick? What would Nick say? Surely nothing personal, now that they were not alone.

Sarah, at twenty-seven, was two years younger than Maggy, though at the moment she appeared older despite the youthfully styled fringed-denim vest and skirt she wore. She was in the midst of an ugly divorce. As a consequence she was both painfully thin and flashily red-haired, neither of which became her. It was her almost desperate need to seek out amusement that had brought the three of them to this little-known country-western bar on the Indiana side of the riverfront.

"Ooh, nice!" Buffy drawled the words as she wedged in beside Sarah and turned to look Nick up and down. Her red-lipsticked mouth pouted provocatively as she glanced from Nick to Maggy and back. "Though I gotta tell ya, handsome, you're wasting your time with Maggy here. She's an old married lady. But I'm available."

"I'll keep that in mind." Nick smiled at Buffy, a very different smile from the one he had bestowed on Maggy. This was a practiced, thousand-kilowatt smile that had once left girls gasping in its aftermath. Maggy had forgotten the effect of that smile on unwary recipients, but watching Buffy's bedazzled response brought the memories rushing back. But then, she hadn't really forgotten. She had purposefully banished Nick and everything about him from her mind.

That was the only way she had managed to survive.

"I'm Buffy McDermott," Buffy said, holding out a slender, perfectly manicured hand with bright red nails. "And you're new in town." Slim and attractive with paper-white skin, chin-length black hair, and small features accentuated by skillfully applied makeup, Buffy was used to being admired by men. Tonight, in a red silk camisole beneath a black leather motorcycle jacket, a black leather mini, and heels, she was dressed to thrill.

Nick took her hand, laughed, and shook his head. "I'm Nick King. And I'm a Louisvillian born and bred. I've just been gone for a while."

"Are you any relation to the Kings who used to live out in Mockingbird Valley?"

As Buffy spoke, Nick released her hand. Without ever taking her eyes from Nick's, Buffy lifted her just-freed fingers to caress the soft white skin just above the neckline of her camisole. Maggy would have had to admire Buffy's technique—if the woman hadn't been aiming her efforts at Nick. As it was, she could only clench her teeth and remind herself that Nick was no longer hers.

"Nope. I grew up in Portland. In the projects."

"Oh." Buffy was momentarily taken aback, and her hand fell to her side. Portland was the worst section of Louisville. It was a dirt-poor, volatile mix of blacks and whites, and nobody with any pretensions to gentility would admit to growing up there. An involuntary half smile curved Maggy's lips. How like Nick to tell the truth and shame the Devil!

"Then you must be a self-made man. How exciting!" Buffy made a gallant comeback after a swift, futile glance that sought to appraise the quality of Nick's clothes. He was wearing jeans and an olive-green crew-neck sweater under a brown leather bomber jacket. Typical bar-hopping garb that gave no indication as to the net worth of the wearer. Buffy clearly chose to be optimistic.

"Isn't it?" His slow smile was calculated to set Buffy aflame, and as far as Maggy could tell, it succeeded. Buffy positively oozed sexuality in response. Maggy's teeth clenched tighter.

"Mr. King, Mr. Casey just walked through the back door." A nervous-sounding middle-aged man in a dark suit came up behind Nick and touched him on the shoulder. "He's in the manager's office. I'm sorry to interrupt, but I thought you'd want to know."

"You're right, Craig. I do want to know. Ladies, if you'll excuse me." His eyes had grown hard, but he smiled at Buffy and Sarah before his gaze collided with Maggy's.

"Magdalena. Stick around. I'll be back."

Before Maggy could decide whether that was a threat or a promise, Nick turned, and, following in the smaller man's wake, made his way through the crowd toward a door at the very back of the room. Unable to take her eyes off his broad back, Maggy found herself fighting a wave of dizziness. Glancing almost blindly around, she discovered Sarah's and Buffy's eyes fixed on her. She knew it was essential that she snap out of it, that she present a normal appearance to her companions. But such poise was, at the moment, beyond her.

The door closed behind Nick, shutting him out of her sight. Awareness of the world around her returned with a jolt. The sound of laughter and the clink of glasses, the growl of a male voice singing ". . . call someone who cares . . ." over a throbbing guitar, the smell of cigarette smoke and the warm crush of bodies packed in around her assaulted Maggy without warning. Faded into nothingness by Nick's presence, they burst upon her consciousness now that he was gone, and she felt as if she were drowning beneath the onslaught.

"Magdalena?" asked Sarah quizzically.

"Who *is* he?" Buffy breathed.

"Nobody, really. I used to know him a long time ago, before I married Lyle." Maggy called on every inner reserve of strength she possessed to present a picture of nonchalance. What she wanted more than anything else in the world at that moment was to turn tail and run as fast as she could. But the surest way to draw attention to herself and Nick was to let her companions see how shaken she was by their encounter.

"And you still married Lyle?" Buffy snickered, clapped a hand over her mouth, and rolled her eyes in exaggerated apology without looking the least bit repentant. Her hand dropped away from her mouth, and she added with a sly grin, "Of course, even I can see that all that money does great things for Lyle's sex appeal."

"Buffy! That's not nice," Sarah chided with a quick glance at Maggy.

"I know it. Lucky for me both you and Maggy already know I'm not a nice person." Buffy glanced at Maggy's still-white face. "I'm sorry, Maggy. I didn't mean anything, you know."

"I know." Buffy's real consternation penetrated the cold shock that held Maggy in thrall, and she managed a smile. "It's okay. I'm not offended."

"He looks like a thug. A divinely sexy thug. Just looking at him was enough to give me the shivers." Reassured, Buffy returned to the subject of Nick with a vengeance. She hitched herself up on the bar stool behind her, crossing her slim legs and leaning avidly toward Maggy. "So tell me all about him. Did he really grow up in the projects?"

The words *so did I* sprang of their own volition to Maggy's lips, but fortunately a distraction kept them from ever being uttered.

With a nerve-jangling crash of chords the band left the tiny stage, and an announcer jumped up to grab the microphone.

"Ladies and gentlemen, or whatever y'all want to call yourselves, this here is amateur night at the Little Brown Cow. Any of you gals out there in the audience, this is your chance to strut your stuff and earn a little money at the same time. Our regulars know how this works. We get a bunch of gals to volunteer, and they get up here and start dancin'. You wanna strip, do a little bump and grind, that's fine, we don't object. Do we, boys?"

A majority of the men in the place clapped and yahooed vociferous approval.

The announcer resumed. "Every few minutes, we'll eliminate a gal by having the audience clap for their favorites. Whichever gal's left shakin' it at the end wins two hundred dollars! Now how's that sound? Where's our volunteers?"

Women were laughing and squealing as some headed for and others were pushed protesting toward the stage.

Maggy, still feeling wildly disoriented, seized the opportunity with silent gratitude and glanced at Sarah. "I can't stand this. I've got to get out of here."

"I'm with you," Sarah said with feeling, turning away from the spectacle to head for the door.

"But what about your sexy friend? If we leave, we'll miss him," Buffy wailed as the other two started to wriggle their way through the crush of bodies swarming to surround the stage.

Maggy heard, but pretended not to. Booming music as the dance contest started drowned out any other protest Buffy might have made as she slithered off the bar stool and followed them.

Once outside, Maggy drew in great gulps of cold night air. It was early April, and they'd been having an unseasonably warm spell, but it was almost midnight and the temperature had dropped almost thirty degrees since sundown. Behind her, the sounds of ribald revelry swelled and then were abruptly cut off as Sarah and Buffy stepped out onto the cracked sidewalk and the bar's double doors swung shut behind them.

Tipton was waiting in the Rolls under a lone streetlamp. Seconds after Maggy spotted it, the sleek navy car purred toward her.

"Don't bother to get out, Tipton," Maggy said as the car stopped and the driver's door started to open. The door continued to open as if she had not spoken. Tipton got out and reached back to open the rear door without a word, his pale face wooden. He was a small, neat man in his late forties, as bald as an egg beneath his uniform cap. A shaggy, grizzled moustache adorned his upper lip. He was Lyle's man all the way, and as such Maggy counted him as her enemy. Tipton was Lyle's spy, and the reason he drove her when she went out was simple: so he could report back to his boss where she had been. Maggy pretended not to be aware of this—to admit that she knew and yet was unable to do anything about it would be to destroy what little dignity she had left—just as she pretended to believe that Tipton had not heard her request that he not get out. She knew that in any confrontation between herself and Tipton, or any of Lyle's hangers-on, she would come out the loser. Lyle would see to that.

Sarah and Buffy, though, were blessedly oblivious of the undercurrents swirling around them as they piled into the soft-leather interior.

Maggy, without so much as another glance at Tipton, slid in behind them, fastening her seat belt as Tipton gently shut the door.

"So tell us about your friend," Buffy said when they were settled. The car had swung about in a wide circle and was just nosing onto the six-lane bridge that spanned the dark waters of the Ohio River. Glancing forward at Tipton—though there was a partition between the front and back sections of the car, and he appeared deaf, dumb, and blind to everything but the road, she had learned that it was impossible to be too cautious—Maggy silently cursed Buffy as she fought to keep her face and voice serene.

"There really isn't much to tell."

"Oh, that's obvious. Especially since you're just now starting to get some color back in your face. You were white as a ghost while you were talking to him, and when he left you couldn't drag your eyes away. So what gives? Is he an old flame? You can tell us. We won't tell Lyle."

Fat chance. Buffy was an incorrigible gossip, Maggy knew. She might not tell Lyle herself, but she would tell enough people so that word would eventually reach his ears. She had to face it: there was no hope of keeping Nick's presence in Louisville a secret. Lyle undoubtedly already knew that Nick was in town anyway. Nick said he had stopped by the house and somehow seen David. Nothing happened at Windermere that Lyle did not know about, not even an unweeded flower garden nor a too-high grocery bill. Certainly the advent of someone like Nick would be reported to Lyle with all speed. But Nick's mere presence, though it would anger and displease Lyle enormously, was not enough to precipitate a crisis. Not *the* crisis, the one Maggy had lived in terror of for years.

With a sinking feeling Maggy realized that too many people—two too many, to be precise—knew about her encounter with Nick at the Little Brown Cow for her to be able to keep it from Lyle. Her best course of action was to tell him about running into Nick herself, in a very casual, by-the-way style, before he heard of it through other channels.

The prospect made her palms sweat.

"Maggy!" Buffy was impatient.

Maggy took a deep, silent breath. "He's a face out of the past, is all."

"That's right, you grew up in the projects yourself, didn't you? I remember Sarah telling me about it, years ago. Was there ever a lot of gossip about Lyle marrying someone from that kind of background! Not that anyone could tell it, now, of course," Buffy tacked on hastily.

"That's rude, Buff," Sarah chided her. Her voice was resigned. Outspokenness was one of Buffy's inherent characteristics, and her friends had long since decided that it was incurable.

"It is not rude. I said no one could tell now, didn't I? Just like no one could tell that that *hunk* came from the projects."

"Maybe that's because you have a few preconceptions about the projects that aren't necessarily true." Maggy's rebuke was mild. She would by far rather talk about the projects than Nick.

"So I'm a snob, right?" Buffy said with the refreshingly honest grin that was the reason people put up with her. "I can't help it, I'm the product of my environment. Anyway, tell me about the hunk."

Maggy repressed an inward groan. Buffy was like a bulldog. There was no dragging her away from a subject once she got started on it. "There's really nothing to tell. We used to know each other, when we were kids. But that was a long time ago."

"Used to know each other? Is that all you're going to say? When he calls you Magdalena in that sexy way?"

"It's my legal name," Maggy replied with a brittle edge to her voice that she immediately strove to banish. Let Buffy get the idea that she was hiding something, and the fat would be in the fire for sure. Every tongue—or at least all the ones that counted—in Louisville would wag. The best defense was a good offense, or so she'd always heard. She tried it: "Besides, I think you would have thought anything he said was sexy."

"The way you were drooling over him was embarrassing, Buff," Sarah agreed.

"I wasn't drooling over him." Buffy sounded indignant. Then she grinned again. "Well, he is a doll baby. If he gets in touch with you, Maggy, do you suppose you could give him my number?"

"I doubt he'll be in touch. But if he does, I certainly will."

To Maggy's relief, she realized they had reached the gates of Windermere. She hadn't even registered that they had left the expressway upon reaching the Kentucky shore and traversed the ten or so miles along River Road to the well-hidden estate entrance, so caught up was she in her own inner turmoil. The car slowed and turned right at the old abandoned gatekeeper's cottage, pausing while the electronic gates opened. Then they edged past the stone pillars and iron gates that marked the beginning of the long drive and headed upward with a whoosh of tires on pavement. The drive was steep and narrow and S-shaped. The first dozen times Maggy had driven herself along it she had done so with her heart in her mouth for fear she would miscalculate and end up a hundred or so yards below in Willow Creek. Over time she had gotten used to the hair-raising approach to the house, and now she scarcely noticed it, except to register in passing that the light that usually illuminated the most treacherous curve was out. But Tipton, well accustomed to the drive, didn't even slow down. Moments later the car reached the level ground at the top of the hill that formed the front lawn. Seconds after that it nosed around the paved circle leading to the wide stone stairway that provided access to the six-columned porch and the heavy oak front door.

The outside lights were on, illuminating the cascading fountain that was the centerpiece of the still-dormant rose garden around which this part of the driveway circled, and shining up on the smooth white stone facade of the three-story house. But except for the chandelier in the front entryway, visible through the leaded glass transom above the door, the inside lights appeared to be off.

Even as Tipton swung open the door beside her, Maggy felt an easing of the tension that had held her in thrall. From the look of the house, Lyle had gone to bed. She would not have to deal with him until morning.

She smiled faintly with relief as she slid out.

Sarah and Buffy didn't move. They were houseguests at Windermere for the festive month leading up to Derby, which in Louisville was a gala event centered around a horse race on the first Saturday in May that eclipsed even Christmas for parties and preparation. They were staying with Sarah's mother, Lucy Drummond, for the duration of the festivities. Lucy, Lyle's only living sibling, had resided for the past six months in the estate's guesthouse, which was a charming, two-story frame farmhouse not far from the main house. She was at Windermere because her and Lyle's mother, Virginia, who lived year-round in her own luxurious apartment in one wing of the main house, was gravely ill. Virginia's doctor predicted she would not survive the summer.

"Good night!" Buffy rolled down the nearside window to wave. Sarah echoed the words and motion.

Maggy, standing on the cobblestoned driveway, waved back with false gaiety as Tipton got in the car. She kept waving until the Rolls pulled slowly on around the curve in the drive and headed east. The guesthouse was located there, beyond the swimming pool and tennis court and dog kennel, hidden from view of the main house by a sheltering stand of shaggy hemlocks. Her smile fading at last, Maggy watched the car until she could see no more than a pair of red taillights glowing faintly through the darkness. Her cheeks hurt from the effort of smiling, and she rubbed them.

A single drop of icy water hit her left hand, splattering just below the huge diamond that was Lyle's brand. Glancing up only to be pelted by a second and then a third, Maggy realized it was beginning to rain. She turned and ran up the well-worn stone steps, key in hand, as the rain commenced in earnest. Though she reached the sheltering portico in seconds, she was already thoroughly wet. It was quite a trick to let herself in the massive door, close and lock it again, and race over the slippery wood floors to the security alarm hidden in the dining room closet before it could notify the police of an intrusion. But she managed it, punching in the code that would pacify the pesky thing with a second or two to spare.

That done, Maggy leaned against the exquisite, hand-painted paper that covered the walls of the dining room, uncaring that her damp clothing might leave a smudge for Lyle to find and scold about, and caught her breath. Shivering as her body registered just how chilled it was, she wrapped her arms around herself and closed her eyes.

Immediately a darkly handsome face appeared on the screen of her closed lids: Nick. Nick was back.

What in the name of heaven and earth was she going to do?

2

$\mathcal{B}$y the time Maggy reached her bedroom—a luxurious suite in the main wing overlooking the huge stone terrace that ran along the back of the house—she had managed to reassure herself to some small degree. Nick would never do anything to hurt her. No matter how angry he might still be.

At least the Nick she had known would not.

But every time she remembered the bitterness of their parting, and the twelve years of silence that had passed since then, she felt a prickle of unease.

Nick had never been one to forgive and forget.

"Guess," he'd said, when she'd asked him what he was doing here.

The various possibilities made her stomach churn.

The bedroom was dark as she walked across the antique Tabriz carpet that covered the polished wood floor toward the small white onyx lamp on the table beside her bed. Unbuttoning her shirt with one hand, she reached to switch the lamp on—then jumped back, gasping with fright, as the sudden light illuminated the man waiting in the chintz-covered chair in the corner.

"Did you have a nice evening, darling?" Lyle smiled at her, enjoying her obvious fright. His thinning blond hair gleamed in the lamplight. His face was long, thin, and bony, handsome at fifty-two despite its rather prominent nose and square chin. His body was long and thin too, and even clad in a silk robe and pajamas, as he was at that moment, he was possessed of an elegance that he took great pride in seeing copied by David. Her son. Their son.

A shiver of foreboding raced along Maggy's spine.

She had to look down to meet his eyes, which, since he was still seated, were somewhere at the level of her chest. They were bright blue, cold as ice, and alive with malice.

"It was all right."

"Meet anyone?"

How could he have found out so fast? Lyle had always been uncanny in what he knew. Sometimes, in her more fanciful states, she imagined he must be a warlock, or a conjurer. He always seemed to know everything she said or did or even thought. It was terrifying.

She took a deep, steadying breath. "Nick King is in town. I—we—ran into him at a nightclub in Indiana."

Assuming an ease she did not feel, Maggy turned her back and walked toward her dressing room, unbuttoning the rest of her blouse as she went. The thought of undressing in front of Lyle made her skin crawl, but she had already begun and to stop where she was would be a mistake. Lyle fed on fear and loathing, and she had learned the hard way to allow him a glimpse of neither. But she could not keep her body from shivering and only hoped that he could not see the fine tremors that shook her. The dampness of her clothes was surely at least one reason why she felt so icily cold.

"Ahh."

So he had known and had expected her to lie. She could tell by the tone of that single, drawn-out syllable. Her shivers increased.

"What did he say?"

"Just a minute." Maggy needed the few minutes it would take her to change to recover her poise. Thankful that Lyle had not followed her, not daring to close the partially open door in case it should provoke him to come after her and watch with malevolent enjoyment of her humiliation while she undressed, Maggy quickly stripped and pulled on the wine velvet robe that hung on a hook behind the door. Tying the satin sash tightly about her waist, she returned to the bedroom, stopping at the foot of the huge canopied four-poster and gripping one of its mahogany posts as she faced her husband.

"I asked you what he said."

Maggy's hand clutched the post as if it were a lifeline. "Nothing, really. Just—hello."

"Did he mention that he stopped by the house this afternoon? I was playing tennis, but he saw David."

"He mentioned that, yes. He—he complimented me on David."

Lyle swore, and stood up so abruptly that Maggy released the post and stepped back a pace. He came around the bed toward her with swift, angry strides. It was all she could do to stand her ground, but stand it she did. She didn't even flinch when his long-fingered hand whipped up to grip her jaw with brutal strength, tilting her head back so that her eyes met his.

"What did you tell him, damn you?"

"N-nothing. I told him nothing! You know I wouldn't!" She was frightened, but angry, too, hotly, healingly angry for the first time in a long, long while. Something about seeing Nick had awakened shades of the girl she used to be. Fiery-tempered Magdalena Garcia, afraid of neither man, nor God, nor the Devil. Until Lyle had taken her in hand and taught her the meaning of fear.

Lyle didn't speak, just searched her face with an expression that would ordinarily have made her cringe inside, though she had learned better than to let her fear and loathing show.

"I don't want him here. Get rid of him."

But this time Maggy refused to be cowed. She even managed a brittle little laugh. "I didn't bring him here. I can't make him leave. It's a free country."

Lyle's fingers dug painfully into her flesh. It was all Maggy could do not to cry out, but she did not. She would not give him that satisfaction. For an instant their eyes clashed.

"If you don't get rid of him, I will."

Lyle released her jaw at last, shoving her away from him in the process so that she stumbled back against the footboard. He walked with angry strides toward the door to the hall. She had still not recovered her balance when he swung round to face her.

"I won't have this piece of trash from your disgusting past messing up our lives. Not mine, not yours, and not David's."

Maggy straightened, holding on to the nearest bedpost for support. From the expression on Lyle's face, the threat to Nick was very real. For years she had felt protective only of David. Suddenly, a barely remembered sense of protectiveness for Nick was there as well.

"He doesn't know, Lyle." Her anger faded, to be replaced by a kind of tired dread. In a physical confrontation between Nick and Lyle, Maggy had no doubts at all as to who would be the winner. Nick was twenty years younger, tough and street smart. But Lyle would never confront Nick himself. That was not how he operated. He would hire thugs to do the job for him.

"And he'd better not find out." There was a threat in the words and in his eyes too as he held her gaze for a pregnant moment. Then he turned on his heel, opened the door, and exited, pulling the heavy wood panel shut behind him with a softness that was more unnerving than a slam would have been.

With a caution born of experience, Maggy watched the closed door. After a moment or two in which Lyle did not return, she crossed to it, quietly turned the deadbolt, and returned to sink down on the edge of her bed. Her fingers were icy as she pressed them to her throbbing jaw. As she did so, she discovered that her hands were shaking.

The briefly risen shade of the young Magdalena Garcia dwindled away into that remote place in Maggy's memory where it had dwelt for so long. Once again she was Maggy Forrest, envied wife of the multimillionaire. What was ironic was that she was living her youthful self's wildest dream: she was rich to the point where money need never concern her, able to buy anything she wanted for herself and her son. Food was still a problem, but not in the same way: instead of worrying each day whether there would be something for supper, she had to watch what she ate to keep from growing plump. She had it all: clothes, jewelry, cars, respect. Everything she had ever longed for.

And she was unhappy to the point of despair. How the fates must be laughing.

Nick's coming had changed nothing. Nothing at all. For her own sake, and for David's, Maggy told herself she had to remember that.

3

Che doorknob rattled.

Maggy jumped, startled, and stared at the door. For one hideous moment she was paralyzed, sure that Lyle had returned.

"Mom, are you in there?"

David. Maggy let out a silent sigh of relief. Thank God. Whatever happened, she musn't let David know that she was upset. Smoothing her hair and her robe, striving to present an appearance of normalcy, she crossed to the door and admitted her son.

"What are you doing up so late?" Maggy asked, closing the door behind him and turning to lean back against it as she smiled at him with aching tenderness. He was so handsome, with his tousled hair and creamy clear skin and tall, straight body, that she took pleasure in just gazing at him. With a peculiar combination of shock and delight and regret, she realized that she was beginning to be able to see the man he would be already present in the boy.

David wore childish Batman pajamas, but the top of his head now reached her chin, though she was tall herself, and his feet and hands were as big as hers. The thick-lashed brown eyes, so like her own that sometimes she felt, when she looked into them, that she was looking into a mirror, held secrets that she could only speculate about. She loved him so much, this child of her flesh and blood and bone, that it almost hurt her to look at him. Yet she hesitated to hug him as she once would have done without thought. Of late he was Lyle's son more than hers in his own heart and mind, slavishly admiring of and devoted to his father. His attitude toward her was more and more a watered-down reflection of Lyle's contemptuous hostility.

She contented herself with touching his hair.

"Don't," he said, as she had known he would, jerking his head out of reach and scowling at her. "What was Dad doing in here? Were you fighting with him again?"

"No, we weren't fighting. We were—discussing something."

It was an odd feeling, being called to account by her own child. But Maggy answered without anger because she didn't know quite how else to deal with the prickly stranger her son was increasingly becoming.

"The man who was here today?"

"What man?" Maggy was startled, and it showed in her voice. But she knew who it had been, who it had to have been, instantly: Nick.

"Some man stopped by to see you. He told me his name, but I forgot. He said he was an old friend of yours. Dad says he's your boyfriend."

"Your dad means he's my *old* boyfriend, David. You know, someone I used to date before I married Dad."

"Did you used to date a lot?" The notion of his mother as a young girl with dates was obviously foreign to David. He looked at her curiously.

"Not very much. I was pretty young when your dad and I got married. Just eighteen."

"But you dated this guy." A hint of jealousy, on his own behalf and that of his father, was there in his voice.

"Yes," Maggy admitted, taking a deep breath. "I dated him."

"I bet Dad thinks you still do."

"I'm sure he doesn't."

"I bet he does. I bet he thinks that's where you run off to at night."

"David, I don't run off anywhere at night. I'm almost always home, and you know it."

"Dad says you sneak out after I'm in bed. He doesn't like you going out at night. He says it's trashy, the way you're always running off to bars and parties and things and leaving me here alone."

"David, none of that is true!" Maggy had to force herself to take a deep, calming breath before she said anything more. For all his life she had sheltered David, doing her best to insure that he would not be injured in the crossfire of her and Lyle's private war. Lyle, on the other hand, used David shamelessly as a weapon against her. He always had, because David was both the chain that bound her to Lyle and the one thing that could pierce her to the heart.

"You went out tonight!" There was accusation in his voice.

"You were hardly alone, sweetheart. Dad was here, and Gran, and Louella, and Herd."

"But you did go to a bar." His tone wouldn't have been out of place in a prosecutor.

Maggy strove for patience. "David, I went out with Sarah and one of her friends to try to cheer her up. You know how sad she's been since she and Tony split up."

"Are you and Dad going to get a divorce, too? He says you might, if you keep running around at night. He says he doesn't know how much more of your shenanigans he can take."

At the fear in his voice that his truculence could not quite hide, Maggy felt a slow anger start to burn in her belly. If there was any justice in the universe, Lyle Forrest would one day suffer the tortures of the damned for what he was doing to David.

"Dad didn't mean it, David. We won't get a divorce. I promise you. Now, you need to go back to bed, darling. You have to get up early in the morning."

"Why? It's Saturday."

"You have a golf tournament tomorrow. Did you forget?"

David groaned. "I wish I could. I hate golf! I don't see why I have to play in that stupid tournament. Anyway, I'm no damn good."

"You watch your language, young man." Maggy frowned, and pointed an admonishing forefinger at him to underscore her words. David shrugged in silent, sulky apology. "And you are too good."

David shook his head gloomily. "Dad says that if I just keep at it I'll improve. He says that every Forrest is just about pro material on a golf course. But I'm not. He should say every Forrest but me."

The hurt in his eyes banished her annoyance. Maggy sighed, crossing her arms over her chest to keep from reaching out and drawing him to her, which she knew he'd resist.

"You don't have to be like Dad, or any other Forrest, David. You're you. A unique individual. Who doesn't have to be almost pro material at golf. Maybe you can be just kind of good, and play because you enjoy the game."

"Yeah, right. Tell that to Dad." Looking dejected, David reached around her for the knob.

"I will, if you want me to. Talk to Dad, I mean. About how you feel about golf." At Maggy's quiet offer as she stepped out of his path, David glanced sideways at her.

"No, don't. I don't want you and Dad to fight anymore. You're always fighting."

Anger was there in his glance and his voice. Maggy felt a stab of pain.

"Does it seem that way to you? I'm sorry."

"No, you're not. It's your fault."

More pain. Maggy tried not to let her son's words pierce her so, but she couldn't help it. As the person she loved most in the world, David possessed the power to wound her as no one else could.

For an instant they were both silent as the aftermath of David's accusation reverberated in the air between them.

"Mom." Without looking around, one hand still on the knob, David spoke to the white-painted door in front of him.

"Hmmm?" Maggy looked rather wearily at the back of his head, knowing herself once again defeated. As always, Lyle had won the battle for David's allegiance. But instead of saying anything David turned suddenly and wrapped his arms tight around her waist, burying his face between her breasts. Surprised, Maggy nevertheless enfolded him against her. With a wordless little murmur she hugged him close, pressing her lips to the tumbled locks atop his head.

"I love you, Mom." The words were muffled, uttered with a kind of fierce defiance that made Maggy ache. A child shouldn't have to tell his mother he loved her in that tone. What had she done, to herself and to him, on that miserably humid night twelve years ago when she had forever linked their future with Lyle's? David was hers, *hers,* and yet Lyle stood forever between them. Lyle, whom she hated and David adored.

"I know, sweetheart. I love you too." It was all she could do to keep her voice steady. But for David, she managed it. He was just eleven years old, and she would not burden him with the pain that was by rights all hers.

David gave her a quick, hard hug before shoving free. Then, turning to jerk open the door, he almost ran from the room.

The force of his shove caused her to stagger back a pace. After recovering her balance, Maggy stepped out into the hall, watching him as he vanished into his own room two doors down from hers. A smallish bedroom suite that had once belonged to the nanny Lyle had insisted on when David was younger was located between them. Since Miss Hadley's retirement two years before, it had been converted into a playroom for David.

David had left his door open. He vanished into his room without looking back, and the door slammed behind him. Maggy stood without moving for a moment longer, hands clasped in front of her, eyes unseeing. Then she turned and reentered her room, locking the door behind her in a gesture that had become automatic over the years.

David had said that he loved her. Well, she loved him, too. Enough to do anything for him. To give up anything for him.

Enough to give up everything for him. Which, she sometimes thought, was just what she had done.

The next day, Saturday, April 11, was Maggy's thirtieth birthday. She rose at six A.M. as was her habit, did her regular twenty minutes on the LifeCycle in her bathroom, brushed her teeth, washed her face and smeared on a little of the creamy sunblock that she used to protect her fair skin anytime she so much as stuck her nose outside. Later she would shower, wash and style her hair, and dress for the day, but these early-morning hours were hers, and she refused to waste a single minute on something as superfluous as an elaborate toilette. Running a quick brush through the tangled shoulder-blade-length strands of her hair, she secured the heavy mass of it with a tortoiseshell barrette at her nape and moved into her dressing room. Quickly she pulled on jeans so old and well-worn that they were faded almost white on the knees and seat, a man's small-size T-shirt topped by a baggy white cotton pullover sweater, and an olive-green hooded anorak, and slipped out of the house. Rubberized boots that came halfway up her calves protected her feet from the soaked ground as she headed toward the kennels where her two Irish wolfhounds, Seamus and Bridey, were already barking in anticipation of her arrival.

The time was just a few minutes past six thirty. The sun, barely up, was a chilly-looking ball hanging low in the lightening sky to the east, just above where the thickly treed hills of the Kentucky and Indiana shores were parted by the Ohio River. The rain had stopped sometime during the night, but the air was cold and Maggy's breath rose in little frosty puffs as she shoved at the latch on the eight-foot-tall fence that enclosed the dogs. At last it shot free, and the dogs came tumbling out, leaping over each other and her in their frenzy of excitement at being released for their morning walk.

"Cool it, guys," she said, rubbing first one importunate gray head and then the other before setting off along the driveway with a sharp whistle that brought them to heel. She didn't really feel like walking this morning, but their early-morning outing was the highlight of the dogs' day, and she hadn't been able to bring herself to disappoint them, so here she was. She was tired, bone-tired, and not just because she had gotten so little sleep the night before. What she was suffering from was not so much physical as spiritual exhaustion. She was tired of her life. Desperately tired of it, and she could see no way out. She was trapped, a prisoner with no hope of parole. The knowledge sucked the energy from her.

Feathers of fine white mist rose lazily from the ground as she turned off the driveway and headed down toward the woods that covered the hillside that made up the bulk of the property. The woods were thick and overgrown except where paths had been worn or cut through them, and she generally confined her walk to a favorite path that wound down and around to the gatekeeper's cottage before meandering back up again. As she reached the path and began to follow it downhill, she flipped the hood of her anorak over her head. It was appreciably darker and colder here where the sun didn't quite reach. But dense as the treetops were, a few stray beams managed to penetrate the gloom with slanting bands of soft yellow light. The effect was eerily beautiful, and it was one of the reasons that Maggy had originally chosen the woods for these early-morning rambles. No matter how bad her life might seem, the sheer beauty of the earth never failed to lighten her heart. She felt the magic begin to work this morning, too, as some of her sense of hopelessness eased.

Scorning the path, Bridey and Seamus bounded ahead through the undergrowth, barking joyously as they chased squirrels and leaves and shadows and anything else that had the poor judgment to move. They knew the morning routine as well as she did, and Maggy had no fear that they would get lost. Most of the twenty acres of the estate was surrounded by a three-foot-high stone wall, with another two feet of iron fence set into the top of that. As the high-profile owner and publisher of *Kentucky Today,* the venerable part-gossip, part-news magazine that had been commenting on personalities and events of interest to Kentuckians for nearly a hundred years, Lyle was careful about security, and the fence and gated entry were part of his precautions. There were always threats, especially when Lyle personally wrote editorials espousing unpopular views. But he had not written any new ones lately, and so, with just the normal degree of hate simmering in the minds and hearts of Lyle's enemies, Maggy really had no fears of being attacked on her own property.

Which was why, when she saw the glowing red tip of a cigarette in a patch of shadows near the path, she kept walking toward it for a couple of paces before registering that, yes, there really was a man leaning against the trunk of a large ginkgo tree, taking a long drag from a cigarette as he watched her approach.

Maggy stopped dead. In the distance, the dogs started to bay as one or the other of them scented a rabbit and took off in hot pursuit. Where she was, the woods seemed very still suddenly. Not so much as a leaf rustled.

"Good morning, Magdalena."

She had known who it was even before he stepped away from the tree and spoke: Nick. Her heart, which had speeded up in response to fear of the unknown, continued to pound with another kind of fear as Nick tossed his cigarette on the damp path, crushed it out with a sneakered foot, and came toward her. Fine beads of moisture glinted in his black hair as he walked through a shaft of gossamer sunlight that shimmered between them. More drops of moisture gleamed on the shoulders of his tan car coat. Like her, he wore well-worn jeans, though his fit the hard muscles of his thighs like a glove. The ancient-looking canvas sneakers on his feet were thoroughly wet, which suggested to Maggy that he had been prowling through the woods for some time.

"What are you doing here?" she asked.

Despite an initial impulse to turn and run, Maggy stood her ground as he approached her and stopped just a couple of feet away where the path was dark and cool. A woodpecker suddenly began its distinctive hammering somewhere high above, but beyond casting a cursory glance upward neither of them paid it the least attention.

"That's the second time you've asked me that. If you'd stuck around last night, I just might have given you an answer. Now I think I'm going to let you figure it out for yourself." He smiled at her, but it wasn't a pleasant smile.

"Nick . . ." she began desperately, only to be sidetracked when he reached into his pocket, pulled out a rectangular package wrapped in plain brown paper and held it out to her.

"Happy birthday, Magdalena." His voice was dry.

"What is it?" Maggy accepted the package gingerly, turning it over in her hands as she stared down at it. It weighed very little, but there was something about the expression on his face that warned her to be wary. Oh, the signs were subtle, the merest crease in his forehead and glint in his eyes, but she had known him too well: whatever was in this package was not something she was going to like.

"A thirtieth-birthday present from me to you." He reached into his coat, fished in an inside pocket, and extracted a pack of Winstons and a book of matches. Tapping out a cigarette, he returned the pack to his pocket then lit the one he held with a flick of a match.

"You never used to smoke." Maggy was surprised at the disapproval she felt as she watched him. For an instant, just an instant, she was the young Magdalena again, and Nick was her mentor and her world. The girl that she had been then would have snatched the cigarette from his mouth and stomped it underfoot, treating him to an angry tirade as she did so. But then, the boy he had been would never have smoked. He hadn't been an angel, but he had never done drugs, never gotten drunk, never smoked. In his vicinity, at least, she'd never done those things either. Nick would have tanned her backside if he'd caught her the few times she had experimented with alcohol and pot behind his back—or at least he would have tried. She would have put up a heck of a fight.

Ah, Nick. Her heart ached suddenly for what might have been. If only —if only—but the die was cast and her path chosen with no possibility of turning back. She'd made her choice twelve years before, and now she had to live with the consequences no matter how painful she might find them.

Another of *Tia* Gloria's sayings was that the wheels of God grind slow, but they grind incredibly small. She felt as if they were grinding her into particles smaller than dust at that very moment.

"I never used to do a whole hell of a lot of things," Nick replied, returning the matches to his pocket and nodding at the package in her hand. "Aren't you going to open it?"

The glint in his eyes warned her again to be on guard even as her fingers ripped clumsily at the paper. And just as well, too, because what spilled into her hand as the paper tore were a videotape, a folded yellow business-size envelope—and four three-by-five, full-color photos of herself at seventeen, dancing nude.

She dropped the package as if it were a live snake. As the contents scattered around her feet, she stared down at the one picture that landed faceup with as much dreadful fascination as if it were a cobra poised to strike.

In it she was onstage in a dive that made the Little Brown Cow seem the epitome of class and sophistication. Her arms, raised over her head, sexily lifted away from her body the heavy fall of red-tinted mahogany hair that then cascaded in lush waves down past her hips. Her skin was pale as alabaster, her mouth pouty, her eyes heavy-lidded and dreamy from the pot she had smoked to get the courage to do what she needed to do to earn the hundred dollars the manager had promised her *every night*. There was a fortune to be made, or at least it had seemed a fortune to the girl she had been then, if she would only dance naked except for a satiny G-string six nights a week for an audience of thirty to fifty drooling men.

They weren't allowed to touch her in the bar—the manager had explained that the owner was afraid of losing his liquor license, and so the rule was strictly enforced—and whether or not she "dated" a customer for more money after her performance was over was strictly up to her. She'd known she never would, so she wouldn't be a whore. She would be only dancing, nothing more.

Thus she had persuaded herself, convinced that in the long run the money would be worth the shame that had twisted her insides whenever she had allowed her imagination to take her as far as actually getting up on that stage. She would make nearly four times the money dancing than she did working split shifts as a waitress at the Harmony Inn, where she got decent tips only on Tuesday nights because of the all-you-can-eat fish special. It would be stupid not to take the job, she told herself with her customary hardheaded practicality, stupid not to cash in on her young, lithe body and pretty face while they were still there to be cashed in on. Yet she couldn't tell Nick what she meant to do, though he was her best friend and her closest family all rolled into one and she told him everything else. Nick would hit the roof if he knew.

When the time actually came for her debut performance on a less than crowded Thursday night, she never would have been able to go through with it if another dancer, more inured to the life, hadn't taken pity on her obvious fright and gotten her high as a kite first.

For three whole nights, she'd been one of the nine beautiful girls and three ugly ones (or so the newspaper ads described them) who had comprised the stable of dancers at the Pink Pussycat. Each night she'd vomited from nerves as she'd gotten ready for her performance, and each night she'd thought she couldn't possibly go out there on that stage again. Smoking grass had gotten her through it. All the girls did, passing joints back and forth as they applied body makeup in the tiny rest room that served as their dressing room. Maggy had deliberately inhaled until she was comfortably lost somewhere in space. Only then had she been able to go on.

Stoned, it hadn't been so terribly hard. She'd felt she was floating as she walked out on the tiny stage and the bright stage lights hit her, all but blinding her. At first it had been easy to pretend she was alone, undressing to music in the privacy of her apartment. The pounding rhythm of the rock anthem "Born to Be Wild" had swelled until it seemed to be right inside her brain, and she had moved instinctively to its beat. For her entrance, her hair was piled high atop her head by one of the other girls. She began her act by removing the pins from the heavy mass and shaking it loose. Then she slowly untied the sash of the scarlet, feather-trimmed robe that was the outermost part of her costume. That first night, when she felt the silk of the robe slide down her arms to puddle at her feet and realized that she was almost completely naked beneath, she suffered an attack of fear and modesty acute enough to pierce the drugged fog that shielded her. Panic assailed her as, dressed in nothing but high heels, black thigh-high stockings, and a black sequined G-string, she faced the audience of dozens of drooling, clapping men. She had glanced down, been confronted with the hard pink tips of her bare breasts and the naked curve of her belly and thighs —and had nearly died of shame on the spot. Quickly, instinctively, she whipped around so that her back was to them, then tilted her chin toward the dusty rafters overhead, because she knew that if she did, her long hair would fall low enough to hide her bare butt. Somehow her feet kept moving in the semblance of a dance while she prayed for deliverance and the audience alternately cheered and booed. The manager hissed furiously at her from the wings—she had to show them *something* —and as she glanced his way her hair had apparently shifted enough to afford the audience a glimpse of the naked cheeks of her behind. The crowd roared approval. Startled, she glanced around at them, affording them another peek. They howled for more. The manager hissed at her again, making frantic turning motions with his hands, inscribing a horizontal circle in the air. Her drug-dulled wits froze, then gave up the struggle for independence. Nauseated with fear, she obediently turned around—but shook her hair forward so that it covered her breasts. The manager growled. The audience stomped its feet. Frightened to death of both him and the crowd, Maggy closed her eyes to shut them all out and swayed to the beat, trying not to hear the thunderous mixture of catcalls and stomping feet and clapping hands that greeted her amateur gyrations. The manager hissed again—*"Show them some skin!"*—and Maggy's eyes opened. She was out there onstage, there was no way off except past the angry manager on one side and a burly bouncer on the other or through the crowd itself, and if she didn't perform she wouldn't be paid. . . .

Getting paid was what it was all about, after all.

Suddenly the crowd was silent. The men licked their lips and sweated and stared as Maggy slid both arms under her hair and lifted the glistening curtain of waves, then dropped it, over and over again, in a somnolent, sensuous sleepwalker's dance born somewhere in her subconscious. The watching men went wild, but the commotion just barely penetrated the haze of nauseated fear and pot that blunted her senses like an anesthetic. Her body was there, dancing nearly naked for money, but she, the part of her that was Magdalena, was not.

On her third night, a busy Saturday, Nick walked in during the middle of her performance. She found out later that he'd been tipped off to what she was doing by one of his friends. When he appeared, she was down to her heels and stockings and G-string, her thick fall of hair all that protected her modesty. Her back was turned to the audience, so she didn't see him when he entered and threaded his way between the crowded tables, didn't see him when he stopped directly in front of the stage, arms crossed over his chest, staring up at her as—once, twice, three times—she lifted her hair and wiggled her bare butt, as he put it later, for all the world to see. Largely over her initial stage fright by that time and high as a kite, she turned around as the audience roared for more and smiled sleepily into the closest pair of male eyes—only to come to the slow, awful realization that they were blazing green with outrage and all too familiar.

Nick.

Shocked sober, she had frozen where she stood. With a single lithe movement Nick jumped up onstage beside her, snatched up her robe from the floor, wrapped it around her body, and picked her up over his shoulder in a fireman's carry, all without saying so much as a word to her.

Then all hell had broken loose. The Pink Pussycat didn't take kindly to having its dancers snatched from its stage right before its patrons' eyes. By the time the melee was over, twenty-year-old Nick had battled his way through the club's three massive bouncers and about a dozen other assorted pugilists, suffered two black eyes, a bloodied nose, and bruised ribs, and barely escaped being arrested when Maggy dragged him out the door just ahead of the arrival of the cops, who were called to quell the disturbance.

And was he grateful? Not he!

Roaring away from the club in his ancient car—Maggy was driving, though as she told him he didn't deserve that she should go to so much bleeping trouble to save his ass—they had had the mother and father of a quarrel. If Nick hadn't been so bloody and battered, Maggy would have slapped him silly herself. Mind your own damned business, she screamed at him. She could do what the hell she wanted with her life and her body! If she wanted to dance naked in the middle of the expressway at high noon, she would! His response, as he'd tilted his head back against the seat and tried to stanch the blood that poured from his nose, was to call her a stupid little fool and tell her to slow down.

After that, the battle had raged at white-hot pitch for a good ten minutes.

Then, because however angry she was at him she hated to see him hurt, Maggy had whipped the car into the parking lot of a closed-down warehouse, slammed the gearshift into park, and started wiping at his bloodied face with the feathered hem of her scarlet silk robe.

He had knocked her hand away, grabbed her by her shoulders and kissed her, bloody nose and all. His kiss—the first time he had ever kissed her in a way that was not entirely brotherly—had rocked her world on its axis.

For an instant, no longer, the memory burned to life in her mind. But she wouldn't let herself remember. She couldn't. That kiss had happened long ago, another lifetime ago, to another girl. A girl who no longer existed.

Now, staring down at the picture of herself dancing before an audience of blurry male faces, Maggy felt the image sear relentlessly into her brain. There she was, beautiful at seventeen, with her high young breasts with their rouged nipples—courtesy of the same girl who provided the pot and the fancy hairstyle—bared for all the world to see, along with her narrow rib cage and small round belly button and flaring hips and the tiny triangle of black sequins that covered her sex. Poised on six-inch-high heels, with her long, slender legs clad in sheer black stockings to the thigh, she appeared to be flaunting her nakedness. She looked somnolent, sexy, as though she were loving every minute of her own performance.

"Remember, Magdalena?" Nick's soft voice flayed her.

She glanced up at him wildly. "No, I don't remember! I don't ever want to remember!"

Whirling, she began to run back the way she had come.

He was upon her in an instant, catching her around the waist with one arm and clamping a hand over her mouth with the other as though he feared she might scream. She would have, too, uncaring at the moment of the consequences of being found alone in the woods with Nick of all people. She struggled and kicked as he lifted her clear up off her feet and carried her away from the path through the underbrush until at last she regained some control and stopped struggling in his arms. Then, in the lee of a just-greening wild-cherry tree, he set her upright again.

"Don't scream," he said, his hand still covering her mouth. Held tight against him, her breasts flattened by his chest, her thighs plastered against his, Maggy registered anew the size and strength of him—Nick was six feet two, and while he had weighed in the vicinity of 180 as a youth, she suspected he was now 200 or more well-muscled pounds—and made a negative movement with her head.

He rather cautiously removed his hand from her mouth.

"Is that why you came back? To blackmail me?" she demanded in a shrill voice, shoving against his chest in a futile bid to free herself. "I have plenty of money now, right? So how much do you want?"

One of his arms was still clamped around her waist, and Maggy felt it harden. Her head tilted back in time to catch the narrowing of his mouth and the icing-over of his eyes. Her words had angered him, she saw at a glance, and she was fiercely glad. She wanted him angry. No, she wanted him to hurt, as he was hurting her.

For a moment he said nothing, just looked measuringly down at her.

"A million dollars or I show the pictures and tape—oh, yes, that's a videotape of your whole performance—to Lyle? Interesting thought, that."

"I—I can't get a million dollars. I don't have access to that much. Nowhere near it."

His gaze met hers, and he smiled, a slow, lazy, taunting smile.

"I bet Lyle could get it, if I threatened to send copies of everything to the local movers and shakers. TV might even be interested. I can just see your little dance ending up on something like *A Current Affair,* can't you? With the appropriate blackouts over strategic areas of your anatomy, of course."

"You son of a bitch."

"You know how I always hated to hear you swear. I still do. Maybe I ought to up the ante for every cussword that comes out of your mouth."

"Go to hell!"

"Watch yourself, Maggy May, this could get expensive."

"Don't you dare call me that!" The once-familiar endearment stung her like the flicked end of a bullwhip.

"In my experience, blackmailers can call their victims anything they want."

"Oh, so you have experience? Is that how you make a living these days, blackmailing innocent people like me?"

"I'd hardly call you innocent, Magdalena. Not then, and not now."

Maggy could feel a hot rush of fury rising inside her. It was a familiar, if long forgotten, sensation. In her teen years she had been renowned throughout the mean streets of Louisville's west end for her fiery temper. She and Nick had once fought like two angry cats swung together in a sack. Since marrying Lyle, the fight had been systematically knocked out of her.

"How much do you want?" She was quivering with shock and outrage and pain. That Nick could do this to her, Nick whom she had once loved with a fierce wild tide, was unbelievable. No, it was very believable. After all, hadn't she learned the hard way that no one was what he or she seemed, and that even the best-known, most trusted person had as many unfathomable layers as an onion?

"What would you say if I told you that I wasn't after money?"

A suggestive glint in his eyes told Maggy what he meant. She laughed, the sound forced and high. "Sex? Is that what you want? Fine. Go ahead, lover. Throw me down on the ground right here and now and get your rocks off. It's a cheap price to pay to get you the hell out of my life again."

His eyes narrowed, darkened. "That's my Maggy May. Foulmouthed and bullheaded." Taut mockery curled his mouth while his arm tightened around her waist, drawing her up on her toes as he pressed her even closer against him. Maggy didn't bother to struggle—she knew from experience that Nick, when seriously annoyed as he was at that moment, possessed the strength of two ordinary men—but she glared up at him with all the rage she had kept stored inside her for the last dozen years. His brows twitched together as he absorbed her expression, and then he bent his head to kiss her.

5

*O*nly he didn't. Maggy, rigid, hating, her arms wedged between them holding him slightly at bay, braced herself for nothing.

Nick let her go and stepped back.

"The pictures and tape are a gift," he said, folding his arms across his chest and watching her like a dog at a rabbit hole. "The negatives are inside the envelope. They came into my possession from someone who did indeed intend to use them to blackmail you, my dear Mrs. Forrest. Luckily for you, I bought them—and they weren't cheap—before anyone else could see them, and now I'm giving them to you, no strings attached."

Maggy stared up at him for a moment, too dumbfounded to speak. She had behaved abominably, and she knew it. But she had forgotten how to trust anyone, even Nick.

"Why?" She thrust her hands into the pockets of her anorak, all at once desperately cold.

"Why not?" The words were flippant.

"That's not an answer."

"It's all you're going to get."

"Nick . . ." Maggy hesitated, searching his face. The features were the same as those of the boy she had loved: the thick straight black brows, the slightly crooked nose with the small bump on its bridge from where it had been broken that fateful night, the broad cheekbones and square chin. Even the elusive dimple on the right side of his mouth was the same. But there were differences, too: lines of experience at the corners of his eyes, a hardness that was new, a certain cynicism in the set of his jaw and in the gleam of those bright hazel-green eyes. He was indubitably Nick, her Nick, but he had changed, inside where it didn't much show. But then, of course, so had she. "I owe you an apology."

"You do—but don't bother. I like you better spitting fire than being reasonable. Brings back old times." He glanced around, his attention attracted by the sound of the dogs barking as they galloped toward them through the trees. "Don't forget to pick your present up off the path before someone else comes across it."

"Nick . . ." But it was too late. He was already striding away. He glanced over his shoulder as she called after him and touched his hand to his brow in a salute.

"Happy birthday, Maggy May," he said, and then he vanished like a shadow through the trees.

Maggy stared after him, feeling her battered heart threatening to break anew. Ah, Nick. How she had loved him. So much that it hurt to remember. And how like him, to appear out of nowhere after twelve years of silence and tease and mock her and drive her crazy even when he meant to do her a good deed. She should have known he meant her no harm. Somewhere deep in her heart she thought she had known it, but she had forgotten how to listen to her heart.

Seamus and Bridey burst through the undergrowth like a pair of bounding moose and leaped on her with doggy ecstasy.

"Down, guys!" She staggered under the onslaught, patting them, glad of their boisterous advent because it distracted her from thoughts of Nick. Now that he had done what he had come to do, would he vanish from her life for another twelve years?

The prospect made her want to wail like an abandoned child.

"Enough of that!" she said aloud, pressing her lips firmly together and forcing her mind to focus on the purely practical, the here and now. She had learned long ago that it was dangerous to give in to maudlin reflection. If she allowed herself to dwell on the negative aspects of her life, she would be forever in tears, and that would do no one any good, least of all David or herself.

As Nick had reminded her, she had to gather up the tape and pictures and negatives and get rid of them before someone found them and gave them to Lyle.

Lyle would use them against her. Maggy knew he would use them against her. She didn't know precisely how, but she knew him well enough to know that he would.

He might even be cruel enough to show them to David.

At the thought, Maggy shuddered and hurried to retrieve the incriminating evidence. Everything was where it had fallen, still scattered across the path, and she scooped the items up without looking at the pictures again, shoving them back inside the ripped package and then tucking them inside her anorak with a hasty, guilty glance around. It would be like Lyle to have spies even here.

But now she was letting herself get paranoid. There were no eyes to see nor tongues to tattle so early in the morning in Windermere's own woods.

She had to get rid of the pictures and negatives and tape.

Standing up, Maggy hesitated, chewing her lip as she considered the problem. Despite her agitation, a tiny glimmer of amusement flickered across her face as the thought came to her that she was pondering the question that must once have tormented Richard Nixon: to burn or not to burn an incriminating tape? But in her case at least, a bonfire of sufficient size to consume every scrap of evidence beyond redemption would be sure to attract the very attention she was so desperate to avoid.

In the end, she walked deep into the woods and buried everything beneath the ground-sweeping branches of a just-budding forsythia bush, scraping out a hole with her hands and a rock and covering it up again with dirt and leaves and a large, half-rotted piece of log to mark the spot. As a permanent solution, the one she had chosen wouldn't work, but it was the best she could do at the moment. If she took the pictures and tape back to the house, even for as long as a few hours while she sought another solution, she was afraid they would be discovered. She suspected that Lyle had her rooms regularly searched, hoping to find evidence that she was having an affair. Not that he would care if she was, except that the knowledge of it would give him one more weapon to use against her.

Unfortunately for him, he could search in vain. Since marrying him, she had never slept with anyone else. The very thought was enough to make her feel ill.

If nothing else, Lyle had cured her of liking sex.

Though she had liked it once, too much. With Nick.

But she would not allow herself to remember. The glorious primal passion that had so briefly and disastrously raged through her life had happened to an altogether different person. The girl she had been then was gone forever.

If the knowledge saddened her, why, then, she would just force it from her head. She had learned in a hard school that there was no use grieving over what was done.

There was David now. She thought of her son deliberately, picturing him in her mind, and as she did so the ghost of that laughing, dancing, love-hungry girl receded to the far-distant reaches of her memory that was her proper home.

David was what was important. She would do anything, endure anything, for David.

Mud and bits of leaves still clung to her hands as she walked back toward the house. She kept them balled in the pockets of her anorak until she reached the kennel for fear that someone might see the state they were in and wonder. With a furtive glance around she called Seamus and Bridey to her, turning on the outside spigot as she did so. If anyone was watching, she hoped he would think that she was merely giving the dogs a drink. Thrusting her hands under the icy stream, she quickly washed the evidence away. Then she dried them on her jeans, turned off the water, and returned the dogs to their runs with the usual quota of apologetic pats. She loved the enormous creatures, but Lyle refused to have pets in or near the house.

She sometimes thought that the only thing Lyle loved, in his own peculiar, twisted way, was David.

The sun was brighter now, and she guessed it must be around eight. Despite all that had happened, she wasn't even behind schedule. She could go in, get dressed for the day, and go about her business as if nothing whatsoever had changed.

Which it hadn't. Nothing had changed. Despite Nick's return, she was still tied to Lyle for life. Unless she wanted to destroy David in the process of breaking free.

Trapped, trapped, trapped, trapped. The word reverberated in her mind with all the helpless frenzy of a butterfly beating its wings against the glass walls of an imprisoning jar. Trapped, forever trapped.

"Goddamn it, David, concentrate!" The raised voice belonged to Lyle, and the annoyance in it was palpable. Seconds later it was followed by the sound of smashing glass.

"I said concentrate! Look at that! The glass in that window is over a hundred years old, and you broke it because you weren't concentrating!"

"Dad, I'm sorry! I tried . . ."

"Tried, tried! I don't want to hear 'tried' from you. I want you to do it! 'Tried' is for losers! Which is what you'll be, if you don't concentrate!"

"I will, Dad. Just give me one more chance." The pleading in David's voice caused Maggy to grit her teeth and hurry around the tall privet hedge separating the driveway from the back lawn. As she had expected,

Lyle and David, each with a golf club in hand, stood with their backs to her scarcely ten feet from where she had emerged at the top of the lawn near the patio. Clearly they had been driving balls in the direction of the woods, and one of David's had gone astray. Lyle was, as always, impeccably attired, this morning in plaid slacks and a navy sweater over an open-necked polo shirt. David, ever his clone, was dressed in nearly identical fashion. The only difference was that his sweater was white instead of blue, and he wore a pine-green turtleneck beneath it instead of a polo shirt. Two well-filled golf bags rested against the low stone wall that bordered the patio. A steaming cup of coffee, Lyle's presumably, waited on the wall near one bag of clubs. She could not see her husband's expression, but David's, as he looked up at Lyle, was both miserable and pleading.

Maggie felt her heart constrict.

"Practicing, gentlemen?" she asked lightly as she walked up to them, meaning to deflect Lyle's attention from David to herself.

"You look like hell." She had succeeded. Lyle's eyes were cold as they swept her from head to toe. One of his "rules" was that she must always be well dressed. No wife of his was going to go about looking slovenly.

"I've been walking the dogs," she replied, refusing to take offense. Her gaze was on David.

"Have you eaten?" she asked him gently.

"Not yet." Only she knew him well enough to detect the misery hidden in his voice.

"He needs practice more than food right at this moment. In case you've forgotten, we're playing in the father-son tournament this afternoon at the Club, and if David can keep up his end of the program, we're going to win." His eyes moved over her again, narrowing with disapproval. "I hope you don't mean to wear that."

"You know I don't. The tournament is not until after lunch." Her answer was quiet. Her gaze focused on David.

"Why don't you go in and grab some breakfast?"

Lyle answered before David could. "He doesn't have time. He has a golf lesson at nine."

Maggy glanced up at Lyle. "Don't you think that might do more harm than good?" She had to fight to keep her voice even. "I should think his game would benefit more from a good breakfast and a relaxed attitude than an eleventh-hour lesson."

Lyle's nostrils flared with disdain. "You would. Fortunately, David knows better. He knows as well as I do that he needs all the practice he can get. He's not good enough, not nearly good enough. I mean to *win.*"

Maggy sensed as much as saw David wince. The look she shot at Lyle was as icy as the one he had earlier bestowed on her, but she did not jump to David's defense as her every instinct urged her to do. If she said what she longed to say, Lyle would retaliate by loosing his vicious tongue on her, and that would upset David more than his father's insensitivity toward him.

"It's okay, Mom. I really do need the lesson."

For an instant David's gaze touched hers, and Maggy read the silent plea in them.

Reluctantly she capitulated to it. She would not oppose his lesson. "You need something in your stomach before you go, then. Run on in and eat. Right now, do you hear?" Though she said it gently, it was still an order. David looked to Lyle for permission before obeying. Lyle nodded once, a jerky, displeased bob of his head.

David turned away. When Maggy would have followed David, Lyle stopped her by grasping her hand. Maggy halted, knowing she was in for it now, but unwilling in front of David to make the scene it would take to free herself. Both Maggy and Lyle stood silent, side by side, hand in hand, for the few minutes it took the boy to return his club to his bag, heft the bag over one shoulder, then walk along the stone sidewalk to disappear around a corner of the house.

"I'll thank you to keep your nose out of my relationship with my son." Lyle's low voice was laced with menace as he glanced down at her.

Maggy couldn't help herself. She had to say it, though she knew she would pay dearly for her outspokenness. "You're putting too much pressure on him. He's only eleven."

"He needs pressure if he's going to succeed. What do you know about success? Where would you be if I hadn't married you? Starving in a flophouse somewhere, that's where. As it is, you're nothing more than a parasite. I won't have your weak genetic traits coming out in David. I'll make a man out of him no matter what it takes."

"You know all about being a man, don't you?" She had gone too far. Maggy knew it as soon as the words left her mouth. His blue eyes flickered, and she just had time to register how they paled when filled with hate. His hand, the one holding hers, twisted viciously. Pain shot up her arm as her wrist bent. Maggy felt rather than heard something pop.

6

*T*he pain of it wrung a small cry from Maggy's lips.

"Oh, sorry, darling, did I hurt you?" Lyle asked with patently false concern as he released her hand. A satisfied smile lurked around his mouth.

Cradling her throbbing wrist, Maggy stared up into mocking eyes that she had once thought were gentle and kind. It was their color that had thrown her off, of course. Who had ever heard of a blue-eyed demon? Which was how, after twelve years as his wife, she had come to think of Lyle. The image even haunted her dreams. For the last few years Maggy had suffered the same terrible nightmare over and over again: she died and went to hell, but had not yet been consigned to the pit of flames where other lost souls screamed in torment. The Devil saw her standing on the sandy shore that led down to the pit, and began to chase her with his pitchfork so that he might spear her on it and throw her into the sea of eternal damnation. She ran and ran and ran, while he laughed and chased her—and then she woke up. But when she lay in her bed, sweaty and scared in the aftermath of the nightmare, the face she always saw superimposed over that of the Devil was Lyle's.

"I think my wrist may be broken. I should go to the emergency room and have it X-rayed. Of course, they might ask me what happened. I wonder what they would do if I told them the truth?" With her memory of that grinning dream-Devil to goad her, Maggy found the courage to challenge him, something she hadn't done in a long, long while.

"Are you threatening me, darling?" Lyle's lips thinned into a predatory smile. "I thought I had cured you of that. If not, I'll be glad to provide another lesson. And, just for your information, I'll tell you what would happen: nobody would believe you. If they should, if you should manage to put me in the position of having to defend myself from a charge of spouse abuse, be assured that I would do so very ably. But there's no telling what little secrets might get spilled along the way."

Maggy met that bland gaze with hatred in her own, clearly understanding the threat that reduced her to impotence. "You are a truly evil man," she said.

Lyle's smile broadened. "Our son doesn't think so."

Maggy turned her back on him without attempting to reply. Words would not move Lyle. Nothing moved Lyle. Where she and David were concerned, he held all the cards, and he knew it. Cradling her injured wrist gingerly against the warmth of her body, Maggy headed for the house, back stiff, head high. Lyle's untroubled voice followed her.

"Why don't you wear that yellow linen suit to the Club? You know how much I like you in yellow."

Maggy pretended not to hear.

She walked around the corner out of Lyle's sight, and immediately wished she had chosen another route into the house.

Her mother-in-law was taking breakfast on the glassed-in porch that ran along the west side of the house. With her was her daughter Lucy, and Lucy's husband of thirty years, Hamilton Hodges Drummond IV, who flew his private jet into Louisville regularly to be with his wife. Louella Paxton, the family's longtime cook-housekeeper, was just setting a basket of homemade biscuits down on the table when Maggy came into view.

Maggy checked almost imperceptibly as she saw the assembled company, and let her injured wrist drop to her side despite the shooting pain that made her grit her teeth. She had too much pride to reveal her injury to these people, who might be her in-laws but were never her friends. She was very much the outsider in this close-knit clan, despite twelve years as the titular mistress of the house. In reality, Windermere remained the family home of the Forrests, just as it had been for generations. The only reason she was even tolerated by them was because of David. Which, when she thought about it, was fair enough, because David was the only reason she tolerated them.

Chin up, Maggy continued on. What other choice did she have? She couldn't very well turn on her heel and head the other way, which was what she really wanted to do.

"Good morning, Virginia. Good morning, Lucy, Ham. I didn't realize you'd arrived already." Maggy addressed this last to her brother-in-law, who was a good-looking man of fifty-nine. He was not much taller than her own height of five feet eight, and he had kept his waistline youthfully slim. He sported a very natural-looking black hairpiece, and a dyed-to-match moustache decorated his upper lip. This morning he was dressed in a navy sportcoat, white open-necked shirt, and gray slacks, and he looked as though he had just flown in from New York's Madison Avenue rather than Houston.

"I got in late last night. How are you, honey?" Ham's thick-as-syrup southern drawl had charmed Maggy when she had first met him. Now she knew exactly what lay beneath that courtly exterior, and she was charmed no longer. Still, she managed not to grimace as he gallantly rose, pushing his chair back from the round table with its gay red-and-white-checked cloth. She even presented a cheek for the obligatory kiss between such close relations.

To think she had once thought this family so civilized, so elegantly affectionate with their gentle endearments and air kisses! That had been long ago when she was young and unable to tell fool's gold from the real thing.

She had grown wiser since.

"David just went up to his room. Were you looking for him?" Though Lucy knew that she didn't have to fear Maggy as a rival for her husband's attentions, she was nonetheless fiercely jealous of anyone in whom Ham exhibited an interest. As a result, Lucy's voice was cool, as was her gaze as it fixed on Maggy. Lyle's sister was a large-boned woman, angular and almost awkward in her movements, with iron-gray hair that she scorned to dye cut in a short, boyish style that, like her bright madras-plaid shirtdress, did not become her. Unlike Lyle, Lucy, two years his senior, wore her age badly. She looked older than her husband, a fact of which she was painfully aware. Lucy had never liked her young sister-in-law, and made no pretense that she did. Still, she was outwardly polite, and that was all Maggy had cared about for some time now.

"I *was* looking for David," Maggy said, making the effort and achieving what she felt was a credible smile. "If you'll excuse me, I'll go up after him."

"You won't join us for breakfast?"

From his tone, Maggy would have thought Ham genuinely disappointed. However, she knew better. She shook her head, and started to move away through the open French doors that led from the porch into the kitchen.

"Maggy, did you hurt your arm?" Virginia spoke sharply. Startled, Maggy glanced over her shoulder at her mother-in-law, who was frail and looked small in the wheelchair to which her heart trouble more and more confined her. Like Lucy, Virginia had once been tall and large-boned, but age and two heart attacks in the past year had left her both physically and spiritually diminished. As always, though, she was very perceptive. Maggy had thought she was doing an admirable job of hiding her injury.

"I—twisted my wrist."

Maggy's gaze met Virginia's, and she saw quick, pained comprehension flare in the older woman's eyes. Virginia probably knew her only son as well as anyone in the world. Though she might deplore many of his attitudes and actions, she loved him devotedly nevertheless. As Lucy had once said, with a small smile but entirely without humor, if Lyle committed a murder, Virginia would bury the body and take the secret with her to her grave. Maggy had suspected even then that hers was the body Lucy had in mind.

"You want me to get out the Epsom salts?" Louella asked with concern, pausing on her way back into the kitchen.

"No, I'll take care of it. It's not that bad, really." Maggy had a genuine smile for the white-uniformed black woman. Louella was thin and small, with graying hair that she wore secured in a severe bun at her nape. Though she was nearing sixty, she had lost none of her deft quickness or her way with a cooking pot. She and her husband Herd had been with the Forrests for forty years, and as Maggy had learned from association with her neighbors' help, they could rightly be expected to be more exclusively clannish than members of the family. But even when Maggy had come to Windermere as a bride, knowing nothing of how to conduct herself in a household such as this and as much out of place as a monkey in a tearoom, Louella and Herd had been kind to her. Maggy possessed a soft spot for the couple as a result.

"There's coffee and doughnuts in the kitchen," Louella told her before disappearing through the French doors.

With a wave for the others, Maggy followed Louella inside, again turned down an offer of a basin of Epsom salts in which to soak her wrist, and escaped from the kitchen. Breakfast could wait until she came down again. At the moment, she feared that anything she swallowed would promptly come back up.

David was not in his room, and she wondered if Tipton had already driven him to his lesson. She had wanted to talk to him before he played in the tournament, but supposed it would have to wait until later. Anyway, there was nothing she could say that would erase the intensity of David's need to please Lyle, or the pain he would feel if he didn't succeed. No matter what David did, or how well he did it, Lyle always wanted more from him. If the boy brought home an "A" on a test, Lyle would demand to know why it wasn't an "A-plus."

If there had been any way to do it, Maggy would have packed up her child and run away right then and there. But it was impossible, of course, quite apart from the fact that at the moment David was nowhere to be found. Her son would fight her every step of the way if she tried to take him from the father he idolized—and Lyle would find them, sooner or later. Maggy had no doubt at all about that. And then, one way or another, she might lose David for good.

Defeated, she went to her room and shut and locked the door behind her. In her bathroom she swallowed two aspirin, then soaked a towel in cold water and wrapped it around her swollen wrist. After several such applications, it felt a little better. The first-aid kit in her linen closet contained an elastic bandage. She bound her wrist tightly with it, secured the little clips, and determinedly ignored the heated throbbing. She was heading toward her dressing room to choose an outfit for the day—anything but the yellow linen—when she saw the clumsily wrapped package on her bed.

It was from David. She knew it even before she saw the card on which he had scrawled "Happy Birthday" and his name. As she pulled the last of the gaily decorated paper away, and the gift itself was revealed to her view, her hands stilled of their own accord. During that first moment of recognition, even her breathing suspended.

It was a small, framed watercolor of herself and David and Lyle, sitting outdoors on a bench in the rose garden, arms around each other, smiling, looking the very epitome of the happy family they had never been. It captured the three of them very credibly, feature for feature, except for the joy in their expressions and the pose which must have sprung from somewhere deep in the artist's heart.

For David had painted it, David with his wonderful talent that Lyle ridiculed as "sissy."

Maggy looked at the painting for a moment longer, then abruptly sat down on the edge of her bed, buried her face in her hands, and wept.

aggy viewed the afternoon and evening as something to be gotten through. Her wrist ached, but the pain was lessening to the point where, if she did not move her arm too rapidly, she could more or less ignore it. As sprains went, it was not so bad, as she knew from bitter experience. A few days, a little home treatment, and it would heal. And once again no one would ever know that Lyle Forrest was the kind of man who abused his wife.

The golf course at the Club was lush and green, meticulously maintained by dedicated staff and zealously used by avid members. The Club had a name, of course—Willow Creek Country Club—but to its members it was simply the Club. If the implication was that there was no other country club in town, then that was fine. To the elite of Louisville, there wasn't. The Club did not even have to rely on its enormous initiation fee to keep out the hoi polloi. One had to be invited to join, seconded, vetted, and approved by all the members. Even one "no" vote was enough to derail an application. Not that the Forrests had ever had to do anything so embarrassing as petition for membership. They had belonged to the Club from its inception in the last century. The membership was handed down from generation to generation, world without end.

To Lyle's oft-expressed disgust, Maggy did not like golf, was terrible at it, and, after a disastrous attempt to learn at the beginning of her marriage to please her husband, never played. Still, she would have enjoyed standing in the sparkling sunlight drinking in the fresh, crisp spring air along with the other mothers and wives and miscellaneous family members and friends who formed the gallery, if she hadn't known how excruciating the experience was for David. Waiting silently by the seventeenth hole, she bit her lip as her husband scowled at her son when David's bungled putt dropped them down to sixth place.

David retrieved his ball, looked up, and met his father's gaze. Though no one who didn't *know* would have noticed anything out of line in Lyle's expression, David did know and his face paled. Observing impotently from the sidelines, Maggy thought that there was no one in the world she hated as she hated Lyle at that moment. The worst part was that there was absolutely nothing she could do to help her son. Watching Lyle's tall, spare body twist as he expertly hit the ball while David looked on with misery in his eyes, Maggy felt a rush of malevolence so intense that she almost vibrated with it. For an instant, just an instant, she wished her husband dead. All of her and David's troubles would be over. . . .

"Good job!" Standing beside her, Mary Gibbons, whose husband and youngest son were currently in tenth place, flashed Maggy a congratulatory thumbs-up sign as Lyle's ball rolled neatly into the hole.

"Thanks." Maggy smiled with false pleasure in her husband's accomplishment and turned her attention back to the game. David's next drive was good, long and straight and hard. Maggy let out a silent sigh of relief. Lyle's, of course, was textbook perfect. Trooping over to the eighteenth hole after them, Maggy gritted her teeth and wished that Lyle would miss his next putt as hard as she had ever wished for anything in her life.

Mary Gibbons's son took six strokes where he should have needed no more than two for par. John Gibbons shook his head in playful reproof at his son, who grinned back at him without repentance.

"Actually, Adam's getting a lot better," Mary confided in a comfortable aside to Maggy. "Anyway, he enjoys playing, and that's what's important to John and me."

Maggy managed to murmur an appropriate reply while never taking her eyes from the game. It was Lyle's turn. His ball was perhaps thirty feet from the hole, and his eyes gleamed with concentration as he plotted the route his putt would take.

Ridiculous as it might be, Maggy couldn't help herself. She focused on him, staring at him so hard that he should have felt her eyes drilling through him, willing him to miss, miss, miss. . . .

Lyle positioned himself, swung—and the ball went cleanly into the hole. A cheer went up from the spectators. Maggy had to swallow a curse. She must have been the only one on the whole course who begrudged him his triumph as Lyle fished his ball out of the hole and held it high in the air, a wide grin splitting his face.

David played next. His handsome young face was grim with determination as he positioned himself over the ball. As fervently as she had tried to derail Lyle, Maggy did her best to mentally aid David, willing his ball to go into the hole with all her might. *Please, please, please* . . .

David swung, the ball rolled toward the hole—and at the last moment it did a neat little fishhook to the left as the putt missed by inches. A sympathetic groan arose from the gallery.

So much for psychic power. Despite *Tia* Gloria's fervent assurances to the contrary, Maggy clearly did not possess any. Maggy watched Lyle catch David's gaze again and felt her fists clench.

How could he be so cruel to the son he claimed to love?

When the tournament was over, David and Lyle took seventh place. Lyle accepted the ribbon for participating that was all they won with a grin and an arm thrown around David's shoulders. But Maggy knew, and knew David knew, that Lyle's good humor was strictly for show. David looked miserable, and Maggy's heart ached for him. She knew how hard David had tried, and how bad he felt about not having been as good as Lyle wanted him to be. She knew also about the coldness Lyle would display toward his son for weeks after this, about the endless hours of golf lessons David would have to endure, about the lectures.

She had been there herself, in the early months of her marriage, when Lyle had been determined to mold her into the kind of wife he wanted and Maggy had done everything in her power to please him, to make her marriage work. Only then, as now, there was no pleasing Lyle. No one on earth was that perfect.

An hour later the children were whooping and playing on the rolling grass in front of the golf course. The adults were sitting in cushioned, wrought-iron chairs on the Club's patio and milling around the bar inside, in the informal dining room. Most of them were starting on their third round of drinks.

Maggy, who had stuck to iced tea as she always did, finally managed to excuse herself, ostensibly to visit the ladies' room but really to find David. Lyle had joined him at the Club that morning for a practice round before the tournament, so she had never gotten the opportunity to say what she had wanted to say to him about winning and losing and how unimportant both were in the whole scheme of life. Now all she could offer her son was comfort, and perspective. Losing a golf tournament was not the end of the world.

After a lengthy search, Maggy found him. David was alone, sitting disconsolately on the grass near the parking lot, his back up against the huge iron incinerator that held the Club's trash, his arms wrapped around his drawn-up knees. The imposing facade of the enormous, turn-of-the-century brick mansion that had been remodeled into the club-house forty years before made an incongruous background for the homely incinerator, which at the moment was belching smelly gray feathers of smoke.

David looked so forlorn that he broke her heart.

"Hi," Maggy said, sitting down beside him without a second thought for the noxious odor or the grass stains that might soon adorn her cream silk shorts. Worn with a matching blazer and a white silk T-shirt, the outfit was as fragile as it was pretty. It was not made for sitting on the grass beside a stinking, smoking incinerator with one's arms around one's knees—but Maggy sat anyway, copying David's posture with long-legged grace.

David glanced sideways at her. There were faint, telltale stains on his cheeks and a certain puffiness around his eyes that told her he had been crying. It was something he rarely did anymore—at eleven he consid-ered himself too old for tears—and the evidence that he had succumbed to his emotions in a way he despised made her ache inside. She longed to put her arms around him—but hugged her knees and smiled at him instead.

"What do you want?" David's greeting was truculent.

"To say 'thank you' for my birthday present. It's wonderful, and I love it."

Another sidelong glance, less hostile this time. "Dad won't like it. He says only sissies paint."

Maggy hesitated, though it was an effort to bite back the words that instinctively bubbled to her tongue. It was always hard to know where to draw the line at criticizing Lyle to David. If she went too far, David would respond by leaping to his father's defense, yet she could not let Lyle's views go completely unchallenged.

At last she said in a mild tone, "Dad's not always right about every-thing, you know, David."

The glance he cast her this time was fierce. "He's right about that. I am a sissy! I can't even play golf right!"

So there they reached the heart of his current misery without any circuitous verbal steering on her part. Maggy abandoned the tactful opening she had planned, and groped for the words she needed.

"You played very well. You and Dad came in seventh, after all, out of twenty. That's pretty good."

"Pretty good's not good enough! Dad said we would have won if I hadn't screwed up!"

It was all Maggy could do not to give vent to what she thought of Lyle for that, but she bit back the words. "You didn't screw up, David. You missed a putt. It happens to golfers all the time, even the great ones. Believe me, your *father* has even missed putts. It's part of the game."

"I let Dad down." David spoke so quietly, in such a miserable tone, that Maggy's heart constricted. She longed to wrap her arms around him, but once again she didn't quite dare. Instead, she was quiet for a moment before she responded.

"David, did you ever think that maybe Dad let *you* down? That maybe he should have been proud that you played well enough so that you two came in seventh, instead of being angry because you didn't play quite well enough to come in first?"

David glanced at her, arrested. For a moment, just a moment, Maggy thought she might have knocked the rosy glasses through which he had always viewed Lyle from his eyes. Then his face twisted into a terrible scowl, and he jumped to his feet.

"What do you know about it anyway?" he shouted. "Dad says that with your background, we shouldn't even expect you to understand about golf. He said you were the next thing to a hooker before he married you, and hookers don't play golf."

"What?" Maggy was dumbfounded.

David didn't answer. He flushed, shot her an indecipherable look, and then without another word turned and ran. Within minutes he disappeared around the side of the clubhouse, headed toward where the other children, whose shouts and laughter echoed faintly beneath the grinding of the incinerator, could be seen tumbling all over a grassy knoll. Maggy was left sitting where she was, feeling as if she had taken a body blow. It was all she could do to breathe.

How dare Lyle say such a thing to her son! Maggy felt a flash of white-hot fury that found vent in mentally calling Lyle every filthy name she could think of. Not for the first time, she took the true measure of just how ruthless Lyle was prepared to be in their war over David. She had to face the truth: Lyle would use any weapon that came to hand to turn David finally and absolutely against her, even if he hurt David in the process. To tell a young boy that his mother had once been the next thing to a whore was absolutely unforgivable.

Maggy remembered the "present" Nick had given her that morning and went cold.

Lyle did not know about her brief career as a dancer. He must never find out. He must never come into possession of those pictures, or that tape. If he did, one use he would make of them would be to show them to David. She knew it now with a hideous certainty. What David would think of her then she shuddered to imagine.

There was one defense left to her, of course. But unless she was prepared to break her husband's hold on the boy by destroying David himself, she could not use it. It was too late now to tell the truth.

"Mrs. Forrest, your husband sent me out to fetch you. He says will you please come in now, as your guests will be arriving soon."

Maggy glanced up, surprised to find a wooden-faced waiter addressing her. She had been so lost in thought that she had never even seen him approach. In honor of her birthday, Lyle was hosting a dinner party for family, friends, and business associates. He did so every year, as an official kickoff to the Derby festivities, and to prove to the world what a devoted husband he was. The hypocrisy of it made Maggy sick, but there was nothing she could do but smile and bear it. She just hoped she didn't overhear any comments about how surprisingly well Lyle's unfortunate marriage had worked out, as she had the previous year.

If she did, she feared she might vomit.

"What time is it?" Maggy was surprised to discover that it was twilight. So intent had she been on David that the sun had set without her noticing.

"A little after six, ma'am."

The party was scheduled to begin at seven. The dress she had chosen for the evening would have been packed by Louella in a discreet garment bag along with appropriate accessories and matching shoes, and passed from Tipton to the ladies' locker room attendant by now. Tipton was then supposed to round up David and convey him home. Louella would be there, as would Virginia, who had pronounced herself too old and unfit for dinner parties several years earlier. David would very likely pass a pleasant evening watching TV and playing cards with his grandmother in her suite, so there was no sense worrying about him. Virginia might not choose to champion her daughter-in-law, but she adored David. She would see at a glance that he was upset, and do her best to cheer him up.

David would be fine. With the resiliency of childhood, he had probably already put their last exchange out of his mind. In the morning would be soon enough to talk to him about what Lyle had said. Maybe she should tell David more about her past, or at least the parts that he could know. He knew she had grown up poor, that she had no family left alive, and that she had never lived the way the Forrests did and had done since time immemorial. But that was really all he knew. Maybe it was time to tell David her own story, or at least the parts of it that were safe for him to hear.

But she would think more about that later. Now she had to put on a happy face for their guests, or face Lyle's wrath.

She was not up to that twice in one day. Winging another mental ill-wish at her husband, Maggy got to her feet.

"Tell Mr. Forrest that I'm getting dressed, and I'll join him directly," she said. The waiter bowed and hurried off.

Not quite an hour later, Maggy emerged from the Club's plush locker room, freshly showered and made-up, her hair washed and blow-dried so that it hung in a thick fall of auburn waves down her back. The diamond drops that dangled from her ears sparkled only a little more brightly than her short, full-skirted, strapless dress of iridescent sea-green taffeta strewn with translucent sequins, which made the dress look as though it were fashioned of shimmering fish scales. Pale hose showed off her long legs, and deeper green satin high-heeled mules were on her feet. A wide, bejeweled gold cuff adorned her uninjured wrist. Maggy knew she looked good, as well as slightly outrageous and very expensive, which would please Lyle no end.

He got a kick out of showing off his beautiful, obviously pampered young wife. Almost as much of a kick as he got out of terrorizing her.

Maggy was unsmiling as she walked along the broad, parquet-floored hall to the party room where, if the sounds that were emanating from it were anything to judge by, a number of guests were already assembled. Either it was later than she had supposed, or people had started arriving early.

She slipped through the wide double doors, hoping to enter unnoticed. But her hope was in vain.

"There she is, the birthday girl! Happy birthday, Maggy!" The voice came from her left, and if she wasn't mistaken it belonged to Sarah. Maggie glanced in the direction from which it had come, forcing a smile as the other guests, perhaps a hundred strong at this early hour, began to clap and yell "Happy Birthday!"

As she had expected, she spotted Sarah, gaunt-looking in a tight black sheath, in a huddle with scarlet-clad Buffy, another woman in a pale blue dinner suit, and two men in dark suits with their backs to the door. Sarah waved, saluting her with a half-empty glass. Maggy, always a little shy in these gatherings of the local bluebloods with whom she had never felt quite at ease, moved to join Sarah and her friends, smilingly accepting congratulations from everyone she passed as she went. She was nearly at Sarah's side, having paused to make an inane reply to a question about how it felt to be on the shady side of the big three-oh, when one of the men with Sarah turned to watch her approach.

Maggy felt the color slowly drain from her face as she glanced up and found herself looking through a drift of cigarette smoke into Nick's narrowed hazel-green eyes.

8

The place was ritzy. Nick had to give it that. He'd never had much use for country clubs, but he could see now, glancing around, that they had their merits. If you wanted to impress the pants off someone, this was the place to bring him. The whole setup reeked of class.

Take the room he was standing in, for instance. They probably called it the ballroom, or perhaps the east ballroom or the little ballroom. A place like this would likely have more than one. It was perhaps forty feet long and half as wide, with a marble fireplace in use at one end and a buffet table crammed with silver and china and all sorts of exotic-looking edibles set up at the other. The ceilings were sparkling white and at least twelve feet high, the walls were a tasteful shade of silver-gray, and the dark, highly polished wood floor sported three bright red Oriental carpets that looked, to his unknowledgeable eye at least, to be ruinously expensive. Two enormous crystal chandeliers sparkled overhead. Champagne flowed as easily as conversation, and the hors d'oeuvres were so fancy that he couldn't identify a single one of them by sight. In one corner of the room a tuxedoed pianist played soft background music next to a sunken pit that was clearly meant for use as a small but adequate dance floor. The advantage of having a live musician over a tape player, which was what they'd usually had at the parties he'd been to, was that a live musician would take requests, if accompanied by a bill of sufficiently large denomination. In this case, a twenty had sufficed to insure that the song Nick wanted would be played when he wanted it.

A half grin curled his mouth as he reflected that he intended to haunt Magdalena as thoroughly as any ghost.

"Would you look at Maggy's dress! I wish *I* had a husband who could afford to keep me in Valentinos," the woman beside him—Buffy—said half enviously, glancing beyond his right shoulder. Nick turned to see for himself. His gaze found Maggy, and his surroundings ceased to exist.

She looked like a mermaid, was Nick's first thought. A drop-dead-gorgeous, redheaded mermaid. The effect the sight of her had on him caught him by surprise. It was immediate and devastating, like a baseball bat to the stomach. It was all he could do not to gasp for air. After twelve years, he hadn't guessed that his emotions where she was concerned were still so raw, so sharp.

He had never gotten over her. He had long since come to doubt that he ever would.

So he'd come back for her. That was the bottom line. He could tell himself all he wanted to that he had come back to wreak bloody vengeance on Lyle Forrest. Not that that wasn't true as well. He meant to destroy Lyle, to explode his world as thoroughly as Lyle had once exploded his. And he had the firepower to do it. He was only biding his time.

Magdalena's little belly dance wasn't the only interesting piece of film that had lately come into his possession.

He'd put out the word that he was looking for dirt on Lyle Forrest, and the amount of sewage that had come rolling back in at him had surprised even him. For a southern gentleman of means and lineage, old Lyle got up to some pretty nasty tricks.

It was the inbreeding, most likely, Nick had decided with a sneer as he went over the material. Like pedigreed dogs, the fine old families from which Lyle was descended had mated with one another for generations, and what they eventually produced wasn't in the original gene pool. Give him a mongrel anytime, Nick thought. Which was how he'd always seen himself, as a mongrel.

Just like Magdalena.

Though no one would have guessed it, the way she looked tonight.

Pride in her was mixed with a certain degree of resentment at her upgraded station in life as Nick registered that in her fancy duds she looked more "to the manor born" than any of the other equally dolled-up women in the place. She'd always been beautiful, of course. Even as a ragged, dirty little girl of seven or eight, she had had a grace and a delicacy of form and feature that set her apart from the rest. But now, adorned in the trappings that came with pots of money, she was dazzling. Just looking at her took his breath away.

She was going to be his again. Hell, she had always been his. From the time they were kids, it was always Magdalena and Nick, Nick and Magdalena, all but abandoned by their respective drunken parents, the two of them against the world. Her marriage to Lyle Forrest had almost killed him in more ways than one, but it had been a mistake, a young girl's mistake. He saw that now. He wouldn't hold it against *her*. For years, he'd been ragingly angry about the way she'd left him, hating her almost as much as he hated *him*. But even then, even when he'd hurt inside as if someone had pistol-whipped his heart and had been crazy with rage as well, he'd understood why she'd done it: for the money. When you never had so much as two quarters to rub together, money became very important, the most important thing in the world.

Finding enough to eat each day had been a major goal of their childhood. The threat of eviction for nonpayment of rent had been a monthly thing. Clothes—his eyes once again moved over Maggy in her drop-dead dress, narrowing this time with wry remembrance—their clothes had come from the Salvation Army. If they were lucky. If they weren't, they'd worn rags.

Especially as Magdalena had gotten older, become a teenager, she had minded about the clothes. Minded so much that he had more than once gotten her some new ones, stylish and pretty and never worn and size six, shoplifting them from tony stores at the malls. She'd been his, and no one who was his ever went without if he could provide. Whatever it took.

So he understood why she had married Lyle Forrest. Hell, back then if some rich old woman had wanted to carry him off to a better life, who was to say that he would not have done the same thing?

But times had changed. He was no longer a dirt-poor kid, stealing cars and breaking into houses and shoplifting and doing any other damn thing he could to provide for himself and his mother and brother as well as Magdalena and her father. He'd made it, financially. Maybe some of the tactics he'd used to pull himself up by his bootstraps had been a little shady, but his business interests were legit now. No grand jury could touch him.

But they were going to have a field day with old Lyle.

Divorce was easy. Magdalena would get one. Just as soon as he had persuaded her that she should.

It shouldn't take long. She was his, just as she'd always been. She knew it, too. He had read it in her eyes, her face, her body from the first moment she set eyes on him again. All they had to do was look at each other, and the twelve years that had passed since they last met no longer existed.

He was even prepared to take her boy, Lyle Forrest's seed though he was, and treat him as his own son. As Nick pondered this last, a glimmer of humor softened his mouth. If he knew anything of Magdalena Rose Garcia—and he had once known her very well indeed—there wouldn't be any question of her running off with him and leaving her son behind. Those she loved, she loved totally.

The way she had once loved him.

No, the way she still loved him, and would love him for the rest of their lives. She was afraid to face it, but sooner or later she would. This time around he was not taking no for an answer. Whatever it took.

Nick reached into his pocket for the pack of cigarettes that he was never without these days, tapped one out, lit it, and inhaled a lungful of smoke as he watched Magdalena approach.

aggy felt her knees go weak. Her lips parted and her eyes widened with disbelieving horror as she registered that it really, truly, was he at her birthday party, in the same room as Lyle, whom she could see out of the corner of her eye not twenty feet away, talking to a business associate and his wife.

Lyle was going to be insane with rage when he caught sight of Nick.

Maggy shuddered. *Hail, Mary, full of grace* . . . The prayer of her Catholic childhood rose unbidden to her lips as her eyes swung from Nick to Lyle and back.

"Happy birthday, pretty lady!"

The speaker was James Brean, president of the Bluegrass Bank and a close friend of Lyle's. Maggy smiled automatically, accepting his kiss on her cheek with a graciousness born of practice, and spent several minutes chatting with him and his wife Ellen. What they talked about Maggy couldn't afterward have said if her life depended on it.

Nick was watching her the whole time.

At last she managed to extricate herself with a murmur about mingling. With a kind of helpless compulsion, she moved toward Nick. His gaze had never left her, and now it reeled her in as surely as a hooked fish. Though the gathering was growing larger by the minute—perhaps two hundred guests now milled around the buffet table, laughing and gossiping as they cadged drinks from the waiters moving among them with loaded silver trays—it would be almost impossible for Lyle to miss Nick. Lyle was ever the attentive host, and he always made a point of speaking to every guest at one of his parties. He loved pressing the flesh and mingling. That was just what he would do, and he would inevitably stumble across Nick.

Perhaps, she thought with scant hope, she could persuade Nick to leave.

"Happy birthday, Maggy!" Sarah said gaily as Maggy walked up to their group. Though Maggy originally had eyes for no one but Nick, this greeting recalled her to a sense of her surroundings. She managed a smile for Sarah.

"Thank you. It's so nice of you all to come." Maggy was surprised at how normal her voice sounded as her smile expanded to include the rest of the group.

"It's nice of you to ask us," replied the woman in the blue dinner suit whom she had noticed standing with Sarah earlier. What was her name? Before Maggy could call it to mind, the woman glanced down at Maggy's bandaged left wrist, and her brows went up. "What happened, if you don't mind my asking?"

Maggy managed a little laugh. "Oh, I fell over one of the dogs. It's not serious, only a very minor sprain."

The woman shook her head in commiseration. "I know how you must feel. I once tripped over our daughter's cat and fell halfway down a flight of stairs. I twisted my knee, and had to spend the next three weeks on crutches."

"During which time she tried very hard to persuade our daughter that she was allergic to cats," the man next to her added with a grin. "With no success, I might add."

They all laughed politely.

"You know Mike Sullivan, don't you? And his wife Joan?" Sarah, belatedly making introductions, seemed to notice nothing amiss in Maggy's demeanor, for which Maggy was thankful. Living with Lyle had taught her the art of public dissembling to a fare-thee-well, apparently.

"Yes, of course. It's good to see you again." Maggy shook hands with the man and his wife, complimenting the woman on her suit's lovely shade of blue as she did so. Joan Sullivan then admired Maggy's dress and was thanked in return. Maggy's face felt stiff with the effort of keeping a smile on it as she struggled to make conversation. Unlike Lyle, she was not at her best exchanging meaningless chitchat with near strangers, and her natural reticence was made even worse by the presence of the man at her side. She was heart-thumpingly conscious of Nick looming at her right elbow, watching her, not saying a word. It was all she could do to breathe, much less engage in social niceties without so much as looking at him, but she forced herself to soldier on. "How is Becky?"

Becky was the Sullivans' ten-year-old daughter, presumably the owner of the cat, who attended the same exclusive private school as David. It was a stroke of luck that put the child's name in Maggy's mouth just when she needed it.

"Just fine," Joan answered with a beaming smile. "And how is David? Is he going to camp this summer?"

The subsequent exchange could not have taken more than a minute or two, but it seemed like an eternity to Maggy. From the corner of her eye she saw that Lyle was on the move, and he could very well spot Nick at any moment. She desperately needed a chance to talk to Nick alone, to see if she could persuade him to leave.

"I hope you don't mind me bringing a guest," Buffy interjected when Joan paused to take a sip from the glass she was holding. As Buffy spoke she slid her hand in the crook of Nick's arm and smiled slyly at Maggy. Maggy, her eyes drawn against her will to those possessive scarlet-tipped fingers, shook her head. What other response could she possibly have made?

"I didn't think you would. After all, Nick *is* an old friend of yours. And when I told him that it was your birthday party I was asking him to, he was positively eager to come."

"Happy birthday, Magdalena," Nick said smoothly as she looked at him at last. His eyes glinted at her over the cigarette he raised to his mouth, but his expression gave nothing away. Only she, who knew him so well, could read the mockery behind the mask.

"Why, Mr. King, I didn't realize you knew the Forrests! How are you?" James Brean joined them, shaking hands with Nick and grabbing a glass of champagne from a passing tray at the same time. "How's the nightclub business these days?"

"Prosperous," Nick said, taking another drag from his cigarette. "We're expanding. We've just bought the Little Brown Cow over in Indiana, and we're looking at a couple of clubs on this side of the river."

"Well, if our bank can be of any help, just let me know."

"I bet you say that to all the rich folk," Buffy purred, batting her eyes at James Brean even as her hold on Nick tightened possessively. Brean might not know when he was being pumped, but Maggy recognized the ploy: Buffy was still trying to determine Nick's financial status, to see if he was worth pursuing as anything more than a toy-boy.

Maggy realized that she was more than a trifle curious on that point herself. Nick said he had bought the Little Brown Cow, but had he really? With whose money? His own? Not likely. When she'd known him, he'd never had a dime. Or, as seemed more plausible, was he running some kind of scam? He certainly looked well-to-do, and he sounded well-to-do, and he had the air of total self-confidence that she had learned came with being well-to-do, but then he had always had the ability to be the consummate con man when he wished. Nobody knew Nick better than she knew Nick, or at least better than she had once known Nick, and in her opinion he was perfectly capable of acting out an elaborate lie if it was in his best interests to do so.

It all came back to that one burning question: What was he doing in Louisville? He had not turned up like a bad penny on her doorstep just to give her the pictures and tape, she knew. Her deepest instinct told her that he was up to no good. But no good for whom? If he meant to fool Brean, or the entire banking establishment for that matter, into thinking he was a legitimate businessman with the wherewithal to buy nightclubs, it was no skin off her teeth. If he was, by some stretch of the imagination, a legitimate businessman with said wherewithal, that was no skin off her teeth either. She wished him well.

As long as he left her, and hers, alone.

But would he? Maggy's stomach started to churn as she faced the truth: If he meant to leave her alone, he would not have turned up at her party tonight.

What did he want from her? Maybe nothing more than an introduction to her well-connected friends. Maybe. And maybe not.

"Not all of them." Brean grinned at Buffy. "Just the ones I think my bank can make money on."

"At least you're honest," Joan Sullivan said with a laugh, while Ellen Brean poked her husband reprovingly, and Buffy looked up at Nick with a beguiling smile.

From the front of the room, the sound of a fork being clinked against a champagne glass drew all eyes. Maggy, too, glanced around, to find that Lyle was standing in front of the buffet table, fork and glass in hand, smiling widely as he got the assembly's undivided attention.

"We have a beautiful birthday cake up here," he announced, "which I for one am dying to tuck into. We can't do that until we wish my wife happy birthday, so let's get her up here, shall we? Maggy, darling, where are you?"

Lyle's eyes swept the room even as Maggy started forward. They found her—"Ah, there she is! Get up here, Maggy!"—then went beyond her, where they fixed and widened. On Nick. Maggy knew it without even having to look around. In that moment of thundering silence, she could feel the tension charging over her head between the locked gazes of the two men like arcing, sparking electricity.

It was a shock to glance around at the smiling, expectant faces of the guests who were waiting for her to reach Lyle's side and realize that she was probably the only one besides the two principals who was aware of their silent, sizzling exchange. Unable to help herself, Maggy glanced over her shoulder at last. She was just in time to watch as Nick lifted his glass and smiled—a slow, insolent, challenging smile—at Lyle. Swiftly Maggy looked back at her husband, and was only one of two-hundred-plus witnesses as all the color drained from Lyle's face and he took a small, unbalanced step backward to fetch up hard against the buffet table.

"Lyle, are you all right?" Ham was the first to reach him, catching his brother-in-law's arm and peering worriedly into his face. A dozen others crowded in behind Ham, including Lucy, who shoved her way to her brother's side.

Maggy joined the clucking circle just in time to see Lyle shake off Ham's hand and stand upright again.

"I'm fine," he said with a touch of irritation. "Don't be an old woman, Ham. I just felt a little strange for a second, is all. Probably I need to eat."

"Well, sit down, man, for God's sake." Ham looked genuinely concerned.

"I tell you, I'm fine. Where's Maggy?"

"I'm right here." Maggy squeezed past Lucy so that Lyle could see her. His gaze held hers for an instant, and she shuddered inwardly at what she read in his pale blue eyes. She would face an awful retribution later for Nick's presence here tonight, she knew.

She felt suddenly chilled to her bone marrow. Then Lyle reached out and caught her elbow, pulling her to his side as he turned her to face the crowd. Maggy smiled automatically at the sea of faces before her, though dread iced her veins. She had seen that particular expression on Lyle's face only once before, not quite a year after David's birth, when she still hadn't known what kind of monster lurked beneath her husband's elegant exterior. She had learned, that night, in terror and degradation, to know the true man, and had never forgotten the lesson.

Now, as Lyle slid his arm around her waist, squeezing her close against him, Maggy offered no protest, though she shuddered somewhere deep inside. Yet all the while she beamed never-endingly at their guests. God forbid they should know that anything was amiss! Keeping up appearances could have been the Forrest family credo, and by now she was as indoctrinated in that as the rest of them.

"As you all know, we are gathered here tonight to wish my wife happy birthday on this, the thirtieth anniversary of her arrival on this planet. If you'll all join in, we'll get the formalities out of the way, and then, in the immortal words of Marie Antoinette, why, let 'em eat cake!"

Lyle signaled to the pianist, who launched into the opening bars of "Happy Birthday to You." Everyone joined in, producing an exuberant, off-key version of the classic. It was the very antithesis of what Maggy was feeling as she smiled in acknowledgment, looking the picture of the happy, well-loved wife while Lyle's affectionate-seeming embrace chained her to his side.

When she contemplated what she faced once they were alone, she felt frightened tears crowd the backs of her eyes.

Maggy blinked them back as the song ended. Everyone applauded, and then Lyle reached into the inside pocket of his suit. He pulled out a small, flat package, tastefully wrapped in shiny silver paper and tied with silver ribbons, and presented it to her with a flourish. Maggy accepted the gift with a smile that hid her gritted teeth, and proceeded to tear off the wrappings with, she hoped, a degree less savagery than she felt. Everything Lyle did was done for show, including the acquisition of a young "trophy" wife and later a son. The annual public presentation of her birthday present was no exception. If there hadn't been an audience to see and be impressed by his thoughtfulness and the expensiveness of his gift, Maggy knew that Lyle would have forgotten the date of her birth altogether.

The leather jeweler's box contained a diamond brooch in the shape of a panther.

"It once belonged to the Duchess of Windsor," Lyle said with satisfaction to everyone within hearing distance, while Maggy dutifully held the box up so that the gift could be admired and exclaimed over. Knowing it was expected of her, she smiled up at her husband.

"It's beautiful. Thank you." Hating herself for playing along, Maggy nevertheless went up on tiptoe to press a quick kiss to Lyle's cheek. His skin felt cold, almost reptilian, beneath her lips. It was all she could do not to shudder in revulsion at the brief contact. But she performed her part in their prescripted little drama without a flaw. Lyle's eyes gleamed with satisfaction as she stepped back.

"I'll keep this for you until we can put it in the safe at home." Lyle took the box from her and restored it to his pocket. Maggy knew that she would see the brooch again only when he wanted her to wear it to impress someone. Lyle kept the jewelry he bought for her under lock and key, and that, Maggy knew, was to keep her as dependent on him as possible. Not that he really feared she would try to leave him—after all, he still had David as the ultimate trump card—but just in case.

Maggy, still smiling though her facial muscles ached at the effort, cut the magnificent, five-tiered chocolate cake, and held out the first piece to Lyle so that he could eat from her hand, just as a bride might feed her new husband cake at their wedding reception. This was an old ritual at her birthday party, one that Lyle insisted she follow every year. The hypocrisy of it used to sicken her, but lately she had grown beyond even being sickened by what her life had become.

If hypocrisy had only been the worst of her troubles, she would have borne it gladly.

Lyle ate his cake, fed her a piece, and the pianist launched into the opening bars of "Blue Skies." She barely had time to wipe her mouth with a napkin before Lyle grabbed her hand and ran with her down the pair of steps to the dance floor, where he swung her into his arms for their ritual dance. Lyle was a wonderful dancer, exhibitionistic in that as in everything else, twirling her around so that her full skirt swirled, dipping her and twirling her again. One hand resting on his shoulder and the other on his waist, a smile pinned to her face, Maggy played her part in the charade just as she did every year. When they finished, the guests applauded.

"Have a good time, folks. The buffet's open and the dance floor's hot," Lyle yelled. Then the ritual was over. Lyle dropped her hand as they ascended the steps. Maggy paused to accept compliments on Lyle's dancing from one of the couples who were already moving onto the dance floor. Most of the guests had descended upon the buffet in a chattering throng, she saw as the couple moved away at last and she was free to glance around. Waiters were dishing up shrimp Creole and beef Wellington and all the trimmings, and slicing and serving the cake. Lyle was huddled with James Brean and a little group of businessmen in the far corner of the room. Lyle always had some deal or another in the works. Rich though he was, he was tireless in his pursuit of more money. Relieved to be freed of his presence, temporarily at least, and completely devoid of appetite, Maggy glanced longingly toward the door. She needed to get outside, get a breath of fresh air, and decide what was best to do.

What could she do?

A tall man in an expensive-looking navy suit planted himself squarely in front of her, blocking her escape. Nick. She knew who it was even before her eyes traveled up over his broad, white-shirted chest and elegant foulard tie past the linebacker's shoulders to his toughly handsome face. His expression was grave as he met her gaze, though there was the merest hint of a twinkle in his eyes that told her he knew she was less than pleased to be cornered by him.

Unable to control the impulse, Maggy swiftly glanced past him to see if Lyle was watching them. He was still far away in the corner of the room, for which she was thankful. His back was turned to them as he talked with his friends.

10

"*C*hampagne?" Nick asked, holding up a crystal flute half full of the golden liquid. An identical crystal flute was in his other hand, and he swirled its contents idly as he waited for her response.

"Please," Maggy said in a low, tense voice, ignoring the proffered glass, her eyes just touching Nick's before darting away toward Lyle again, "just leave."

He downed the champagne in his glass in a gulp—Lyle would have been outraged at the lack of respect for the expensive vintage—and then downed the contents of the second glass too. With a jerk of his head he caught the attention of a passing waiter and set the glasses down on the tray he bore, not caring that it held only newly poured drinks. Wooden faced, the waiter disappeared.

"Run out on your birthday party? Not on your life."

"Please, Nick."

"Afraid my presence will upset old Lyle?" His eyes narrowed on her face. "You're right: it might. But what do you care?"

"I care." Never had she ever spoken a truer statement, Maggy thought with a bubbling up of what was almost hysteria. Of course, Nick didn't understand. No one did.

"Why? You don't love him. Do you?"

"No." She couldn't lie anymore. Not to Nick. Not when she was almost sick with fear—and light-headed with the sudden need to walk into Nick's arms and have them close around her as they used to do. He had always protected her. Always. But however much every instinct she possessed urged her to, she couldn't turn to him now. She was on her own. With her own actions she had put herself forever beyond his reach. "Now would you please go away? You're making my life difficult."

"If you don't love him, why don't you leave him? It can't be the money keeping you. After twelve years, you'd get a fat settlement. Or did he talk you into signing a prenuptial agreement?" The satirical edge to his voice as he said this last stung.

"There's David." Her response was cool.

"So? Plenty of kids' parents get divorced. He'd adjust."

"This really isn't the time or place for this discussion, is it? Anyway, why I choose to stay married to my husband is no concern of yours."

"Isn't it, Magdalena?" Nick's voice was very soft. She glanced up, met his eyes. They were disturbingly intent, and his mouth quirked in the faintest suggestion of a wry smile.

Ah, Nick. How often had she seen that expression on his face before? It was so familiar, so beloved and dear, that her heart gave a sharp, painful throb.

"Go away," she said between stiff lips and turned her shoulder to him, meaning to walk away.

"Not without you. Not this time." He caught her arm just above the elbow. His palm was warm and large, his fingers long, his skin faintly callused. His hand was big enough to easily encircle her upper arm with room to spare. She glanced down, absorbing the swarthiness of his skin, which seemed even darker compared with the lily-whiteness of hers, the size and power of the hand that held her, the faint scattering of silky black hairs across its back, the gold of his expensive watch just peeking from beneath the gleaming white cuff of his shirt.

His hand, bold and possessive, curled around her arm as though it had every right to do so. She wished, oh, how she wished, it did.

"Please let me go." She did not try to pull away, afraid that they would attract undue attention if he refused to release her. Instead, she turned toward him to lessen the appearance that he was detaining her, and even managed a brittle smile.

"I don't think I can." He smiled at her, and the wryness she had noticed moments earlier was there in force. "I don't think you want me to. Tell the truth for once, Magdalena. Do you really want me to go away?" His grip loosened, became almost a caress as his fingers moved against the soft skin of her arm. She steeled herself against him, and pulled her arm free.

"Yes, I do," she said with cold, clear decision for all she spoke in an undertone. "You're a complication my life doesn't need."

He laughed suddenly, surprising her.

"You don't exactly simplify my life either, you know."

"So do us both a favor and leave me alone."

Despite the curt dismissal of her words, he reached out and caught her hand. Twining his fingers in hers, he pulled her toward the dance floor, pausing only to tap the pianist on the shoulder on the way.

"Damn it, Nick, let me go!" Maggy said in a furious undertone as they reached the dance floor and he turned to face her, his hand still imprisoning hers. Conscious of the other dancing couples, some of whom were watching, Maggy kept a smile glued to her lips. Though she had no doubt that it did not fool Nick, who was more accustomed than most to reading the danger signals in her eyes.

"Don't swear, Magdalena," he chided her on a tender note just as the pianist began a new song. Then he pulled her into his arms.

" 'Hey, where did we go days when the rain came, . . .' " Nick sang the words softly in her ear as Maggy subsided against him in shock. " 'Laughin' in the hollows . . .' "

She hadn't listened to that song in years. Twelve years, to be precise. On the few occasions when she had been in a car and it had been aired with a selection of oldies, she'd asked that the radio be switched off. It had been too painful to listen to, because it brought back so many memories. Wonderful memories. Heartbreaking memories. And he knew it. Damn him, he knew it, and he was deliberately having it played so that she would remember things he knew she'd rather forget.

Nick had always loved that song, because he'd said it made him think of her. Magdalena's song, he'd called it, just as he had once called her "My Brown-Eyed Girl."

"Do you remember when we used to sing sha-la-la-la-la . . ." Nick's arms were wrapped around her waist, holding her close against his body. Her arms were looped around his neck. The song had shocked her so that she hadn't even realized what she was doing until she was plastered against him, dancing like a want-wit in his arms. Now it was too late. To pull away from him would, she feared, cause more comment than finishing out the dance, especially if he wouldn't easily let her go. Which, knowing Nick, he wouldn't.

Maggy tried to put a modicum of space between their bodies, and realized he wasn't going to let her do even that. Turning her head, she rewarded him with a furious glare, to which he responded with a twinkle and a naughty smile. No shame there. Maggy resigned herself to the dance. If only, she prayed, Lyle stayed at the far end of the room.

Nick had never been a great dancer—his forte was a standard box step—but then, he'd never needed to be. The thrill in dancing with Nick came from having his arms around her, feeling the hardness of his chest pressing against her breasts, feeling the brush of his thighs against her own as he moved her with him. When they were kids, all the girls had wanted to dance with Nick. He had usually obliged them, too, until the last few months they'd been together. Then she'd been the only one. . . .

" 'You, my brown-eyed girl . . .' " Nick sang the words into her ear, pulling her even closer as he did so and executing a less-than-graceful turn. "My brown-eyed girl."

Despite the best will in the world to do so, Maggy couldn't prevent the memories from washing over her. She'd taken him to her junior prom, at Manual High School. They'd sneaked in, because the twenty-five-dollars-a-person cost of a ticket had been as out of reach for them as the price of the Hope diamond. She was sixteen, he was eighteen. She wore a white dress with a tulle skirt and a silver flower in her hair, both courtesy of Nick's skill as a thief. He wore a tuxedo that he'd borrowed from a friend who ran a funeral parlor. In it he was so handsome that just looking at him had made her heart speed up. When he took her in his arms, he had made her shake—and this was while he was still treating her like a well-loved but sexless little sister. As far as she knew, he'd remained oblivious of her mad crush on him until that night.

It had been a magical night. He had even kissed her goodnight. The chaste peck on her lips had kept her dreaming of him for months of nights.

"Remember your prom, Magdalena?" he whispered. Maggy was surprised and yet not surprised to realize that his thoughts were running parallel with hers. It had always been like that, with Nick. He had known what she was thinking almost as soon as she did.

Maggy closed her eyes and let her head rest against his shoulder.

Like that, they finished out the dance.

When the song ended, her eyes didn't open until Nick put her away from him, his hands resting on either side of her waist. Maggy blinked at him, feeling dazed. Nick smiled broadly down into her eyes.

Around them people were glancing their way. Maggy caught some of the looks, flushed, and experienced a frisson of pure panic. Please God Lyle hadn't witnessed that dance. . . .

"Keep away from me," she said through teeth that were bared in a travesty of a social smile, and jerked free of his hands. Turning her back on him, she marched to the edge of the dance floor and up the shallow steps. Nick was right behind her. She could feel his eyes boring a hole through her back. The pianist was already playing another song. Everyone was dancing again, and no one was paying the least attention to her and Nick. If she could just get away from him, Lyle need never know. Two steps beyond the dance floor, she turned on him.

Furious brown eyes met teasing hazel-green ones and shot him a look that should have stopped him in his tracks. But Nick, remembering her temper of old, merely crossed his arms over his chest and looked ready to enjoy the attack.

"Maggy." Lyle's arctic voice behind her made her jump sky-high, and she glanced back over her shoulder like a startled fawn. He'd seen her dancing with Nick. She knew it as soon as she caught a glimpse of his face. The rage went out of her like air from a deflating balloon, and burgeoning fear took its place. Lyle's hand clamped over her elbow, bringing her back to reality with a shock. His touch made her skin crawl.

"Lyle." She started to sweat. Nerves set her pulses to pounding as, still keeping her arm imprisoned, he moved to stand beside her. Glancing up at her husband again, Maggy was surprised to find James Brean just beyond his shoulder, beaming jovially at her. With them was Brean's wife Ellen, and Buffy. All were smiling. Even Lyle's lips were curved upward. Only his eyes were cold.

Maggy thanked God for the presence of outsiders.

"Shame on you, Maggy, for trying to steal my date," Buffy said with playful reproof, and slid over to Nick's side, where she tucked a hand in the crook of his elbow and smiled up at him with kittenish charm. Then her gaze shifted to Lyle. "You know Nick King, don't you, Lyle? I assume you must, if he's an old friend of Maggy's."

Maggy wondered if she was only imagining the malice in Buffy's voice.

"We've met," Nick said after an instant's silence in which the two men's gazes locked. "But it was just briefly, and many years ago." He paused and smiled a killer-crocodile smile while looking directly into Lyle's eyes. "It's a pleasure to have the chance to renew the acquaintance."

"The pleasure is all mine." Was Maggy the only one who heard the danger that underlay Lyle's reply? Even Nick seemed impervious to the threat, maybe because it was veiled by a thin veneer of courtesy. Of course, Nick didn't know Lyle as she did.

"Mr. King just purchased a nightclub we were getting ready to foreclose on over in Indiana. Didn't you also make us an offer on that, Lyle? The Brown Cow?" James Brean glanced at Lyle for confirmation.

"The Little Brown Cow," Lyle said smoothly. "But unlike Mr. King, who I believe makes his living by running sleazy nightclubs, my interest was purely in the property's intrinsic value as an investment. I happen to think that the Indiana waterfront is hugely underpriced."

"What a tip!" Brean said with a laugh, smoothing over the tension that only Maggy and the two men involved seemed to be aware of. "If I only had a few hundred thousand to spare, I'd start snapping up property over there. Do you think the bank would notice if I gave myself a loan?"

"Don't even make jokes like that!" his wife admonished him with a poke.

"Oh, everybody knows I'm just kidding. You take things too seriously." Brean rubbed his side where Ellen's forefinger had dug in.

"So you bought the Little Brown Cow? It's such a—cozy little place! So country! Will you be running it yourself?" Buffy sounded delighted as she gazed up at Nick.

"I'll put in new management who will eventually take over completely, but until the place is profitable I'll oversee things." Nick extracted his cigarettes from his pocket, put one to his lips, and lit it before repocketing the lighter and pack.

"Oh." Buffy looked fascinated.

"So how long do you expect to be in Louisville?" Lyle asked.

Nick took a drag on his cigarette, and let the smoke drift from his lips before replying.

"For just as long as it takes," he said. Maggy shivered as Nick's gaze met Lyle's again. Were the others totally insensitive, that they didn't pick up on the undertone to the conversation? Couldn't they feel the hostility in the air? Couldn't they see the enmity that surged between the two men?

At Nick's answer, Lyle's hand tightened so viciously around Maggy's elbow that it was all she could do not to cry out. She bit her lower lip, and felt a fresh wave of chills run down her spine. Lyle was going to go crazy with rage as soon as they were alone. The prospect made her feel nauseated.

"Do you feel well, Maggy? You look pale." Ellen Brean spoke with concern.

Maggy opened her mouth to deny any illness—and then realized that here was her salvation. At all costs, she wanted to avoid being alone with Lyle tonight. She knew his moods, and this one scared her.

"You know, I *am* starting to feel ill," she said. "I think I must be coming down with the flu. David was sick with it all last week." She sent her best for-appearances-only smile up at Lyle. "I hoped I'd be able to make it through the party, but I don't think I can. I'm afraid I'm going to have to go home and lie down."

"Do you feel that bad, Maggy?" Buffy asked with a little smile. Of course, Buffy would be glad if Maggy went home so she could have Nick all to herself.

"You don't want to miss your birthday party," Lyle said. Maggy caught the warning edge to his voice, though she didn't think anyone else did. He knew that she was trying to slip away from him, but in public there was little he could do to foil her.

"I'll drive you home." Nick's offer was abrupt. Maggy glanced up at him with sudden alarm—she had never intended this—and shook her head.

"No, I . . ." she began.

"I'll take you myself," Lyle interrupted her. He was not glaring at Nick—Lyle was far too subtle for that—but his dislike was expressed in every tense line of his body. Was she really the only one who could see?

"You have to stay and see to our guests," she said to Lyle firmly. "I wouldn't dream of taking you away from the party. For both of us to leave would be just too rude." Her eyes flickered up to Nick's, and away. "And I wouldn't dream of breaking up your date. I'll borrow Sarah's car. She can ride home with Lucy and Ham. Or Lyle." She glanced at Lyle again as she finished.

For an instant, no longer, his gaze met hers and promised an awful retribution for her night's work. Then he surrendered with outward grace. "If you are truly ill, then driving yourself home is not a good idea. And you're right, it would be rude for both of us to leave the party." A triumphant gleam appeared in his eyes. "Tipton can fetch you. If you-all will excuse me a minute, I'll give him a call."

Lyle pulled the small phone he was never without from his pocket, unfolded it and, turning his shoulder on the group, placed the call. Maggy knew he had agreed to allow her to leave only because he could count on Tipton to convey her straight home. She would be under guard all the way, and, with the cars locked up, would presumably have no way to leave the estate once she got there. Lyle could exit the party at his leisure, and when he did he would know where to find his errant wife.

The prospect made her shiver.

11

It was not yet nine o'clock when Tipton dropped Maggy off at the house—absurdly early to be returning from a party. Usually her birthday celebration lasted until the wee hours of the following morning. Maggy slid out of the backseat and went inside without a word to Tipton, who stood silently watching as she entered. On Lyle's orders, no doubt.

The first thing Maggy did was to reset the alarm. That it be kept on at night was one of Lyle's rules. Supposedly the purpose of the elaborate system was to protect the household valuables from burglars, but in reality Maggy suspected that Lyle had had it installed to keep track of her. There was a monitor by his bed that beeped whenever a door or window was opened, and a computer logged the exact times the system was turned off and on. Thus Lyle would know precisely when she had arrived home tonight, and that she had not gone out again.

Shedding her coat and leaving it on a chair in the front hall—Maggy had gotten spoiled by knowing that Louella would pick up after her, and never gave her action a second thought—she headed toward the west wing, where Virginia's apartment was located. She meant to look in on David before she did anything else.

The house was huge, with twenty-one rooms, including eight bedrooms, each of which came complete with a private bath and sitting area. The first time she had walked through it she had been thoroughly awed, and not a little intimidated. She'd been eighteen years old, and three months married to a man who seemed more instead of less of a stranger with every day that passed. She was his legal wife, but Maggy felt she didn't know Lyle Forrest at all.

Worse, she was even starting to feel like a stranger to herself. A stranger in a strange land, wasn't that how the quote went? That was how she felt. Nothing—her surroundings, her husband, her pregnancy, herself—seemed quite real. She was no longer the wild, heedless girl she had been, no longer the girl who had laughed freely and sworn freely and said frankly what was on her mind. For the first time in her life, she didn't know who she was. She wasn't Magdalena Garcia any longer— but she wasn't Maggy Forrest, either.

She felt like a nonentity. Lyle had stripped her identity from her as ruthlessly as he had had an anonymous maid at a hotel they had stayed in throw away her old clothes while she slept. He had then summoned a personal shopper to select a whole new wardrobe for her from Bergdorf's in New York, and despite her annoyance at his high-handedness, she had to admit that the new outfits had looked fabulous on her. Unfortunately, she discovered that she couldn't reclothe her spirit as easily as she could her body. To her surprise, she found that she valued the person she had been, and it had been both a shock and a blow to learn that Lyle apparently did not.

Yet twelve years ago she had been too young, too needy, too dazzled at the unbelievable Cinderella twist her life had taken to resent Lyle or what he was doing to her. She'd been so poor—and suddenly she was rich. Money for rent wasn't a problem. Money for food wasn't a problem. *Money* wasn't a problem. It was plentiful. Great mountains of it had suddenly been erected between her and the harsh realities of the world. The worries she had faced every day of her life no longer existed. Lyle had houses, and cars, and servants, and investments. And as his wife, *so did she.* The security of it was mind-boggling. Like Prince Charming in the fairy story, Lyle had rescued her from a grim life, and she was grateful. If her Prince Charming demanded that she transform herself into a princess worthy of him in return, that seemed fair enough.

But some of the things she had to do to earn his approbation were hard. Her half-Mexican heritage was no longer to be a source of pride to her, but something to be hushed up, she learned, because her husband wished it. Her father (a drunken bum, according to Lyle) was not welcome at Windermere, and was not to be mentioned in polite company. Her clothes were all wrong, and her taste in them—jeans and T-shirts, basically, and maybe sequins for dress-up—was a subject for derision. Even her hair, with its unsuitable length and stubborn waves, was attacked and tamed. She felt as if she was constantly being subjected to the same process as her hair. Yet she didn't protest, because she felt Lyle was right. She was, basically, unworthy to be his wife. That he had married her at all must be counted among life's minor miracles.

It had probably come about, Maggy had thought since with a touch of black humor, because she'd been praying to Saint Jude, the patron saint of impossible causes, for assistance just seconds before Lyle drove up in his champagne-colored Jaguar coupe. He was a regular customer of hers at the Harmony Inn—one of a group of businessmen who frequently met there for lunch—and the other girls had told her that he was filthy rich. He was always nice to her, and he always left a big tip, and she liked him. So when he saw that she was crying, and called her over to his car to ask if he could be of assistance to her, she had climbed in, barely noticing the luxurious vanilla leather upholstery that would have thrilled her at any other time, and spilled the whole ugly mess in his lap. His solution had astounded her—and yet she was not as surprised as she would have been had she not just prayed to Saint Jude.

Sending her a kind, handsome multimillionaire who proposed marriage on the spot was the kind of miracle Saint Jude was renowned for.

So she had said a prayer of thanks to the saint and married her millionaire the same afternoon. As soon as the ring slid on her shaking finger, her life was altered as drastically as if she'd been Alice tumbling down the rabbit hole. Nothing was to remain the same, not even her name.

"Magdalena?" There'd been no mistaking the distaste in Lyle's voice when he saw the name she gave on their marriage license. "At the restaurant they called you Maggy."

"People do, sometimes."

"As my wife, I prefer that you go strictly by Maggy. Magdalena is not a name for a Forrest."

She'd married him anyway, never even seeing his dislike for her name as the warning sign it would have been to an older, wiser woman.

Her name was only a small issue. There were other, larger ones. Lyle knew what he wanted in a wife, and he made no bones about remaking her to fit his wishes. Within twenty-four hours of their wedding, when she briefly protested having the dress she got married in thrown away and he went into an icy rage, she learned that her life would be smooth only as long as she did precisely as he wished.

A control freak, that was what he was, among other, even worse, things, though it had taken her years to identify them all. Maggy shook her head at her younger self as she remembered how naïve she had been, and the lengths to which she had once gone to appease him.

Their honeymoon had been spent in wonderful, fantastic places that she had never even imagined visiting—London, Paris, Rome, Geneva, New York. Lyle made no bones about the fact that he considered her ignorant, uneducated, and, as he put it, as lacking in culture as a mule. He was determined to remedy that. Consequently, she hardly saw the cities themselves. Instead, during the days while he conducted business, she toured every museum and cathedral and art gallery in the area while a hired escort lectured all the time. When there were no museums, she had lessons in etiquette, lessons in table manners, lessons in walking and sitting and standing, lessons in how to dress, how to apply makeup, how to shake hands, and even a brief lesson in using foreign rest rooms (she'd never seen a bidet in her life, and after inadvertently making one's acquaintance didn't care if she never saw one again). She learned how to make small talk, which books to read (or say she'd read), which painters, politicians, writers, and movies to express appreciation or disapproval of.

At night she stayed alone in the hotel, which in itself was not a hardship. They were five-star hotels with room service and every imaginable and previously unimaginable luxury, and she would have been less than human had she not enjoyed them. She did enjoy them. The only problem was that when she was left alone for any length of time, homesickness threatened to overwhelm her. But she never told Lyle that, because the idea of her being homesick—for what? he would have asked with a contemptuous laugh—infuriated him.

While she stayed in, he went out with associates to conduct deals over dinner. (She was not yet "ready" to meet his associates, he said.) The few times they dined together, he curled his lip over her lack of appreciation of fine food and wine and deplored the fact that she was a gourmand, not a gourmet like himself.

What he didn't understand was that she could remember scavenging her dinner from garbage bins. Having enough food, much less such wonderful stuff, all swimming in cream sauces and thick with mushrooms, was such a treat that, looking back, she had to admit she'd made something of a pig of herself. After watching her eat a few times, Lyle had even threatened her with dire consequences (divorce had seemed dire to her then) should her gluttony ever make her grow fat. This threat had taken on increasing potency as her pregnancy began to be obvious, and her stomach began, quarter inch by inevitable quarter inch, to expand. The situation worsened when her husband made no effort to conceal the fact that he was repulsed by her increasing girth.

It seemed almost funny now, when Maggy remembered how much she had feared he would divorce her.

But she hadn't *known*, then. Hadn't grasped the full implications of what she had done when she married Lyle. She had been too young, and, just as he accused her of being, too ignorant. Only it wasn't education she so sorely lacked, but knowledge of what really mattered in life.

Well, she had learned, and the learning had been slow and painful.

Snatched from dire poverty where the only future she could foresee grew bleaker with each passing day, thrust into a world of unbelievable luxury, she had been insecure, overwhelmed, frightened—and determined to be the best wife she could be to her new husband. Despite his distaste for her rounding body, he was happy about her pregnancy. He fiercely wanted a child.

She hadn't been precisely happy during those long-ago days—despite her best efforts to forget about her previous life as Lyle insisted she do, Nick and her father were too often in her thoughts for that, and she found herself missing the most ridiculous things, like the smell of the cabbage that was always being cooked by the family in the apartment next door—but she hadn't been miserable, either. She had been too dazzled by the 360-degree turn her life had taken. Having money to spend was a thrill that she was sure would never grow old. Calling up and ordering things from even the most ordinary of catalogs, going out to stores and buying whatever she wanted and saying grandly "Charge it," even having the money for an ice-cream sundae or a new pair of panties when she wanted them was such a novelty that it made up for a lot. Also, as the child inside her made its presence felt, her every thought began to focus on the coming baby. He was going to have everything life could give him, everything Maggy herself had never had, she vowed inwardly. He was going to be a little prince.

So she and Lyle returned to Windermere, not too unhappily, on a foggy November day. Maggy had been awed into silence as the chauffeur-driven Mercedes dropped them off in front of the house. She'd never seen it before. Her eyes had grown wide as she climbed out of the car, and she could remember as if it had just happened yesterday how she had felt standing on the cobblestoned driveway looking up at her new home.

"Well?" Lyle had asked, glancing down at her, impatient as she paused.

"It's beautiful," she said, and it was—so beautiful that it scared her. She'd seen places like it only in movies or magazines. The blue slate roof with its many gables, the ivy that twined like twisted green ribbons over the pale stone facade, the dozens of glistening, lead-paned windows, the huge, round white columns that soared up for two stories to support the porch roof, were ritzier than anything she had ever imagined. She, who had grown up in a two-room apartment in which the plumbing had worked only fitfully and where the joke of all the residents was that the only pets allowed by management were fleas and roaches, would now be living in a house with twelve-foot ceilings and Oriental carpets and gleaming mahogany furniture that she learned later was all antique.

Ah, the workings of Saint Jude. As she had walked through Windermere for the first time, she silently vowed that she would publish her thanks in the newspaper the very next day.

Lyle, saying that she spoke English less well than most people for whom it was a second language, was telling her that he had already hired a vocal coach for her to continue her lessons in elocution as he led her through a maze of connecting rooms. Maggy was able to register only fragmented impressions of the house, because she was busy listening to Lyle. The walls—smooth plaster walls painted or papered in exquisite colors—bore massive oil paintings that looked as though they belonged in a museum. Ornate cabinets were everywhere, bursting with gleaming collections of china and crystal. The upholstered furniture—a pair of brocade couches here, wing chairs on either side of a fireplace there—were fat and pristine, as if no one had ever even thought about sitting down. There seemed to be a fireplace in every room, enormous chandeliers hung from every ceiling, and vases of fresh flowers bloomed on stands in all the corners. Maggy felt very small as she absorbed her surroundings, and completely out of her element. It was unbelievable that this mansion that Lyle was herding her through so unceremoniously was, from that day forth, to be her home.

Then Virginia had emerged from somewhere in the bowels of the house.

"Lyle . . ." Virginia had looked as surprised to see them as Maggy was to see her. Maggy hadn't even known who she was. Lyle had never mentioned the other residents of the house, or that his mother lived with him.

Virginia's eyes focused on Maggy, slid over her once, then darted to Lyle. Maggy simply stared at her, so scared upon being confronted with this white-haired patrician that her tongue stuck to the roof of her mouth and her knees started to shake.

"Mother, this is Maggy. She's my wife—and she's going to be the mother of your grandchild."

Thus Maggy found out that Lyle hadn't bothered to inform any of his family about his marriage or the coming baby.

Lyle's mother paled, her hand flying to her throat.

"My God, what have you done?" she whispered.

Virginia's words, and the stricken expression that accompanied them, had returned to haunt Maggy many times since. Virginia knew everything there was to know about Lyle, of course, far more than Maggy could ever have imagined at the time. But Maggy thought she was protesting her son's unsuitable choice of wife. If she had been alone, just herself, she probably would have slunk away from Windermere like a whipped dog right there and then. But there had been her baby to think of. No one, *no one*, was going to make her baby feel *less than*. Maggy had felt that way all her life, and for her child's sake it was time to stop. They—the two of them—weren't *less than* anymore. Never again. Her baby was going to be a Forrest, and the Forrests were the richest, most powerful family in Louisville.

For the baby's sake she had stood her ground. Her chin had come up, and her knees had stopped shaking.

"How do you do, Mrs. Forrest?" she'd said in the best superior manner she'd so recently been taught by one of Lyle's etiquette experts and held out her hand. Both Lyle and his mother had stared at her. His mother had been surprised, while Lyle was clearly dumbfounded. Then Lyle had laughed and put his hand on her shoulder in approval. Though she still looked shocked, Virginia had very slowly come forward to take her hand.

If Maggy had only known then what she knew now, she would have turned at that moment and run screaming as far from Windermere as it was possible to get.

But she hadn't known, and so she allowed Lyle to escort her in to lunch with his mother, and the web began to inexorably tighten around the unwary little fly that she had been then.

Maggy stopped outside the very same rooms where she had eaten lunch that first day and knocked.

"Come in," Virginia called from the other side of the door.

Maggy turned the knob and went inside.

*V*irginia's apartment consisted of a sitting room, two bedrooms, a small kitchen, and a bath. The upholstery was all cheery English chintz, and the Savonnerie rug on the sitting room floor was cream and rose and pale blue. Long windows opened out onto the back lawn. Curtains in a rose-colored floral print on a deep yellow ground had been drawn across the windows. Virginia, clad in a pink satin robe, reclined on a small, overstuffed chaise longue in front of them. A pale blue afghan lay across her legs. She had been reading by the light of a single floor lamp that stood at her elbow, though she glanced up as Maggy entered. The rest of the apartment was dark and quiet.

"Has David already gone to bed?" Maggy asked, glancing around. Bed before nine was enough unlike her son to worry her.

Virginia shook her head, looking surprised. "He's spending the night with the Trainors. I assumed you knew."

Mitchell Trainor was David's dearest friend. Maggy didn't really object to her son sleeping over at his house—but she did object to not being consulted about it.

"No, I didn't."

"Mitchell called and invited him after David got home from the Club, and David called Lyle. Lyle said he could go."

"Lyle just neglected to inform *me.*"

Virginia looked at her steadily. "Men can be thoughtless."

Maggy gave an unamused little laugh. "Can't they just?"

Virginia's brow furrowed. She glanced down at her book and then up at Maggy again. "You're home very early. Where is Lyle? Did anything —happen?"

For an instant Maggy stared at her mother-in-law, tempted to tear away the veil of pretense that had always existed between them and tell the exact, unvarnished truth. The words bubbled to the tip of her tongue, but she bit them back. Virginia was old, and in frail health, and she didn't really want to know.

Besides, there was nothing Virginia could do to help her. She had no control over her son—and, though she might deplore some of Lyle's actions, she was ultimately on his side, at the expense of Maggy or anyone else who might get in Lyle's way. Maggy knew her mother-in-law well enough to suspect that any serious accusations Maggy raised against Lyle would be passed on to him, probably in a chiding way as his mother asked him if his wife's stories were true. Virginia would no doubt mean it for the best, but the harm she would cause would be enormous.

Maggy's tone was light as she replied. "I felt ill, is all. I didn't want to ruin the party for everyone else, so I came home alone. Since David isn't here, I think I'll take a sleeping pill and go to bed. You might tell Lyle when he comes in, so he doesn't bother trying to wake me. Those things make me dead to the world."

Lyle always looked in on his mother when he came in at night. At first Maggy had thought it was a charming habit, and then, later, when he showed such brutal indifference to her, his wife, she had resented it. Now she merely accepted it, and even found it occasionally came in handy. It allowed her to communicate with her husband through his mother, without facing him herself.

Virginia looked at her steadily for a moment. "I'll tell him. How is your wrist?"

"Better, thanks."

"Maggy . . ."

"Yes?"

"Nothing." Virginia looked very old and tired suddenly. The dark smudges that lodged perpetually beneath her lower lids seemed more pronounced than usual, circling her eyes like two grayish bruises. In the unforgiving glow of the floor lamp, her too-white skin was a dry web of wrinkles. Her mouth was drawn and almost colorless. Her neck, thrusting up from the vee neck of her robe, was so thin as to appear scrawny. Maggy caught a glimpse of her collarbones and was shocked to notice how prominent they were through Virginia's paper-thin skin.

Maggy felt a rush of concern. "Are you all right, Virginia?"

Virginia waved a hand in the air as though to shoo the question away. "I'm fine. A little tired, but fine. Why don't you go along to bed, if that's what you came home to do? I want to get back to my book." Her tone bordered on the brusque.

Maggy was not offended. She knew how much Virginia, a robust sportswoman for most of her life, hated admitting to the physical weakness that was so much a part of her condition. It embarrassed her. Consequently, Maggy's smile at her mother-in-law was warm. "I will. If you're sure you don't need anything."

"I don't. If I did, I'd call Louella." Virginia's tone softened as her gaze met her daughter-in-law's. "Thank you for asking. Good night, Maggy."

"Good night."

Maggy lifted a hand in farewell, turned, and left the apartment. As she closed the door behind her, she experienced a momentary sadness. She always felt a twinge of regret in her dealings with Virginia. Had her marriage worked out differently, she thought they might have been friends.

But under the circumstances there was nothing she could do for Virginia, just as there was nothing Virginia could do for her. Reminding herself of that as she wound her way back through the endless corridors toward the center of the house, Maggy succeeded in putting her mother-in-law out of her mind.

As she climbed the wide, curving staircase toward the second floor, Maggy's steps lightened. A few more minutes, and she would be free! She was suddenly almost giddy with anticipation, like a prisoner about to be let out of jail. Of course, she had just a couple of hours. Then she had to come back. And sooner or later, she would have to face Lyle.

The realization brought fear in its wake. But she refused to let it dampen her rising spirits. She would enjoy the moment, and worry about the future when it was at hand.

If Lyle ever found out what she did on the occasional nights when she supposedly retired to bed early with a sleeping pill, he would be livid with rage—but with luck he would never find out. He hardly ever came to her room anymore. Even if, by some dreadful mischance, he should happen to do so on a night when she was gone, she thought—hoped—he would go away when his knock wasn't answered. As angry as he was, though, it was quite possible that he would come to her room tonight, which was why she meant to be inside it with the door safely locked by the time he got home. She knew that he would dislike making a noisy scene to gain admittance, and in the morning she could always plead the effect of the sleeping pill as the reason why she did not hear him. He did not possess a key to the deadbolt she had had installed on her bedroom door, supposedly as a general safety precaution but really to keep him out. At least, she assumed he did not, though she was never 100 percent positive of anything with Lyle. Thank goodness she had managed to come home from the party on her own. If he had accompanied her, there would have been no escaping his rage.

Tomorrow she would have to face him, but there would be ways to avoid being alone with him then. Church, for instance, and lunch at the Club afterward. Then he would play golf with his friends. With luck, she would once again manage to be safely locked in her bedroom before he came home for the night.

But the next few hours were hers. Like the other ten or so nights a year when she locked her door, turned out the lights, and slipped out her window, she was already counting the minutes until she could escape.

Tonight she had a mission as well. She had to dig up Nick's "present" and take it to the one place in the world where she knew it would be safe. The one place where everybody was on her side: *Tia* Gloria's house.

Maggy had bought the house for her father. Even now, almost nine years after his death, it gave her comfort to reflect that whatever else her disastrous marriage might have done, it had enabled her to support her father in comfort for the last two years of his life. Shortly after David's birth, by means of cash advances on her credit cards and by scraping together all the pin money that Lyle, in his euphoria over David, had showered on her, Maggy had managed to come up with the funds required to purchase a small, dilapidated house on the Indiana waterfront that she knew her father would love. Deed in hand, she had gone to fetch him from the public housing project where she'd grown up and where he still lived. He had cried when she handed him the deed— and he had never returned to the projects.

Thus her father, Jorge Luis Garcia, the first generation of his family to be born a U.S. citizen, became a homeowner. It was his dream come true.

The son of itinerant farm laborers who had sneaked across the border from Mexico in search of work, Jorge had lived all his life in conditions of extreme poverty. His family had moved constantly, rotating with the seasons from Florida's orange groves to Georgia's peanut farms to Kentucky's tobacco fields. As the years passed, his parents left children who matured to adulthood and formed their own families behind at every stop along the way. Finally having died within three months of each other in Georgia, his parents were buried in that state's red clay. After their demise, Jorge, their youngest, continued to travel from state to state with the crops, until one season, when he was working in the tobacco fields of central Kentucky, he fell in love with the third of the farm owner's five daughters. Mary Kramer was just seventeen years old when they ran off and got married. Jorge was twenty-five.

If the Kramers had gotten their hands on Jorge, they would have lynched him.

Magdalena Rose was the result of that union. She was born within the year.

Disowned by her parents, shocked by the harsh reality of grinding poverty that came hard on the heels of her whirlwind romance, Mary Kramer Garcia had nevertheless rallied, rolled up her sleeves, and done what needed doing. The itinerant life was not for her, she decided after a single season on the road, and it was she who insisted that Jorge give it up. Their little family moved to Louisville—Mary's Kentucky roots sank deep—and with Mary and Magdalena to provide incentive Jorge worked two jobs, nights in a dairy plant and days as a street sweeper. Mary had taken in laundry and cared for Magdalena. Maggy's sole visual memory of her mother was of looking up at a redheaded, pale-skinned woman who leaned tiredly against a wringer washer as she endlessly twisted the white sheets that came through the wringer, day after day. To the present day, Maggy had only to smell laundry detergent to be reminded of her mother.

Mary was hit and killed by a car when Magdalena was four. Jorge was crazed with grief, and it was then that he turned to the bottle. Within a year he had lost both jobs and they were kicked out of their little house for nonpayment of rent. Had it not been for a kindly priest, Maggy guessed that she and her father would have ended up in the streets. But Father John had taken pity on them and arranged for them to live in public housing. Always too proud to accept charity before, Jorge had accepted it then so that Magdalena would have a roof over her head. Later, his pride drowned in a tide of alcohol, he had made no protest when Father John arranged for them to get welfare.

Jorge never recovered from the loss of his wife. For the rest of his life, Maggy couldn't remember a period of more than two consecutive days when he'd been sober. But she loved him. And she had never doubted that he loved her. He just couldn't cope with his pain.

Had it not been for Nick, who first happened across six-year-old

Maggy rooting through a fast-food outlet's trash, Maggy didn't know how she would have survived.

She could still remember the first words Nick had ever spoken to her: "Hey, kid, get out of the garbage! Don'tcha know there's rats in them things?"

It had been dark, maybe eleven o'clock or so because the burger joint down the street from where she lived had just closed, though the red-and-yellow neon light in the shape of a giant *M* was still illuminated. It was summer, because it had been warm. The too-small, faded pink dress she'd been wearing had barely reached halfway to her knees, and its short sleeves had been uncomfortably tight around her upper arms. She'd been perched precariously on a stack of boxes in a dark corner of the parking lot, bottom upended as she pawed through discarded Styrofoam containers piled high in a Dumpster, looking for something edible. Already she had found a cheeseburger with nothing wrong with it at all and half a pack of fries. That would do for herself, but she needed to find more if she was to also feed her *papi,* who was at that moment lying on the floor of their apartment recovering from a week-long drunk.

"Mind your own damned business!" she'd shot back, after a quick, initially scared glance had told her that the threat was not a threat at all, but only a skinny black-haired boy not much older than herself. She'd gotten back down to business, turning her back and sifting through the trash with single-minded concentration.

"You got a hole in your underpants! I can see your tushie through it!" was the taunting response. This assault on her modesty and dignity was too much. Maggy's hand closed over the first promising missile that came to hand—a large paper cup almost full of Coke, lid still on, straw still protruding—and with a cry of rage she turned and hurled it at her tormentor.

It hit, dead on.

The boy shrieked as the cup smacked into his forehead and burst, drenching him with icy liquid. Maggy, triumphant yet knowing when she was in deep trouble, leapt down from her perch and bolted for home.

A flying tackle brought her down. Maggy hit the concrete and saw stars. But by necessity she'd learned to take care of herself. Biting and clawing and kicking and yelling, she squirmed over onto her back and fought like a little tigress.

He'd won in the end. Sitting on top of her, his hands pinioning her wrists to the ground, his wet black hair plastered to his skull where she drenched him, scratches she'd given him beading with blood on his left cheek, he unexpectedly grinned.

"You fight pretty good, for a girl."

"Go to hell!"

"You live at Parkway Place, don't you? So do we—me and my mom and my brother. I've seen you around."

"Ain't none of your business where I live!"

"You hungry?"

"No, I ain't. I just poke around in Dumpsters 'cause I like 'em."

"I got some spaghetti at home I can cook. Ain't nobody there. My mom's at work—she's a waitress, she works nights—and my brother's gone out somewhere. You want some?"

At the word spaghetti, Maggy's stomach growled. She hadn't eaten since the night before—and she loved spaghetti.

"I got to take some home for my *papi*."

"Your what?"

"My daddy. He's—sick, and I gotta take care of him."

"He's that old drunk that's always fallin' down the stairs, ain't he? I had to jump over him once, 'cause he was sleepin' right in front of the entrance to our building."

"*Papi*'s not a drunk!" She stiffened, glaring, ready to fight again, all the good feelings brought on by the thought of spaghetti vanished in an instant.

"My mom gets drunk, too. Not as much as your dad, but I know what it's like. We got lots of spaghetti, I can make enough for him. You want to come?"

"Not till you take back what you called my *papi*!"

"Okay, I take it back."

Maggy relaxed slightly. The boy got off her. She scrambled to her feet and stood facing him while the big neon sign bathed them both in shades of red and yellow. She didn't know whether to stay or to run.

"So you want spaghetti?"

In the end, the lure of spaghetti proved too strong to resist. "Yeah."

"Then come on." The boy started walking toward the cluster of apartment buildings at the far end of the street. He looked around to see if she was following. She was.

"What's your name?" he asked.

"Magdalena. What's yours?"

"Nick."

Nick. He'd looked out for her ever since, until she'd left him behind to marry Lyle.

How he must have hated her for that. She knew, had he done it to her, she would have hated him.

And now he was back. Unbidden, his face as it looked now rose in her mind's eye: dark, dangerous, charming, a little hard. A stranger's face, though it bore an outward likeness to that of the boy she had loved. She had to keep reminding herself that that boy was gone forever, just as Magdalena was: vanished in the mists of time. Although, perhaps, not entirely. Maybe shades of the boy lived on in the man, remembering. Just as the part of her that was still Magdalena Garcia remembered, too.

Memory could be a dangerous thing. She had to keep reminding herself of that.

13

Once in her room, Maggy locked the door with the key, threw the deadbolt, and leaned back against the wooden panel for a moment while she planned what she had to do. Then she began to shed her clothes, hurriedly, because she suddenly couldn't wait to be out of them, kicking off her satin mules and shimmying out of her pantyhose and leaving them where they fell, tossing the four-thousand-dollar dress across a chair, dropping the even more expensive diamond earrings in a saucer on her dresser. Crossing to her dressing room, she pulled on a pair of black stirrup pants, a black turtleneck, black running shoes, and a black leather motorcycle jacket. She ran a quick brush through her hair, caught it at her nape with a wooden barrette, and was ready to go.

The security system did not extend to the upstairs windows. She had discovered that years ago, when she had been desperate to find a way to leave the house without being found out. From the beginning, Lyle had insisted that Tipton drive her wherever she wanted to go. For security reasons, he said. In case some nut should get it into his head to kidnap her to get at him. At first she had defied him by occasionally taking a car out herself. Her father had still been alive at the time—he had died three years after her marriage—and he and *Tia* Gloria were the only family she had left. Not even her fear of Lyle was going to keep her from them.

At first she had gone to see them openly, at times driving herself and at other times having Tipton drive her, hoping that that would appease Lyle. Sometimes she had even taken little David to see his *Papi* Jorge, though Lyle threw a fit at that. But Lyle had found ways to punish her every time she went, subtle, cruel punishments that escalated to physical abuse when she dared to take David with her. Facing Lyle afterward became such an ordeal that Maggy at first stopped taking David, then found her visits growing less and less frequent, so much so that her father complained of her neglect. That was before she discovered the lifesaving combination of the flawed security system, her bedroom window, and *The Lady Dancer.*

The Lady Dancer was a twenty-year-old, fifteen-foot powerboat that was kept moored at Windermere's small dock on Willow Creek. The boat was never used by anyone except Herd, who liked to fish the creek and river. Often in the summer Louella would cook up his catch of bluegill or catfish or a mess of crawdads for supper. If Lyle remembered the boat's existence, Maggy would have been surprised. He had a huge, luxurious yacht he used for entertaining, which he kept moored at an exclusive enclave about five miles farther along River Road.

Maggy hated the yacht almost as much as she loved *The Lady Dancer.* In its luxury, its silent testimony to the perquisites of wealth and position and power, the yacht was so very *Lyle* that she could hardly stand to set foot on it. Fortunately, he rarely required that she do so. The people he entertained on the *Iris* were his guests alone.

It was time to go. Maggy turned off the light, plunging her bedroom into inky darkness. Crossing the room, she pulled aside the heavy curtains of fringed ruby brocade that the decorator had insisted would contrast beautifully with the pale pink silk walls (in Maggy's opinion, they clashed) and cranked open the window farthest to the left, one of a half dozen abutted casements at the far end of her bedroom. Beneath the casements were the huge bow windows that graced the library. Many-paned, curving twins, the bow windows jutted out from the house with majestic grace—and the tin roof of one of them rested not two feet below her window.

Each casement was eight feet tall and a little more than two feet wide. Though Maggy cranked the window open only the bare minimum that was required for her to squeeze through, getting out was ridiculously easy. More than once she had thought that a burglar could have a field day with those windows. Though she supposed, to give Lyle's highly paid security consultant his due, getting in from the outside without the benefit of a previously opened window probably would have been much more difficult than getting out.

Maggy crouched on her bedroom floor, stuck a foot out into space, found the tin roof with it, and then shifted her body weight through the casement until she was standing on top of the bow window. The brisk night air surrounded her, caressing her skin, filling her lungs, making her feel alive as she glanced cautiously around.

The view from up there was magnificent. Pale wisps of clouds scuttled across the sky, aiding dozens of tiny twinkling stars in their game of peekaboo with Earth. The small, frosty-white crescent of the moon rode low over the rounded dark forms of swaying treetops and cast an eerie light over the stone patio below. Beyond the patio, the rose bushes, which were still mounded with mulch against the early spring chill, thrust bony black fingers toward the sky. The bench depicted in David's painting sat in the middle of those rosebushes, its white wrought-iron form looking skeletal in the darkness. The just-greening lawn that surrounded the rose garden was washed silver by the moon. Maggy's gaze swept the lawn as it sloped toward the dense wall of shadows that was the woods.

She could see no one. Turning, pushing against the casement so that it closed as far as possible (there was always a small danger that someone might spot the opening, although in the darkness she felt it was a very remote chance), she sat on the edge of the bow window's roof and lowered herself, feeling for a toehold with her foot. Her bandaged wrist throbbed as it was forced to bear some of her weight, but it did not give way, and the pain was not so severe that she couldn't ignore it.

In her twelve years with Lyle, she had learned to ignore worse.

The natural protuberances of the stone were jaggedly uneven at the angle where the wall met the window, creating niches and crannies for her feet and hands that over the years had become as familiar to her as the treads of the stairs inside. In seconds she was on the ground, almost completely shielded from the view of any who might be looking by a large Taxus bush, which grew taller than her head. It was one of a thick row of identical bushes that grew along the back of the house.

The night was still except for the cries of night animals and the sounds of branches rustling in the wind. It was not really cold yet, but the wind promised lower temperatures later.

Maggy set off at an angle from the house, following the trajectory of the driveway without getting too close to it and skirting the dog kennel for fear her canine friends would somehow sense her presence and bark.

She headed for the path through the woods she had taken that morning. The first item on her agenda was the retrieval of Nick's "present."

There was a small penlight in her jacket pocket, kept there in case of necessity. The moon provided ample light until she was deep beneath the trees. Then she pulled the penlight from her pocket and turned it on. She would not leave it on continuously—the fear that Tipton or some other of Lyle's minions might be lurking about the grounds just when she least wished them to be never left her—but she flashed it when she needed it and turned it off again. Thus she was able to locate the place where she had left the path, and, with only a little backtracking, find the forsythia. The log beneath it was undisturbed, she saw with another quick flare of the light. Relieved, she pocketed the light, crouched before the log, and worked to unearth what she had buried earlier in the day.

The darkness of the woods was far more intense than the darkness of the lawn. Without moonlight to alleviate it, it was heavy, portentous, almost menacing. Which was ridiculous, of course, Maggy scolded herself even as she paused in what she was doing to glance uneasily around. She had never been afraid of the dark, and she was not about to start now.

Still, the woods were not silent. They creaked, and groaned, and rustled, and moaned. Insects whirred and chirped, birds muttered to themselves high up in the branches overhead, and small nocturnal animals squeaked and shrieked and scuttled among the fallen leaves. All of which would have been mildly charming by daylight. By night it made her spine prickle.

Maggy shook her head at herself and turned her attention back to the job at hand. Scooping out the last of the loose dirt and leaves was the work of only a moment. Everything—package, tape, pictures, envelope—were just as she had left them. Apparently Lyle and his spies were not as omnipotent as she had feared.

Maggy let out the breath that she had not realized until that moment she was holding, and got to her feet.

She was standing there, tucking the package inside her jacket for safekeeping, when a sudden, sharp noise rent the night.

Maggy jumped, then glanced almost guiltily around. Of course it was nothing. A dry branch breaking, perhaps, as a larger animal stepped on it—but what kind of larger animal would be abroad in Windermere's woods?

The noise had come from her left. Maggy zipped up her jacket to secure the items inside it, her eyes boring past the solid gray of the closer trees as she tried vainly to penetrate the blackness beyond.

It was impossible. She could see nothing except the shadowy trunks of oaks and maples and walnuts and pines for five feet in every direction. Beyond that was utter darkness.

The sound came again—the snap of a dry, brittle stick breaking as it was stepped on. Maggy was almost sure that was what it was.

The hairs rose on the back of her neck. Someone—or something—was in the woods with her. She knew it in her gut. At that moment she couldn't decide whether she would prefer to come face-to-face with Lyle and his minions or some hideous, night-stalking monster. Then, remembering the pictures and tape, she decided. She would take her chances with the monster anytime.

For the minute or so that had elapsed since Maggy had heard the first sound, she had stood frozen with fear like a rabbit mesmerized by the headlights of a car. Regaining her wits along with the use of her feet, she began to back away, her movements quick and stealthy. Her eyes remained glued to the shadowy blanket of darkness that hid whoever or whatever was lurking in the trees.

Five steps back, six—another snapping sound, about twelve feet to the right of the last. Closer, much closer. Maggy's head jerked around and her eyes searched vainly through the night. Her pulses jumped, her heart pounded. She knew, as well as she knew her name, that someone or something was in the dark with her, and very near.

Pressing one hand over the objects in her jacket to keep them safe, Maggy took a deep breath and pivoted. Then she bolted like a scared colt from a burning barn.

An enormous dark silhouette stepped out of the woods directly into her path.

Maggy couldn't help herself. She screamed like a fire engine. Immediately an arm whipped around her from behind, and a hand clamped down hard over her mouth.

14

*M*aggy's heart stopped even as her scream was cut off in mid-blast. Her blood froze. For an instant, a dangerous instant, her muscles refused to work and she was not fighting but shocked motionless in her assailant's hold.

"Christ, Magdalena, who are you expecting? It's only me."

The familiar voice in her ear made her go limp. Her knees sagged, and for a moment she rested weakly against him. Against Nick.

As fear swept away, sudden fury rolled in to replace it. She hadn't forgotten that coerced dance, and he had no business scaring her to death, either. Maggy bit the hand that still covered her mouth, closing her teeth over the meaty part of his palm with relish. Nick yelped, jerking his hand away. Maggy wrenched herself out of his arms.

"You scared the *crap* out of me!" she hissed, turning on him and delivering a hard, swift punch to his unprotected belly, the kind she hadn't thrown in years. The muscles were taut there beneath his clothes, but he was not expecting her attack and the punch connected with satisfying force.

"Ouf," he said, bending, his arms coming out in front of himself to ward off further assault.

"You almost made me pee in my pants!" she raged.

Nick was laughing, the sound rich and low and full of amusement. Listening to him made Maggy wild.

"Stop laughing, you son of a bitch!" She punched at him again, and when her fist connected with nothing more promising than his hard forearm she aimed a kick at his shin. In the nick of time he jumped back out of range. "I said, stop laughing!"

"She hasn't changed a bit," said a disapproving voice behind her.

Maggy had forgotten the huge man who had originally stepped out of the darkness to confront her.

"Not much," Nick agreed, amusement still plain in his voice, as Maggy whirled openmouthed to gape at the second man.

"Link!" Maggy gasped, one hand flying to her mouth as she stared up at him. In the darkness it was impossible to make out his features, but the sheer size of him left her in no doubt that it was really he: Travis Walker, Nick's half brother. Five years older than Nick, he was otherwise known to the street kids he used to run with, courtesy of his size and the blunt ugliness of his face, as the Missing Link.

"Link, is that you? I thought they sent you up for thirty years."

"They did. I do a little dope, get busted three times in four years, and they go calling me a persistent felon. It wasn't like I was dealin', for God's sake. That persistent-felon rap had me doin' big time. But Nicky here got big bro a good lawyer, and the guy sprung me. Sentence commuted to time served. I been out for eight years."

"I'm so glad!"

"Me, too." Link was looking her over, though she doubted he could see much in the dark. "How ya been, baby girl? Last time I seen you, you was a little bit of a teenager. Nicky tells me life's been treatin' you pretty good since."

The last time she'd seen Link was when she'd gone with Nick to visit him at the prison in Jesup where he had been an inmate. Nick had been torn up over his brother's fate and hadn't wanted to go alone. Twelve years ago, when Link had been inside for just a few months.

"I'm doing okay."

"That's great."

It suddenly occurred to Maggy just how absurd the conversation was under the circumstances.

"Nick King, what are you and Link doing prowling around my woods in the middle of the night?" She turned her head to scowl at Nick.

He had lit a cigarette and was puffing away as he listened to her and Link. The tip glowed bright red in the dark.

"And put that out! Somebody might see it!" Irritation sharpened her voice.

"Still bossy," Link observed sotto voce to his brother.

"Link's my, uh, driver tonight. When you left, I left too, and had him follow you to make sure you got home okay."

"Yeah, then he made me park and walk up this damned hill so he could stare up at your window and make sure you got tucked in for beddy-byes all right and tight."

"Shut up, Link." Nick took another drag on his cigarette. Its red glow illuminated his face, and Maggy could see that he was frowning at his brother.

"Only you happened to be coming out the window," Link continued with a grin, disregarding Nick's annoyance completely. "We watched you, then followed you into the woods."

"Do you make a habit of leaving parties claiming you're sick and then climbing out your bedroom window?" Nick asked.

"What hubby don't know won't hurt him, right?" There was an innuendo in Link's voice that Maggy didn't like.

"I'm only going to visit *Tia* Gloria. Lyle—doesn't like me to, so I sneak out sometimes. It saves an argument."

"*Tia* Gloria?" Nick sounded surprised. "Don't tell me the old lady's still kicking!"

"She is indeed. And I'm on my way to see her right now. If you gentlemen will excuse me, of course."

"*Now* she sounds like a rich bitch," Link observed. "Hoity-toity."

"I do not!" Nettled, Maggy turned on her heel and strode off through the trees. When she emerged from the woods, some distance down the slope and out of sight of the house, Nick and Link were right behind her.

"Go away," she said over her shoulder to them.

"Not on your life," Nick answered while Link grinned companionably down at her.

Maggy walked on, ignoring them. Not that it did any good. She didn't even have to look around to know they never got farther from her than three paces away.

Windermere was built atop a wooded hill. To the east of the house where the driveway was, and to the rear, where the three of them now walked along a grassy verge, the hillside had eroded into a rocky cliff, obviating the need for a wall such as surrounded the rest of the property. About three hundred feet below, at the base of that cliff, was Willow Creek, and the dock where *The Lady Dancer* waited.

"You got a car out here?" Link sounded confused when he saw that they were headed toward what appeared to be a sheer drop-off.

"Not a car. A boat," Maggy responded.

"You visit *Tia* Gloria by boat?" Nick asked, surprised.

"I told you, Lyle doesn't like me to visit her. This way I can do it in secret."

"To hell with Lyle." Nick's voice was hard.

"That's easy for you to say."

"You never used to let anybody tell you what to do. What, did ol' Lyle buy himself a slave when he forked over twenty bucks for that marriage license?"

"Where's the boat?" Link intervened hastily as Maggy glared up at Nick. Years ago, when Maggy's and Nick's verbal exchanges had consisted for a time of nearly endless bickering under the throes of adolescent growing pains, Link had gotten into the habit of running interference between them when necessary. He fell back into the role easily now. Just as easily as Maggy and Nick slid back into the grooves of their previous relationship. Being with Nick, even after so long a time apart, came as naturally to Maggy as breathing. So naturally that it scared her.

"Down there." Maggy, glad of the distraction, pointed toward the glinting strip of black cellophane far below that was the creek. The stone walls of the cliff glistened palely in the moonlight, seeming to defy any attempt at descent.

"Down *there*?" Link was aghast.

"You sound like Horatio, repeating everything I say," Maggy said, shooting Link a part amused, part irritated glance.

"Horatio?" Nick's attention was caught. "Do you mean *Tia* Gloria still has that horrible bird?"

"He never liked you much, either," Maggy sniffed. Then, because she couldn't help it, she started to giggle. Horatio was *Tia* Gloria's beloved parrot, an Amazon double-yellowhead who had been *Tia*'s closest companion for most of her life. The bird, like the woman, was probably over fifty by now. For some reason, he'd taken a fixed dislike to Nick the first time he ever laid eyes on him. Nick had reciprocated that dislike with interest.

"Do you remember when he chased you down the stairs?" Maggy asked Nick, the memory surprising her into a giggle.

"Hoo-boy, I do!" Link said, chortling. "Nicky came running out of the building screamin' like his pants was on fire with that bird screechin' 'Bad boy, bad boy!' and flappin' after him! When he landed on Nicky's back, I thought the kid was gonna pass out! It was the funniest thing I ever saw in my life."

"Ha, ha," Nick said sourly.

"What'd ya do to him, Nicky?"

"He threw a ball at Horatio's perch. When Horatio came after him, he got exactly what he deserved. Even if the other kids did call him Junior Birdman for weeks afterward."

"Until I beat 'em up." Nick grinned. "If I hadn't been afraid to go near the damned bird after that, I would have fricasseed him for Sunday dinner. Do you mean to tell me the thing's still alive?"

"Very much so."

"I can't wait."

"I don't recall inviting you to accompany me."

"There she goes again," Link muttered.

"Do you really not want us to come with you, Magdalena?" Nick asked softly.

Maggy hesitated. She knew from experience that that soft voice didn't mean anything at all, and that ninety-nine times out of a hundred Nick would do as he damned well pleased whether she liked it or not. She knew that she ought to at least try to send him away, for her own sake and David's. But it was such fun, laughing over old times, and it felt so good to have him near, just for a little while. Out here, where she didn't have to watch everything she said, everything she did for fear Lyle would find out. What harm could it do, if she took him with her to visit *Tia* Gloria? Once, long ago, *Tia* had had one heck of a soft spot for Nick. Though he was nothing else any longer, surely Nick could still be her friend. Just for a little while, here out of sight of everyone else. Maggy discovered with a rush of feeling that was almost painful that what she most hungered for was a friend. And Nick had always been her dearest friend in the world.

"You're still wearing your suit," she said as if stating an objection, her eyes running over him and registering this discovery for the first time. "*Tia* Gloria won't know you."

Indeed, she hardly knew him herself. In all the years of their acquaintance, she didn't think she'd ever seen him in a suit except that once at her prom, and that had been a rather ill-fitting tuxedo. This suit fit him as though it had been custom-made. She had noticed it at the party, thinking that his broad-shouldered, narrow-hipped, hard-muscled workingman's physique lent the traditional businessman's attire a sexiness that it rarely possessed. Now, with his black hair tousled into unruly curls by the wind, a pronounced five-o'clock shadow darkening his cheeks, his shirt collar unbuttoned, and his tie at half-mast, he was so dangerously attractive that it made her heart speed up just to look at him.

"I'll remind her." Nick grinned down at her, clearly reading her capitulation in her words. Maggy did not smile back, not with her mouth, but her eyes were smiling as she turned her back on him with a toss of her ponytail and headed straight for the sheer side of the cliff. Thought he was clever, did he? She would show him.

"Whoa!" Nick grabbed her arm from behind just as she reached the edge. "You may not have noticed, but you're about to run out of ground."

"There's a path, silly," she said, pulling her arm free of his hold and sitting suddenly, so that her legs dangled over the three-hundred-foot drop. Her smile had reached her mouth by the time she shoved off without warning, scooting on her rear end over the eight or so yards of steep shale track that was the only way down the cliff face to the chiseled rock ledge that marked the beginning of the footpath.

"Magdalena!" Nick sounded as if he were on the verge of a heart attack. He had apparently grabbed for her again and missed. As she reached her destination in a shower of rocks and looked saucily up over her shoulder at him, she discovered him squatted by the cliff edge, one hand still extended as though to catch her, his face unnaturally pale against the backdrop of the night sky.

"Come on," she called, a taunt in her voice as she stood up and brushed off the back of her jeans. "You wanted to visit *Tía* Gloria, didn't you?"

"You little brat, you did that on purpose to scare me," he said. The accusation was true, so she didn't dispute it, instead grinning widely as he stared down at her for a moment as though debating the wisdom of following her example. The shale slope was off-putting, but it wasn't nearly as dangerous as it looked, as she had discovered when Herd had first shown her the way. And it was by far the fastest way down to the creek. Just as she was opening her mouth to jeer at Nick for cowardice, he sat and shoved off. Maggy stepped quickly back out of the way as he came rocketing toward her on his backside while a mini-avalanche of small rocks rained down in his wake.

"Good boy!" She clapped her hands in mock applause, moving toward him again as he slid to an ungainly halt.

"Damn, I've ripped the seat out of my pants," he growled, standing and brushing his hands over his rear end.

"Let me see." Trying not to laugh, Maggy moved around behind him, lifting the tail of his coat out of the way so that she could inspect the area in question. The seat of his navy wool suit pants was indeed shredded. She could see white cotton jockey briefs through the tears in the cloth. The pale skin of his small, hard, and nicely rounded butt was also clearly visible through a rip in his shorts.

"You've got a hole in your underpants. I can see your tushie," she said in a taunting singsong of a little-girl voice, in almost exact imitation of the words he had once used to tease her.

"What?" He felt his backside, discovered the hole, and burst out laughing. Maggy couldn't help herself. She laughed, too.

"Shame I don't have a Coke to throw at you," he said, grinning at her.

"Thank goodness." Like his, Maggy's laughter had subsided, but a lingering smile curved her mouth. She felt happy suddenly, lighthearted and carefree and *young*. It had been years since she had felt that way. She discovered that she liked the sensation very much.

"Now what do I do?" he asked half humorously. "I can't go visiting with my butt hanging out."

"With your coat on, you can't even tell your pants are ripped," Maggy said, but the grin that lurked around her mouth robbed the words of any comfort value.

"Oh, yeah, sure. Suppose I have to bend over for something? Suppose it's hot in there and I want to take off my coat? Suppose you decide to have a laugh at my expense and tell everybody?"

Maggy burst out laughing again. "Would I do that to you?"

"Yes," Nick said. "You would."

"Well, if you've changed your mind about going, all you have to do is climb back up there." Maggy pointed toward the top of the cliff. The twenty-odd feet of the shale track that rose from where they stood to the grassy verge overhead looked smooth as glass and nearly perpendicular.

"Hell," Nick said, looking up.

"It's your choice."

"You," Nick said, eyeing her, "are loving every minute of this."

Maggy was surprised to discover that his words were the absolute truth. "Yes, I am."

Nick grinned. "So am I."

For a moment they beamed at each other in perfect amity, coconspirators, partners in crime. That was how it had always been between them. It was as if the years that had passed since they had been together had vanished, and they were once again Nick and Magdalena, Magdalena and Nick, best friends, *family,* world without end. Always, growing up, they'd loved each other best.

"I'm glad you're back, Nick," Maggy said suddenly in a low voice, the smile dying from her face, wiped away by a flood of emotion. "I've missed you."

Nick reached for her, appeared to change his mind at the last moment, and folded his arms over his chest instead. His eyes were very green suddenly as they gleamed through the night at her.

"I've missed you, too, Maggy May," he said.

The name, which she suspected he used deliberately, made her wince. She would have turned and walked away, but there was nowhere to go. The ledge they were on was less than six feet wide, and no more than eight feet long. She was stuck, stuck with him and the memories he deliberately invoked. Memories of the night they had become more than best friends, more than family to each other. The night they'd become lovers. Rod Stewart's hit "Maggy May" had blasted out over Nick's car radio. She could still remember lying curled in Nick's arms afterward, listening to that song. Nick had sung along—he'd always fancied himself a singer—and afterward he'd started calling her Maggy May. For what little afterward there'd been.

She searched his eyes to see if he remembered, and saw that he did. His gaze held her immobile, reminding her silently of just how much they had shared. Yet he never touched her. His arms stayed crossed over his chest. And she never touched him. Her hands were thrust deep into the pockets of her jacket. A distance of a good two feet separated them, but Maggy felt as though every part of their bodies was in contact. They stood unmoving, hazel-green eyes boring into brown, a pair of small dark human silhouettes suspended against the pale stone of the cliff, for an instant out of time.

While their souls embraced.

Without words or touch or anything except the memories in her eyes, Maggy finally welcomed Nick home.

And he told her how glad he was to be back.

15

"*W*ait a minute, folks. If you think I'm sliding down this here mountain on my butt, you've got another think comin'. No, sirree."

Link's voice, heavy with disapproval as he crouched at the cliff edge peering down at them, roused them from their reverie. As Nick's eyes left hers to focus on his brother, Maggy felt strangely disoriented. Dizzy, almost. As if she'd been journeying in another world and now found herself rudely returned to reality.

"He's afraid of heights," Nick said to her, but loud enough so that Link could hear.

"I'm smart, is what I am," Link growled in reply. "Only a lovesick fool with more hair than brains would go shimmying down that cliff on that little gal's say-so. You miss that ledge, and you can kiss your ass good-bye."

"I told you, he's afraid of heights," Nick said to Maggy.

"Damn it, Nicky, you're not going to shame me into doin' this. I'll wait for you in the car."

"But, Link, we'll probably be gone for a couple of hours," Maggy recovered enough to protest.

"So I'll grab a burger and be back. The car'll be waitin' where it is now."

"See ya, bro." Nick did not sound particularly upset.

Link's reply was a grunt. Then he stood up and disappeared from view.

Maggy was suddenly very conscious of the fact that she was all alone with Nick. The realization made her nervous.

"Come on then," she said gruffly, and, turning, headed toward the north end of the ledge where it narrowed into a rocky footpath. The path, a little less than two feet wide, had been carved into the stone by a combination of man and nature some hundred years before, according to Herd, who had shown it to Maggy the summer after David was born. It snaked down the cliff in a rough Z-shape, eventually depositing the faithful not ten feet from where *The Lady Dancer* was docked.

"Christ, this is suicide," Nick muttered behind her. Maggy glanced around. A faint grin appeared and hovered around her mouth as she watched him cautiously follow her onto the path. His left side hugged the cliff, and his eyes focused on the rocky trail just in front of his feet.

"It's safer than it looks. I come this way all the time."

"I always knew you were crazy."

There was silence for a few minutes after that while Maggy blithely trod the route she had covered many times before and Nick inched his way after her. Then Maggy peered back over her shoulder again.

"What did Link mean by calling you a lovesick fool?" The question popped out of its own volition, but she wouldn't have called it back if she could have. She wanted—no, needed—to know.

Nick glanced up at her for an instant before returning his attention to his feet. "That I was getting his goat. He wanted to get mine back."

"But why a *lovesick* fool?"

Nick glanced up at her again. She had twisted around, watching him, and their eyes met. His foot hit a rock, dislodging it. He swore and froze as it skittered away from his feet, to roll over the edge of the path and plummet toward the creek below.

"Magdalena, I'm two-hundred-odd feet in the air with only a tiny little ribbon of rock standing between me and eternity. Could we talk about this on solid ground?"

"Oh. Sure."

There was silence between them after that. Maggy wasn't altogether sorry to be cut off. She knew she was tampering with something that was better left alone, but like Pandora with her box, temptation was almost impossible to resist. Why shouldn't she talk about feelings with Nick— just for tonight?

Because feelings, like memories, were too damned dangerous to play around with, she warned herself savagely.

Maggy reached the ground and turned to wait for Nick. She watched as he came down the path, moving slowly and carefully, bracing himself against the solid rock wall. The moonlight touched his hair, adding blue glints to the rich black waves. It washed the hard planes and angles of his face with silver. Clad in his elegant suit with his face turned away from her, he did not look like her Nick at all.

Of course, she reminded herself, he wasn't. He had stopped being "her" Nick twelve years before.

Then he reached the ground and glanced up, grinning as he saw her watching him. Maggy met his eyes and realized a fundamental truth: in the only way that mattered, he hadn't changed at all. He still occupied a room in her heart that had never, could never, belong to anyone else.

"I just have one question: how the hell do we get back up?" he asked as he joined her.

She clamped down hard on the emotion that was starting to bubble to the surface. Allowing herself to fall in love with Nick again could very well be the bomb that exploded her life. And David's. She must never forget David.

"Oh, we go up the other path. Down the creek, over the wall, and through the woods." Pardonably proud of her apparent insouciance, Maggy was already walking across the narrow dirt road that allowed the occasional pickup truck access to the dock as she replied.

"Are you telling me there's another path? One that doesn't involve a near-suicidal climb down a sheer cliff?"

"Yes." Maggy smiled sunnily at him over her shoulder. "But this one's much faster."

"Shit. Next time I'll take the overland route."

He was right behind her. Unable to help herself, Maggy grinned but didn't reply. As long as she remembered that Nick was, could be, no more to her than a very dear old friend, she would be fine.

"So, you want to talk about why Link thinks I'm a lovesick fool?" He spoke nearly in her ear when she was only a few paces from the dock. Maggy jumped, startled, then turned to face him, backing up a pace, shaking her head.

"No, I don't."

His eyes narrowed.

"It was a mistake to ask," she said hurriedly, wrapping her arms around herself to ward him off, though again he'd made no move to touch her. His hands were thrust deep into his pants pockets. "Being with you—brings back old memories. Old times. You know. That dance." She took a deep breath. "For a little while there, I guess I forgot I was married. With a child."

She made that point to underline it in her own mind. David, David—

he was both her reason for keeping her present life intact, and her talisman against exploding it.

"So you're telling me you choose ol' Lyle, huh? Whether you love him or not." Nick's response was surprisingly mild. Her eyes met his, then fell. He looked pensive, not angry—but she felt as if her heart was being wrung.

"Yes, that's exactly what I'm saying. And—I think I'd better go see *Tia* Gloria alone. If you hurry, you can probably still catch Link."

"I haven't laid a hand on you, have I?" He pointed this out in a perfectly reasonable tone.

"I—no."

"So what are you worrying about? You're not being an unfaithful wife just because you're standing here in the dark talking to me. Are you?"

"No." He was confusing the issue, as he'd always managed to confuse the issue. Nick had always been the slickest talker she'd ever known. A moment ago, she'd been so sure that she knew what to do for the best. But now . . .

"We're old friends, remember? Practically family. And you're taking me to see more family. What's wrong with that?"

"Lyle wouldn't like it." The objection was wrenched out of her before she could catch it. She waited for Nick to say "To hell with Lyle" as he had before. In a way, she would almost welcome a quarrel. To make parting with him easy . . .

"So don't tell him," Nick said, neatly taking the wind out of her sails. Maggy pursed her lips.

"So are we going to see *Tia* Gloria or not? You have to get rid of your present, remember."

Her eyes widened, and one hand moved automatically to rest over the items in her jacket. "How did you know?"

"I can read you like a book, Magdalena, remember?" Then he grinned. "Besides, I felt the things when I grabbed you back in the woods."

"Cheater." But she had to smile, too.

"So?" Nick's brows lifted. "Do we go or not?"

Maggy hesitated.

"Don't worry, fair maiden, you're safe with me." His stagy whisper made Maggy laugh again.

"You're impossible. Come on," she said and turned away, already knowing that she was making a mistake.

But she simply did not have the strength of will—or the time—at that moment to deal with Nick. He was a bulldog when it came to getting what he wanted, and she was weak, emotionally, just at present, where he was concerned. Besides, she had to get the tape and pictures to a safe place and get home again before she was missed.

Not that there was one chance in a million that she would be missed. But where Lyle was concerned, she didn't even like those odds.

The soft rush of the quarter-mile-distant river and the louder lapping of the creek nearly at her feet overlay the other sounds of the night. Glancing to her left, Maggy could just make out the serene darkness of the mighty Ohio as it flowed past Willow Creek's mouth. The unmistakable signs of the river's nearness permeated the air: the fishy smell, the dampness of the breeze, the sound of a barge horn floating over the water.

The moon had risen so that it now floated at a 45-degree angle in its setting of midnight-blue velvet sky. It was reflected in the dark mirror of the water, along with dozens of tiny twinkling stars, so that the night sky seemed to stretch on without end.

The opposite bank of the creek was wooded and quiet, with no cliff such as the one on which Windermere was built. That property belonged to another twenty-acre estate, Hagan's Bluff, but the huge brick house was located far away from the creek, and anyway it was empty. Old Mrs. Hagan, a widow, had died in the early part of the fall. The property would soon be up for sale. The vegetation across the water was thick and tangled, showing no signs of having been touched by human hands for years except for the path that led down to the small but shipshape aluminum dock. Mrs. Hagan had a teenage grandson whose passion was boating, and she had had the dock kept up for him. Two boats were tied up there still, one about the size of *The Lady Dancer* and one a little larger. Both were Fiberglas, and new-looking, their hulls gleaming brightly in the moonlight. Compared to them, *The Lady Dancer* was a derelict wreck.

On Windermere's side, their own wooden dock was ramshackle at best, kept from collapsing into the creek only by Herd's constant repairs. The dock jutted about ten feet out into the water, and *The Lady Dancer* bobbed at the end. The creek itself was perhaps forty feet wide, and not particularly deep. But it was deep enough to allow river access to a fifteen-foot runabout like *The Lady Dancer*.

Maggy, with Nick following, walked out along the dock to the very end.

"Hop in," she said, striving to strike a note that was friendly but impersonal. As she bent to untie the rope that secured *The Lady Dancer* to the dock, he moved to stand beside her.

When he didn't do as she said, she straightened to discover him, narrow-eyed, looking from her to the boat and back.

"Hop in?"

"Yes, hop in."

"What about you?"

"I'm coming. I don't want to let her loose until you get in because your weight is going to push her away from the dock. So when you're in, I'll unwrap the rope and jump in myself. See?" To illustrate her point, she loosened and held up the metal-tipped end of the rope while she left the middle still wrapped securely around the pole to hold the boat in place.

He still hesitated.

"Nick, would you get in the boat!"

He grimaced, then capitulated. "I'm trusting you, Magdalena. Don't blow it."

"That's a brave boy."

Nick clambered in with something less than his usual grace, holding carefully to the side as *The Lady Dancer* rocked and swayed. Just as Maggy had predicted, his weight sent the boat scooting away from the dock. The still-secured rope prevented it from going more than a few feet.

"Magdalena . . ." There was an edge to his voice as, crouched in the bow, Nick glanced up at her still standing on the dock.

"I'm coming. Hold on tight." Maggy released the rope, and, holding it, jumped. She landed on the balls of her feet smack in the center of the boat, bending her knees to maintain her balance as *The Lady Dancer* bucked under her weight. Nick, grabbing both sides, said something explosive under his breath as Maggy regained her balance and went aft with the agility of a cat.

"Are you sure you know what you're doing?" he asked.

"Just sit tight. We'll float out to the center in a minute, and then I can start the engine. Haven't you ever been in a boat before?" She tossed this back over her shoulder.

"No." His simple answer had the effect both of silencing Maggy and reminding her where she and Nick had come from. If she had not married Lyle, she probably would never have ridden in a boat, either. Boats were not plentiful in Louisville's west end.

Maggy secured the line to the hook Herd had set into the hull for just that purpose, then moved to where the engine was mounted on the stern. *The Lady Dancer* was an old boat made of solid wood; it had once been used as a ship-to-shore vehicle for a previous Forrest-family yacht.

When that yacht was sold, *The Lady Dancer* had been deemed useless, and Herd had been allowed to take it over as his own personal vessel. He had stripped the interior, outfitting it as a fishing boat with two simple plank seats, one across the stern and one nearer the bow. Steering was done by means of a rudder from the rear. To start the engine, it was necessary to pull on a rope attached to the motor, just as one would start a small lawn mower.

Maggy pulled on that rope now, once, twice, and the engine roared to life.

"Sit down," she called to Nick, who had started up as though he would come to her assistance when the motor did not start on the first try. He sat rather abruptly on the bow seat facing her as *The Lady Dancer* took off, sliding slickly through the waters of Willow Creek toward the river. After the initial burst of noise that always accompanied its ignition, the engine subsided to a dull sputter.

"Are you sure we ought to take this thing out on the river? It's a cold night for a swim." Nick's slightly raised voice sounded dubious as his eyes slid over *The Lady Dancer*'s ancient fittings.

"She's perfectly river-worthy. Trust me."

"You keep saying that. I wonder why it doesn't reassure me."

"Because you can't stand not being the man in charge."

Nick grinned. "You know me so well."

"I know."

There were logs floating near the mouth of the creek, and more logs and other jetsam wedged into the mud shoal that made negotiating the transition from creek to river a little tricky. Maggy had gotten hung up on those shoals more than once when she had first started taking *The Lady Dancer* out alone. But after twice having to jump overboard and wade in muddy water up to her neck to push the craft free, she had learned to stay just slightly to the right of the center of the channel. That was where the water was deepest.

"Grab a flashlight out of that tackle box by your left hand, turn it on, and set it in the bracket in the bow, would you?"

Nick looked at her suspiciously. "Why?"

"We don't have lights. Without lights no one can see us. It's not a good idea to be invisible on the river at night, what with the barges and everything. I don't know about you, but I'd hate to get run over by a barge."

"Christ," Nick said, but he did as she asked while Maggy hid a smile.

The beam of the flashlight was not strong enough to help with navigation, but that was not its purpose. Even on the darkest nights the river reflected enough light to make it easy to see where one was going. Herd had rigged up a way to use a flashlight as a headlight strictly as a safety device, just in case he or someone else should ever want to take *The Lady Dancer* out after dark. Not that he ever did. No one did, to her knowledge, except herself.

They chugged out of the mouth of the creek and into the wide, black expanse of the Ohio River without a hitch.

The water was choppy, due to the brisk wind that was always stronger over the water, but not as choppy as it had been other times when she had made the crossing. No white-tipped waves menaced the boat, and the wind was not strong enough to keep her from setting and keeping to a northeastern course, which, given the drag from the current, would bring them to landfall precisely where Maggy wished to be.

In the distance, the yellow lights of a barge moved steadily in their direction. Maggy could just make out the barge's huge black bulk riding low in the water perhaps four or five miles away. Between the barge and *The Lady Dancer* rose Six-Mile Island, a small, crescent-shaped island closer to the Indiana than the Kentucky side of the river where pleasure boats sometimes docked on hot summer days for picnics and swimming. Boasting three muddy beaches with overhanging grapevines for swinging and jumping, lots of circular rock bonfire pits, and acres of tangled woods, the island was one of two dotting the river. Its larger twin, Twelve-Mile Island, was, just as its name implied, some six miles closer to Cincinnati. During the summer, power boats would race figure eights around the islands, slowing down in the narrow channel between Indiana and Six-Mile before roaring out into the open river again at full throttle for another lap. Six-Mile Island wasn't a popular destination among the moneyed crowd the Forrests ran with. But for young families with access to a boat but little cash, it was the cooling-off spot of choice. No boats were docked there tonight, at least not on the Kentucky side, which wasn't surprising, given the nippiness of the air. Sleeping out on one's boat was definitely a summer activity.

"If you want to check, I think Herd keeps a change of clothes in the port compartment. In case you really don't want to go visiting with a hole in your pants."

"Who's Herd?" Nick looked where she pointed, spotted the wooden cabinet, edged off his seat and headed toward it in a crouch, clearly not comfortable with moving about on the bouncing boat.

"The gardener."

He gave a short whistle through his teeth. "Ritzy."

"Isn't it?" Maggy watched while he opened the compartment, rummaged around, and extracted a pair of jeans and a beat-up-looking army jacket.

"Think they'll fit?" Maggy asked as he held them up for inspection.

"Close enough. Think your gardener will mind if I borrow them?"

"No."

"Too bad if he does, right? One complaint, and off with his head?"

"No." Maggy had to laugh. "The Forrests consider Herd and Louella —Louella is Herd's wife, and the housekeeper—family. They wouldn't dream of letting them go, and even if they did I don't think Herd or Louella would leave. They'd just continue to work around the place like they've always done, waiting for somebody to come to his senses and realize Windermere couldn't be run without them."

"You speak of the Forrests like you're not one of them." Seated again on the forward bench facing her, Nick kicked off his tasseled loafers.

"I'm not, really. I'm an outsider, and I always will be. Not so much because I wasn't born into the family, but because I wasn't born into their world. When I first married Lyle, I didn't—oh, know the difference between a fish knife and a dinner knife, for example. That kind of thing drives them nuts."

"You mean they have a special knife for fish? What about peanut butter? Is there a knife for that, too? Or Cheez Whiz?" Nick shed his suit coat and tugged his tie free.

"The Forrests," Maggy said with her nose in the air, "don't eat anything as plebeian as peanut butter, much less Cheez Whiz."

"Dull bunch."

"Yes," Maggy said, grinning suddenly. "Yes, they are."

"Too dull for you, I would have thought." Nick unzipped his pants. The sound was surprisingly loud, rising sharply above the thud of small waves hitting the hull and the dull throb of the motor. "Was it worth it, Magdalena?"

He asked the question casually, sliding out of his pants and sitting there for a minute in his underwear, watching her as he waited for her answer. Maggy looked at him, at the large, very masculine feet in sober black socks, at the hard muscularity of his hair-roughened bare calves and thighs, at the gleaming white shirt that covered his lap and his strong arms and his wide chest, at the darkly handsome face. And she knew the answer. *No,* she wanted to scream. *No, it wasn't worth it.*

"Was what worth it?" she asked in a cool voice, averting her eyes to the nearing Indiana shoreline as he began to pull on Herd's jeans.

"Don't give me that, Magdalena." She couldn't help sneak a peek at him as he thrust one leg into the jeans and then the other, pulling the pants up with easy efficiency. She caught just a glimpse of him in his underwear—white jockey shorts, as she had surmised from what she had seen through the hole in his pants—but it was enough to awaken something in her that had not stirred in a long, long time.

A tiny spurt of lust? No, Lyle had cured her of that. She hadn't had any sexual feelings for years.

Getting them back with Nick was not a smart idea.

She focused again on the Indiana shoreline as he tucked in his shirt, zipped up the jeans, and threaded his belt through the loops.

"Do they fit?" she asked in as composed a tone as she could muster.

"A little short, a little big around the waist, but they'll do." She heard the zip of a second zipper and looked back at him to discover that he was now fully clad, jeans, army coat and all, and was sitting down to pull on his shoes.

"So, was marrying an old guy for his millions worth it?"

Nick was not going to give up. Maggy knew him well enough to recognize the note in his voice that told her so.

"At the time I thought it was." Her voice was remote.

"And now?" Her tone deterred him not at all. Not that she had really expected it to. After all, she knew Nick.

Now I'm trapped, she wanted to cry. Instead, the words that came out were, "Now it's done."

"It can be undone."

"No."

"Magdalena." Fully dressed now, Nick moved, coming to sit on the seat beside her. Only the sticklike rudder, with her hand resting atop it, separated them.

"You're making the boat stern-heavy," she protested.

"You asked me earlier why I came back to Louisville."

"Could you move back to where you were?"

"Want to hear the answer?"

"No." She made the mistake of looking at him then. His eyes were intent on her face, gleaming green as a cat's in the moonlit night.

"Don't lie to me, Magdalena. You never could lie to me. I always know. You do want to hear the answer. You're just afraid."

She wet her lips, tossed her head, tried to look away from him and gave up. "All right, then, tell me: why did you come back?" The question was supposed to sound lighthearted. She wasn't sure that was how it came out.

Nick's voice was very quiet as he replied, "For you, Magdalena. I came back for you."

16

"**N**ick . . ." Maggy wet her lips with the tip of her tongue, swallowed, and with the best will in the world not to do it, dropped her eyes. Which, when she thought about it, was probably just as well. He had always possessed the uncanny ability to read her mind. And the jumble of thoughts and emotions that filled it at his words were not for him to divine.

With every atom of her being, she longed to lean her head against his broad chest and feel his arms come around her. She ached to pass her troubles on to him and let him make everything right. . . .

Only he couldn't. He could not do it. Her world was past being fixed by the arrival of a knight in shining armor, even so redoubtable a knight as Nick. Every scrap of her intelligence told her that. The only dissenter was her wayward heart.

"I hope that isn't true," she said in as composed a fashion as she could muster, dragging her gaze back up to his at last. Her training in proper social niceties and her years of dissembling as Lyle's wife served her well. Her attitude was a masterpiece of dismissal.

Only he refused to be dismissed.

"It is true, Maggy May. And you know it. Did you ever really doubt that one day I'd be coming back for you?" The tenderness in the words was almost her undoing.

"I hoped you wouldn't." In a way, her answer was sincere, and some of that sincerity must have been apparent in her voice, because his eyes darkened.

"That hurts my feelings," he said after a moment. His tone was light, but she knew him well enough to realize that he was deliberately making it so. "Or at least, it would if I believed it. I don't believe it, Magdalena."

"Believe it." She took a deep breath, glanced around to make sure they still had a wide expanse of clear river around them, and looked back at him. He was watching her, his heavy-lidded eyes both hooded and intent, sitting very still with his hands resting on his knees. Only one who knew him as well as she did would realize that his very stillness was a mask for an incredible tension that he was having to fight to control.

"You love me, Magdalena." The flat statement was quiet. His eyes never left her face. "You always have."

Maggy's eyes didn't even flicker as she took a deep, silent breath and prepared to lie as she had never lied in her life.

"I loved you *twelve years* ago. That's a long time, and a lot of water under the bridge." Belying her calm words, her hand gripping the tiller shook, sending the little craft skittering to port. Correcting their course gave her the precious time she needed to finish armoring her heart.

"So you're saying you don't love me anymore."

He would never believe her if she denied it outright.

"I'm not saying that. What I'm saying is that I do love you: as a very dear old friend. And that's all."

Nick looked at her without speaking for a moment, his expression impossible to read. Unable to hold his gaze for more than a few seconds, Maggy turned her eyes to the dark Indiana shoreline slipping past, on the pretext of watching where they were going. In reality, she hardly saw anything, so focused on Nick and his response was she.

"Bullshit," he said.

Surprise brought her gaze back to him. His jaw was set hard, his eyes gleaming green as they met hers. He looked tough, aggressive, and utterly disbelieving. Her teeth clamped together, and her chin came up. She would not let him rattle her. He had always been good at that.

"Believe what you like." She did her best to feign indifference.

"You already admitted that you don't love *him.*"

For a moment, she silently cursed her loose tongue. Then she thought, *I couldn't have pretended otherwise. Not with Nick.*

"So? Does that mean that I automatically have to love you?"

"You've always loved me. From the time you were a little bitty girl. You've never stopped. You never will." His voice held cool certainty.

"You always were a conceited thing. Still think you're God's gift to women, do you?" The glance she shot him was withering.

"Sometimes." A teasing grin flickered over his face. "Remember how mad you used to get? When we were teenagers, and I started seeing other girls? You'd throw a hissy fit every time I went out. You'd punch me and kick me and call me everything in the book when you caught me, then stomp off in a rage. Once you even followed me, and slapped the girl I was with. What was her name? Melinda something?"

"Melissa Craig," Maggy said icily, not realizing how telling her perfect recall of the busty blonde was until it was too late. She bit her tongue, wishing she could stuff the words back into her mouth.

"Ah, yes. Melissa." He sighed reminiscently. "Sixteen years old and already a thirty-six double D. And hot as a firecracker."

"She was a slut." Maggy couldn't help it. The memory of Melissa Craig hanging all over Nick was still enough to make her blood boil.

Nick grinned wickedly. "You were just jealous because she was a thirty-six double D and you hadn't even started to bud."

"I was only fourteen! And I wasn't jealous! I was trying to save you from her! I didn't want to see you make a terrible mistake."

"From the viewpoint of a sixteen-year-old boy, Melissa Craig was not a terrible mistake. She was sex on the hoof."

Maggy sniffed. "That's all you care about."

Nick shook his head. "Even then, it wasn't *all* I cared about. If it was all I cared about, I would have had sex with you. Don't think the thought didn't occur, with you making goo-goo eyes at me all the time. But you were too young, and I cared about you too much. I wouldn't have done it. I *didn't* do it."

"You did." Maggy could have bitten her tongue off as soon as the words left it. She didn't dare look at him after that.

Still, she could feel it as Nick's focus on her face sharpened. "You were grown-up by then. I held out as long as I could. And, believe me, the last couple of years were sheer hell. You deliberately tried to drive me nuts, didn't you? Seeing you do your little belly dance was the last straw. I realized then that you weren't a little girl anymore, and I might lose you if I didn't stake my claim. So I did."

Maggy took a deep breath as memories threatened to swamp her.

"I don't want to talk about it, all right?" Her eyes shifted away from him, to sweep the dark, rolling water as the boat cut through it.

"We had great sex. The best I've ever had."

Every muscle in her body tightened. Her gaze swung back to his face. "Is that what you want from me? More *great sex*?" Her voice mocked him bitterly.

He shook his head. "If that was all I wanted, I would have taken you up on your very interesting suggestion of the other day. Remember?

You offered to let me throw you down on the ground and get my rocks off on you right there and then."

"Oh, shut up." Maggy's face was red.

"I came back for *you*, Magdalena, not sex. Great or otherwise."

"Then you're wasting your time."

"I don't think so."

"Don't you care that you're causing trouble for me? With Lyle? He hates you, you know." There was a hint of desperation in her voice.

"Yes, I know." If he recognized her despair, he did not take pity on her and abandon the topic. "Just what did you tell him about me, Magdalena, to make him hate me so?"

Maggy's lips compressed, and with the best will in the world her eyes flickered away from his face. "Not a lot."

"He obviously knows we were once lovers. He wouldn't hate me so much otherwise."

"Yes," Maggy said. "He knows that."

"Not a wise revelation to make on your honeymoon, I wouldn't think. Or did you tell him later? You certainly didn't have time before."

Maggy gritted her teeth. "What makes you think I told Lyle at all? He could have found out on his own. He could have had me investigated, and found out that way."

"That's possible," Nick said with a shrug. "But you're too honest not to have told him about us. Did you tell him how much in love we were, or did you only tell him about the sex? In one of those let's-reveal-our-previous-bed-partners conversations that always turn out to be a mistake?"

"I don't have to answer that." She was angry suddenly, and the look she sent him showed it.

"Does he know you married him for his money?" Nick was relentless. When she disdained to reply, he thought for a second, then answered the question himself. "Of course he does. He's an asshole, but he's not stupid."

Again Maggy said nothing. Nick continued in a musing tone. "So the question is, why did he marry you? You were young, and beautiful, but hardly his type. Unless he fancied some great sex himself. Was that it?"

"Go to hell."

"What happened to spoil it, I wonder? Did having sex with a man older than your dad become too much of a chore? Or did he lose interest in you?"

"My marriage is none of your damned business."

"Don't dodge the question, Magdalena. I want to know what happened."

"I want a lot of things I'm never going to get."

Nick studied her for a moment. "When did it start to go bad, baby? Was it soon?" His gentled voice was almost her undoing.

"I am not going to discuss my marriage with you." Again she fought the urge to crumple, to give up and tell him the whole story. Then the fat would be in the fire, indeed, she reminded herself fiercely. Nick would never let her go back to Lyle—unless she told him *everything*. He very well might then, because he would probably hate her forever after that.

"Is it the money? Is that why you won't leave him?"

"No!" Nick's relentlessness was goading her into too-hasty replies. And he knew it, damn him, just as he knew her. It was the effect he was hoping for, to get at the truth. "Well, yes. Partly."

"Partly?" The breath Nick drew in was audible. "I have money now, Magdalena. Not as much as he has, but enough. I've done well over the last twelve years. I could keep you in comfort. And the boy, too."

"His name is David."

"All right, David. You don't have to be afraid that I wouldn't welcome him. I would."

Hearing Nick say David's name was almost more pleasure than pain despite the circumstances. Maggy thanked God for the darkness that kept Nick from reading the more subtle nuances of her thoughts as they flickered across her face. He knew her so well that he might guess. . . . He must never guess.

"Nick—" Maggy took a deep breath and tried again. "Nick, I can never leave Lyle. Please just—accept that, for all our sakes, would you?"

He was silent for a moment. Tearing her eyes from him, peering upriver to see if she could spot their destination, Maggy hoped against hope that her flat statement would be enough to persuade him to let the subject drop. Of course, she should have known better. She did know better.

"Now, that's a curious choice of words," he said. "You can never leave him. Not that you won't, not that you don't want to, but that you can't. Are you afraid of him?"

That hit so close to home that Maggy flinched. Terrified that Nick might see and correctly add two and two to guess something of what she had been through over the past twelve years, she hurried into speech, hoping to throw him off the scent.

"No, of course not!"

"Now why doesn't that convince me, I wonder? Does he hurt you, Magdalena? If so, all you have to do is tell me. Believe me, he won't do it again."

His voice was so soft that Maggy felt a shiver run down her spine. Nick would murder Lyle with his bare hands if he ever learned the truth. Nick had always taken care of his own.

Only she wasn't his any longer. She had to convince him, and herself, of that.

"Nick." She took a deep breath. "It's not the money and it's not that I'm afraid of Lyle. It's more complicated than that." She hesitated, and decided to go for a partial truth. "It's David. David worships Lyle."

"So? Lyle would still be his father. The boy could continue to see him."

Maggy shook her head. "Lyle would fight for custody. And he would probably win. Every judge in Kentucky is his friend. If I left Lyle, I would in all likelihood lose David. I couldn't bear that."

"I always knew you'd be a hell of a mother." The words, uttered after a brief pause, were grudging.

Maggy's breath caught in her throat. She was afraid to look at him.

There was another, longer, pause. Maggy eased the rudder over, heading toward the center of the river as the distance between their boat and the barge lessened. It was never wise to get caught between a barge and the shore. The barge's wake was enough to push a craft as small as *The Lady Dancer* into the rocks.

"So tell me about him—David."

The question was unexpected. Maggy glanced over at Nick, and hesitated a moment. Then she said slowly, "He's—a great kid." She took a deep breath, then continued. Why shouldn't she tell Nick something, just a little something, about David? "He does well in school, and everybody likes him, and he's handsome and funny—oh, and he is a wonderful artist! You should see some of his paintings! His teachers say he has a really exceptional talent."

"He must get that from the Forrests, then. As far as I recall, you couldn't draw so much as a stick figure."

"No, he didn't get it from me." Maggy's voice was constricted.

"You love him a lot." It was a statement, not a question.

"He's the joy of my life."

"I'm glad you've had him, then, all these years. I would hate to think of you without anything to bring you joy." Nick's gaze searched her face. "You've been unhappy, haven't you?"

"Sometimes." The admission, massive understatement though it was,

was such a relief that Maggy felt it leave her like a weight lifting off her soul.

"You did it for the money." It was a flat statement.

Maggy barely hesitated. "Yes."

"I understand. Offered the same chance, I probably would have done the same thing myself."

"Thank you for saying that." She managed a small smile at him. For a moment neither of them said anything else. Then Nick spoke softly.

"The day before you ran off with him, we'd had a fight, remember? A real humdinger. I brought you a present—a winter coat, because you didn't have one—and you looked at it and started screaming that I had stolen it and was going to end up in prison like my brother and you wanted more out of life than to be hooked up with a hood like me. Your reaction floored me. I'd brought you lots of things before, and you'd never questioned where they came from. Hell, you knew."

"Yes, I knew," Maggy agreed softly, remembering the scene in vivid, excruciating detail. It had been a beautiful coat, fine black wool with a dyed-to-match fox collar and cuffs, and a label from an exclusive store. She'd known instantly that it had cost the earth. She'd also known that Nick, who had worked construction when there was work and done whatever he could, legal or not, to earn a buck when there wasn't, was not able to afford a coat like that. He'd stolen it, just as he had stolen lots of things for her in the past, and one day he was going to get caught stealing and go to prison like Link. But, although she had tried her best, he could not be brought to understand that. Presenting the coat to her, he had been cocky in the way a young man is cocky, proud of himself and his gift and eager for her to try it on despite the raging summer heat. She had taken one look, thrown the coat in his face, and followed it with her shoe and harsh words.

He continued: "So I came over the next night to see if you were over your little snit. You weren't there, but your father was sitting at the table, guzzling Jack Daniel's and crying. You know how he always used to cry about your mom when he drank? That's what I thought he was doing. It took me about twenty minutes to pry out of him that you weren't home because you'd run off to Indianapolis to marry some rich guy he had never even met. That was why he was crying."

Nick glanced at her to see if she would say anything, but Maggy couldn't. She had heard the story of Nick's questions and his rage from her father. In her mind's eye she had pictured the scene a thousand times. . . .

When she remained silent, Nick went on. "I went nuts when your father told me that. I couldn't believe it. When I finally did, I jumped in my car and hightailed it for Indianapolis as fast as I could go. The damn thing threw a rod fifty miles out of Louisville. No way was it going another inch. I hitched the rest of the way. It was after midnight when I got there. I knew that if your old man had his facts straight I was too late. I thought you might be spending your wedding night in a hotel in the city. I went to a couple of them, raised hell when they wouldn't let me look at their registers. Finally one of the managers called the cops, and I got arrested. I was in jail for a week, on a charge of disturbing the peace. I didn't have any money for bail."

He stopped then, his eyes still fastened on her face. Maggy could hardly look at him, so awful did she feel. She could see his rage so clearly, feel his anguish as if she had experienced it herself. . . .

In a way, she supposed she had.

"Did you ever think of me, querida, when you took off on your honeymoon with that rich old guy?" Old anger hardened his voice. The name, the pet name that her father used to call her and that Nick had gleaned from him years before, was a weapon that he used on purpose to wound. And Maggy knew that if Nick was deliberately trying to hurt her, he must be in pain himself. Dreadful pain.

"Oh, Nick." Maggy couldn't help it. Her heart broke for him, and for herself. Tears sprang to her eyes. "Of course I did. All the time. Even when I—tried not to."

"You tried not to." Sarcasm edged the words. "For a long time, I tried not to think about you, too, but in the end I couldn't think of anything else."

"There was David . . ." Her voice was almost pleading.

"Ah, yes. David. David, who was certainly begat in the biblical way. Tell me something, Magdalena: how did it feel to screw old Lyle when you were crazy in love with me?"

Maggy felt as if he had punched her in the stomach. Her eyes went wide, and she felt the color drain from her cheeks. She could only stare at him speechlessly.

"Was the sex good for you, at first? Did you like it? I used to almost go crazy, wondering."

"Stop it, Nick!"

"All right," he said, his voice rough and low. "As you said, it's all water under the bridge now, anyway. I've had a few chicks since you, too, baby—but I could never get you out from under my skin. I don't think you ever got me out from under yours, either. Did you? Not in twelve years. What does that tell you? That we belong together. You belong to me. We've wasted twelve years. Let's not waste any more."

"It's too late for us, Nick." Her quiet rebuttal made his eyes harden on her face. He stared at her without speaking for a moment. Maggy could not hold his gaze. Instead she glanced away, across the dark water toward the barge that was within half a mile now, between *The Lady Dancer* and the Indiana shoreline.

"Do you still sleep with him?" The question came at her out of nowhere, ripping her composure like a stray bullet.

"What?" Her head whipped around so that she was looking at him again.

"Do you still sleep with him? Lyle?" Nick's face betrayed no emotion. Only his eyes were a bright, glittering green.

"I—no." She shifted her gaze to the river again. It was safer to watch the progress of the barge.

"No? Since when?"

"Not—for years." Maggy took a deep breath, and fought to keep her voice steady. "Look, can we drop the subject?"

"No." The word was brutal. "I didn't think you slept with him, Magdalena. You don't have the look of a woman who's been well-loved. You don't sleep with anybody else, do you? No boyfriends?"

"No!"

"Ah." There was a satisfied quality to the sound. Maggy glanced at him then, to find that he was smiling at her rather grimly. "Remember what it was like? With us?"

"Nick, I told you, I don't want to talk about this."

"Too bad, querida. *I* want to, so we're talking about it anyway. Are you telling me that you're prepared to spend the rest of your life without ever feeling that way again? Without ever feeling your blood boil and your skin steam and your body burn until it bursts? You were so passionate. I remember how you used to love what I did to you. How you used to beg me: 'Don't stop, Nick! Don't stop! Please—' "

"Damn you, will you let it drop!" Her words were fierce as her whole body quivered, partly in outrage—and partly in reluctant remembrance.

" '—please don't stop!' And how you'd wrap your arms around my neck and your legs around my waist and hang on as if you were never going to let me go. . . ."

Maggy slapped him. She let go of the tiller and leapt to her feet and slapped him, all in a movement so quick that he didn't even have time to duck. At her action the boat heeled violently. Water sloshed over the side in an icy wave, soaking her shoes and the bottoms of her pant legs.

She lost her balance, teetering wildly. Nick caught her arm just as she would have pitched overboard and yanked her back. She landed in his lap.

"The passion's still there, querida. You can feel it again—with me."

He kissed her. Hard. Her head sank back against his shoulder, pushed there by the force of his mouth. His tongue slid past her lips to fill her mouth, then plunged in and out, in and out, while his arms around her tightened like iron bands, holding her in place for his kiss. He tasted of toothpaste, and more faintly of champagne—that was the last rational thought that ricocheted through her stunned brain. His hand was suddenly on her breast, squeezing, kneading. Even through the layers of leather and cotton that separated his flesh from hers she could feel that hand. Her breast swelled beneath it, tightening, hardening. Her body quaked to shivering life. Taken by surprise, her response was purely instinctive. Maggy's back arched, and she moaned against his mouth.

Her arms went around his neck. And she kissed him back.

His hand abandoned the front of her leather jacket to delve down into the zippered opening, seeking closer contact with her breast. She was ready for his touch, aching for it, quivering for it. His hand covered her breast with only the thin cotton of her turtleneck and bra between his fingers and her flesh. He pressed, squeezed, kneaded while she kissed him back with a hunger that had been waiting inside her forever.

He rolled her nipple between his thumb and forefinger, and then his hand left her again. Still kissing her, he shifted her so that she lay back along the plank seat with him looming above her. She could feel the hardness of the wood against her back and bottom. He reached under the flap of her jacket for the fastening of her jeans. The snap was easy, but he fumbled with the tab on the zipper.

His jeans-clad knee slid between hers, parting her thighs. For a moment she was willing, eager even, and her clutching hands and hungry mouth proved it. Then, without warning, the memories came flooding back, as vividly horrible as if they were a first-run movie playing in her head. Not of Nick, but of the other, the night when Lyle had taught her what fear truly meant. Hideous memories, that she now did not doubt would scar her for life.

"No!" she screamed, the sound swallowed by his mouth, and began to fight.

The warning blast of a barge horn rent the night.

"Jesus!" Nick lifted his head, let her go, and grabbed for the tiller. *The Lady Dancer* made a sharp 90-degree turn that sent Maggy tumbling off the seat.

She struck her injured wrist on the edge of the seat, and it hurt. The discomfort zapped her back to the present quicker than anything else could have done. The horn blasted again, indignantly. As *The Lady Dancer* spun away from the sudden threat, the running lights of the barge swept past Maggy's line of vision, and then were out of sight.

"I'm sorry, baby. Are you all right?" With danger past, Nick reached down a hand to pull her up. Maggy ignored it, scrambling to get her feet beneath her. She crouched there in the bottom of the boat, rubbing her bandaged wrist, glaring up at him. Her face was utterly white in the darkness of the night.

17

"*D*on't you ever, ever touch me that way again." Her voice was as hard and brittle as a pane of glass.

His brows knit.

"Not if you don't want me to," he said after a minute. His eyes were keen on her face. "Did you hurt your wrist?"

"No."

Maggy let her injured arm drop to her side. She hesitated, her gaze fixed warily on him as the last of her panic dissipated. Ignoring the hand he offered her, she slid back into her seat. She reached for the tiller, then drew back her hand when it would have brushed his. With the part of her mind that was functioning rationally, she knew this was Nick, and that Nick would never hurt her. But the memories, freshly awakened, were too strong, too potent, to be dismissed by mere knowledge. Buried for years in her subconscious, never willingly acknowledged by her with so much as a conscious thought, they nevertheless lived on. The sexuality of Nick's kiss had resurrected them. Suddenly they loomed, atavistic and threatening, in the forefront of her mind.

If she had to touch Nick, or any man, just at that moment, she thought she would be sick.

"I've got it," she said, her manner brusque. He relinquished the tiller without comment. She refused to look at him as she placed her hand where his had been, though she knew that he was watching her. Instead she confined her gaze to the Indiana shoreline as she brought the boat around. She needed time to calm her shattered senses, time to banish the terrifying dinosaurs from her past back to the swamp of forgetfulness. Time to remember that the man beside her was Nick . . .

But there was no time. Nick was looking at her curiously. She could feel his gaze even though her face was averted. He would want an explanation—and she could not talk about what had happened all those years ago if her life depended on it.

Her shiver had nothing at all to do with the chill of the night air. Thank goodness *Tia* Gloria's house was just around the bend in the river, and they were approaching the bend.

"Magdalena . . ." For one of the few times since Maggy had known him, Nick sounded almost hesitant.

"Leave it alone. Please." Her reply was rigid.

"I didn't mean to scare you."

"You didn't."

"I did. We both know that. The question is, why?"

"I don't want to talk about it." Her words were fierce. She glanced at him finally, anger in her gaze, to find him studying her like a scientist examining a specimen. How long would it take him to come up with something perilously near the truth? she wondered. He had always been too smart for his own good. And hers.

The expression on his face enabled her to get herself under control. She was not ready for what would happen if he were to suspect what had caused her to be the way she was about sex.

"I just don't like being mauled, is all. Caveman technique does nothing for me," she added with a haughty lift of her chin.

"I see." Nick's reply was bland, but his eyes weren't. They were bright with speculation.

Uncomfortable, she shifted her gaze back to the water. *The Lady Dancer* chugged around the bend in the river, and *Tia* Gloria's house was finally in sight.

It was a funny-looking little house, set not twenty feet back from the river. A living room, kitchen, and bath occupied the first level, and two tiny bedrooms took up the second. All five rooms were wedged into a structure that was as asymmetrical as it was possible for a dwelling to be and still remain standing. From the outside, the second floor appeared larger than the first. The windows were a variety of shapes—round, octagonal, triangular, square—set haphazardly into the walls, as if the designer had stood over the blueprints, tossed paper shapes representing the windows up in the air, and placed the actual windows wherever the paper facsimiles landed. The house itself was built of wood that had never been painted and had thus weathered, over the years, to a silvery shade of gray. The pitch of the wood-shingle roof was dizzyingly steep, and a black metal stovepipe, unevenly joined at the seams, jutted from it at a crazy angle. The house was perched about twelve feet above the ground on a quartet of telephone-pole stilts to keep out the water should the river ever rise, which it did about once a year. Maggy had dubbed it "the Crooked House" the first time she set eyes on it, because it reminded her of a nursery rhyme that she had loved when she was little:

> *There was a crooked man*
> *who walked a crooked mile*
> *and found a crooked sixpence*
> *beside a crooked stile.*
> *He bought a crooked cat*
> *who caught a crooked mouse*
> *and they all lived together*
> *in a little crooked house.*

"There it is," she said to Nick, pointing.

"That?" As the boat chugged toward the shoreline, Nick looked up at the dark shape of the birdhouselike structure that she indicated. Silhouetted against the shifting canvas of the night sky, the house rose above the scrub trees just beyond the muddy beach, and his eyes widened.

"We call it the Crooked House." She recited the nursery rhyme for his edification.

"Name fits."

"Papi loved it."

Nick chuckled suddenly. "I bet. He always did like anything out of the ordinary. And he loved the river. From up there, he must have had a hell of a view." He sobered, and cast her a sideways glance. "I would have come home for his funeral, but I didn't hear about it until a couple of months too late."

There was no accusation in his voice, but nevertheless Maggy felt heat rise to her cheeks. She should have notified Nick, who had been considered family by Jorge. But she hadn't known where he was, and even if she had, she probably wouldn't have had the courage to contact him. The obstacle that was Lyle had seemed insurmountable.

"It was—very sudden. A heart attack. *Tia* Gloria was with him, but there was nothing she could do. They were eating supper on the balcony, talking and watching the sunset, and—he just keeled over. He was dead before they got him to the hospital."

"It must have been hard on you. I know how you loved him."

"Yes." Maggy took a deep breath and willed herself not to cry. She never did anymore, for her father. Her sorrow at his loss was with her still and would be for the rest of her life. But it had been tempered over time by loving memories and by the sure knowledge that he was happier reunited with her mother than he ever had been since Mary's death. Nick's presence brought Jorge's memory back sharply, and suddenly the pain of her loss was new again. Jorge had loved Nick almost as a son in the days when Nick and Magdalena were inseparable.

But if she cried, Nick would comfort her, and she could not bear his touch.

"Is your mother—how is your mother?"

"Fine. She lives in Detroit now, with husband number four. Link and I spent this past Thanksgiving with her. Rob, her new husband, isn't too bad. He treats her good, and she's happy."

"I'm glad."

Her father had built a tiny dock just for *The Lady Dancer*. Approaching it, Maggy eased back on the throttle until the boat was just barely moving through the water. With years of practice behind her, it was the work of only a few minutes to sidle in next to the dock, secure the rope, and cut the engine.

"Come on," she said without looking at Nick. With a nimble leap she was on the dock before he could reply or, as she feared, touch her.

"Looks like she has company," Nick observed, clambering after her, his gaze fixed on the half dozen or so cars that were parked in the gravel driveway that curved around behind the house.

Glancing up at the tiny, faint light just visible through one of the octagonal windows—the rest of the house was in complete darkness—Maggy nodded, unsurprised.

"She's probably having a séance."

"Oh." Though Maggy's statement undoubtedly would have given a stranger pause, Nick took it in stride. He had once known *Tia* Gloria, self-proclaimed seer, mystic, and psychic, well. "She still get ten bucks a head?"

"No." Maggy was already stepping off the dock and heading up the pebble-strewn beach toward the stairs that led to the front door. "She retired when she moved in with *papi*. This must be a group of her friends."

"Fantastic."

Maggy ignored this unenthusiastic mutter and swiftly climbed the stairs.

"What do we do, knock? They'll probably think we're spooks." Nick was two steps behind her as she reached the balcony. It ran all the way around the house and the front door opened off it.

"I have a key." Maggy reached in her pocket and produced it. "Shhh. We don't want to interrupt if they're in the middle of something."

Making as little noise as possible, Maggy unlocked the door and motioned for Nick to precede her into the small kitchen. It was utterly dark except for the moonlight wafting in behind them, because the swinging door that separated the kitchen from the living room was shut. A faint whitish glow showed beneath that door.

"I feel like a cat burglar," Nick whispered as Maggy closed the front door behind them. With the moonlight cut off, the darkness was almost impenetrable. A burning smell permeated the kitchen, causing Maggy to wrinkle her nose.

Sepulchral music began to play in the other room.

"Calling the spirits . . . I'm calling the spirits . . ." A high-pitched, moaning voice that Maggy recognized only with difficulty as belonging to *Tia* Gloria was just audible through the closed kitchen door. "I'm calling the spirit of one dearly departed, one beloved by a still-living entity present in this room. I'm calling the spirit of Alice Kannapel. Alice Kannapel, speak to your niece!"

This dramatic pronouncement produced dead silence except for the rolling music. Even Maggy, in the act of tiptoeing to the pantry to flick on the tiny light that hung from the ceiling there, was affected. She paused, listening, before she caught herself, mentally shook her head at her own gullibility, and continued with what she was doing.

"Glory, glory, glory . . ." a hoarse croak of a voice suddenly warbled from somewhere nearby. Maggy jumped, whirling, but could see nothing except Nick's large bulk not far behind her, apparently frozen in place by the same sound. Heart pounding in reaction, Maggy swallowed and fumbled for the light switch.

"What in hell . . . ?" growled Nick, no longer rooted to the spot. She could feel him looming behind her, protectively close. Where was that light switch? She groped for it as hysterical laughter bubbled inside her.

". . . Lord God Almighty . . ." The hymn gained strength.

"Do you hear that?"

"It was Aunt Alice's favorite hymn!"

"And the smell!"

"Sulfur!"

"Gloria, by golly, I think you may have finally done it! You've got in touch with a real spirit at last!"

"What are you talking about, you foolish old man? I always get in touch with real spirits!" The jumble of excited voices from the other room coincided with Maggy's discovery of the light switch.

". . . God in three persons . . ."

The light, a tiny yellow bulb with no more wattage than a single candle, sprang to life. Its glow was just enough to reveal the singer—and Nick's face.

He was staring at her, face pale, eyes wide, as the ghostly hymn filled the little house from a source not three feet behind his back.

". . . Blessed Trinity!" This triumphant conclusion, the sheer volume of which could have rattled the rafters if there had been any to rattle, immediately dissolved into a degenerate cackle of laughter.

Nick was already swinging around when Maggy said, with soft hilarity, "Look behind you."

He did, saw the large, wrought-iron cage and the parrot in it pacing its perch, head bobbing, green-and-yellow feathers ruffled, and muttered something explosive under his breath.

"Hello, Horatio." Maggy, grinning widely, slipped around Nick toward the cage.

"Damned bird. I should have guessed." Nick stuck his hands in his pockets, his expression self-conscious as the tips of his ears took on just the slightest tinge of red.

"There's a light in the kitchen!"

"Someone's in there!"

"It's Aunt Alice!"

"More likely a burglar."

"Do you smell that? Could it be—the scent of the netherworld?"

"Smells more like something burning to me."

The voices from the other room were punctuated by the sounds of chairs scraping over the floor as the occupants apparently rose with haste. The music was abruptly cut off. Footsteps pounded toward the kitchen door.

Maggy had no time to do more than exchange a look with Nick before the door swung open. A group consisting of a single elderly gentleman brandishing a silver-headed cane and five sixtyish ladies, one armed with a furled umbrella and another with a tall brass candlestick, which she waved threateningly in the air, confronted them. For a moment no one moved.

Then, "Magdalena!" came a placid voice from the back of the group, and the knot of potential gladiators parted to let *Tia* Gloria through. Her plump form clad in a purple silk tunic and pants embellished by silvery crescent moons, blond hair piled high in a neo-beehive atop her head, *Tia* Gloria sailed across the kitchen, arms thrown wide to embrace Maggy. Maggy, despite being nearly suffocated by a cloud of Chloe perfume, returned the shorter woman's hug with enthusiasm. Though no bonds of blood bound them, ties of the heart did. For most of Maggy's childhood, she had thought of Gloria as a close family friend. It was only when Gloria moved into this house with Maggy's father that she had realized the truth: of course they had been lovers for years. Dearly as Jorge had loved his wife, his sexual needs had not died with her. Gloria had met those needs. Jorge had been fond of Gloria, but Gloria had loved him deeply. Her one goal in life had been to persuade him to make her wife number two.

Jorge had died before her single-minded persistence could prevail. Afterward, at Maggy's insistence, Gloria had stayed on in the house. Though nearly a decade had passed, she had never, to Maggy's knowledge, had another boyfriend.

"You got my message," *Tia* Gloria said, drawing back from the embrace to beam at Maggy. Anyone listening might have been forgiven for supposing that she was referring to a phone call, or a letter. Maggy knew better. *Tia* Gloria meant a psychic message, which she had sent and had expected Maggy to receive. With her long experience of Gloria's eccentricities, Maggy merely nodded.

"Your father was here, and he left a note for you. Now, where did I put it?" Gloria glanced around with a perplexed expression, as if she expected the note to materialize out of thin air. Maggy, catching a glimpse of Nick's face out of the corner of her eye, could not help smiling. It had been a long time since he had seen *Tia* Gloria. Clearly he had forgotten her penchant for the paranormal.

"That smell . . ." One woman sniffed the air.

"My cookies are burning!" another wailed, rushing toward the stove.

"Told you it wasn't the netherworld," the gentleman said to a third.

"Hmmph!" this woman replied, while the second one opened the oven door and, fanning away smoke, pulled a tray of nearly black cookies to safety.

"So much for tea and cookies," the gentleman grumbled.

"We can still have tea," his conversational partner said with dignity and turned her shoulder on the wet-blanket gentleman.

Tia Gloria watched this byplay with only mild interest before her attention returned to Maggy.

"You brought me a visitor, I see. I've been expecting you to. You remember a couple of months back when I told you that a tall, dark, handsome gentleman would soon be entering your life? This fellow certainly is that, isn't he? And you brought him to see me, just as they said you would. The spirits are never wrong." She broke off to study Nick. "My land, is it really—Nick? Nick King, is that you?" *Tia* Gloria's eyes widened, her mouth dropped, and she flew to envelop him in a hug.

"It's really me, *Tia,*" Nick said, hugging her back. *Tia* Gloria looked absurdly small and plump when enveloped by Nick's six feet two inches of solid muscle. She giggled as she strained up on tiptoe to plant a kiss on his cheek, then left a red lipstick smear in the five-o'clock shadow that darkened his jaw and had to wipe it off with her hand.

"I haven't seen you for—how long? Years. Years! You bad boy! Jorge missed you, and Magdalena's needed you! Where have you been?"

"Oh, here and there."

"Have you said hello to Horatio?"

"I said something to the stupid bird."

"Don't call him that," *Tia* Gloria chided. "You'll hurt his feelings. He's very sensitive."

"Bad boy! Bad boy!" The indictment came from the bird. Maggy looked around with everyone else to see Horatio clutching the bars at the front of his cage, the pupils of his orange eyes rapidly shrinking and dilating, shrinking and dilating as they fixed on Nick. His beak thrust through the bars, and he seemed to be fumbling with the latch on his cage.

"Horatio remembers you!" *Tia* Gloria said with delight. "Here, let me let him out."

"No!" Nick visibly recoiled.

Maggy had to laugh as *Tia* Gloria glanced at him in surprise. "Oh, that's right, you always were afraid of him, weren't you? But you're a grown man now." Her voice reproved him. "He won't hurt you. Will you, Horatio?"

"Bad boy," Horatio said, working at the latch. "Bad, bad boy."

"You shouldn't have thrown a ball at his cage," Maggy murmured wickedly to Nick. The glare Nick bestowed on her in reply should have wilted her on the spot. Instead it made her grin.

18

"*W*ell, I won't let him out then, if you'd rather I wouldn't," *Tia* Gloria said comfortably. "Besides, he can open his cage himself if he's of a mind to. Come in, Nick, come in, Magdalena, and sit down! The cookies may be burnt, but I have some coffee cake in the pantry, and Lois here makes wonderful green tea." She nodded at one of the other women. "Oh, I haven't introduced you. My friends, this is Magdalena. Jorge's daughter." She turned to Maggy. "They've heard me talk about you for years, it's nice they finally get a chance to meet you and see for themselves that you're not a figment of a crazy old woman's imagination." Gesturing at Nick, who stood beside Maggy, she added, "And this is Nick King. Remember, I told you about Nick?" She exchanged a significant look with her cronies.

"Oh, yes!" The women chorused, and from the collective expressions on their faces Maggy had to wonder just what *Tia* Gloria had told them. They looked at Nick as if the mere sight of him was enough to make them swoon.

"This is Lois Branson, Renee Sharer, Betty Nichols, Harvey Nichols, and Dottie Hagan."

Everyone nodded and made polite murmurs. Though Maggy would have resisted if given the opportunity to do so, she was not given the opportunity: *Tia* Gloria took her arm and Nick's and propelled them toward the living room by main force.

The gaggle of guests stood back to let them pass, then followed them into the small living room.

"Bad boy!" A swoosh of wings behind them made them all duck.

Horatio swooped toward Nick, wings flapping as he landed, claws extended, on Nick's upflung arm.

"Would somebody please get this stupid bird off me?" Nick demanded as Maggy giggled uncontrollably. The rest of his audience was laughing, too, as the bird stalked down Nick's arm toward his face. Nick cowered. *Tia* Gloria hurried to Horatio's rescue.

"Come up," she said, holding out two fingers to the bird. Horatio glared at Nick for a moment.

"Bad boy!" the bird said again, and then, in response to *Tia* Gloria's admonishing fingers, he stepped onto her hand. With a cluck of sympathy for him, she turned and headed back toward the kitchen.

Maggy snickered. "And I thought *elephants* never forgot." Nick, straightening, gave her a withering glance.

Tia Gloria returned in a matter of minutes, and they continued on into the living room.

Ordinarily it was furnished comfortably, if not elegantly or expensively, with a brown tweed couch, matching leather recliners, an oval-shaped braided rug, early-American coffee and end tables, orange bean-jar lamps, and a TV. Tonight a large round table—the dining table that ordinarily occupied the far end of the room, Maggy realized—had been dragged to the center of the floor and draped with green felt. Around it were six chairs, each of which bore evidence of having been haphazardly pushed away from the gathering. In the center of the table a single short, thick candle in a glass globe guttered in its own tallow, casting a feeble yellow glow over the immediate area. The rest of the room was dark.

"We were trying to contact Dottie's aunt," *Tia* Gloria explained, as she saw Nick cast a quizzical look at the setup.

"She's put her jewelry somewhere, and I can't find it," one of the other women, presumably Dottie, complained. "Gloria's been trying for three months, but Aunt Alice just won't come through."

"Your father has, though." *Tia* Gloria beamed at Maggy. "He had to sneak away from your mother, who, I'm sorry to say, seems to be a very jealous wife. But he made it twice. The last time he left you a message."

Nick looked slightly amused by this interchange. Maggy, who had not had twelve years to forget *Tia* Gloria's easy interactions with the spirits, took the information in stride.

"Did he?" she replied as both she and Nick, gently but inexorably, were pushed side by side down onto the couch.

"Yes—oh, there it is. I knew I had it somewhere."

Somewhere turned out to be the front of the wood-burning stove, which fortunately was not in use at the moment. *Tia* Gloria triumphantly removed a white envelope that was affixed with a clip magnet to the iron door and handed it to Maggy. Her name was scrawled on the outside. When she tore it open, she found a yellow self-stick note folded in thirds, so that the note sealed itself. She opened that too.

"Your father writes you letters?" Nick's question, muttered in Maggy's ear as she smoothed out the paper, was both skeptical and amused.

"Automatic writing," Maggy whispered back. "You know, where the medium sits down with paper and pencil and goes into a trance and the spirit uses the medium's body as a conduit. *Papi* contacts me all the time."

Nick rolled his eyes. Maggy read the note. "Magdalena," it said. "Danger is at hand. Beware of harm . . ." The message was written in a black, spidery script that she knew for *Tia* Gloria's automatic-writing hand. The last word—*harm*—trailed off until it was a barely legible scribble.

Despite years of dealing with *Tia's* eccentricities, Maggy couldn't help it: as she read the message through a second time, a chill ran down her spine. Folding the note in half, she stuck it in her pocket.

"Of course, he doesn't say precisely what he means," *Tia* Gloria said fretfully. "What harm should you beware of? I asked him if he could be a little clearer, but your mother was calling him and he had to go. Said he'd be in *mucho* trouble if she found him down here with me."

"She shouldn't be so jealous," one of the women—Betty?—said, as if the subject was one that the group had discussed many times before.

"Women are always jealous," Harvey muttered. From the less-than-loving looks the couple traded at that, and their identical last names, Maggy felt safe in assuming they were husband and wife.

"Only if they're given cause," Betty snapped.

"Perhaps you're in danger of suffering an accident." *Tia* Gloria ignored the bickering pair to frown at Maggy. "Of course, Jorge left that message for you nearly a month ago. If you were going to have an accident, it might already have happened. They can't see that far in the future, you know. Not infinitely, like a lot of people think, but just a few weeks. *Have* you had an accident?"

"She hurt her wrist," Nick supplied. Maggy glanced at him, surprised. She had thought her small injury had barely registered on Nick.

"Did you, dear? How?" *Tia* Gloria focused on Maggy.

"I fell down some stairs," Maggy answered, instinctively touching her bandaged wrist.

"I thought you tripped over a dog." Nick's voice was sharp.
Caught off guard, Maggy barely managed not to stutter.

"I did. I tripped over a dog, which caused me to fall down the stairs,"
she said, recovering fast. She had forgotten what she had told Joan
Sullivan at the party, and that Nick had been listening. Damn him for
having such a good memory and for being so quick to catch her up.
Until now, no one had ever really paid attention to the stories she told
to cover her injuries, so it hadn't mattered if she'd occasionally mixed
them up. But then, Nick cared.

"How awful!" *Tia* Gloria clucked. "Is it sprained? I hope you soaked
it in camomile tea. That keeps it from swelling so badly, you know."

"I did," Maggy lied, because she feared that if she didn't *Tia* Gloria
would insist on soaking her wrist in tea there and then. "It's fine, really.
Nothing at all."

"Which stairs did you fall down?" There was a casual note to Nick's
question that belied the lurking alertness in his eyes.

"The front ones, by the driveway." It was always possible that Nick
knew that Lyle wouldn't permit animals inside the house. "A friend
stopped by with an invitation that it was too late to mail, and when she
left I ran up the stairs to put it on the table just inside the door. I didn't
realize the dogs had followed me, and when I turned around I tripped
over one of them and fell down the stairs."

"Which dog?"

"Seamus," Maggy snapped, glaring at him. "Is there anything else
you'd like to know?"

"Lots of things." He smiled at her, a long, slow smile that alarmed
her. Maggy got the feeling from that smile that he knew everything
there was to know about the circumstances of her life—but of course
that was idiocy. If Nick knew that, he would not, in a massive understatement, be sitting so calmly beside her on *Tia* Gloria's couch. He had
always had the knack for making her think he knew more than he did, so
that she would confess her misdeeds, imagining that he already knew of
them. And he didn't. She had to remember that. He never did. Until she
told him herself.

Well, this time she was not telling.

"Who wants tea?" The interruption, in the form of a sprightly question from the kitchen doorway, was welcome. Maggy turned away from
Nick, relieved to be off the hook, as one of *Tia* Gloria's friends—Lois?
—carried in a tray crowded with a china teapot and cups.

"We'll continue this very interesting conversation later," Nick whispered meaningfully in Maggy's ear as cups were passed out and tea was

poured. She tensed, her fingers tightening over the handle of the delicate cup, causing a small amount of fragrant green tea to slosh into the saucer.

Then she realized what she had to do. Setting the cup and saucer down on the coffee table, she stood up.

"If you all will excuse me, I'm going to run upstairs for just a minute."

As the sole bathroom was upstairs, this occasioned no comment. Maggy left the living room and climbed the narrow stairs to the second floor, where she headed straight for the bedroom that had been her father's. Though *Tia* Gloria had lived with him, in every sense of the word, for years before his death, they had maintained separate bedrooms. Maggy had always supposed that one or the other of them was sensitive to the proprieties. Since Jorge's death, *Tia* Gloria had informed her that her assumption was wrong: he had been afraid even then that Maggy's mother was watching him from above, and thus decided to play it safe by not taking another woman into his bed on a permanent basis. And, *Tia* Gloria added, it turned out he had been right: his wife had been keeping an eye on him for all those years. Lucky for Jorge they hadn't shared a room, or he would have caught hell in heaven. He caught enough of it as it was, over the mere fact of Gloria's existence. Maggy's mother—begging Maggy's pardon—sounded to *Tia* like a jealous witch. It was a mystery to *Tia* how Jorge could love her so.

Far from offending Maggy, this pronouncement amused her so that she had to hide a grin. To *Tia* Gloria, the spirits were as alive as her friends down the street. Such matter-of-fact conviction helped keep Maggy's parents alive for her too.

There were twin bookcases in Jorge's room, flanking the door. Jorge had built them himself. The bookcase on the left had a trick bottom shelf. If one lifted it up, one would find a small space between the shelf and the floor. Anyone looking at the shelf from the outside would not guess the existence of the extra space, because the baseboard molding, which had been carried on around the shelves as though they were original to the house, hid it. The space was only about nine inches wide by twenty-four inches long by three inches tall, but that was room enough for what Maggy had to hide. Quickly she lifted all the magazines off the bottom shelf—they were piled in flat stacks, with books, paperback mysteries, and true crime mostly, on the upper shelves. Then she pried up the shelf itself, not without some little effort since it was wedged in pretty tightly. But finally she got it up, and the hiding place was revealed.

It was empty, except for dust and an errant cobweb. Maggy had expected it to be. On her own, *Tia* Gloria would never use it, although she knew of its existence. Jorge had been the careful one, wary of burglars, stashing away small valuables whenever he left the house. Having lived so long in a public housing project, he could not quite get over the notion that a break-in was just a walk around the block away. No one ever was burglarized in the rural area where the Crooked House was located, but to Jorge that didn't matter. What mattered was that they might be.

Tia Gloria, on the other hand, had never bothered to hide her treasure trove of mostly costume jewelry even when she had lived in public housing. She'd never been robbed, either, probably because Horatio had been notorious in the projects. No burglar who knew of its existence wanted to mess with the bird. Give 'em a snarling German shepherd anytime over a feathered devil with claws and beak who was known to attack those he disliked and could shriek for help and fly at the same time.

Maggy had often thought that if she were a burglar, she would have felt the same way. She knew Nick would have.

Unzipping her jacket, she removed the package with the pictures and tape and placed it inside the space. Then she replaced the shelf on top, wedging it down firmly. She was in the act of returning the magazines to the shelf when *Tia* Gloria appeared in the doorway.

"Don't worry, nobody will find it there," *Tia* Gloria said placidly.

"What?" Startled, Maggy glanced up, her hands dropping away from the just-replaced magazines.

"Whatever it is that you want to keep hidden, of course. Nobody knows about that compartment except you and Jorge and I, and Jorge and I aren't telling." She twinkled at Maggy. "So, you're back with Nick? That's as it should be. He is your other half, you know. You two belong together like—like bacon and eggs, pencils and erasers, oil and water . . ."

"Oil and water don't mix," Maggy said dryly, getting to her feet. "And neither do Nick and I anymore, except as old friends. I'm married, remember?"

"But the marriage is wrong for you," *Tia* Gloria said, frowning. "All wrong. You should be with Nick. Now, *he* is handsome. Don't tell me you don't agree."

"I agree." Maggy zipped up her jacket.

"So?"

"So I have to go home now. Without Nick. If Lyle knew I was with him, he wouldn't like it. He's a little—jealous—of Nick. You can see why. As you said yourself, Nick is handsome, and Lyle is—older. So I want you to do me a favor."

"Anything, dear."

"Drive Nick home for me, would you please? He came with me in *The Lady Dancer,* but I'd rather leave without him. If Lyle found out I was with him—well, it wouldn't be pleasant. Lyle can be—very possessive."

"Mean as the devil, you mean," *Tia* Gloria said darkly.

Maggy managed a laugh. "That, too," she said, knowing that *Tia* Gloria had no idea how close to the truth her words were.

"Of course I'll drive Nick home, if you want me to. But are you sure he is not going to be angry with you for leaving him here?"

"Probably." Nick's anger didn't worry Maggy. She was not, and never had been, afraid of Nick. Nick would never hurt her . . . "Just tell him I had to go, would you please? He'll understand why."

"If I had a man like that wanting me, I would fly to him so fast that you wouldn't see my feet for the dust."

Maggy made a face, but other than that didn't reply. What reply could she have made? If there had been any possible way to do it, she, too, would have flown to Nick so fast that no one would have seen her feet for the dust. But there was no way.

"I've got to go now. I'm sorry I couldn't stay longer, *Tia.*"

"That's all right, dear. I understand."

She didn't, not really, Maggy knew. Though Jorge had suspected that Maggy was not happy in her marriage, she had never told him even so much as a fraction of the truth. There was nothing he could do to help her, and she saw no point in upsetting him. He had so enjoyed the change in his financial circumstances that her marriage to Lyle had made possible. Even being able to afford a daily paper had been, for Jorge, something to savor. How could she have put a damper on his pleasure? The answer was, she couldn't. And after Jorge's death, she had never told *Tia* Gloria, either. The woman's continued concern for her was based on a sixth sense rather than any actual knowledge.

"I'll try to come again soon."

"I know you will. Maybe we can talk, the next time."

Tia Gloria stepped aside so that Maggy could pass through the doorway. As Maggy went quickly down the stairs, the older woman followed.

Nick's low rumble mingled with other voices from the living room. Maggy breathed a sigh of relief as she slipped through the hall, past the living room doorway, to the relative safety of the kitchen.

"Are you sure you won't change your mind about Nick?" *Tia* Gloria whispered with a jerk of her head in the direction of the living room.

"I'm sure," Maggy said, kissing her soft cheek. "Give Horatio an extra peanut for me, would you?"

"Sure." *Tia* Gloria followed her to the door. "You be careful, Magdalena, you hear? Maybe Jorge wasn't just talking about your wrist."

"I will. Bye." With a wave, Maggy headed across the rocky beach toward the dock. She wanted to be safely on the river before Nick missed her. She had had all of him she could take for one night.

Tia Gloria stood in the doorway until Maggy had *The Lady Dancer* under way. Chugging away from the dock, Maggy waved again at the small figure silhouetted against the light. *Tia* Gloria waved back, and then at last closed the door.

Maggy was surprised at how bereft she suddenly felt. She was all alone in a small boat on the river on a cold, dark night. Such a circumstance had never bothered her before, but it bothered her now. She was lonely and afraid.

Maybe that was because of the note. Though it was foolish, she could not help feeling her father's presence when she thought of it. Was he truly looking out for her from the afterlife? *Tia* Gloria was firmly convinced that it was so. Being around someone with such strong convictions could sway even the staunchest nonbeliever, and Maggy was never that. Her Catholic childhood had predisposed her to believe in all manner of otherworldly mysteries and miracles. And on some few occasions, *Tia* Gloria's messages had hit the nail squarely on the head. Like the time when the note had read, "Sickness will strike your house," and David had come down with chicken pox the next day. But, Maggy reminded herself, anything, from a cold suffered by Louella to Virginia's heart trouble, could have qualified as sickness striking her house, thus fulfilling the prophecy. Or the time when the message had said, "Good news will come to you," and Sarah had called to say that she had found Maggy's diamond engagement ring on the sink in the bathroom of the guesthouse, when Maggy had been sweating bullets in case Lyle should notice that she had lost it. But again, that message had been vague enough that almost any positive event would have made it seem to come true. The notes were always vague, always ambiguous, and if she thought about it, did not this undermine their credibility most of all? If her father was truly watching out for her, and if he could see into her future from where he was, would he not write something like, "Don't worry about the diamond, it'll turn up?" Yes, he would. Of course he would.

Not that Maggy thought that *Tia* Gloria deliberately intended to mislead anyone with her forays into the spirit world. *Tia* Gloria sincerely believed that Jorge spoke through her pen. Intellectually Maggy knew better. But still some part of her, some gullible, yearning part, wanted to believe.

"Danger is at hand. Beware of harm . . ." Remembering the warning that Jorge had supposedly sent this time, Maggy felt a chill run down her spine. Danger was Nick, and harm was Lyle. . . . The thought popped into her mind as full-blown knowledge given to her on some intuitive level.

Hogwash. Poppycock. Bullpatties. But still, she shivered again, unable to help it. Then she scolded herself: how idiotic could she be, to give credence to such drivel? Maggy deliberately called to mind the fifteen-year-old palm reading that had told her that she would marry happily and have six children, five of them boys. She dredged up the memory of the tarot cards that had foretold a life lived far from the place of her birth. She thought back on a prediction based on the leaves left in the bottom of her teacup that had told her she would be divorced or widowed within the year—made seven years ago. None of them had come true.

Nonsense. It was all utter nonsense, and she knew it. She thought back over the further psychic misfires of *Tia* Gloria and her friends and thus almost managed to shake the mood of dread that threatened to overwhelm her.

Automatic writing, indeed. That was about as likely to happen as her ill-wish toward Lyle at the golf tournament had been likely to come true.

How foolish could she be? The answer was, pretty foolish, apparently. But still, despite her inner bravado, she could not totally shake the sense of foreboding that circled her looking for a weak spot in her defenses like a hungry beast hoping to home in for the kill. She steered *The Lady Dancer* toward Windermere and blamed her edginess on the dark spookiness of the river at night. Whose nerves wouldn't be on edge, with a ghostly moon floating high overhead and a cold wind whipping white froth into the waves and showering her with icy spray? Who wouldn't see ghosts and goblins in silvery-white clouds running before the moon, and in the shifting of the dappled moonlight on the water?

A less imaginative soul than she, that was for sure.

Thus she tried to laugh at herself, as she made the crossing. Still, it was a relief to reach the dock, to tie *The Lady Dancer* up and get away from the river.

Going up to the house, she didn't have to walk through the woods. Instead she followed the road, and then the driveway.

By the time she reached the house, crept around back, and climbed back up to her window, she was feeling almost herself again. Tired, a little nostalgic, but normal.

Automatic writing, indeed . . . she even managed a rueful smile at the thought as she slithered through the casement window like a snake, to end up lying on the floor of her bedroom on her stomach.

"You stupid, lying little bitch! Where the hell have you been?" a voice growled out of the darkness not far above her head. Lyle's. Maggy recognized it and was galvanized, scrambling to her hands and knees in a panic, eyes straining against the thick gloom of the room to see . . .

She never even made it up off her knees before he kicked her brutally in the ribs, and she went down.

19

$\mathcal{T}$he next morning Nick stood in a cold gray drizzle for almost two hours, but she didn't come. The dogs remained in their kennels, unwalked. They were restless, two enormous rough-coated beasts stalking the confines of their runs, barking occasionally. Like him, they were growing impatient, waiting for her.

It wasn't like her not to come. The information he had on that point was specific as hell: Mrs. Forrest always walked her dogs between six thirty and seven in the morning. His own experience bore that out.

So where was she?

He paced the woods, enumerating the things that could have delayed her. Perhaps she was merely sleeping in; after all, it was Sunday. Though from earliest childhood she had been a lark, not an owl, and she had not stayed out particularly late the night before, not if she had gone straight home, which he was willing to bet every hair on his head she had. He himself had gotten in no later than midnight, and that was after turning down *Tia* Gloria's offer to drive him home and waiting for Link, summoned via car phone, to fetch him.

So exhaustion from her late night was out.

Maybe she was sick, though she had been fine just a few hours before. And Magdalena had always been healthy as a mule. No, he would lay odds she was not sick.

Maybe she was avoiding him.

It was possible. More than possible, probable. After all, she'd run out on him, left him stranded at *Tia* Gloria's. He wasn't happy about it, and she would know it. She would also know that he was not so easily gotten rid of, and that he would be in the woods this morning waiting for her. But more than that, what might keep her away was the way they'd connected again, last night. Before he'd made the mistake of kissing her. Big mistake, that. Nick acknowledged it to himself with a grimace.

He hadn't meant to do it. But she'd made him angry, and then there she'd been in his lap, and the temptation had been too great to resist. He'd been burning for the taste of her mouth, for the feel of her body against his, ever since he first laid eyes on her again in the Little Brown Cow. She had kissed him as if she felt the same. For him, the kiss had been mind-blowingly good—until she started to fight. He had scared her, no doubt about it. Scared her silly. But hell, who could have guessed that she would react to the touch of his hands and mouth like a cat with its tail caught in a door?

Magdalena had once been hot as a chili pepper for him. Who the hell had scared her of sex?

The answer was obvious, glaringly obvious, even if it made him boil with anger to consider it. Had Lyle Forrest, the sick son of a bitch, turned his perversions on Magdalena?

If Forrest had, he would kill him.

But Magdalena was a fighter, the fightingest woman he'd ever known. Pinch her ass and you'd get a punch in the nose for your trouble. Grab a tit and you'd lose the use of a couple of fingers for life. He couldn't see her as a victim. Magdalena had too much fire, too much spirit, too much sheer guts, to be a victim.

At least, she did twelve years ago. Had something happened to her since?

But he was ready to swear that she hadn't changed that much. Oh, there were differences, but they were all on the outside. She might wear fancy clothes and talk with a soft, refined accent that he found alternately annoying and wildly sexy, but inside she was still the same fiery-natured little girl from the projects. The same spit-in-your-eye, curse-you-up-one-side-and-down-the-other hellion.

He'd back his Magdalena against half a dozen Lyle Forrests, any day.

What was keeping her inside the house?

He smoked a cigarette, swore, and smoked another one. Glancing at his watch, he saw that it was nine thirty. Almost time for her to be leaving for church. She and old Lyle always went together, with his mother and their boy. Sort of a family tradition. Even as Nick pictured it, his mouth twisted into a sneer.

The image was as pretty as it was false. Magdalena didn't belong in it. She belonged with him.

It was hard to imagine Magdalena as an ice-water-veined Episcopalian, too, but that was what she had become. Because the Forrests had been Episcopalians since they had first dirtied their aristocratic boots on the shores of this country some three hundred years before. To be one of them, Magdalena had had to shed her Catholic skin.

He was starting to despise the Forrests collectively, instead of just hating Lyle.

He shifted his position so that he could watch the front door. The chauffeur drove up in the navy Rolls, right on schedule. The front door opened—and the mother emerged, leaning on her daughter's arm. Lucy Drummond, the daughter's name was. A big woman, she towered over her shrunken mother, holding her arm, helping her carefully down the stairs. Both women were dressed in their Sunday best, complete with hats. Two other, younger, women and a man emerged from the house in their wake. He recognized them only after a few seconds of careful scrutiny as Lucy's husband, Hamilton Drummond, and their daughter Sarah. The fourth woman was Buffy McDermott, his date of the night before, shamelessly abandoned when he had left the party without a word.

Nick hunched his shoulders, stuck his hands in his pockets, and withdrew farther into the trees as he waited for Magdalena to join them.

The chauffeur got out of the car and came halfway up the stairs to take the old lady's other arm. The mother was helped into the car, the women slid in after her, Hamilton Drummond joined the chauffeur in the front seat, and the door of the house shut with a moneyed click on them all. Seconds later, the Rolls pulled away.

Where was Magdalena?

Nick controlled an urge to stride up to the door, hammer on it, and demand an answer. Discretion was the better part of valor, as he'd once heard someone say.

Lips compressing into a hard line, he turned on his heel, walked back around the house to the woods, and headed down and across the road toward the graveled turnaround where he'd left his car.

Thank God for car phones.

Link was sitting in the driver's seat of the lipstick-red Corvette, smoking a cigarette and staring out over the gray expanse of the river. A few months before, person or persons unknown had tried their damnedest to blow Nick away. Nick had his suspicions about who was behind the attack, but with nothing concrete to back them up, all he could do was watch his back and hope they wouldn't try again. Since then, Link had designated himself as his brother's keeper and hardly let him out of his sight. Link took his self-imposed duties so seriously that Nick sometimes considered himself lucky to be able to go to the bathroom alone.

It was a minor miracle that Link had considered him safe enough with Magdalena to take himself off last night.

Such protectiveness, while funny at first, had grown damned irritating with the passage of time. But Link would not be dissuaded by anything short of a baseball bat to the head. He couldn't even be shamed out of it. Link's standard reply when someone kidded him about this excessive display of brotherly love was, who would authorize the paychecks if Nick bit the big one?

As the taunts were invariably made by one or another of the small circle of Nick's employees, that tended to work pretty well as a means of shutting the perpetrator up.

"Took you long enough," Link grunted, barely looking around as Nick let himself in the passenger side. Nick, knowing his brother as he did, wasn't fooled: Link had been well aware of his approach since he had first emerged from the woods. His senses, never dull, had been honed by the years he'd spent in prison, as had his ability to defend himself—and his brother if necessary—against all comers. That sleepy-eyed pose of his was an act.

Nick said nothing, just reached for the small cellular phone that rested on the console between the two bucket seats and started punching in the number.

"You and Magdalena kiss and make up?" Link was watching him out of the corner of his eye.

"Didn't see her."

"What? You've been up there for almost three hours! What the hell have you been doing, if you didn't see her?"

"Waiting."

"God save me from true love," Link muttered in disgust as the phone began to ring in Nick's ear.

"Forrest residence." The voice on the other end was a woman's, but definitely not Magdalena's. The housekeeper, most likely.

"I'd like to speak to Mrs. Forrest, please."

"The elder or the younger?"

"The younger."

"She's not available to come to the phone right now."

That caught him unprepared. Nick frowned. "She's there, isn't she? Why can't she come to the phone? Is she all right?"

The woman's tone grew frosty. "I'll be glad to take a message."

"No message," Nick practically ground out the words and pushed the disconnect button.

Link chuckled. "Magdalena don't want to talk to you, hmmm? Too bad, lover boy."

"Why don't you just shut up?" Nick fought the urge to shove the phone down his brother's throat. Two things stopped him: the first was that he really was extremely fond of Link despite his obnoxious ways; the second was that he was not entirely sure that his brother couldn't kick his ass.

"Grumpy, are we?" Link was still grinning as he turned the key in the ignition and put the car in reverse. "What you need is food, little brother. Didn't somebody once say that man can't live by love alone?"

"I think it was bread alone, and whoever said it didn't know you," Nick growled.

Link only chuckled again and headed for the nearest waffle house to assuage his enormous appetite. Nick was convinced that his brother ate twice as much and twice as slowly as usual just to aggravate him.

He called Magdalena twice more during the course of the day, only to be given the same response by the same housekeeper. The younger Mrs. Forrest was not available to come to the phone. The last time he left a message, requesting that Mrs. Forrest call Mr. King, and gave the housekeeper his number.

She didn't call. He waited until almost midnight before he was sure she wasn't going to, and then, when he went to bed, he couldn't sleep. Even in his dreams, anger and worry wrestled each other for the upper hand. Was she deliberately avoiding him, or had something happened to her? By the next morning he was as touchy as a bull elephant deprived of its mate, and chewing his nails with concern.

"Gettin' up at the crack of dawn to visit your ladylove is wearin' kinda thin, little brother." Link looked almost as disgruntled as Nick felt as they pulled into the graveled turnaround at six fifteen the following morning.

"Nobody asked you to come. In fact, I'd rather you didn't."

"Without me, you'd probably get your ass blown off." Link swung the car around so that it faced the way they had come, and then slid the transmission into park. "Whoever tried to kill you back in January's still out there, you know."

"That was in Syracuse," Nick said dismissively, though he knew even better than Link did that the danger had almost certainly not passed.

"You think they can't buy bullets in Louisville?"

Ignoring Link's sarcasm, Nick got out of the car.

"Why don't you go feed your face or something?" he said, leaning in to scowl at his brother. "I may be awhile."

"Like I don't already know that." Link crossed his arms over his chest and leaned his head back against the leather headrest, for all the world as if he meant to take a nap. "Just take your time, Romeo. I'll be here."

Nick slammed the door so hard it made Link's head bounce, for which he was very meanly glad.

This time he waited only two hours. As he climbed back into the car, he gave Link a look that dared him to say a word and picked up the phone.

Same housekeeper, same message. Again he left his number, and again Magdalena didn't call him.

He already knew she wasn't going to show up on Tuesday morning before he went, and he was right. Even Link, reading murder in his face when he slammed back into the car at just a few minutes past eight, wisely confined himself to driving rather than talking as he headed toward his favorite waffle house.

It was shortly after one o'clock, and they were headed from a prospective purchase on the Indiana waterfront toward a business meeting in downtown Louisville when Nick swore out loud and snatched up the phone again.

He shot Link a look that dared him to say a word as he punched in Magdalena's number for what must have been the dozenth time in three days. As always, the housekeeper answered, her words exactly the same: Mrs. Forrest the younger was still unavailable to come to the phone, but if he liked she'd be glad to take a message. Nick saw red. If the housekeeper wanted a message, then he'd damned well give her one.

"You go tell Mrs. Forrest the younger that Nick King is on the line again. Tell her that if she doesn't get on this phone within five minutes and speak to me, I'm going to be up there to pay a Goddamn personal call on her five minutes after that. Can you give her that message?"

There was a pause.

"Please wait," the voice said grimly, and then there was silence at the other end.

"That's a hell of a message to give to a housekeeper." Link's expression was reproving. "You forget about the husband, or what?"

"I wish I could forget about the bastard," Nick said through gritted teeth. "I can't."

"That's a sweet setup she has up there. A mansion complete with chauffeur, housekeeper, the works. Have you ever thought that maybe Magdalena don't want to give it all up for you?"

"What makes you think I'm asking her to?"

"I know you, Nicky boy."

Nick scowled into the phone, though no one was on the other end. "Something's wrong up there. I can feel it."

"Maybe her husband's mad 'cause you're after her like a fly after honey." Link's voice was dry. "If I was her husband, that would do it for me."

"Are you telling me you think I should lay off?" Nick transferred his scowl to his brother, who held up a placating hand.

"Hey, man, chill out, we're blood, remember? I know what you two had—once. But that was a long time ago. I ain't heard nothin' that makes me think Forrest forced her to marry him. She did it of her own free will. What I'm sayin' is, maybe you should respect that. If she keeps tellin' you she wants you to get lost, maybe you should believe her. Maybe you should let her alone."

"Screw that. She only did it for the money."

"Maybe she wants to stay with him for the money, too." Link's tone was gentle, as it always was when he broke what he considered to be unpalatable truths to his kid brother. That was the tone he'd used when he told Nick that the reason they had different last names was because they had two different fathers. That was the tone he'd used when he told Nick he was going to jail, maybe for a long time. That was the tone he'd used when he told Nick that Magdalena was gone for good and advised him to get on with his life without her.

Nick heard that tone and winced before he thrust the recollections from his mind.

"Something's wrong up there," he repeated stubbornly, just as Magdalena spoke into the phone.

"Nick?"

There was no mistaking that it was she. Nick released the breath he hadn't realized he'd been holding. He had been starting to toy with the idea that she might even be dead, that Forrest might have killed her in a rage, and the whole tribe of them up there might be involved in concealing the crime. Where the notion had come from he couldn't be sure—probably from that damned message *Tia* Gloria had given her—but he could have sworn that something bad had happened to her. He'd felt it every time he'd thought of her, as if he had ESP or something, and not being able to see or speak to her for three fricking days had made the feeling worse. Now that he actually had her on the phone, the feeling was subsiding a little, but while it had lasted the sensation had been downright eerie. Shades of *Tia* Gloria's spook fest, he'd thought more than once, and hoped like hell that looniness wasn't contagious.

Maybe Magdalena had just been avoiding him after all. Instead of bothering him, as it should have done, the idea was a blessed relief.

"Magdalena! Long time no see." His voice was artificially affable.

"What on earth did you say to Louella? She was outraged."

"I told her that if she didn't let me speak to you, I'd be up there in person five minutes after she hung up the phone."

He heard her quick indrawing of breath and wondered.

"You can't do that." Her words were swift, urgent. He got the impression that they tumbled out of her mouth before she could stop them.

"Why can't I?"

"Lyle wouldn't like it." She was in control of herself again, but there was something he couldn't quite put his finger on in her tone. He couldn't describe what it was, but he didn't like it.

"To hell with Lyle," he said cheerfully and listened hard.

She laughed, a brittle, three-note sound that was unmistakably bitter agreement. Nick felt his ears prick up like a hound's.

"You didn't walk the dogs this morning. Or yesterday, or Sunday either."

"How do you know?"

"How do you think I know? I stood out there in your damned woods for three hours with rain trickling down my neck on Sunday. Monday I froze my ass. At least today it's sunny."

"It wasn't raining Sunday."

"It was at six thirty in the morning."

"Oh." Her voice softened. "I'm sorry you waited for nothing. The truth is, I won't be walking the dogs again for a while. I'm in bed with the flu."

"You're in bed with the flu?" Disbelief made it a question. The ugly suspicions that had been flickering inside him almost since he had first laid eyes on her again were strengthening with every beat of his pulse. "Actually in bed?"

"Yes. I'm speaking to you from the phone on my night table."

"You've never been in bed with the flu in your life." He spoke with absolute certainty. This was a girl who had never slowed down through chicken pox, measles, mumps. He'd seen her get her head split open by a glass light fixture that gave up its tenuous grip on a hall ceiling just as she passed beneath it, lose a pint of blood in the process and get fifteen stitches for her trouble, and go out to play kickball in the street later that same afternoon. There wasn't a flu bug in the world that could keep her in bed for three days.

"Well, I am now." She sounded cross.

"Right." Nick tried another approach. "So when do you expect to be out walking the dogs again? I mean, can you set a date to it? Then I won't have to hang around your woods every morning twiddling my thumbs."

There was a brief pause. "Nick . . ."

"Hmmm?"

"I don't want you hanging around the woods. I—don't want to see you anymore."

"Why not?" He wasn't hurt or angry, because it was more or less what he was expecting.

"You know why not."

"Maybe you better spell it out for me. Sometimes I can be a little dense."

"You know why not," she repeated, sounding cross again.

"Are you brushing me off, Magdalena?" he asked.

"If you want to call it that." Her voice was wintry.

"You're going to have to do it in person."

"What?"

"You heard me. If you want to get rid of me, you're going to have to tell me so in person. I'll be at your front door in twenty minutes. You can tell me to go straight to hell, if that's what you want. And you know what? If you tell me to my face, I'll go."

"Nick . . ." There was panic in her voice. "I don't want you here. *I do not want you here.* Can't you accept that?"

"Why not, Magdalena? What are you afraid of? Lyle?" he asked, his voice soft with perception, and again he was rewarded by that sharp indrawing of her breath. And he knew. It was as simple as that. He knew.

What had kept her in bed for three days was not the flu. He wanted to see her for himself, make sure she was essentially all right and check out how bad the damage was. Then he was going to make sure it never happened again. Whatever it took.

"If you come, I won't see you."

"Oh, I'm coming, Magdalena." His tone was gentle but inexorable. "You can either see me, or call the cops to come meet me at your front steps and haul me off to jail. That's the only way you're going to get rid of me without telling me in person to go."

"I'm not dressed, Nick!"

"So get dressed," he said grimly, and pushed the disconnect button. Link was frowning at him. "We got a meeting at the Galt House in less than an hour."

"Cancel it."

"It's with those dudes from Lexington, man. Everything's all set up."

"To hell with that! I said cancel it."

"Shit," Link said and picked up the phone. Seconds later he was explaining to someone that his brother was in bed with the flu. Nick was so absorbed in his own thoughts that he didn't even wince at the wimpy excuse.

"Didn't you ever learn to take no for an answer, little brother?" Link asked as he hung up after telling whoever was on the other end that they'd call to reschedule. "From what I could hear, Magdalena don't want to see you."

"He's been knocking her around. That bastard's been knocking her around."

"What?" Link cast him an incredulous look.

"You heard me."

"Son of a bitch!" Link's face slowly reddened. He glanced at his brother. "You sure?"

"Pretty damn sure. Step on it, would you?"

"You got it."

For a little while both men were silent. Then Link flashed Nick a look. "She didn't say so, did she? Maybe you got it wrong."

"Maybe. I don't think so."

"You gonna beat the crap out of him?"

"What do you think?"

"Hell, yes." Link sounded almost cheerful suddenly as he pulled off the exit marked River Road. "You need any help, you let me know."

"I won't. But thanks."

"Anytime, little brother. With pleasure. Any asshole that hits on our baby girl's gonna have to answer to me."

"My sentiments exactly."

They didn't speak again as they drove alongside the Ohio. When they reached Windermere's driveway, Nick was surprised to find that the gates were open. He and Link exchanged glances. Link shrugged, and pointed the Corvette up the hill.

When they emerged from the trees onto the flat ground at the top that served as the formal lawn, the first thing that caught their attention was the dozen or so fancy cars parked around the circular part of the driveway just in front of the house.

"Don't look like none of them belong to cops," Link said with a fleeting grin.

"Nope." Nick had been thinking the same thing.

The cars were all parked on the left side of the pavement with two wheels in the grassy circle, so there was room for Link to pull the Corvette past them right up to the foot of the front steps. Both of them got out.

"Hey, at least we're dressed for payin' calls on rich folks." Coming around the trunk of the car, Link glanced down at himself, then over at his brother.

Until that moment, Nick had forgotten they were both wearing suits.

"Yeah," he said, and with Link behind him headed up the steps toward the imposing front door.

20

*T*hank God Lyle had barely touched her face. The yellowing bruises on her right cheekbone and above her right eye had been easily covered with makeup and were invisible even under close scrutiny. Reassured on that point, Maggy turned away from the elaborate gilded mirror that hung on the yellow-silk-covered wall of the front sitting room. The cut on her head where he had kicked her was hidden beneath her hair, which was brushed into shining waves around her face. The bruises on her neck where he had strangled her were concealed by the high ascot tie of her white silk blouse. Her loose-fitting navy cardigan covered the slight swelling over her ribs, where the damage from his fists and feet was the worst. Tight navy pants gave the illusion that she had nothing to hide. As Maggy completed this mental inventory of her appearance, she grew increasingly confident that Nick wouldn't find a visible sign of what Lyle had done to her. Still, she clasped her fingers together and twisted them as she walked to one of the big windows overlooking the driveway. Nick knew her so well, and he already suspected. Would he somehow be able to sense what he couldn't see?

A bright red Corvette was just pulling up to the top of the drive. Maggy knew that it was Nick's, though she had never seen his car before. None of the Forrests' acquaintances would drive something that flashy, and, anyway, Nick had always wanted a red Corvette. At the memory, the ghost of a smile just touched her lips before vanishing. It belonged to another girl, another lifetime. It was not hers to enjoy.

She had to convince Nick that he must go away, now, today, and not come back.

If she didn't, the price she would have to pay would be unbearable. It would break her heart.

Her throat ached with unshed tears as she watched him slide out the passenger side door and stand up. It was a gorgeous spring day, all blue skies and shining sun and grass that was newly green. Bright yellow daffodils and scarlet tulips vied for position around the tinkling fountain in the grassy center of the drive. Through the window she could see Nick clearly. He was dressed, most improbably for him, in a charcoal-gray suit with a gleaming white shirt and maroon tie. With his black hair combed into smooth waves and his bronzed cheeks freshly shaved, he looked like an impossibly sexy banker, or lawyer. He also looked very familiar, and very, very dear. The ache in her throat intensified. For an instant the pain that attacked her heart and soul far exceeded anything her body had endured.

But she could not cry. She would not cry. Crying did no good at the best of times, and just now, when Nick was taking the front steps two at a time, it would be a disaster. Not for nothing had she been a Forrest for twelve long years, she thought with a deliberate lifting of her chin and stiffening of her spine. If it had done nothing else for her, it had taught her the fine art of self-control.

The doorbell rang. She turned away from the window, crossing nervously to stand before the marble fireplace at the opposite end of the room from the door. The green velvet upholstery of the small wing chairs on either side of the hearth beckoned, but sitting was a chancy proposition. She could sit with relative ease, if she held on to the chair arms for support, but the soreness in the muscles over her rib cage made her movements tellingly stiff when it was time to stand up.

"Mrs. Forrest is in here."

She heard Louella's voice, stiff with disapproval, an instant before one half of the double doors opened. Nick was deep in the doghouse with Louella after three days of persistent phone calls and his final less-than-tactful message, and the thought of him suffering her black looks was vaguely funny. Thus Maggy had a small smile playing around her mouth when Nick strode into the room.

He stopped short at the sight of her, his eyes running comprehensively over her. What he suspected was there in his face, in the grim set of his mouth, in the aggressiveness of his stance. But she was confident that there was nothing for him to see, no way he could *know,* and thus she was able to face him coolly.

Link was behind Nick, half a head taller, impossibly broad. Funny, she'd been so blinded by Nick that she hadn't even noticed Link getting out of the car or coming up the steps. But his presence at what should have been a private meeting told Maggy something: Nick's suspicions were so strong that he had come prepared to take Lyle apart.

If only it were possible. But it was not. Lyle wasn't even here, and if he had been she still couldn't allow it. There was David to consider.

Her heart quivered at the thought.

For David's sake, she had to play her role brilliantly. Why did it seem so impossible? She'd played it many times before.

But never with Nick. Nick, who knew her so well . . .

Louella still hovered in the doorway, clearly uncertain about whether or not to leave Maggy alone with two such unprecedentedly pushy visitors. Maggy caught her eye and nodded. Louella sniffed and closed the door.

"So I'm telling you to your face: go away," Maggy said to Nick as soon as the three of them were alone. The best defense was a good fast offense, as she had learned the hard way when she was a little girl. Head up, eyes unflinching as they met his, she was as coldly unwelcoming as it was possible to be. She didn't move from her stance beside the fireplace. If her fists were clenched, he would never know it because they were thrust deep into the pockets of her cardigan.

"Whatever happened to 'Hello, come in, sit down'?" Far from being intimidated, Nick moved toward her with the prowling intensity of a cougar. Though it was bright outside, the early-afternoon sun struck the house in such a way that the room they were in was murky with shadows, which was one reason why she had chosen it. His eyes gleamed green through the soft gloom as they roamed every inch of her face and body, searching for visible evidence that he would not find.

"You said if I told you to your face to go to hell, you'd do it. So I'm telling you: go to hell." She yielded not an inch.

He was close, by then, standing in front of her looking down at her almost quizzically.

"You know how much I hate to hear you swear," he said, a faint glimmer of humor softening his face, which until that moment had been set in unremittingly harsh lines. "I ought to wash out your mouth."

Maggy pursed her lips, thrown for a moment by this unexpected flicker of levity in the face of a situation that she considered deadly serious. "Why do you insist on making this difficult? I'm telling you I don't want you here. Please leave and don't come back."

"You almost sound like you mean it."

"I *do* mean it! What do I have to say to convince you? Shoo, scram, beat it, take a hike!"

"He hurt you, didn't he, Magdalena?"

She had not expected a full frontal attack. The very gentleness of his question was almost her undoing.

"No! I mean, I don't know what you mean! You said you'd go away!"

"I lied," Nick said, coming closer until he practically loomed over her, his eyes searching every millimeter of her exposed skin with frightening intensity. The fireplace behind her gave her no room to retreat.

"Get out of my face, you pigheaded bully!" cornered, she verbally lashed out.

"Tell me the truth, Magdalena. This is me, Nick. I'm on your side, remember?" His hands came up to grasp her head, burrowing deep into the heavy fall of hair behind either ear as he tilted her face so that, short of closing her lids, she had no choice but to meet his gaze.

The pain as his fingers encountered the laceration in her scalp was so sudden, so unexpected, that Maggy was taken by surprise: she yelped and jerked her head from his grasp.

Their eyes met. For a moment neither of them said anything, just stared at each other in a kind of mutually horrified comprehension.

The thought that ricocheted through Maggy's mind was *There's no point in lying now.* What he knew was there in his face, in the immobility of his stance, in his suddenly suspended breathing.

Then, "Come here," Nick said grimly, reaching for her.

"Don't!" Hopeless as it was, her every instinct screamed at her to resist. His hands cupped her shoulders, pulled her close.

"Don't be a fool, Magdalena." Nick's voice was impatient and tender at the same time as he dealt with her stiff resistance with the minimum of necessary force. Link, looming up behind him, scowled down at Maggy over his brother's shoulder.

"Let him look, baby girl." Belying his expression, Link's words were soft. "We both love you, remember?"

She did remember, and the remembrance was what sapped her strength at long last. She had no will to resist as Nick carefully searched through her hair, parting it at last to expose the cut that she knew must be awful to look at, long and jagged and discolored. It had bled profusely, so profusely that before Lyle had left her he'd thrown her a towel and ordered her to wrap it around her head so she wouldn't bleed all over and ruin the expensive carpet.

"Would you look at this," Nick said to Link. Link looked, and the brothers exchanged grim glances.

"Where else did he hurt you, querida?" Nick let her hair drop back into place. Like his voice, his hands were very gentle.

"It doesn't matter. Really." It was all she could do to hold on to her composure. Now that Nick knew, she felt weak suddenly, as if her skeleton had turned to jelly. And she knew why: with one of the deepest, darkest secrets of her life suddenly out in the open, the steely resolve that had enabled her to hide so much all these years was draining away, as if her strength of will were a container that had unexpectedly sprung a leak.

"It matters to me. *You* matter to me."

She did. She had no doubt about that. It was there in his face, his voice, his hands. She felt shaky suddenly, as the emotions she had battled for years to control broke for the surface. At last someone knew, and cared, what she had suffered.

Nick knew. Nick cared.

Of their own accord, her hands fluttered up to touch her ribs, her neck.

"Did he hurt you there? Can I unbutton your blouse?"

Maggy was too beset with emotions to do more than nod. She was trembling all over, and her knees felt weak. Nick's hands very gently pulled her blouse from the waistband of her pants. When he started to undo her buttons from the neck down, Link, like the gentleman no one would ever guess that he was, turned his back.

"He tried to choke her." The bluish marks on her neck where Lyle had wrapped his fingers and squeezed elicited that, which was addressed to Link. Then, as Nick's fingers continued downward and the full purple-and-yellow splendor of her battered rib cage beneath her delicate lace bra was exposed, he swore, viciously. The single word he used was succinct, ugly, and very filthy. Maggy had never, ever heard him use it before.

"What is it?" This came from Link, who still had his back turned.

"He beat the crap out of her." Nick's voice was near normal, but his face was not: it was awful. Murder was there in his eyes, in the set of his jaw, in the sudden ashen shade of his skin. Maggy had never seen him look like that in her life, and it scared her. She reached up and took the two edges of her blouse from his grasp, pulling it closed. Their eyes met.

"Where is he?"

There was no doubt whom he meant. Maggy's gaze dropped, and she tried to fasten her blouse, but her hands shook so much that she couldn't force the first button through its hole.

"Where is he, Magdalena?" The terrible gentleness was more frightening than any amount of cursing and threats would have been.

"He's gone. He left early Sunday morning, for three weeks. And he took David." Her voice broke as she said her son's name. "They're looking at boarding schools abroad. Lyle said that if I don't get rid of you and start behaving myself, he'll put David in boarding school as early as June and make sure I never set eyes on him again till he's grown."

"That son of a bitch." Link whipped around at this, face apoplectic, fists clenched.

"He can't do that." The more reasoned response came from Nick, elicited by the heartbreak that feature by feature claimed Maggy's face. Her bottom lip quivered, her cheeks crumpled, her eyes filled. When he pulled her close she went unresistingly. Enveloped by the solid strength of his arms, the warmth and never-forgotten scent of him, the security of him, Maggy leaned her forehead against his chest like a tired child. He spoke into her hair. "Don't worry, baby, he can't do that. I give you my word. You trust me, don't you? He can't do that."

"Lyle Forrest can do any damned thing he wants," Maggy said bitterly into the soft silk of his tie, and to her amazement felt a gush of hot tears spring from her eyes like erupting geysers.

She heard the opening of the door behind her, but she didn't dare look around. Denied for so long, the tears would not be stopped. They flowed like torrential rivers, complete with sobs that shook her body and helpless, grasping hands that clung to Nick's shirt.

"I must have left my glasses in here . . ." a woman's fretful voice said. Nick, looking over Maggy's head, stiffened even as the voice broke off in surprise. Maggy pictured how they must appear to anyone who saw them: herself, the young Mrs. Lyle Forrest who wasn't quite one of *them,* you know, blouse awry, weeping bitterly in the arms of a tall, dark, tough-looking stranger, while another, equally tough-looking stranger stood guard. The juiciness of it would entertain Louisville's high society for weeks to come—but she couldn't even bring herself to care.

For the first time in twelve years, her defenses were all gone.

"To hell with this," Nick muttered. Then, to her surprise, she was swung off her feet and up into his arms. Holding her so that her face and the unbuttoned state of her blouse were hidden against his chest, he carried her from the house.

He was running down the stairs with her, his tread as light as an acrobat's, when she happened to catch a glimpse, over his shoulder, of the stunned group who crowded through Windermere's front door to watch. Her mother-in-law, of course, and Lucy, with their bridge group. Maybe twenty women altogether, all appearing absolutely stunned, all wide-eyed and openmouthed.

Then Link opened the door of the Corvette, and Nick slid in with her cradled on his lap. The door slammed shut. Seconds later Link was beside them, the engine was engaged, and the Corvette purred down the drive.

21

$\mathscr{M}$aggy couldn't help it. She cried all the way to their destination. With her face buried in Nick's shoulder and sobs racking her, she had only the vaguest sense that they were crossing the bridge into Indiana, then following numerous twisty back roads that led God knew where. Not that she was worried. She trusted Nick with her life, and more.

"Shh, now, it's all right." Nick crooned soothing phrases in an endless variation in her ear as he cradled her against him, but still she wept bitterly. He and Link might have exchanged a few words, but if they did the sense of them went over Maggy's head. All she could do was cry.

When the car stopped at last, Nick slid out with her in his arms without ever once turning loose of her. Which was a good thing, because Maggy continued to sob against his shoulder, her arms wrapped around his neck as though she would never let him go. One of his arms cradled her back; the other was beneath her knees.

"Clear 'em all out, would you?" Maggy heard Nick say to his brother, who had opened the car door for them and still stood there holding it as Nick spoke to him over Maggy's bent head.

Link's reply escaped Maggy, but apparently it was in the affirmative, because Nick turned and walked across the grassy yard with her without saying anything more. Maggy got just a fleeting impression of an ancient two-story farmhouse, sadly in need of another coat of white paint, and perhaps three or four strange men poring over a map on the front porch. They all looked up with identical surprised expressions as Nick came up the shallow flight of stairs. But something, the look on his face or the fact that he carried a helplessly sobbing woman in his arms, prevented them from saying anything to Nick, or at least anything that she could hear. Link must have followed right behind Nick, because the door magically opened for them without any impediments to slow them down. It closed again just as magically. She was borne through a shadowy hall before Nick reached what seemed to be the living room and sank down in a shabby, overstuffed chair with her on his lap.

Cuddled close to him, Maggy sobbed and gulped and wheezed for maybe another ten minutes before the storm began to subside. Nick held her the whole time, murmuring things like "Shhh, baby" and "Hush, now" while he gently stroked her hair and her back.

When it was over, Nick still held her. She lay against him like an exhausted child, body spent and limp, eyes closed. Then she must have fallen asleep, because when she next became rather groggily aware of her surroundings, the room, which had been filled with dusty-looking sunlight, had grown dark. Through an uncurtained window behind the chair, she could see that it was dusk outside.

She was still on Nick's lap, her face burrowed into the space between his neck and shoulder, her left arm draped around his neck, her right curled between them, her body utterly relaxed. His arms curved around her, holding her against him.

Slowly, exquisitely, Maggy absorbed the details of her position as she came fully awake. Nick's shoulder was broad and strong beneath her head. Against her ear, she could hear the steady beating of his heart. The smooth cotton of his shirt covered a chest that was wide and solid and radiated heat. Linked around her waist, his arms were thick with muscle, as capable of defending her as they were of comforting her. Beneath her bottom, his thighs felt reassuringly substantial. He was a strong man, she thought, a man capable of caring for his own. And she was his. She always had been.

Curled against him, Maggy thought, *I've come home.* The realization shook her.

She stirred, sat up, and discovered that he was watching her.

As she blinked at him, he stubbed out the cigarette he had been smoking and smiled at her, his eyes tender. His head rested back against the faded floral upholstery, and his body felt heavy and relaxed beneath hers. She thought he looked tired.

"Better?" he asked, and she nodded. With any other man, she would have felt the need to apologize for crying all over him. But this was Nick. He would get no apology, because it was unnecessary: he was her twin soul. Apologizing to him would be like apologizing to herself.

"You must be uncomfortable," she said. "I feel like I've been asleep for hours."

"About three," he confirmed. "If the chimes in the kitchen are anything to go by, it just turned six o'clock."

"You could have woken me, or at least put me down. There's a couch right here." And there was, just to the left of the chair, an enormous piece of furniture covered in ancient gold velveteen. For all its apparent age, it looked comfortable enough.

"I could have. If I'd wanted to, I would have."

"Where are we?" Settling back against him with as little self-consciousness as if he'd been a chair, she glanced around the room.

"Starlight, Indiana. Link and I've been staying over here. We've rented this farm."

"Oh." She felt lazy, almost boneless, as if her strength had drained away with her tears. Her ribs ached, but the pain was nothing compared to what it had been, and she could ignore it. "Remember when we were kids, we always wanted to live on a farm?"

"I remember." He smiled a little. With the back of her head resting against his shoulder, she couldn't really see his face, but she caught the reminiscent curving of the near side of his mouth. His jaw and cheeks were dark with five-o'clock shadow. The roughness of it scraped lightly against her temple as he turned his head. "Your big ambition in life was to feed the chickens every morning."

"It was a nice, simple ambition, you have to admit." She sighed as reality began to rear its ugly head. "Too bad I didn't stick to it. I've really made a mess of things."

"Nothing that can't be fixed." His arms tightened around her, but not too tightly, probably because he didn't want to press her bruised ribs. Despite everything, Maggy felt absurdly safe in his hold.

"I wish I was as sure of that as you. You shouldn't have carried me off like that. That was Lyle's mother's bridge club, for goodness' sake, and you can bet the story's already all over town."

The shit's going to hit the fan was what she didn't say, because she didn't want Nick to scold her again for swearing. At the moment, she wasn't in the mood to annoy Nick.

"So? You're getting a divorce." It was a flat, blunt statement that left no room for argument.

Maggy said nothing. She could feel him tensing.

"Damn it, Magdalena, you can't even be considering going back to that bastard! I forbid it, do you hear?"

Despite everything, that made her smile. "You always were bossy."

His arms dropped away from her waist. Watching his hands grip the arms of the chair until his knuckles turned white, Maggy guessed that he had released her because he could no longer trust himself to keep his hold on her gentle. Beneath her back and thighs, she could feel his body stiffening with anger. So much for not wanting to annoy him. She didn't even have to say a word to do it, because he knew what she was thinking. He knew her too darned well.

Her head still lolled against his shoulder, and she turned it just in time to watch bright scarlet color creep high into his cheekbones and the tips of his ears. That, in her experience, meant Nick was starting to get really, really mad.

"I'll give you a choice," he said, his gaze sluing down to her face. "You get a divorce, or you get widowed. It's as simple as that."

"Nick," she said gently, "there's David."

"To hell with David!"

"Don't say that," she said. "Don't ever, ever say that. He is my son."

"And you're his mother," Nick said through gritted teeth. "How do you think he would feel if he could see what his father did to you? Do you think he'd want you to be beaten black and blue? If the tables were turned, if, in order to stay with you, David had to endure a vicious, violent man using him as his own personal punching bag, what would you want him to do?"

There was a pause. Maggy had never thought of it quite like that before. "That's different."

"Like hell it is."

It was a measure of Nick's agitation that he was starting to swear freely. He did so only when something really upset him. Swearing, especially in front of women, wasn't usually one of Nick's vices. He didn't like to hear her swear, either. When they were kids, she used to get a kick out of memorizing the most colorful bits of profanity that came her way, just so she could use the words on him and watch him get mad.

"It's not usually this bad. He's only beaten me up like this once before, years and years ago. When David was little. Sometimes he'll slap me if I do something he doesn't like, or punch me once or twice, or twist my wrist like he did the other day, but nothing as severe as this in years. He much prefers to control me through fear."

"By God, I *am* going to kill him!" Nick's response was passionate. "Why didn't you leave him years ago?"

"Because of David," Maggy said wearily, already knowing that Nick was not going to understand. "He would never, ever have let me have David."

"Does he hit the kid?" Nick sounded as if he was having to work hard just to keep his voice even.

Maggy laughed, the sound sharp and unpleasant. "I'd leave him in a heartbeat if he ever laid a violent hand on David. I'd steal David and run, and to hell with the consequences. But I am as morally certain as it is possible to be that Lyle would never do anything to harm David. In his own twisted way he loves the child, and David worships the ground that he walks on. Sometimes I think David is—almost—more his son than mine."

It hurt to say it, to have Nick hear it. But it was true. One reason that she was afraid to try to take David from Lyle was because there was always the possibility that David, if given the choice, would choose Lyle over herself. Lyle was a consummate athlete, proficient in every sport he tried: golf, tennis, swimming, sailing, skiing. He was handsome, confident, always very much the man in charge. Practically everyone in Louisville asked *how high* when Lyle said *jump.* David was dazzled by these facts, by Lyle's aura of power and invincibility. And David had been raised as the heir, the lion's cub. Windermere and everything that went with it would be David's one day, and David knew it. How could the mere fact that she was David's mother and loved him compete with that?

She hated Lyle, was afraid of him, and was miserable as his wife. She feared his influence over her son. With every atom of her being, she wished she could use some of *Tia* Gloria's much-vaunted psychic power to zap Lyle out of existence. But she couldn't, and in any contest between them, including a divorce, she would come out the loser, and she knew it. Lyle held all the aces. Her own hand held only one trump, and it was pitifully weak compared to his. Using it would involve badly, perhaps mortally, wounding David. And in the end, it might not do any good at all.

She could not take her own happiness at the expense of her son's. She would not.

"Does anybody else know about him beating you up? His mother, the housekeeper?"

Maggy shook her head. "I—don't think so. I—didn't want them to know. I cleaned up the blood where he kicked me in the head, and then when I found I couldn't move around very easily, I stayed in bed. As far as they know, I've had the flu."

"Didn't you scream? Call for help?"

"I didn't want Virginia to hear." The words were so low that they were barely audible. "I didn't want anyone to hear."

Nick muttered something explosive under his breath.

"You probably ought to see a doctor," he said after a moment, as if thinking aloud. "That cut on your head needs to be looked at, and he may have cracked a rib or something."

"No!" Maggy's voice was sharp.

"Why not?"

"Because I don't want to!" Maggy hesitated, then decided to tell the truth. She added more quietly, "I'd be too ashamed."

"Ashamed! You?" Nick sounded both furious and dumbfounded. *"You* haven't done anything."

"I know, but . . ." Maggy sighed, suddenly weary of the discussion that she could already see might continue fruitlessly through the night. "Could we save the rest of this conversation for later, please? My head hurts, and I have to use the bathroom, and I'm starving."

"You are not going back to Forrest if I have to handcuff you to my wrist for the rest of your life." Nick sounded as if he were on the verge of choking with suppressed fury.

"I'd like that," Maggy said with a flickering smile, hoping to lighten the atmosphere before Nick totally lost his temper with her.

"I'm serious, damn it!"

"I know. So am I."

Nick stared hard at her. "Magdalena, you've got a nasty-looking cut on your head and bruises over most of the rest of you. We've already established that your bastard of a husband has scared you good and proper of sex. So why the hell are you batting those big brown eyes at me all of a sudden, and cooing at me like you're daring me to kiss you?"

"Because old habits die hard?" Maggy ventured with a twinkle. With her, Nick had always been safe as a church and steady as a rock, and she knew perfectly well that he wasn't about to try to throw her down on the rug and have his wicked way with her. Therefore, she saw no danger in teasing him just a little. She was so tired of feeling depressed, and scared. The last three days had been among the most miserable of her life. She wanted to be happy while she could. Since half of Louisville probably knew by now how Nick had carried her off, and the other half would surely know by this time tomorrow, there was no way she was going to be able to keep it from Lyle. Lyle would be beside himself with rage. The prospect frightened her, but it had its up side: he was going to be so furious over that that nothing she did now could possibly make it worse.

He was out of town for another two and a half weeks. She was going to steal this time with Nick.

Then she would decide what she had to do. If she had to take her lumps from Lyle, she would. But for now, just for a little while, she was going to put Lyle and all her troubles out of her mind. She was going to snatch a little happiness.

Surely two weeks worth was not too much to ask after twelve years.

"Get off my lap, witch."

Sensing her change in mood, Nick surrendered to it, though she knew, as the expression went, that he'd be back to fight another day. He gave her rear a gentle swat—she figured it would have been harder if he'd been sure she didn't have bruises there, too—and she slid to her feet, surprised to find that she was not quite steady on them. He stood up behind her, grimacing as blood rushed into muscles that had remained in one position for too long, and steadied himself and her with his hands on her shoulders.

"Bathroom's through there," he said, pointing toward a door that was just visible along the hall. "I'm going to go out to the kitchen and see what I can find for us to eat. If you feel dizzy, or need help, give me a shout."

"Yes, sir," she said with a glimmering smile over her shoulder for him and went along to the bathroom.

After taking care of business, she did up her blouse at long last, washed her hands, and grimaced into the mirror. Her hair stood out all around her head like a squirrel's nest made of bright reddish autumn leaves. Crying had left her eyes swollen and puffy, and her face as white as if she'd just risen from an encounter with Dracula. The makeup she had carefully applied to cover the bruises on her face had vanished, presumably on the front of Nick's suit. Not a trace of lipstick remained on her, but a smear of black under one eye bore silent witness to the fact that her mascara was not as waterproof as the ads claimed. She looked a fright, and she couldn't stand it.

Twisting her hair into a knot at her nape, she washed her face with plain soap and cold water, figuring that it didn't matter if Nick saw the bruises on her forehead and cheek now. They were nothing, compared with the injuries he had already seen. That done, she swished a swallow of mouthwash around in her mouth and spat. Then she carefully (because of the cut, which was still very sensitive) smoothed her hair with a comb she found on the back of the toilet. Hunting through the medicine cabinet for anything she might possibly use as a cosmetic, she had no luck. But she did find a bottle of Tylenol and took two of the tablets, swallowing them with a handful of water. In a few minutes, she hoped, the pounding in her head would begin to subside.

Feeling better than she had in three days, she left the bathroom and headed for the only room with light blazing through the door.

It was a typical farm kitchen, with white-painted cabinets and appliances, a speckled linoleum floor, and red gingham café curtains at the windows. A big chrome-legged table straight out of the fifties claimed pride of place at one end beneath a bank of small windows. Nick had already set two places on it, and a plastic tub of butter and cardboard containers of salt and pepper adorned the middle. Nick himself was bending to peer into the open oven, a cooking mitt on one hand and a long-handled fork in the other. As she watched, he flipped the second of a pair of sizzling steaks, then slid the pan back under the broiler, and straightened, shutting the oven door. He wore just his white shirt and gray suit pants, with the shirt unbuttoned at the collar and its sleeves rolled up past his elbows to expose hard-looking, hairy forearms. His face was flushed from the heat of the oven, his hair was mussed, and his cheeks and jaw were dark with stubble.

He looked handsomer to her like that than any other man ever had in her life.

"Smells good," she said, walking into the kitchen. He glanced around at her, smiling.

"Hey, unlike you, I'm a good cook, remember? Unless you've improved since I last ate one of your burnt offerings."

"Not much," she admitted, wandering close to peer interestedly over his shoulder at the contents of the pots on the stove. Ears of corn bubbled in one, while butter melted into peas in the other.

"I'm impressed," she said, and her stomach growled to prove it.

"Go sit down. This'll be ready in a minute."

Maggy moved toward the table, then hesitated. "I need to call Windermere, and let them know I haven't been kidnapped or anything. Before they get really alarmed, and do something stupid like phone the police, or Lyle." She hated to even bring up the subject of Lyle again, before it was absolutely necessary. But she needed to make the call, too, and she wasn't going to do it behind Nick's back. She was never going to tell another lie to Nick as long as she lived.

Nick turned around, fork in hand, to frown at her. Maggy met his gaze unflinchingly.

"So call," he said finally. "But you're not going back."

"Did I say I was?"

Nick's mouth twisted. "Phone's on the wall," he said, and turned back to the stove.

22

"Who was that man?" Lucy demanded shrilly as soon as Maggy identified herself. Maggy, wincing, wished she had hung up as soon as she heard her sister-in-law's voice. She would rather have talked to Virginia. But maybe not. Maybe Virginia would have asked her questions she wasn't prepared, just at the moment, to answer.

"A friend." Her voice was cool.

"Are you having an affair with him?"

"No, I'm not. Not that it's any of your business, is it?"

"Everyone thinks you are. You should have seen Linda Brantley's face! Oh, and Connie Mason's! They were shocked—shocked! We all were! Mother was nearly prostrate, and it's weakened her so that she has already gone to bed. At six o'clock! Not that I blame her: you were embracing that man in our house with your blouse half off! And for him to carry you out of the house like that in front of our friends—we'll never live it down! Lyle will just die when he hears! I've already placed a call to him, though they say he's in transit right now and it may be a couple of days before he gets my message. Mother keeps begging me not to tell him, but I think it's my duty to. I don't want to cause trouble for you, Maggy, but he'll hear it from someone, believe me, and I think it best that he hear it from family first. . . ."

"Lucy," Maggy interrupted, unable to listen to more as her stomach tightened with nerves. She could almost feel Lyle's tentacles reaching out for her, as if he could snatch her back even over the phone line. "I called to tell Virginia I won't be home for a few days. I'm going to be staying with friends."

"Friends!" Lucy snorted. "Don't insult my intelligence! You're with that man! Who *is* he, anyway? Sarah said it was probably that old boyfriend of yours Buffy brought to your birthday party, but she can't remember his name. She's going to call Buffy and ask."

"Tell her not to bother," Maggy's voice turned to ice. "His name is Nick. Nick King. *K-i-n-g,* got it? And yes, he's the friend I'm staying with. So now you can tell Lyle all about it when you talk to him."

"You—you blatant *adulteress,*" Lucy gasped.

"Tell Virginia I'll be in touch, will you please?" Maggy said, and hung up the phone. When she let go of the receiver she was surprised to find that her hands were shaking.

"Bitch," she said to the wall. Then, more viciously, "Bitch!"

"Hey. You okay?" Nick's arms came around her from behind, pulling her against him. For a moment she stood stiffly in his embrace, and then she relaxed against his chest. His arms were warm around her middle. Almost unconsciously, her hands folded over his forearms, noting the heat and hardness of them, the silky texture of the hair over the warm satin of his skin, and the size and sheer masculinity of his hands.

"That was Lyle's sister. She's just like him."

"Bitch," Nick echoed her description companionably. Something about the way he said it made Maggy start to smile in spite of herself.

"She is," she insisted.

"I don't doubt it for a minute."

"She wanted to know who you are."

"I heard. Nice of you to spell it for her."

Maggy hesitated, then put into words the thought that had been troubling her since she hung up the phone. "Nick—maybe I ought to go to a hotel. I don't want to cause trouble for you with Lyle. He can be—ruthless."

"Magdalena, get this through your head: I am not afraid of Lyle Forrest. And you're staying right here. Unless—do you want to go to a hotel?" He asked the question in an altered tone, as if it had just occurred to him that she might not want to stay with him.

"No," she said, to disabuse him of that notion.

"Well, then." There was a smile in his voice.

"She called me an adulteress." It was ridiculous, she knew, but the accusation stung.

"Did she?" Though his arms didn't tighten around her—clearly he was mindful of her bruises—the muscles in his forearms tensed. Maggy could feel them grow harder beneath her hands. "Don't worry about it. She's wrong."

"I wish she wasn't." Passion blazed suddenly in Maggy's voice and in her eyes as she turned in his arms to look up at him. Though she was tall herself, he was taller by nearly a head. His shoulders were wide, his arms strong, his body muscular. Pugilist's face or no, he *was* handsome, with his black hair and sleepy, hazel-green eyes and hard, bronzed face. And sexy. And very, very male. Any normal woman would be panting with desire for him. Once upon a time *she* had panted with desire for him. But not now. Lyle's abuse seemed to have knocked physical desire clear out of her emotional range. "I wish I *was* an adulteress. I wish I was having a hot, hot affair with you."

Her hands rested on his shoulders. His hands slid up her back.

"You could be."

His face was very close. Maggy looked up at him, up at the square, bristly chin and high flat cheekbones, up at the long, thin mouth and crooked nose and broad forehead, up at the eyes that gleamed pure emerald green at her from beneath drooping lids. She met his gaze and read his hunger for her. And she saw, not an amorous, predatory man, but only Nick. Her heartbeat quickened. Her arms slid around his neck.

"I love you, Nick."

"I know." His lips, just touching her mouth, were withdrawn. "I love you, too."

"I *want* to have an affair with you."

"Not as much as I want you to, believe me." He was smiling tenderly, ruefully, down into her eyes.

"Kiss me."

"Magdalena . . ." But his protest, if protest it was, was silenced by her mouth. She went on tiptoe to press her lips to his, and found them very warm, very firm. Very kissable. Her mouth slanted across his, and the tip of her tongue came out to stroke his lips. His arms tightened around her, and suddenly he took control of the kiss. He gathered her against him, one hand moving up to cradle the back of her head as he tilted her face for his kiss. Maggy greeted the warm caress of his mouth eagerly, parting her lips to accommodate his tongue as it slid between them, her arms twining around his neck.

His tongue explored her lips, the roof of her mouth, the inside of her teeth, and was withdrawn. It entered again with a careful, slow stroke, sliding softly against her tongue, coaxing it to play. She trembled as she answered him, her tongue slipping at last inside his mouth.

She had not yet closed her eyes.

As if he could feel the weight of her gaze, Nick's eyes flickered open. For an instant, just an instant, Maggy thought he looked dazed. Then his eyes focused sharply on her face. And his eyes smiled into hers.

Still he kissed her, his tongue staking claim to her mouth. He watched her watching him all the while. Her breasts were pressed against his chest. She felt the pressure as pleasure, and her body responded of its own accord: her breasts swelled, nipples tightening. Against her abdomen, she could feel the corresponding engorgement of his body as he got hard.

For an instant her senses froze as she assimilated what was happening to him. Then, before she could react, he lifted his head, freeing her mouth, though with a deep physical reluctance that she could feel.

His arms around her, which had hardened and tightened like the rest of him, dropped away. He set his hands on her hipbones instead, his long fingers not quite steady as he eased her body away from his.

Contrarily, now that she knew that he was not going to force the issue, Maggy felt almost sorry that he had stopped. In mute protest her arms stayed looped around his neck. Her fingers threaded through the hair at his nape, enjoying the crispness of the curls there and the warmth of the underlying skin.

For a moment Nick's gaze searched her face. Then, with a quirk of his lips that was almost a grimace, he rested his forehead against hers. His breathing had quickened. Dark color had risen to stain his cheekbones. His body was tense, his hands on her hips restless.

"That wasn't bad at all," Maggy murmured, relieved that she hadn't panicked.

A ghost of a laugh shook him. "Somehow that's just what I thought you were thinking."

"So why did you stop?"

He lifted his head to meet her gaze. "Because it's going to be better than that between us. One day soon. But there's no rush: we've got all the time in the world. We're back together for good this time, Magdalena. I'm not going to let you go."

"Oh, Nick . . ." The sudden ache in her heart was almost a physical pain. Her hands tightened on his neck, and she tilted her face up to press her lips to his bewhiskered chin. "I don't want you to let me go."

"Good," he whispered, his mouth seeking and finding hers. This time his kiss was brief, a quick foray into her mouth before he abruptly lifted his head.

"The steaks!" He abandoned her as unceremoniously as if she'd been a rag doll, whirling to dash to the stove and jerk open the oven door.

Clouds of smoke billowed out around him. He snatched at the pan, burned his hand, swore, and grabbed the oven mitt. Seconds later he was depositing the rescued steaks atop the cutting board near the stove.

Maggy looked at them, looked at Nick looking at them, and started to laugh.

"Talk about burnt offerings," she said.

"You distracted me on purpose." He turned off the burners under the saucepans, then picked up his fork and poked dispiritedly at the charred meat. "They're probably still edible, if we scrape off the worst parts."

Maggy cast a dubious glance at the steaks. "Do they have pizza delivery out here?"

Nick grinned and shook his head. " 'Fraid not. But we could go out for pizza, if you want to."

Maggy hadn't gone out for pizza in years. Pizza wasn't something the Forrests ate. Except for David, and then only when he and she were out alone together and stopped by a Pizza Hut for a quick meal, or when he spent the night at a friend's house.

"I'd love to go out for pizza." A thought occurred to her, and she hesitated, touching her face with a tentative hand. "I forgot—I don't have any makeup with me. While you were in the process of carrying me off, I wish you'd remembered to bring my purse."

"Sorry, but purses are not something I normally think about. Anyway, you don't need makeup. You look great without it. About fifteen again."

"Thanks." She sent him a quick smile. It was a casual compliment, uttered sincerely, and she was surprised by how much it pleased her. Probably because Lyle had spent the last few years telling her that her looks were fading fast, and that she'd better thank God for cosmetics because without them she was about as beautiful as one of her dogs. Hesitantly she asked, "But what about the—bruises? Do they look too bad?"

Nick's eyes hardened as they moved over her face. "It'll be dark in the restaurant. And no, they don't look too bad. What, does he take care not to hit you in the face?"

"Yes," Maggy whispered, humiliated, and glanced away from him.

"Magdalena," he said softly, coming close. One hand clasped her waist, while the other cupped her chin and tilted her face up. "Look at me."

Unwillingly, her gaze met his.

"If you got hit by a car, would you be ashamed because you happened to be crossing the street when it came by?"

"N-No."

"If you were in a plane crash, would you be ashamed because you'd bought a ticket on that particular flight?"

"No."

"If you were robbed at gunpoint, would you be ashamed because the robber picked you to steal money from?"

"No."

"Why not?" he asked. Then, before she could reply, he answered for her, "You would not be ashamed if any of those things happened to you, because they would not be your fault. What that bastard did to you falls into the same category. Lyle Forrest is the one with the problem, and he's the one who should be ashamed. Not you."

"Oh, Nick . . ." A smile trembled and died on her mouth. The ache was throbbing in her throat again, the one that warned of impending tears. She felt as though she'd been spinning in an endlessly whirling vortex for so many years that she couldn't even begin to count them, and suddenly he'd reached in and grabbed her and yanked her out onto firm earth. Her head was steadying at last, and with it her perspective. With her mind, at least, she knew his words were the truth.

She was grateful, so grateful, for that. But crying on him twice in one day would be a poor way to show her gratitude. Swallowing, she willed the ache to disperse.

He was watching her keenly. "I want you to say, 'That bastard Lyle Forrest is a brutal criminal with psychiatric problems, and *he* did this, not me. I have done nothing to be ashamed of.' "

A quavering smile touched Maggy's lips. "You're being silly."

"I am not. Say it."

"I feel ridiculous."

"I don't care. Say it."

Maggy swallowed as the words seemed to stick in her throat, and then she got it out. "That bastard Lyle Forrest is a brutal criminal with psychiatric problems, and he did this, not me. I have done nothing to be ashamed of."

"Do you believe it?"

His eyes blazed intently into hers. Maggy reached up to curl the fingers of both hands around the wrist that supported her chin, and nodded. "Yes."

"That's my girl." His hand left her chin to entwine with one set of fingers. "Every time you start feeling ashamed that he hit you, I want you to say that. Okay?"

"Okay." Maggy smiled rather tremulously up at him, and his eyes darkened. He brought her knuckles to his lips for a brief kiss, then rubbed her curled fingers back and forth over his cheek. His whiskers rasped like sandpaper against her hand. The combination of prickly bristles atop warm, smooth skin was quintessentially masculine, and it appealed to her. She freed her fingers from his to lay her hand against his cheek. The small contact seemed as intimate to her as any touch she had ever shared with a man, because of the trust involved.

As always, Nick seemed to be able to read her thoughts. He covered her hand with his, pressing her fingers into his skin. His eyes took on a sensuous, somnolent gleam as they met hers. For a moment Maggy thought that he was going to kiss her mouth and found herself almost hoping that he would. But he didn't.

"Still feel like pizza?" Nick asked instead. When Maggy nodded, he entwined his fingers with hers again and turned away, heading through the darkened hall toward the front door. With her hand in his she was towed willy-nilly after him. He paused only to hook his suit coat from the back of the chair in the living room where he had left it, and toss it over his arm.

When they stepped out onto the porch, Nick cast a quick glance around. It was full night. A sudden swoosh of chilled air caught the remnants of autumn's fallen leaves that still lurked along the fence line and sent them rustling across the flat, patchy turf of the front yard.

"It's colder than I thought," he said, releasing her hand. Instead of shrugging into his coat as she would have expected, he dropped it over her shoulders. A glinting glance forestalled her when she would have protested. Knowing Nick as she did, Maggy swallowed her words. Pointing out the fact that she already had on a thick-knit cardigan while he was in his shirtsleeves would not have made a bit of difference. Nick had always been concerned for her comfort over his own.

And it was cold. Not bitterly, but certainly no warmer than 55 degrees, with a stiff breeze blowing from the east. Maggy was glad of the coat's warmth as she waited for him to lock the door.

"You must be freezing," she said, her glance touching his rolled-up shirtsleeves and unbuttoned collar, and his black hair as it was ruffled by the wind.

He slid the key ring into his pocket, wrapped an arm around her shoulders, and grinned.

"When you're around, I don't feel the cold," he said, and she smiled at his absurdity, as he no doubt intended that she should.

But at the same time she felt ridiculously warmed.

23

*O*ver pizza they talked about everything and nothing. Instead of a chain restaurant Nick took her to a small, one-of-a-kind place owned and operated by an immigrant Italian family, improbably located at a country crossroad with no other commercial establishment in sight. Even on a Tuesday night it was busy, and Maggy felt lucky that they had managed to procure a booth in the corner. The food, served by the owner's teenage daughter, was excellent. Maggy savored every bite. For the past three days she had eaten scarcely anything at all, and it was good to feel hungry again and to satisfy that hunger. It was good to sit at a table over such simple but delectable fare and laugh and talk and say whatever came into her head. It was good not to have to be afraid of what might be waiting for her when she got home. It was good not to have to care about her lack of proper manners as strings of chewy cheese stretched between her mouth and the slice of pizza she was eating. It was good not to feel self-conscious over her scrubbed-clean face and lack of lipstick and mascara, or the faint bruises that marred her skin.

It was good just to be with Nick.

"Tell me what you've been doing over the past twelve years," Maggy ordered as she bit into her pizza.

"Besides pining for you, you mean?"

Maggy laughed. "Yes, besides that."

Nick told her. He had joined the service, done his stint, gotten out, gone into business for himself. Basically, he said, that about covered it.

"What branch of the service?" Such a bare-bones description of how he had spent the time they'd been apart was not like Nick, with his prodigious memory for detail and gift of gab.

"Navy." He answered briefly and took another bite of pizza.

"You were in the navy? I bet you looked cute in one of those white uniforms." Maggy twinkled at him.

"Must have. You've heard the old saw about sailors having a girl in every port? With me, it was at least three."

Because she knew he was teasing, she kicked him under the table and went on with her meal, unperturbed.

"So what exactly do you do for a living now?" Maggy asked with growing curiosity as she watched him devour the last slice of pizza.

Nick took a swallow of beer. "I buy nightclubs that are losing money, turn them around, then sell them again for more than I paid for them."

Maggy glanced at him suspiciously. She'd known Nick a long time, and she knew when he wasn't being up-front with her. His answers were too brief, too glib. What was he hiding?

"Truth?" The single word came out automatically, and Maggy felt a flicker of surprise as she heard herself utter it. Then she thought with an inner smile that in Nick's presence she was reverting to childhood again. It was a question they'd often posed to each other as kids, and they even had a never-to-be-doubted oath they'd sworn in response.

"You don't believe me? Why on earth not?" His glance at her was wary. And he, at least, seemed to have forgotten their oath.

"Because I know you, Nick King, and that doesn't sound like you at all."

"I'm thirty-two years old, Magdalena. I've changed."

"When pigs fly," she said cheerfully.

He laughed and took another large bite of pizza.

"Will you believe me if I tell you that I'm financially comfortable? I'm not rich, but I make good money. Enough to take care of you, and me, and your kid, and put a little away for our old age at the same time."

"I'm not interested in money anymore," she said with perfect sincerity. "Take my word for it, I've learned the hard way that money does not buy happiness. The last twelve years I've had more money than we ever dreamed of having when we were little, and I've been miserable. It's been a nightmare."

"It's over now." He was chewing the last bite of pizza, but his eyes were suddenly keen on her face. "You're never going back there again."

Maggy sipped her Coke.

"How come you've never married?" She was genuinely curious about this, but she also wanted to change the subject. Her future was something she didn't even want to think about at the moment. Even considering going back to Lyle made her stomach tighten with fear and her skin crawl with revulsion, but David was the stumbling block. She could not, would not, abandon David. And Lyle would never let David go. But she wouldn't think about that now. Later, a few days from now, a week, she would have to calmly consider her options, and weigh them, but not yet. She wasn't ready yet.

"Now why do you think, Magdalena?" Nick shot her a wry glance, chugged the last few ounces of beer, and signaled for the waitress.

"That's not an answer."

"Because I never met another woman who could fill the hole you left in my heart."

It was charming, but, "Truth?" she asked again with a flickering smile.

"Cross my heart and hope to die, may dogs chew on my bones if I lie."

There it was, the answer. The oath they had sworn as children whenever something was the absolute, unvarnished truth. Maggy stared at him as he handed the check and a twenty-dollar bill to the waitress, who came up just as he finished speaking.

He hadn't forgotten the oath. So there was something he was not telling her about his employment. Maggy thought about it, uncovered a stray hope that he wasn't a thief or a con artist or worse, and then decided that it didn't really matter very much after all. If she did find a way to divorce Lyle, she could always get a job. Twelve years ago, she'd been the best waitress the Harmony Inn had ever had.

What mattered was that for richer or poorer, better or worse, honesty or deception, what she wanted was to spend the rest of her life with Nick. Too bad she hadn't come to that realization twelve years ago. She would have spared them all a lot of grief.

"Ready?"

Maggy nodded. Nick stood up and waited for her to precede him out the door.

The dusty Ford pickup truck that had been the only vehicle left at the farm awaited them in the parking lot. Link had apparently taken the Corvette, and Nick had muttered a string of irate animadversions on his brother's character when he discovered the loss. Fortunately, the key had been in the truck's ignition, or they would have been condemned to eating burned steaks after all.

The truck's cab was so high off the ground that Maggy had to literally climb onto the bench seat. She winced as she bent too far forward and a pang of discomfort sliced across her rib cage, but fortunately the pain subsided as soon as she sat upright. Pulling Nick's coat closer around her shoulders as protection against the chill in the truck, she slid across the blue vinyl upholstery to unlock the driver's side door for Nick, who had already slammed her door and was walking around the cab. Mission accomplished, she scooted back toward the passenger door as he swung up behind the wheel.

"Whoa." He stopped her in mid-scoot with an arm dropped around her shoulders and a roguish smile. "Haven't you noticed how couples ride in pickup trucks around here? People'll think we're not natives if you go hugging the door."

"We wouldn't want them to think that." Given the fact that there was not a soul in sight, and she knew perfectly well that Nick wouldn't have cared what anybody thought in any case, it was a ridiculous argument. But she was perfectly content to be pulled back over to sit next to him. After he fished one end of the seat belt out from where it had slipped into the crack in the seat, she fastened the thing. By the time it clicked into place the truck was in motion. The heater blasted out warm air almost instantly, and Nick turned it down. Nick's body put out a heat of its own, and soon Maggy was too warm. She discarded his coat, throwing it over the back of the seat between herself and the door. Without the coat, she could feel Nick's right arm as it brushed hers every time he turned the wheel.

Maggy found that she thoroughly enjoyed the contact.

"Want to go for a ride?" he asked.

"Where to?"

"Oh, down memory lane."

"If you want to." She didn't know what he was talking about, and he didn't explain, but she didn't care. She was perfectly content to go wherever Nick took her. They hit the interstate, then crossed the bridge into Kentucky in companionable silence. It was only when he pulled off the Algonquin Parkway exit that she realized where he was heading.

"Parkway Place." She hadn't been back there for years, not since she had moved her father out of the projects. She had never wanted to go back, because to do so would be too painful. Not because of all that she had suffered when she lived there, but because of all she had lost when she left.

"I drove by here when I first got back into town. It hasn't changed a bit."

"I haven't been back in ten years."

Nick glanced sideways at her. "Roots, Magdalena," he said softly. "Sometimes you've got to get back to your roots."

She said nothing, but with growing eagerness searched for familiar landmarks. There was one, the Church of the Assumption on the corner, where Father John had once presided. The windows were boarded up now, and what was left of the roof was blackened and open to the night. The small wooden spire that had once served as a neighborhood beacon was missing entirely.

"Oh, look at the church," she caught his arm, pointing. Nick looked and shook his head.

"Burned out."

"I'm surprised they haven't fixed it—or torn it down."

"Not here, baby. You've been living in the white-bread world too long. Things don't get fixed down here."

It was so true that Maggy couldn't refute it. Looking out the window, she was jolted back into the past by the sights that met her eyes. Shacklike houses were jammed in next to factories, stores, and warehouses. Many of the buildings appeared to be deserted. A few, like the church, bore signs of having burned. More were boarded up. The smell from nearby industries permeated everything, even managing to waft through the rolled-up windows of the truck. Green space was at a precious minimum, and what little there was was jealously guarded by rusty chain link fences. Uneven sidewalks ran the length of the streets, but though it was only about nine o'clock, there was no one out. This was a high crime area. Only shadowy types scurried about in the darkness, back away from the streets where the chances of being seen were less. Prudent folks stayed inside, out of harm's way.

Maggy had forgotten what it had been like.

Suddenly, ahead and to the left, loomed Parkway Place. Maggy's eyes widened as she took in the barrackslike cluster of buildings. Built around a small courtyard that then had managed to grow only the scraggliest of grass, the yellow-brick buildings were even grungier than she remembered. The boxlike structures were adorned with ugly aluminum windows, a few of which sported battered air-conditioning units jutting from their sills like blunt metal noses, and tired-looking concrete stoops beneath drooping V-shaped roofs. The residents had gained more parking since Maggy had resided there: the concrete around the buildings was all encompassing now, with not a blade of grass nor, God forbid, a tree in sight.

Sharp popping sounds from the direction of Seventh Street Road caused her to stiffen instinctively. The sound was familiar, though she had not heard it in years: gunshots. Exposure to not-too-distant gunfire had once been an unremarkable part of her existence.

From the next street over came the rumble of semis. That sound, too, was part and parcel of her childhood. If one lived in Parkway Place, the constant noise made by the big trucks was an inescapable fact of life.

A stooped old man pushing a grocery cart full of unidentifiable items emerged from between the buildings, staring blindly down at the sidewalk in front of him as he made his way up the street. About fifty feet behind him followed three teenage boys in denim jackets and backward baseball caps, poking each other in the ribs and laughing.

It didn't require a lot of imagination to guess that somewhere farther along the street, perhaps in front of a closed warehouse or an abandoned store, a confrontation would take place, with results that might prove disastrous to the old man.

"There's your apartment." Nick had turned into the complex and was pointing. Maggy looked up at the three pairs of lighted fourth-story windows behind which she had passed her childhood and felt a shock of recognition. In a sudden explosion of long-forgotten emotion, she remembered in exquisite, excruciating detail what it had been like to be a child in this place, remembered how it had felt to have her father passed out on the floor and no food in the house, remembered being cold and hungry and alone, remembered being scared.

But she remembered good times, too, when her father was sober. And most of all, she remembered Nick.

"Your apartment's over there." She pointed across the complex. Lights blazed from the windows of his former residence, too. In fact, lights shown through nearly all the windows. The apartments were poor, and dingy, and small, but they also had a crucial redeeming feature: they were unbelievably cheap, with rent based on the tenant's ability to pay. Her own father had been committed to the ridiculous sum of five dollars a month. She was sure the amounts had gone up some since then, but not much. As a result, Maggy doubted that a single unit was empty.

"It hasn't changed much, has it?" Nick spoke ruefully, his expression almost sad as he took in the concrete wasteland in which they had grown up. "When I was a kid, I couldn't wait to get out of here."

"Me either," Maggy said. They were both silent as he circled the parking lot and headed back to the street.

"There's the ball field." Nick nodded off to his left. "Remember when you used to come watch me play ball?"

"Remember how none of you guys would let me play on your team because I was a girl?" There was half-humorous accusation in her tone as she poked him admonishingly in the ribs. "I could hit as well as most of the guys, too, and I ran faster than all of you."

"That's why we didn't want you to play," Nick said, grinning. A yellow-and-red neon sign loomed up on the right.

"Oh, look, the McDonald's is still here," Maggy squealed. Like everything else she had seen, the restaurant where she and Nick had first met as children was a little dirtier and looked a little more dilapidated, but was basically unchanged. A large blue Dumpster still claimed pride of place in the back. A skinny black mongrel nosed hopefully around its base.

"Wonder if that's the same Dumpster?" Nick had spotted it, too.

Maggy shrugged. "Surely not. This one's got a lid."

"Good thought. Keep hungry little girls out at all costs."

Maggy sobered at the thought. "I wonder if there are very many hungry children around here tonight."

She thought of David, her brilliant, beautiful, beloved boy, and shuddered. Whatever evils had resulted from her actions, and they had been many and varied, at least her child was not growing up in the grinding poverty she had once known. The cost to herself had been great, but she had saved him from that.

Maybe what she had done had not been so hideously terrible after all. Oh, it had been wrong, she knew that now clear through to her bone marrow, but maybe it was not completely unforgivable. She had done what she felt she had to do at the time to provide for her child. And she *had* provided for him. David had had the best of everything, always. Even love. Lots of love, from his mother and grandmother and even Lyle. David had never lacked for anything in his life.

Then her glance swung to Nick, and she mentally amended that. Still, she felt a lightening of her spirit and realized that it was because she was at last beginning to forgive herself.

"Remember this place?" Nick asked softly. Lost in her own private ruminations, she hadn't realized that he'd once again pulled off the street.

"The warehouse," she said, as a quick sweep of her surroundings told her where they were. The warehouse where she had parked with Nick after the debacle in the Pink Pussycat and tried to stanch the blood pouring from his nose. The warehouse where he had kissed her for the first time.

"I told you, memory lane," he said with a flickering grin and pulled the truck around to the back, where he parked far away from the single yellowy light that was attached to the warehouse roof and provided the only illumination.

He unfastened his seat belt and reached over to unfasten hers. Then he lifted her carefully, gently, onto his lap.

*M*aggy could have stopped him at any time, but she didn't. It was as if their journey to Parkway Place had been a trip back through time as well. For however long the feeling lasted, she was the young Magdalena Garcia again, and she was wild about Nick.

When he kissed her mouth, she wrapped her arms around his neck. When his lips slid down to the underside of her chin, she tilted her head to give him greater access. When his hand moved across her silk blouse to cover her breast, she shivered and arched her back.

His hand was warm and strong, his hold on her possessive. He rubbed his fingers across her nipple, and the sensation of pleasure was so intense that Maggy's toes curled in their shoes.

She kissed him then, quite of her own volition, her lips finding his and opening over them, her tongue sliding into his mouth. He responded, but no more, letting her escalate the kiss. Maggy could feel the growing tension in his body as he held himself in check, waiting for her to set the pace.

Nick would never force her to do anything she didn't want to do. The knowledge had always been there, a fact of which Maggy was absolutely certain, but now it emerged to give her a new sense of freedom. She was half lying across his lap, her nape resting on the arm that curved around her, her knees tucked against his side. The back of her head pressed against the driver's side window, but she wasn't even aware of the hard cold glass. The steering wheel brushed her shoulder, but she wasn't aware of that, either, any more than she felt the slight soreness around her ribs when she moved.

Every atom of her being was focused on Nick.

"You smell good," Nick whispered in her ear as he caressed her lobe with his lips.

"White Linen," Maggy replied, her brain still able to function though her voice was less than steady.

"What?" He didn't seem to be quite as lucid as she.

"It's the name of the perfume I wear."

"Oh. You must dab it behind your ears."

"Yes, I do."

"I can tell." His mouth was nuzzling the tender spot directly beneath her ear, which meant that his nose would be in just the right position to get the full effect of the expensive perfume that she applied every day as automatically as lipstick. Always before, she had done it for herself, just because she liked the smell. From this night forward, she would do it for Nick.

"The scent makes me dizzy. *You* make me dizzy," he said.

"Do I?" It was a mere breath, stopped by his mouth moving to cover hers again. He kissed her, his lips warm and ardent, his tongue growing more insistent as it explored her mouth. He tasted a little of cigarettes and a lot of beer, and the latter taste triggered a memory that she had long ago almost forgotten: when he had kissed her that first time, here in this very parking lot, he had tasted of beer, too. The recollection was suddenly crystal clear, and as it unfolded in her mind Maggy felt a rush of warmth, along with an odd sensation of bonelessness. He was kissing her gently, considerately, holding himself in check, and he was thrilling her down to the ground.

Her hand roved up over the smooth cotton of his shirt to the vee opening. Her fingers touched his neck, found the warm hollow at its base, and slid down to discover the uppermost reaches of the wedge of black hair that covered his chest. Below that, the buttons of his shirt waited. She toyed with one, unable to make up her mind what she should do. His breathing suddenly rasped in her ear. Then his hand was brushing hers aside, and he was undoing the buttons himself.

"Touch me," he whispered, taking her hand and pressing it against the hard masculine flesh he had partially bared. With her hand flattened over his heart, Maggy could feel its thudding beat. He held her hand there, and for a moment, just a moment, she started to panic at being constrained even in so small a thing. But then he took a deep breath and withdrew his hand.

Her hand stayed where it was.

His skin was warm and faintly moist, his pectorals firmly defined and covered with crisp black hair. She moved her fingers cautiously. When nothing frightening happened she grew bolder, sliding her hand from one side of his chest to the other, feeling the dips and valleys, the tensile strength of the muscles that underlay the hairy warmth of his skin.

Her exploring fingers found his left nipple, rubbed across its surface, felt it spring to pebbly attention. Entranced, she glanced down at her handiwork, and flicked her pink-painted thumbnail back and forth over the stalwart nub.

Watching too, he gave what sounded like a strangled groan and grabbed her hand.

"Bad idea," he said in a tone that was completely unlike his normal one.

"Really? Why?" She was all melting innocence as she looked up at him, but she knew what she was doing to him perfectly well, and he knew she knew. It was there in the hot gleam of his eyes, in the almost grim set of his mouth. She was teasing him, toying with him, trying to rouse his passion, and he was willing to let her without any intention of making her pay the usual price.

"Because you're really, really turning me on." He returned her hand to the relative safety of his shoulder. She grinned in delight. He grimaced at her. Even as she was deciding what other naughty delights to sample, he dipped his head to hers again.

For an instant, the merest instant, there was nothing at all gentle about his kiss. He kissed her as if he could never get enough of her, as if he were starving for the taste of her mouth. He kissed her hotly, he kissed her passionately, he kissed her as if he meant to take her straight to bed.

Maggy stiffened. And then, before instinctive fear could do more than lift a cautionary head, his kiss deliberately gentled.

The gentleness did it, because she knew how dearly it cost him. He was holding himself on an iron leash for her. Maggy absorbed the thought and measured the depth and breadth of the emotion that prompted it. As she did, she felt a nearly forgotten fire flicker to life inside her, growing in nanoseconds to a heat so intense that it threatened to melt her bones.

She curled her arms around his neck and kissed him back with sudden wild excitement. Pressing her still-covered breasts to the bareness of his chest, she closed her eyes as the pleasure of it made her feel light-headed. She threaded her hands through his hair, and the sensation of his crisp curls twining around her fingers was intoxicating.

The place between her legs throbbed. The throbbing demanded immediate attention. She pressed that part of herself against him too, and to her mingled pleasure and frustration encountered the hard bone of his hip.

With an instinct as old as the human species, she rubbed herself against that unyielding surface.

"Jesus H. Christ!" His groan sounded pained. His mouth slid from her lips down the length of her neck, nibbling and sucking and licking over her yielding flesh. At the same time, so swiftly that she was taken by surprise, his hands were on her bottom. He cupped her cheeks through the soft knit pants, squeezing and kneading as he shifted positions behind the wheel so that he was stretched out along the seat as much as possible. With his hands on her rump he pulled her on top of him, maneuvering her so that she was lying full against him, her breasts on his chest, her legs between his bent knees. Her hands clutched at his hair as he kissed the throbbing pulse at the base of her neck.

His hands slid under her armpits, lifting her above him. His mouth moved down the front of her blouse, over the swell of her right breast, and stopped at the crest. For a moment his lips rested there, pressing into her and parted against her but not moving. Maggy felt the heat of his mouth through two layers of cloth and tingled all over. Her breasts engorged in fierce response, and her nipples hardened until they were stiffly erect, straining to experience more fully the promise of his mouth. He bit down on her nipple, sending a bolt of erotic pleasure rocketing clear down to her toes.

Maggy moaned, and her fingers tightened on his scalp.

He bit her nipple again, sucked on it, drew it inside his mouth. The sensation of his hungry lips nuzzling at her breast, along with the hot wetness of her blouse and bra against her erect nipple, was so exquisite that she felt a sudden clenching in her loins.

His mouth left her breast to travel up over her throat as he slid her back down his body. At the friction of her body against his, Maggy moaned again, the sound blatantly sexual, and, as such, shocking to her own ears. Nick glanced up, and the hot green glitter of his eyes made her melt inside. With a sound that was a cross between a curse and a growl he pulled her head down to his.

He kissed her wetly, deeply, his hands once again seeking for and finding her rump. He stroked the soft roundness, and then his hands molded her shape, fingers meeting in the crevice between the curving halves. His grip on her bottom tightened, and his palms flattened over her cheeks, pressing her down, so that she could feel the steel-rod bulge in his pants against the apex of her thighs.

"I want you. Christ, I want you." The words were growled into her mouth, and Maggy swallowed them with her kiss. Her head was spinning so that she was incapable of conscious thought. Her body was quivering with need, wonderful, glorious, burning need.

She wanted him. The realization burst inside her like a rocket on the Fourth of July.

The hands that had been cupping her buttocks slid down between her thighs. Without ever touching bare skin, they caressed the weeping heart of her through her pants, running back and forth over her quivering flesh until, mindless, she opened her legs and moaned for more. He was sweating, his tongue in her mouth, his heart galloping against her breasts.

With one hand he continued his erotic game, rubbing between her legs. The barrier of the cloth between his fingers and her body added to the excitement. His other hand she completely lost track of, until suddenly it was between them, squeezing her breasts, tormenting her nipples anew.

Time rolled back. Everything was as it had been before. It was as if she were a teenager again, and Nick was the neighborhood stud she had panted after for years. She wanted him—and he was obliging, making her crazy with his hands and mouth and body.

Maggy was on fire. Her legs writhed helplessly as his hard thighs slid between them, parting them so that now her legs lay along the outside with his bent between them. The sensation was mind-blowing. Her arms locked around his neck in a stranglehold of desire. The kiss she gave back to him was avid and hungry and begging all at the same time.

When his hand left her breasts, she felt the loss almost as a physical pain—until that same hand turned up again, this time sliding down inside the waistband of her pants.

The feel of his warm, strong fingers stroking down the softness of her belly, discovering the silky edge of her bikini panties, and sliding inside, was so unbearably exquisite that she trembled all over, gasping her pleasure into his mouth.

Suddenly his hand was deep inside her panties, covering the silky triangle of curls, stroking and squeezing as it reawakened her to the shattering imperative of a woman's desire.

The aching within her intensified until she was squirming with it, her thighs quivering, her breath coming in great wheezing gulps—and then he found the tiny pulse point from which her greatest pleasure radiated, and touched it.

Maggy dissolved in a hot sea of bliss.

As she melted in his arms, his kiss turned fierce, demanding. His hold on her tightened, keeping her still, and his fingers slid inside her body, penetrating deeply, invading her. She gasped, and still his fingers moved in and out while his body suddenly thrust upward, ramrod stiff. . . .

"No!" Maggy shrieked the protest into his mouth, fighting against the imprisoning arms, the tongue that threatened to gag her, the fingers that impaled her. His iron-hard pelvis ground into her again, and she knew that he was just moments away from throwing her onto her back and mounting her. "No, no, no!"

"Jesus!" It was part curse, part prayer. Unbelievably to Maggy in her moment of extremism, the hand that violated her withdrew abruptly, and the arm that imprisoned her pushed her away. Still in the grip of that unreasoning fear, Maggy scrambled to her knees, scooting back along the seat to hug the passenger door as he dragged himself into a sitting position. Then, after a brief, glittering glance at her, he opened the cab door and almost fell out into the dark parking lot. Crouched at the far end of the bench seat, Maggy watched tensely as he sucked in great gulps of cold air.

25

*H*is shirt was unbuttoned to the waist, allowing her to glimpse a wide vee of solid masculine chest, well covered with hair. His heaving shoulders were almost as wide as the open truck door. His torso was lean and hard, his legs long and powerful. His arms were thick with muscle, his hands, curled into fists at the moment, large and capable.

If he had not wanted to let her go, she could not have escaped him. The fact of it was there, stated implicitly in the tall, strong body. But he had released her, despite the discomfort it had obviously caused him, at her protest.

These thoughts jumbled together in her mind as she eyed him warily. Gradually she became aware of other, less threatening attributes of his: the night-black waves of his hair, disordered now by her hands, washed with silver by the rising moon. The ruggedly carved symmetry of his features, the deep dimple at the side of his mouth, the sheer outrageous handsomeness of him.

Nick.

"Oh, God, I'm sorry." Maggy said it quietly, her hands pressing hard against her cheeks.

He turned to look at her then, one hand braced against the open door, and saw how she huddled on the seat, her knees drawn up to her chin, her hands almost covering her face.

"It's all right." He drew in another great gulp of the cold night air. "I'm all right. Hell, the question is, are you all right?"

"I couldn't help it." Her voice was tiny. "It just—happens. It isn't you."

"I know. I'm not mad about it. Just give me a minute to pull myself together, okay?"

"Okay." He shut the door, and she watched, through the windshield, as he took a quick jog to the end of the parking lot and back. When he opened the door again, he was flushed and windblown, but calmer.

"I'm going to get in now, and we're going home. Nothing for you to worry about at all." He said it in the kind of soothing tone one might use with an edgy wild beast.

"I'm not worried." She was still too shaken to find the humor in the cautious glance he cast her before he swung up behind the wheel.

"Put your seat belt on." He shut the door and glanced over at her. Maggy, still curled into the farthest possible corner of the seat, put her feet on the floorboard and drew the shoulder-and-lap belt around herself. A good two feet of blue vinyl separated them this time as Nick set the truck in motion.

For a long time they were silent. The truck was on the bridge, with the black waters of the Ohio flowing serenely far below and the glittering backdrop of Louisville's well-lit skyline receding behind them, when Nick looked her way.

"Okay?" he asked softly.

Maggy nodded.

"Magdalena . . ."

She glanced at him.

"Don't you think it's about time you told me what he did to scare you so of sex?" His voice was unbelievably gentle, his expression warm and caring. Maggy cringed.

"I can't."

"I think you should."

"I can't bear to remember."

"Please. For both our sakes."

"Nick . . ." It was a mumbled plea for mercy.

"Would it help if I told you that I already know he's gay?"

"What?" Startled, Maggy turned to stare at him.

"Lyle Forrest is gay."

"No," she said. "No. That's not true."

"Magdalena, I've seen pictures . . ."

"They're wrong," she said numbly. "He's not gay. He's not even bi, really. He's basically—asexual, and a voyeur, I guess the word is. He likes to watch, and cause—pain."

"I have pictures . . ."

"Look at them again," she said quietly. "I'm sure they don't show him engaging in actual intercourse with anyone. Do they?"

His brow wrinkled as he tried to remember. "They show him in leather, with a variety of—sex toys, is the best way I can think of to describe them. Different ones, basically, in each shot. He's with a naked man, who's bound to some sort of contraption that has him bent almost double, right in front of ol' Lyle. Couldn't identify Mr. Bare-ass, because the shots we got were of his backside." A faint grin flickered over his face and was gone. "But ol' Lyle was unmistakable. We assumed from those pictures, and some other information that we had, that our boy was gay, and into some kinky stuff—sort of his own interpretation of the gay-biker-bar scene."

"We?" Magdalena's response was sharp as she grasped at every available straw that would enable her to postpone having to tell Nick what he wanted, and yes, she even admitted, needed to know. Her nerves were suddenly, screamingly on edge, because she realized that sooner or later she was going to have to tell him everything. Things she had never told another living soul. Things she could hardly bear to think of herself. Things that it made her sick to remember.

But she wouldn't tell him *everything*. Not all at once. One piece of the puzzle she would keep to herself. One piece she would hide for as long as she could, until she had figured out how best to tell him, or even if to tell him.

She had to tell him. She already knew it, no matter how much she might fear his reaction. And she did fear it. Because the fact that Nick was back and loved her was the closest thing to a miracle God had sent her for a long, long time. She didn't want to jeopardize that one second sooner than she had to.

"Link and I." Nick's response took a shade too long, and the glance that accompanied it was guarded. It was almost as if the "we" had slipped out by accident, and he was trying to cover his mistake. But Maggy was too focused on something else he had revealed to take any real notice. She registered the impression of deceit, and filed it away, without considering it consciously for more than a split second.

"How on earth did you get pictures of Lyle doing—that? He—he's very secretive about his sex life. Not many people have the slightest idea what he is, and I can't imagine him letting anyone take pictures."

"He didn't exactly *let* anyone. He didn't know it was being done."

"You spied on him? When? Why?"

"*I* didn't. He's got plenty of enemies besides me. One of them did."

Nick's eyes were focused ahead of them as he turned off the interstate onto the twisty roads that led into southern Indiana's back country. The rolling hills through which they traveled were dotted with farms, and cows and chickens outnumbered human inhabitants by about fifty to one. Around them the night was still, with only the occasional light in a farmhouse or barn to push away the dark. Nick drove cautiously, as befitted one who was just becoming accustomed to the hazard posed by free-roaming deer and wandering cattle. The bright beams of the truck sliced through utter blackness to reveal what was ahead—but they were useless for anything farther than twenty feet away.

"I imagine the original intent was to use the photos as leverage, you know, blackmail. Just like someone meant to use the ones of you dancing for blackmail. But before the pics of Lyle could be used, the guy who set it up took a powder. The pictures didn't, though, and when I started doing a little research into your hubby, they surfaced. Cost a pretty penny, but worth every bit of it."

"Just like the tape and pictures of me surfaced."

"Just like that." He cast her a quick, weighing glance.

"What are you doing here, Nick?" she asked quietly. "Really?"

"I told you, baby, I came back for you."

"That's a load of crap."

He sent a quick, unreadable glance her way. "It's the truth, Magdalena, I swear to God."

"Don't lie to me, Nick. Please."

He sighed. "All right. You want the whole truth, and nothing but the truth? I did come back for you, to see you again, to see if you could possibly be as beautiful and bright and funny and strong as I remembered, to see if there was anything left of 'us.' I knew that coming back would have one of two results: you would have been his wife for so long that the girl I remembered was gone, or you could be—as you are. Mine. My girl, always and forever. You know it, too."

Maggy chose not to acknowledge that last for the moment, though she knew without any doubt at all that it was so. Hadn't she always been his girl? The twelve years they'd been apart were beginning to seem no more substantial than a dream—no, a nightmare. But something less than real.

"I still don't understand how—or why—you came across those pictures—the ones of Lyle and the ones of me—and bought them. Where did you get them, and what were you going to do with them?"

"There are all kinds of sleazy individuals in the nightclub business, and news travels through it like a brush fire. When I put out the word that I wanted information on Lyle, and was willing to pay, material flowed in thick and fast. The pictures, all of them, were just the tip of the iceberg. The ones of you I was going to make sure never saw the light of day. The ones of him—I was going to use them as needed. They are a weapon, Magdalena, as powerful as any gun."

"Blackmail."

"Persuasion—and revenge. Did you know that I came to see you, after you got back from your honeymoon? Married or not, did you really think I would let you go so easily? I was going to throw a jealous fit, drag you away and all that—but I never got the chance. You were nowhere to be seen, but your husband was. He had me thrown off his property. I think I even did something dramatic like yell 'Magdalena!' at the top of my lungs a dozen times as I was dragged away."

"I didn't know." Maggy's stomach churned. The idea that Nick had come for her and she hadn't known—if he had seen her, would it have changed everything?

"I realize that. I figured out pretty fast that he would never tell you. He was afraid he'd lose you if he did. And he would have, sooner or later. You would have come to your senses, realized that you belonged with me, not him. I knew it, and I wasn't going to give up. I was going to come back again and again until I was at least able to talk to you. To tell you that I would change, do anything you wanted, if only you would come back to me."

He glanced over at her as if to gauge her reaction to what he was saying, and continued. "That night four punks were waiting when I came out of the apartment and got in my car. They forced their way in after me, dragged me into the backseat at gunpoint, and drove me north. I thought it was your garden-variety senseless crime for a while. I didn't get the picture until we made Cleveland and pulled into a deserted park overlooking some river. They yanked me out of the car, said, 'This is a message from Mr. Forrest—you should have stayed the hell away from his wife!' and started working me over. When they finished with me, I was unconscious. They stuffed me behind the wheel of my car, wedged my foot down on the gas, and put it in drive. It was parked on an overhang some twenty feet above the water, and the water there was deep. When the car went over with me in it, I'm sure they thought I'd never see daylight again. But the shock of the water woke me up, and I managed to get out of the car. I don't remember a lot after that, but I was told that a fisherman found me clinging to a log not far from shore and took me to a hospital. It took six months for me to recover enough to get back to Louisville. The first thing I did was hotfoot it to Windermere. There were blue balloons tied with ribbons all over the front gates. Your child had just been born."

Nick took a deep breath, remembering, while Maggy stared at him in growing horror. She hadn't known. *She hadn't known.*

"I decided to leave you alone. You had his baby. That made you his more than mine."

Guilt and pain combined to twist Maggy's insides like a sheet being fed into a wringer. She was utterly speechless, but something of what she was feeling must have shown in her eyes, because he gave her a wry smile.

"I couldn't ever get you out of my mind. Not a day went by in twelve years that I didn't think of you. None of the women I was with meant a thing, compared to the way I had felt about you. I almost got married once, until I realized that I'd leave the girl behind in a heartbeat if the Magdalena I remembered crooked her little finger at me. Then I knew —I had to lay this thing that was between us to rest once and for all, or I had to get you back. It took a while, I had to make plans—but here I am. Like I said, I came back for you."

"Oh, Nick." She couldn't find any other words. There *were* no words, to express the emotions that were warring inside her: love and thankfulness and shame and guilt, all mixed up together.

"Glad I did?" he asked, striving for a lighthearted tone and failing utterly.

"Yes," she whispered with tears in her eyes. "Oh, yes."

Unbuckling her seat belt, she slid across the seat to wrap her arms around his neck and press a kiss to his sandpaper cheek.

He slipped an arm about her shoulders and dipped his head to kiss her. The truck swerved toward the side of the road. He jerked back to attention, righting the truck just as a horn blared behind them. A car swept by on the left in a blinding glare of headlights, oblivious of the fact that passing was illegal on the two-lane road.

"Damned lovesick kids!" the driver yelled out the window. With another cheery honk it proceeded to roar off into the night.

"Link," Nick said in disgust. "In my car. If he wrecks it, I'm going to wring his neck."

Maggy had been too wrapped up in Nick to identify either car or driver. But Nick's tone made her laugh, though her laugh was shaky. With both hands she reached up to wipe the incipient tears from her eyes. She felt as though she'd already shed enough tears to last a lifetime. She certainly wasn't crying any more today.

"I'm glad I have you guys to kick around with again," she said in as light a tone as she could muster. "It's been boring around here with you gone."

"Oh, so that's all we're good for, eh? Comic relief?"

Maggy poked him in the ribs. Nick flinched away from her fingers, flicked a glance at her, and smiled.

26

$\mathcal{T}$he Corvette was parked in front of the farmhouse when they pulled up, and every light in the house appeared to be on. Nick made a face as he cut the engine and doused the lights.

"If we're lucky, he's alone," he said.

"And if we're not?"

"He's got a bevy of babes with him. He says that the Corvette is better for attracting 'em than a six-inch-thick roll of hundred-dollar bills." Nick glanced at her and grinned. "But he wouldn't bring chicks like that around with you here. I don't think."

"Great. You're giving me so much to look forward to." Maggy scooted away from him and reached for the door handle.

"Magdalena," he said softly, catching her arm.

"What?" She glanced around.

"Wait a minute, would you please? I meant to save it till we got inside, but Link's being here killed that. I want to know what Lyle did to scare you of sex."

Maggy's hand froze on the handle. "I don't want to talk about it, Nick," she said in a tiny voice. "Please."

"Querida, can't you tell me?" His voice was very gentle.

Maggy took a deep breath and closed her eyes. She didn't want to see the pictures in her mind again—but she was going to tell Nick. It was inevitable. If not now, then soon, and it might as well be now. Then she would have it over and done with, and maybe, just maybe, without his constant irritation of the wound she could once again bury the night-mare deep in her subconscious where it had dwelt for so long.

"He beat me up, held me down, and let his brother-in-law rape me," she said in a flat voice. Then she pulled her arm free of his slackened grip and got out of the cab. The cold air caught her in its icy fist. She never even felt it.

Nick was beside her before she had gone two feet.

"Magdalena." He caught her by the shoulders and turned her to face him. "My God, Magdalena, do you mean Hamilton Drummond?"

"The very same." She laughed bitterly. "Can you believe it? I couldn't. Sometimes I still can't."

"My God," he said again, sounding nearly as stunned as she'd felt all those years ago. But she wasn't going to remember how she'd felt. She wasn't going to let herself remember. She slammed a mental door on the reel that was starting to unfold of its own volition in her mind, crossed her arms over her chest to ward off the memories as much as the chill, and averted her face from Nick. She couldn't stand to watch him as she spoke.

"I'm going to tell you this once, and then we're never going to talk about it again, understand?" she said in a fierce whisper that was all she could force out past her aching throat. "During my pregnancy, Lyle never touched me. No sex, understand? I thought it was because he was afraid of hurting the baby, or maybe because he was repelled by my body. Who knew? While I was pregnant, it was no big deal. Afterward, I was so wrapped up in David that I never thought about it for about eight months. Then I started to worry. I wanted my marriage to work, and how could it work if Lyle never touched me? He was not physically abusive then—I was being a good girl, doing everything he said, being meek and quiet and adoring, and of course there was David—and I foolishly thought he was holding back to spare me. Well, I wasn't in love with him, but I thought that if our marriage was normal, I might learn to. So I started trying to seduce him. You know, slinky nighties, the whole bit. Nothing worked. One night I put on this fancy black negligee, did my hair and makeup, doused myself in perfume, and went along the hall to his room. It was about two o'clock in the morning, and my grand plan was to climb in bed with him and turn him on so much that he would stop thinking about me solely as David's mother. He always slept with his door locked—I knew, because I had tried the midnight seduc-tion bit once before—but I had taken care of that. I conned a key out of Louella."

Maggy took a deep breath and focused on the light that was pouring out through the farmhouse's front window. She hugged herself tighter, but not because of the cold. Memories were flooding her mind, jumbled images of horror, and she couldn't look at Nick in case her reaction was mirrored in his face. He stood as unmoving as she, his hands curled around her shoulders, his eyes fixed on her averted face. She knew they were, because she could feel the weight of them. But as she spoke she never once looked at him. She could not, would not look at him. It was all she could do to continue speaking.

"Quiet as a mouse, I unlocked his door and slipped inside. He has a suite, you know. A sitting room with a bedroom adjoining it. The sitting room was dark, but there was a faint light under the bedroom door. I thought he might be reading in bed. I thought it was kind of sweet, if he was. I almost chickened out because he was awake, but then I decided to go for it. For David's sake, I really wanted to be a wife to my husband."

Maggy paused again, steeling her courage, then plunged on. "I crept across the sitting room, opened the bedroom door as quietly as I could —and nearly died there and then. Lyle was awake, all right. He was standing in a corner of the room, naked, watching as Ham humped one of the teenage gardener boys in his bed."

Nick made an indecipherable comment under his breath. Still unable to look at him, Maggy gripped her own elbows and took a deep, shuddering breath. "They saw me—how could they not? I would have run, but Lyle grabbed me. The boy snatched his clothes and left. I said some things to Lyle—I don't remember what, I was pretty much in shock— and he slapped me. I hit him back, and then—he beat me up. And—and the rest."

"He let his brother-in-law rape you." Nick's words were a mere thread of sound, but incredulity and rage both came through.

"Yes. He—he watched, telling Ham what to do, cheering him on the whole time. Af—afterward, Lyle told me that if I told anyone, he'd kill me. By that time, I believed him. When they—let me go, I crept back to my room. I was in shock, I guess, because I don't remember much. I know I got dressed and put on a coat and shoes and got my purse, which had some money in it. Then I went along the hall to get David. I wasn't going to leave without David. It was just dawn, because light was starting to filter in through the window at the top of the stairs. Lyle caught me coming out of the nursery. He took the baby, slapped me around, told me that I could leave if I wanted but not with the baby. The baby was his, and I would never see him again if I left him. And he went back in David's nursery and locked the door."

Maggy closed her eyes. "How could I leave without David? I couldn't.

I went back to my room, meaning to try to slip away the next day, or the next, whenever I could sneak David out of the house. But Lyle knew what I was going to do. He hired a woman, a dragon-lady type, named Miss Hadley. She was to be David's nanny. Lyle told her not to let the baby out of her sight, that I was a little deranged and might do him harm. Miss Hadley guarded him night and day. She was always, always with us."

The memories were coming back now, thick and fast. Maggy's stomach churned, and her mind shrank from the images that whirled through it. "I called a lawyer, anonymously, and asked what my legal situation was. Lyle found out—he always finds out everything—and told me that if I started spreading malicious gossip about him, he'd have me committed to a mental institution. He would, too. And he could. Still."

Her voice shook on the last word, and she jerked away from Nick and headed toward the house. Whether he followed or not she didn't know, because she broke into a run. Link, probably anticipating their arrival, had left the front door unlocked. She burst through it, stumbled past a surprised-looking Link, and barely made it to the toilet before she vomited.

Maggy stayed in the bathroom for a long time, kneeling in front of the toilet, eyes closed, head resting back against the cool tile wall as the spasms subsided. Weakly, she wished that she could empty her mind as easily as she emptied her stomach.

But the memories of that night were never going to completely go away. All she could do was rebury them and hope that the passage of time continued to dull their impact. How long had it been already? Ten years? And she had finally told someone, told Nick. She hadn't even cried.

Maybe, given enough time, the terrible wound might heal.

The fear that raised its head on the heels of that thought was as ugly as any that had gone before: would Nick feel differently toward her, now that he knew?

No, not Nick. Her heart knew it instantly, instinctively. Nick would be outraged for her, not with her. As he had said, he was on her side.

Still, it was a long, long time before she finally got up the combination of strength and nerve that she needed to leave the bathroom.

Nick was sitting in the living room, the big easy chair moved from its previous position so that he could see the bathroom door, a floorlamp behind the chair providing the only light. The TV was on. She heard its noise, though she couldn't see it from where she stood. All she could see was Nick. He was watching the bathroom door as she emerged, and he looked tired and drawn as he met her gaze.

"It's all right, baby," he said, getting to his feet and coming swiftly toward her. With shaky knees she crossed the small space that separated them to meet him halfway. As she reached him his arms opened for her, and with a wordless murmur she collapsed into them. They closed around her, hugging her close, while he buried his face in her hair. Then he swept her up off her feet and walked back into the living room with her, where he sat down with her cuddled on his lap.

For a long time they stayed like that, holding each other, unmoving, unspeaking, as the TV blared in the background. If Nick had any idea what was on, it was more than Maggy did. But she didn't think he knew any more than she.

"Run her a bath, would you?" Nick said after a time. Maggy hardly stirred, certainly did not look around, but she knew he was talking to Link. Link's reply was inaudible, but moments later she heard the hum of water rushing through the pipes overhead as water filled what was presumably an upstairs bath.

"Magdalena," Nick said then, as if Link's entry into the room and then the sound of the water running had brought him back from wherever his thoughts had taken him. "You know I love you."

Maggy nodded, her face still hidden against his shoulder. She'd always known that.

"You trust me, don't you?"

Again she nodded.

"Then listen here: you don't have to be afraid of Forrest or any of that bunch anymore. I give you my word. Something's coming down—don't ask me what, because I can't tell you—that's going to take care of the problem. They are going to get, maybe not what's coming to them, but close enough. You won't ever have to see Forrest again. And he won't be in any position to argue over custody of David."

"Nick . . ." Maggy absorbed all that, frowned, and sat up. "What are you talking about?" A dreadful suspicion popped into her mind. She had known Nick almost all her life, and, while he was not a quick-tempered man, his anger, when it was aroused, was formidable. And he never forgot anything. Not any kindness, not any insult. Certainly not something like what Lyle had had done to him all those years ago, let alone Lyle's offenses against herself.

"You're not going to murder him, are you? Or hire a hit man?" she asked anxiously.

Nick actually laughed. "It's tempting," he said. "Real tempting."

"But if you get caught . . . Nick, I couldn't bear it if you got caught."

"Relax. I'm not gonna get caught, because I'm not going to murder anybody. Forrest and his cronies are going to be taken care of another way. Perfectly legally."

"How?"

"Now that I can't tell you. You'll just have to trust me," Nick said. "I wouldn't have told you anything about it, but I don't want you to be afraid anymore. No more, do you hear?"

"Are you sure—about Lyle?" Maggy whispered, wanting but hardly daring to believe.

"I'm sure. Trust me, Magdalena. I'm sure."

"Bath's ready," Link called from upstairs.

Nick glanced toward the open living room door, then back at Maggy's face. Pale and tousled and woebegone and unattractive as she knew she must be, his eyes still softened when they looked at her. His hands came up to smooth the hair back from her forehead and cheeks, and then his arms were sliding around her back and under her knees as he stood up with her in his arms.

"I can walk," Maggy protested as he headed toward the hall with her.

"I know," he said mildly, and when she would have protested more, he silenced her by dropping a kiss on her parted lips.

Later, after she was finished with her bath, she dressed in the over-sized white T-shirt Nick had given her for use as a nightgown. From its very hugeness (it hung to her knees and could easily have wrapped around her torso twice), she guessed it must belong to Link. She combed her hair, brushed her teeth with a new toothbrush she found in the cabinet, and washed out her underthings for the morrow. A pang of self-consciousness assailed her as she draped the delicate white lace panties and bra over the shower bar, because, after all, she was sharing living quarters with two *men,* even if she had known them both from earliest childhood and was madly in love with one. But she could think of no alternative, so she shrugged and put modesty from her mind. It was, all things considered, a very minor concern.

She was, Maggy realized as she left the bathroom, getting very good at putting unpleasant things from her mind. The thought faintly worried her.

Nick was waiting for her in the narrow hall, his shoulders propped against the wall. As she came out, he straightened and held out a small plastic cup with a noxious-looking green liquid in it. In his other hand was a paper cup.

"Here," he said. "Take this."

"What is it?" She regarded the liquid with deep reservations.

"I thought you trusted me." He actually managed a crooked smile.

"With my life, yes. With my future, yes. With some kind of medicine, no. What is it?"

"Nyquil. It's the closest thing to a sleeping pill we've got. Neither Link nor I suffer from insomnia as a general rule—but he did have a cold two weeks ago."

"I don't need any Nyquil."

"You've had a rough day. You need to sleep. And you won't. Don't forget I know you, Magdalena. You have trouble sleeping at the best of times. Without this, you'll be up all night."

Maggy scowled at him. He was perfectly right, of course, but that didn't make her any more reconciled to drinking his cough medicine.

"Please?" he added with a coaxing smile. Her scowl deepened, but she took the medicine cup and drank. He removed the empty plastic cup from her grasp and passed her the Dixie cup, which held water. She drank that too, with considerably more pleasure.

"Now that you've got me all doped up," she said when he had disposed of both cups in the bathroom, "where am I supposed to sleep?"

"In here." He led the way to one of the two upstairs bedrooms. It was small, with the minimum of furniture: a double-size spool bed with crisp white linens and a blue-and-white patchwork quilt, a nightstand with a blue ginger-jar lamp, a dresser with a mirror, a wicker rocking chair. Small seascapes in inexpensive gilt frames hung on the walls. All the furniture had been painted white, probably because, having been collected piecemeal, none of the original finishes matched. Simple white lace curtains adorned the window, drawn over a pulled-down white shade that provided privacy. A blue, pink, and white rag rug covered the wide pine boards of the floor.

What touched her was the state of the bed. It had obviously been freshly made up, because the used linen still lay in a crumpled pile in the hall. The sheets had been changed, the pillows plumped, and the coverings turned back for her. By Nick, whose only claim to domestic accomplishment was cooking. He had always particularly hated making beds.

"Thank you, Nick," she said softly, turning to face him, her heart in her eyes.

"For what?" His voice was gruff, but his hand was gentle as it rose to circle her nape.

"For taking such good care of me."

"Anytime, baby." He dropped a kiss on the end of her nose and

released her, pushing her gently to the room. Then he ushered her over
to the bed.

"Hop in," he said.

She did, because he looked so expectant and because she was too
worn out to do anything else.

"Where are you going to sleep?" As she crawled between the sheets,
it occurred to her that she was probably taking his bed. Unless he
planned to join her—and she didn't think so. Not Nick. He knew she
was not ready.

"With Link. There are twin beds in his room. Don't worry. We've
shared a room before."

She knew that was true. As children, Nick and Link had even shared a
bed, because there had been only one in their whole apartment. Their
mother had slept on the couch.

Remembering, Maggy snuggled her head deep into the softness of the
pillow and stretched out along the bed, feeling physically more comfortable than she had for days. Her aching rib cage had been soothed by
time and the hot bath. Her stress-induced nausea had subsided, as had
the niggling headache that had accompanied it. Even better, the worst
pain of all, her psychic pain, had been eased. She felt relieved now that
she had told Nick about that night that had haunted her for years. And
her fear of Lyle and for herself and David was no longer so acute.

Nick had said to trust him, and she did. If he said she had nothing to
worry about, then she would not worry.

At least, not for tonight.

With that inner vow, Maggy sighed, snuggled, and turned onto her left
side, stretching and appreciating the clean smell and cool feel of the
sheets. Nick watched her all the while, his eyes hooded, his expression
unreadable. When she was settled at last, he tucked the covers around
her and turned off the light.

"Sleep tight, Maggy May," he whispered and dropped a quick kiss on
her mouth. Then he turned and left the room, closing the door behind
him.

He was barely gone before she was fathoms-deep asleep.

Hours passed. The clock in the kitchen chimed midnight, then one
A.M. Sometime shortly thereafter, Maggy began to dream.

27

*I*t was the same dream. The one she always had. In the farthest reaches of her mind, Maggy recognized that, knew she was dreaming, even. But it didn't stop the full-blown terror from assailing her. She was sick with fear even as she saw herself standing on that familiar sandy shore.

A pit yawned not six feet in front of her, a gigantic, malodorous pit that belched black smoke and orange flames. Screams came from the pit, hideous screams that made her want to cringe and cover her ears.

But she did not. Instead, as she always did, she craned her neck to see what was in that pit, and with a shock that turned almost immediately to panic she realized that she was looking into hell: the screams she heard came from the souls of the lost. Endless numbers of men, women, and children held up their arms for succor that never came, and shrieked in agony as flames consumed them. It occurred to her then, with a burst of horror that was almost sickening, that she was about to become one of them: one of the damned.

She heard something behind her and glanced around. What she saw made her heart freeze in her breast. The Devil was running toward her, his pitchfork poised, to throw her into the pit with the rest. She knew if he did she could never escape. He was laughing dementedly, this red Devil complete with horns and lashing tail. But what terrified her more than anything else was his face.

It was Lyle's face, Lyle's pale blue eyes.

She ran. And screamed, and screamed, and screamed.

"Magdalena! Magdalena! My God, Magdalena, what is it?"

It was only as she heard those words that she realized that she was sitting bolt upright in the bed she had fallen asleep in hours before and was screaming the house down.

The bedside lamp clicked on. Nick loomed over her, shaking her awake. Link, holding a pistol that looked as if it meant business, hung back in the doorway, darting suspicious glances around the shadowy corners of the room.

"Did you see something? Are you hurt?" Nick's questions were sharp. Maggy could tell from his pallor that she had scared him badly. His hands gripped her shoulders hard, and his gaze as it ran over her was dark with anxiety.

"It was awful," she said thickly, still caught up in the horror of it. "Oh, God, Nick, it was so awful."

"What was?" There was tension in his voice. Across the room, Link opened the closet door and jumped back as if he expected someone to be hiding there.

"The dream."

"The dream?" Nick repeated, his grip on her shoulders easing as comprehension dawned. "What dream, baby?"

Blindly Maggy reached for him, feeling that she would be safe only if he held her in his arms. He bent toward her, and her hands touched bare, muscled shoulders, slid around his neck and clung, pulling him down with a strength she hadn't realized she possessed.

"What dream, baby?" he asked again, his voice gentle, as he surrendered to her insistent tugging and sat down on the bed beside her, casting a significant glance at his brother as he did so. Link snorted and abandoned his search of the room, retreating toward the hall and closing the door behind him as he went. As the click of the latch announced that they were alone, Nick transferred his gaze to her face.

"I was so scared." The words were muttered shudderingly against his throat. Her hands clutched him as if she would never let him go. Pulling aside the quilt and top sheet, he came fully into the bed with her, drawing her against him, pulling the sheet back over her. His arms came around her shoulders and waist, pressing her to the long, hard length of him. The heat of his body burned all the way down her side. It warmed her, though she still shivered. But then, her shivers were not from cold.

"Can you tell me about it?" He stroked her tumbled hair soothingly.

"It's Lyle—Lyle's the Devil."

"I know." His voice was dry.

"In my dream," Maggy insisted, her shivering intensifying as she had another vision of those demon-blue eyes. Nick's arms tightened comfortingly around her. She wrapped her own arms around his middle as she got as close to him as she could.

"Tell me," he said again. So she did. She poured out the jumbled story of her nightmare while he held her, stroking her hair, her shoulders, her back. When she got to the part about the Devil's having Lyle's face, she trembled and his grip tightened comfortingly. Maggy buried her face in the hollow of his neck as she finished, drawing a deep, shaking breath and closing her eyes.

Nick listened and said nothing, just continued to hold her, his hands never ceasing their gentle caresses.

"I've been having the same dream for years," she concluded in a near-whisper, her lips moving against the warm skin of his neck. He was leaning back against her pillows now, still in a sitting position but more comfortably so, with her huddled against the length of his body. One of his arms encircled her back, while he petted her with his free hand, caressing hair and shoulder and back indiscriminately. Her arms were wrapped around his chest just below his armpits. Both of her hands clutched his bare back. "It scares me to death."

"Remember, querida, I told you you didn't need to be scared of Lyle anymore? You're safe from him forevermore. I'll protect you from him now, and very soon he won't be in a position to bother you or anybody."

"Oh, Nick, are you sure?" Maggy wanted so badly to believe. She had thought she did believe, but in the aftermath of her terror she discovered that there had been chinks in the armor of her faith in Nick all along. After all, Lyle Forrest was a very, very powerful man. Nick was handsome, sexy, charming, strong, intelligent, and absolutely wonderful in every way, but could he really pluck the stinger from a hornet as vicious and cunning as Lyle?

Believing in his words required more than a leap of faith: what was needed was on the order of a swan dive.

"I'm sure. *He'll never hurt you again.* Say it, Maggy. 'Lyle Forrest will never hurt me again. Nick says so.' "

Maggy hesitated, her nails digging into the strong, resilient muscles of his back. But she believed in Nick's determination to protect her, if nothing else. As she realized that, she took the plunge. Obediently she repeated, "Lyle Forrest will never hurt me again. Nick says so."

To her surprise, she felt better as soon as she said it.

Still shivering, she huddled against him, her head pillowed on his chest. Her fear gradually lessened, leaving only a muted memory of what had been heart-thumping terror. Nick's arms were around her, warming her, soothing her, and his hands stroked her hair.

Slowly, infinitesimally, her body began to relax. She lay against him more heavily, feeling comfortable and safe. The musky scent of him was pure man, and she breathed it in every time she inhaled. Mixed with his own natural scent was the smell of the same soap she had used, and she deduced from that that he had showered not too long before. His chest hair felt crisp against her face.

She moved her hand until it rested against the hard muscles that pillowed her cheek, twining one manicured finger in a wiry black curl. Then, and only then, did it truly dawn on her that the chest beneath her head was naked.

Maggy frowned slightly, and sneaked a glance down his body. He had pulled the quilt around her shoulders, but hadn't bothered to cover himself. He was clad only in a pair of white jockey briefs, she saw. The rest of him, chest, legs, feet, everything, was completely bare.

The knowledge should have unnerved her, but it did not. After all, this seminaked man was Nick. She curled closer to the warm comfort of his body, her face snuggling deeper into the soft mat of hair as she allowed her eyes to drink their fill of him.

He had a great body. That was the thought that took on shape and substance in Maggy's mind as her gaze ran over him. Dreamily she registered the linebacker's shoulders that loomed above her, the strong brown arms that held her, the wide, heavily muscled chest that pillowed her head and tapered down in a classic V-shape to a muscle-ridged abdomen that in turn disappeared beneath the jockey briefs. The briefs were almost more interesting than his bare flesh, she decided. The soft cotton of which they were made clung lovingly to every curve and hollow of his body, providing no concealment for the growing bulge that was tenting his underwear.

Her face turned away from his scrutiny, Maggy smiled a secret smile as she watched him get hard. He wanted her badly, there was no hiding that. But Nick, her Nick, would suffer the tortures of the damned before he would do anything about it. Whatever the cost to himself, he would put what he perceived as her needs first. He always had. Her eyes traveled down past his briefs, over hairy thighs and powerful calves, to large, thoroughly masculine feet. And retraced their journey.

The swelling in his briefs had not abated. Maggy regarded it thoughtfully. Evil as the notion probably was, she couldn't resist the sudden temptation to tease him, just a little.

She rubbed her cheek against his chest. He stiffened.

"Feeling better?" It was a barely audible murmur, uttered as he dropped his arms from around her.

"Ummm." Maggy wriggled closer with wicked pseudoinnocence, her hold on him tightening. When his arms still failed to return to their previous position, she whispered, "Hold me, Nick."

She thought he complied rather slowly, but he complied.

Once again Maggy rubbed her cheek against the curls that covered his chest, closing her eyes, enjoying the tickling sensation of his chest hair against her soft skin. Her hands moved against his back lightly scoring his flesh as she tested the strength and resilience of the underlying muscles.

Nick shifted uncomfortably. Maggy bit back a grin.

Maggy's eyes opened, though her lowered lashes and bent head concealed the fact from Nick. He couldn't see the gleam in her eyes as she evaluated the state of his briefs. He was so hard and swollen now that she could see the tip of his erection peeking out at her from beneath the elastic of his underwear. Some people might accuse her of being cruel, she supposed, and the dreaded epithet *cock-teaser* flitted through her mind. But it was so wonderfully liberating to feel free to play, to have sexual fun with a man. Nick would not begrudge her her enjoyment at his expense, she knew. In fact, he would applaud it, if it helped her heal.

Her bare legs lay against his. The T-shirt she wore had ridden up almost to the point of indecency, so that she could feel the heat and hair-roughened abrasiveness of his legs against her own. She moved her thigh over his experimentally and felt his legs go taut. She watched the bulge in his briefs swell until it was obvious that only the stretched-to-the-limit confines of the cotton was keeping it from standing stiffly erect.

"I'd better let you get back to sleep." If there was a hint of desperation in Nick's voice—and there was—Maggy refused to let it sway her.

"Don't leave me, Nick." Her voice was a piteous murmur. She thought she heard him grit his teeth, but his arms came back around her, though his embrace felt almost cautious.

Smiling to herself, Maggy relaxed, letting the full weight of her body rest against him. She felt more and more content, like a cat curled on a radiator and ready to nap. Here, in Nick's arms, was where she belonged. His nearness, the solid strength of his body against hers, the warmth of him, his scent, were as intoxicating as a fifth of the finest whiskey. The very stillness of him held her in thrall. It told her how urgently he desired her—and yet he would do nothing, make not so much as a single overture, that he didn't feel she was ready to welcome. The knowledge chased away the last vestiges of her fear. With him, she need only go as far as she wished.

His chest hair tickled her chin, so she wrinkled her nose and blew it aside. The satin-over-steel texture of his skin fascinated her, so she tested it with her fingers, slowly stroking his well-developed pectorals. The tactile pleasure of simply touching him was amazing. How could she have forgotten how good a man's chest beneath her fingertips could feel? Her movements lazy, almost somnolent, she let her fingers slide over his rib cage, rub back and forth across his rock-hard abdomen, dip into his belly button. As she conducted her tactile perambulations, his briefs appeared ever more strained, and the amount of erection that peeked out at her grew ever larger.

She knew perfectly well that she was pushing him to the brink, and she reveled in the knowledge. Because she knew she could stop what she was starting at any time. Nick would never force her—and Nick would never blame her.

He tolerated her exploring fingers without moving, without the slightest verbal response, but he lay rigid as a board against her, his arms taut as they curved around her shoulders, his heart thudding in ever-increasing intensity beneath her ear.

He was sweating, just slightly, his body growing damp where she touched it. Maggy had always heard that sweat tasted salty, and she decided to find out if that were true. Turning her head, she pressed her lips to his chest, and touched the surface of it with her tongue.

The kiss was butterfly light, delicate as a dewdrop.

"Don't," Nick said sharply, sliding his hand between her mouth and his chest.

"Nick?" she questioned, peering up at him.

"Shit," he said in disgust and began to tremble.

28

*S*he was driving him crazy. The feel of her against him, her soft tits pressing against his chest with only the washed-thin cotton of one of Link's old T-shirts between them, the silkiness of her thigh lying atop his, the weight of her head on his chest. Everything about her, her sweet, seductive scent, the pale luminosity of her skin against the bronze of his, the way her cascade of auburn waves looked as they tumbled over the bareness of his chest, the pale, delicate profile, the touch of her hands . . .

Oh, God, the touch of her hands.

That had been when he had first known he was going to lose it: when she started touching him with those slim white fingers, scoring his flesh with pink-painted nails that looked as luscious as candy. There was only so much he could stand, after all. He had all the normal impulses. He was a red-blooded American man.

But he loved her, desperately, fiercely, with a grand wild tide capable of sweeping mountains out of its path. Too much to let anyone else hurt her. Too much to hurt her himself.

Damn it, she was scared of sex. She'd gone nuts in the truck, screaming at the end as if she'd forgotten who he was, as if he was some stranger bent on rape.

Nick felt grim as he remembered. Hell, she had cause. She'd been through more than any woman should have to bear in twenty lifetimes, and he was not going to add to her burden. He was going to be loving and gentle. He was going to take his time with her, coax her over the bad memories, make her happy and unafraid before he started panting after sex. He was going to do it that way if it killed him.

Which, at the moment, it seemed it just might.

But not before he killed Hamilton Drummond right along with that bastard Lyle.

She had entrusted him with her secret, the secret she had never told anyone. He knew that she was scared of sex, knew why she was scared of sex, and granted that she had reason.

So what was he doing? he asked himself with disgust. Lying here in this damned over-warm bed with her, holding her tenderly as she recovered from a nightmare so hideous that it had waked her screaming from a deep sleep, trying his damnedest to think of everything in the world but making love to her while his damned dick got big and hard as a telephone pole.

Whoever said that men kept their brains in their pants must have known his dick.

It knew only what it wanted, not what it couldn't have.

The spidery touch of the tip of her nail rasping over his belly made him clench his fists in her hair, but gently, so she wouldn't feel it. He controlled his breathing—in, out, in, out—in an effort to control his bodily urges.

In, out—*don't think about that candy-tipped finger in your belly button* —in, out—*don't think about how you'd like her fingers to go just a few inches lower*—in, out—*don't think about how hot the touch of her soft, sexy mouth against your chest is making you get* . . .

Jesus, he couldn't stand it. In self-defense he pushed his hand between her mouth and his chest, but it was already too damned late.

His balls were aching, and his dick was so hard that it could drive nails. He fought against the overwhelming need to yank her T-shirt over her head, flip her onto her backside, and bury his aching member between her thighs—and he won, by the skin of his teeth.

But the effort of it made him tremble like a horny seventeen-year-old.

"Shit," he said, gritting his teeth. There was no way she could miss his reaction, no way to keep her from realizing exactly where his mind had been wandering while she clung to him for comfort.

Magdalena looked up at him then, tilting her head so that her eyes met his. Those great beautiful brown eyes shone like soft warm velvet through the veil of her long black lashes, so innocent, so concerned. If he'd been in his right mind, he might have wondered if she didn't look just a little *too* innocent.

"Are you cold, Nicky?" she asked.

Cold. Hell, no. Not hardly. The pit of a volcano had to be colder than he felt at that moment. The realization drove every other thought—like the sudden suspicion that she was deriving a great deal of amusement from his distress—from his mind.

"A little," he lied through clenched teeth as another long shiver racked him.

"You should get under the quilt, then," she said, smiling openly now, and her hand flattened over the tortured muscles of his abdomen as she spoke . . .

And slid down to touch with the tip of a slim forefinger the superheated head of his dick.

"Sweet Jesus," Nick groaned and grabbed her hand away.

"You used to like me to touch you," she said, entwining her fingers with his. He held tightly to her hands so that he wouldn't completely lose his head. She was teasing him, he was sure of it now, and that was a good sign. He just had to keep his self-control. The last thing on earth he ever wanted to do was to scare her. But this particular game had to stop—now. He was too close to the edge.

"Magdalena, baby, querida, I still like it. I do like it. So much so that if you touch me that way again, I won't be responsible for what happens next." He clenched his teeth and tried not to crush her hand. "I've got to get out of here."

"Maybe I don't want you to be responsible. And maybe I don't want you to get out of here."

"Christ, you're killing me," he muttered through teeth clamped so tightly together that they ached. He knew he should roll off the bed now, that very instant, but was totally unable to move.

"Am I?" She slanted that sleepy, innocent smile up at him again. He realized then that it was totally fake, that the little witch knew exactly what she was doing to him, that she was doing it *deliberately.* His heart tripled its beat. Lifting her head from his chest, she shook her hair back from her face so that it swirled around her shoulders in a gorgeous auburn cloud, and pulled her hand from his. Her gaze ran openly over him, from his face to his feet and encompassing everything in between.

Then she touched his dick again.

"Magdalena, for God's sake!" he groaned as her hand slid down inside the waistband of his briefs, but he made no move to stop her. He couldn't. He was paralyzed, literally, with the force of his desire.

"Make love to me, Nicky," she whispered as her hand closed over the huge, granite monolith that threatened to explode at any second. "I want you to. Please."

"Magdalena . . ." With a last desperate burst of true nobility, he battled the urgency of his desire.

Her hand moved, warm and velvety soft as it slid along his shaft. "Please."

He gritted his teeth as his balls clenched and his loins boiled. With the best intentions in the world, he couldn't hold out any longer. Hell, only for Magdalena could he have held off as long as this.

"I love you," he said, guilt and tenderness roughening his voice as his shoulders came off the bed in a lunge. He caught her under her armpits, turned, laid her down, and yanked his briefs and her T-shirt out of the way in the same series of frenzied movements. "Love you, love you, love you."

"I love you, too," she whispered, opening her legs for him.

The sight of her lying there naked and willing and unafraid, her skin creamy satin against the white sheets, her eyes wide and luminous and smiling as she reached for him, completely stopped his breath.

He wanted to go slowly, to make it good for her, to excite her to the point where she could think of nothing but him.

He plunged inside. Nothing he had ever experienced had felt so good. Groaning at the sheer exquisite pleasure of it, he clutched her tightly and lost his head completely.

The ride was fast, wild, and like none he'd ever taken. The feel of her hot, wet sheath hugging him drove him insane. He lifted her legs till they were wrapped around his waist, thrust his tongue into her mouth, and fucked her brains out.

It was good.

When the release came, he buried himself inside her, shaking as if he had palsy, as his loins exploded in fierce hot bursts that were pure ecstasy.

It didn't come any better than that.

For a few minutes afterward he couldn't even think.

Then he could. And that was worse.

Had he scared her to death? Rapidly conducting a mental review of what had just transpired between them, he could recall no shrieking, no fighting to be free, no indication from her that she was not perfectly happy to be where she was.

Had she fainted? Not his Magdalena. She wasn't the fainting kind. But why, then, was she so quiet? Nick summoned all his resources, lifted his head, and looked rather shamefacedly down into her eyes.

29

It was over, Maggy realized jubilantly. She'd done it. No, Nick had done it. Nick had broken through the barrier that had strangled her sexuality for years. She was free, free to be a normal woman again, free to love her man.

The idea was exhilarating. She hadn't realized how heavy the burden of fear had been until it was smashed.

When Nick lifted his head to look down at her, she smiled at him. He looked so guilty that she couldn't help it, though the urge to tease him had not entirely dissipated. Looming above her, the weight of his upper body braced on his bulging arms, his shoulders were broad enough to block her view of the rest of the room. His chest with its thick mat of black hair was only a few inches from her eyes, and she admired its masculine beauty before shifting her gaze to his face. Her eyes ran lovingly over the blunt pugilist's features, the square jaw that was almost black now with whiskers, the wide, thin mouth that was unsmiling as he watched her. She absorbed the crooked nose, the broad cheekbones, the thick black eyebrows, the wildly tousled black hair. Then, and only then, did she meet his eyes. The hazel-green depths were dark with worry.

And that was when she smiled at him.

"Are you okay?" he asked, not sounding particularly relieved by her expression.

She nodded.

"I didn't hurt you, did I? I didn't even think about the bruises."

Maggy shook her head.

"Did I scare you?" He looked guiltier than ever as a frown pulled his brows together over his nose.

Maggy shook her head again.

"Damn it, Magdalena, talk to me," he ground out. "I feel like three kinds of heel, and you aren't helping."

With that he rolled off her, flopping over onto his back and lying with one arm bent under his head as he glared up at the ceiling.

"I'm sorry," she said meekly, coming up on one elbow to look down at him.

His eyes slid to her face. "No, that's my line: *I'm* sorry," he said with contrition in his voice. "I didn't mean it to happen like that."

"It was fine." Maggy was feeling more cheerful by the second.

"Well, thanks a whole heap of a lot." Nick, on the other hand, sounded positively grumpy. His eyes rolled up to once again contemplate the ceiling.

"I didn't mean it like that," Maggy said placatingly, and giggled, which was something she probably shouldn't have done. From the expression on his face it was clear that his masculine pride was now thoroughly affronted. This, for some reason, she found hilarious.

"Actually, it was great. Really great. I mean it," she said. He gritted his teeth, and she giggled again.

"Don't give me that." If his expression was anything to go by, his temper was turning sour faster than day-old cream. She'd better cut the chuckles in a hurry, Maggy thought. Or else he'd be stalking out of there buck naked before she had a chance to explain what she meant. But she felt so good suddenly, so young, so *normal*, that it was hard not to laugh from sheer joy.

"It *was* great," Maggy insisted softly. Then, as his gaze slued down to her face and he glared at her, she clarified: "I didn't get scared. I didn't scream. I didn't even *think* about anyone but you. And that's what made it great for me."

An arrested expression flickered for a moment in his eyes, and then he smiled, a slow, rather grudging smile, but still a smile.

"You're telling me you didn't come." It was an accusation, but a humorous one.

"Not this time." Her admission was meek. A roguish smile quivered around the edges of her mouth, and she all but twinkled at him. "In the truck, now, was a different story."

"Oh, yeah?" He lifted his eyebrows interestedly at her.

"Yeah." Maggy nodded, and grinned down at him.

He sat up suddenly, caught the edge of her T-shirt, which was twisted around her hips, and pulled it over her head. Maggy lifted her arms for him, shaking her head to settle her flying mane of hair as, tossing her night attire on the floor, he left her naked and smiling at him.

"My women *always* come," he growled, turning on her, his hands on her shoulders bearing her down onto the bed. "Are you trying to spoil my record?"

For a moment he held her down, his expression mock ferocious as he took in the tangled clouds of auburn hair that spread capelike around her body, the delicate beauty of her features, the smile in her eyes, the softness of her generous mouth. Then his gaze moved down over her smooth white neck to her slender shoulders and the lush bounty beyond. Though she was a slim woman, she had always had plenty on top, and Maggy felt a spreading warmth begin inside her at the gleam in Nick's eyes as he looked at her. Full, round, creamy-smooth breasts with pinkish-brown nipples already erect and clamoring for his attention—Maggy knew what brought that look to his face. And, to her surprise, she reveled in it.

But then he froze, not moving, hardly seeming to breathe as his expression darkened.

For a moment Maggy was at a loss. Then she glanced down at herself, at where his eyes rested. The bruises on her rib cage stood out in all their purple-and-yellow glory against the creamy whiteness of her skin. That was what had brought that terrible look to his face.

Funny, she'd almost forgotten.

"They don't hurt," Maggy said. "Not now."

Then she reached over and flicked off the bedside lamp. The room was immediately plunged into darkness so dense that she couldn't see the tip of her nose, much less him.

"So get busy," she said, her hands lifting to encircle his neck and pull him down. "Make me come. You don't want to spoil your record."

"Magdalena . . ." He held back, sounding almost somber.

"Shut up, stupid, and kiss me," she whispered, tugging, and at last he did. Maggy felt the impact of his big, naked body pressed intimately to hers all the way to her toes.

His mouth found hers, kissing her with loving care. His tongue penetrated the sweet depths of her mouth, exploring the wet darkness, teasing her tongue with his. She kissed him back without urgency, with a warm sense of rightness. Her hands stroked over his broad shoulders, down his back. The warm dampness of his skin tantalized her. She loved touching him.

He put his hands on her breasts. Maggy almost ceased to breathe as he caressed her nipples. The soft mounds swelled, and the peaks grew hard.

His mouth left hers, took over from his hands. He suckled gently at first one needy breast and then the other. At the touch of his mouth, Maggy felt a throbbing ache spring to life in her loins.

As if he knew, his hands went in search of it. She caught her breath as his hands slid down over her stomach, stroking the silky skin there, and then moved to rest lightly on the vulnerable triangle of curls between her thighs. He stroked her there, petted her there, teased her there, while his mouth continued to make a leisurely meal of her breasts.

With a wordless murmur of pleasure, Maggy clasped his head to her breasts, her fingers threading through his thick black curls. Her eyes closed and her legs trembled as she grew hopelessly, helplessly aroused.

His mouth slid down to take over from his hands. Maggy felt the warm wetness of it trail down to her belly button, where his tongue paused for a minute to delve inside. She shivered, then grew momentarily still as his mouth went lower yet. Her fingers clenched in his hair as he nuzzled her triangle of curls, while his hands slid beneath her to cup her buttocks and lift her up for the full possession of his mouth.

"Please, Nick," she begged as she felt his mouth burning intimately against her, felt the slick caress of his tongue. But whether it was said as protest or prayer she was too far gone to sort out.

Maggy was aware of nothing but the heat of his mouth on her, the strong possession of his hands holding her and serving her up for his delectation, the aching pleasure that was coiling ever tighter inside her, wound by that devilish mouth.

Her hands were flat against the sheets, clutching them, tugging at the cool cotton with fingers that shook. Her eyes were closed, her lips parted, her head tossing restlessly from side to side.

God, she loved what he was doing to her! She never wanted him to stop. . . .

But he did. Just as she thought she couldn't bear it for so much as another instant, he lifted himself away from her, sliding his hard length back up her writhing body, his mouth stamping a hot, wet brand over her clamoring flesh every inch of the way. He paused to savor her breasts, and she cried out.

He moved up again, his hard, hair-roughened thighs sliding between hers as if they had been made to fit there, the red-hot tip of his shaft probing at the throbbing entrance his mouth had just thoroughly claimed. Maggy felt him there and made a little mewling sound. She heard it without even realizing that it came from her own mouth.

"Not yet, baby," he whispered, and kissed her mouth. She kissed him back, panting with eagerness for his possession, her arms clutching him, her nails scoring his back. Still he wouldn't be hurried, easing slowly, so slowly inside her, filling her inch by maddening inch until she was squirming beneath him, thrusting herself up against him to hurry him up.

But he wouldn't hurry. With his hands on her breasts, his tongue in her mouth, he filled her and pulled out, filled her and pulled out, in slow deliberate strokes designed to drive her out of her mind.

When she came, it was with an earth-shattering intensity that made her lock her arms and legs around his body, arch her back, and sob out his name.

"Nick! Oh, yes! Yes! Nick!"

The shock waves of ecstasy that racked her pushed him over the edge as well. Maggy felt him stiffen against her, and then he shuddered. She could feel his climax as he plunged deep inside her, and the knowledge of his pleasure intensified her own.

For long moments afterward they were still, locked together, his body a dead weight pushing her down into the mattress. She held him, stroking his hair, a dreamy smile curving her mouth. Finally she turned her head and brushed his unshaven cheek with her lips.

"I came," she whispered into his ear.

"Told ya," he answered with a cockiness so reminiscent of the boy he had been that she had to smile. Lifting his head to drop a quick kiss on her lips, Nick rolled off her, taking her with him, cuddling her against him with one arm as he pulled the covers over both of them. He found the pillows that had been shoved back against the headboard, pulled one under his head, left the other for her, and kissed the tip of her nose.

Moments later, the steady rasp of his breathing told Maggy that he was asleep.

Worn out, poor thing, she thought. And fell asleep with a lingering grin on her face and her head pillowed on his chest.

30

*T*he thought that woke Maggy was that they hadn't used birth control. Her eyes popped open, wide with horror as the enormity of her deed struck her like a baseball bat to the head. She of all people should know better than that. Unless Nick had had a vasectomy during the last twelve years, which she very much doubted, he was fertile. And so was she.

It had been years since she'd even thought of having sex with a man, so birth control was something she hadn't needed to worry about. Feverishly she counted back to the date of the end of her last period. Eight days ago. Did that mean she was safe? She didn't know.

Nick was opening up a whole new world for her, she thought sourly. Unplanned pregnancy, birth control, sexually transmitted diseases—she hadn't had to worry about them in a long, long time.

She and Nick were going to have a frank talk on the subject that very day.

In the meantime, it occurred to her that she was in bed alone. There was an indentation in the pillow beside hers that indicated where he had been, and the covers on his side of the bed were thrown back. But there was no sign of Nick himself.

It was full daylight, of course. A single beam of brilliant sunlight had managed to sneak through a crack where the drawn shade did not quite cover the window. Dust motes floated lazily in its brilliance.

From outside came the muted slam of a car door, and then, a few minutes later, the corresponding slam of the front door to the house. Masculine voices spoke briefly—she couldn't understand the words, but there was no mistaking the gender—and then she heard footsteps coming up the stairs two at a time.

It was Nick, and he was whistling. Maggy absorbed those facts even as she scrambled beneath the covers, pulling them up to her armpits and tucking them around her so that only her shoulders were left bare. What had passed between them the previous night notwithstanding, she could not just be sitting here stark naked when he walked in.

Just as Maggy had expected, Nick didn't even knock. The knob turned, the door opened, and there he stood. He was wearing a blue-plaid flannel shirt tucked into a skintight pair of jeans, cowboy boots, and a tooled-leather belt. His hair, clearly having emerged fairly recently from the vigorous ministrations of a brush, waved glossily back from his forehead, and he was freshly shaved.

"Sleepyhead," he said, breaking off the cheerful tune he'd been tootling to grin at her.

"You didn't use a rubber," she said accusingly. Her ire was increased by the thought of what she must look like: her face needed washing, she lacked even the faintest trace of makeup, and her hair hung in a tangled mess around her shoulders and down her back. She caught a handful of hair that hung over her forehead, pulled it back from her face, and scowled at him.

Nick paused, looked hard at her as if to weigh the degree of her displeasure, and came on into the room, nudging the door shut behind him.

"I didn't have one on me at the time," he replied with unimpaired good humor, crossing to the bed to drop a kiss on her mutinous mouth and a small brown paper bag that she hadn't even noticed he was carrying into her lap at the same time. "Don't worry, querida, you're safe with me."

Magdalena understood from that that he knew he was disease free. But disease was not her major concern at the moment. Knowing Nick as she did, she was sure that if he'd had the slightest doubt about his status he would never have touched her. Pregnancy was what she was worried about.

"I'm not on the pill." At his apparent lack of concern, her scowl grew fiercer.

"Neither am I."

Maggy almost gnashed her teeth. "Would you be serious?"

Nick crooked his thumbs around his belt loops and looked down at her reflectively. "I'd forgotten what a little shrew you used to be. Do I want to let myself in for a lifetime of being yelled at before I even get a cup of coffee inside me?" He appeared to ponder for an instant, and then that deep dimple appeared beside his mouth. "Well, you're worth it. I guess."

Maggy snatched the pillow from behind her back and threw it at him. He ducked, laughing, and opened the door, calling back over his shoulder as he headed down the hall: "Coffee's on downstairs. Food'll be ready in fifteen minutes. Try not to chew any furniture before then."

Beast. But Maggy had to smile even as she thought it.

The bag he had dropped on her lap contained a few vital cosmetics, shampoo, toothpaste, toothbrush, and a comb and hairbrush. Maggy's eyes lit up as she saw her booty. Nick had obviously gone to the drugstore for her, for which she was grateful. Armed with clean hair and a lipstick, she felt she could take on the world.

Clothes were a different story. She could wear the clothes she had arrived in, but they were crumpled and dirty and she preferred not to. Maggy pondered the problem for a moment, and then got out of bed, retrieving her T-shirt from the floor and pulling it over her head so that she wouldn't have to cavort around naked while she rounded up something to wear. Since this was Nick's room, it stood to reason that his clothes would be in the closet. She would borrow something of his.

She found a sweat shirt and sweat pants, both in heavy black cotton, folded on the closet shelf. Carrying them and the bag Nick had given her to the bathroom with her, she showered, shampooed her hair, and then rubbed herself dry, wrapping a thick terry towel around her head turbanlike as a final measure. If either Nick or Link possessed anything as convenient as a hair dryer, she would be surprised. At any rate, there wasn't one around that she could find.

Her underthings had been moved, and as she pulled them on, she blushed faintly at the idea of Nick—she hoped it had been Nick—handling them. Which was silly, of course. He had handled the body that they clothed, for goodness' sake. Which was more intimate?

She stepped into the sweat pants, which were far too large. Fortunately the ankles were elastic, and the waist had a drawstring. She tied the string tightly about her own waist, and was left with a billowy pair of sweats that nevertheless fit well enough to be wearable. The shirt, too, was overlarge. The hem hung almost to mid-thigh, and the fit was definitely loose. The sleeves were a good eight inches too long. She hadn't realized what a large man Nick was until she tried wearing his clothes. Probably because she compared him with Link, who was even larger.

Pushing up the sleeves almost to her elbows solved the problem of the sweat shirt. The outfit was big—fortunately oversize was in—but serviceable. With her own flats, she could be seen outside the house.

Maggy looked in the mirror, was pleased to note that the bruises on her face were fading, and applied lipstick and a light dusting of powder on her nose from the supplies Nick had brought. He hadn't thought to buy mascara—what man ever did?—but her lashes were naturally long and dark, and today her eyes were wide and sparkling without any need for enhancement. Her cheeks had a faint rosiness too—she supposed blusher was also outside his realm of experience, because he hadn't brought her that either—and her skin had a creamy quality that it had lacked twenty-four hours before.

It occurred to her then that being madly in love was the best cosmetic of all. Maggy smiled at her reflection and unwound the towel from her hair.

Combing the thick mass out and crimping it with her fingers in crucial places to encourage the natural waves to form where she wanted them was all she could manage in the way of hairstyling without a blow dryer. Slipping her feet into her flats, she headed downstairs, drawn by the tantalizing smell of frying bacon.

Nick was at the stove, deftly cracking eggs into a skillet of sizzling grease. A plate loaded with bacon covered with a paper towel rested on the counter next to the stove. Link leaned against the counter a little farther along, munching a piece of bacon as he said something to his brother.

They glanced up as Maggy hesitated in the doorway.

"One egg or two?" Nick asked her, while Link eyed her up and down and grinned hugely.

"One," Maggy answered, wary of Link's grin.

"You're looking a considerable bit better this morning, baby girl." Link's eyes twinkled knowingly at her as he stole another slice of bacon from the plate. Nick waved his fork at him in a silent warning to lay off the food.

"I feel better," Maggy replied, refusing to rise to Link's teasing.

"A good night's sleep'll do that for you," Link said with a wise nod.

This was too much, even for Maggy's good intentions. "Oh, shut up, Link," she said witheringly and opened the refrigerator to search for juice.

Link grinned but wisely shut up, busying himself with putting bread into the toaster as Maggy set the table and poured orange juice into three glasses. It was not until she was returning the carton to the refrigerator that she realized what song Link was humming so cheerfully under his breath: "Hello, Young Lovers, Wherever You are. . . ."

"Does he have a girlfriend?" she asked Nick, with a jerk of her thumb toward his obnoxious brother. "Wait till you see what I'm going to do to embarrass him in front of her."

"He's got an army of them. I told you, he trolls for them in my Corvette."

"Man, it's not the Corvette, it's *me*. I'm ir-re-sistible." Link grinned. "Besides, what good's a hot car like that if you never use it? Little brother here's been moonin' after you for so many years that he's never really realized its full potential."

"Shut up, Link." This time it was Nick's turn to direct a quelling frown at his brother. Link merely grinned in reply. Nick scooped the eggs out onto plates, while Link tossed them each a slice of toast. Maggy, just catching hers before it hit the floor, put it on her plate, carried her plate to the table, and sat down. The men followed suit.

They ate and talked about nothing, really. This trio had eaten meals together on many occasions in the old days, and they fell back into the groove without missing a beat. Maggy didn't even feel particularly uncomfortable with the idea that Link knew precisely how she and Nick had passed the night. Link had always known how it was between her and Nick.

"Where are you going so fast?" Nick asked when Link stood up as soon as he had shoveled the last bite of his meal into his mouth. Maggy wasn't more than half finished with hers, and Nick wasn't much further along. Of course, they'd been doing most of the talking, while Link had been steadily eating.

"Places to go, things to do. Know what I mean, little brother?" Link answered with a shrug.

"Yeah. Tell 'em I'll be along later." Nick glanced at Maggy. "A lot later."

"Nah." Link shook his head and grinned. "I'll tell 'em you're in bed with the flu. See ya."

With a wave of his hand Link left the kitchen. Maggy heard him going up the stairs. Ten minutes later, as Nick was washing the few dishes and she was drying and putting them away, Link reappeared in the downstairs hall, gave a brief wave in her direction as he caught her eye, yelled, "Bye, flu!" and vanished from sight. Seconds later she heard the opening and closing of the front door. A few minutes after that came the roar of a powerful engine.

"Damn it, he's taking my car again," Nick groaned, pausing in the act of rinsing the final glass to glare futilely out the window toward the empty spot where the Corvette had been.

"Doesn't he have a car?" Maggy couldn't help grinning at this all-too-typical byplay between the brothers, but she was tiptoeing to put the plates back on the top shelf and fortunately Nick didn't see.

"Six months ago he bought a brand new Range Rover. You know, four-wheel drive, the works. He took it everywhere, and I do mean everywhere, through woods, streams, up mountains, down valleys. Last month he got cocky and went up a slope that turned out to be just a little too steep. The thing flipped, and ended up sliding down on its top into a gully. Lucky for Link he was thrown out, or he probably wouldn't be with us today. The blasted car's been in the shop since then. He wanted them to total it so he could get a new one, but it's not quite that bad, they said. They're fixing it. He may be an old man before it gets finished, but they're fixing it. In the meantime, he bought that old truck to drive around. But what does he use? My car."

"Oh." Maggy couldn't help it. She giggled, then clapped her hand over her mouth.

"Think it's funny, do you?" Nick turned and handed her the glass he'd rinsed for drying.

"Only a little," Maggy said meekly, unable to put into words how the interaction between the brothers warmed her. It was nice to be in the thick of a normal family again, one where family members bickered and teased and argued—and loved each other. That was what she wanted for herself, and David.

She dried the glass and put it away in the cabinet. When she turned back toward him, he thrust a small brown paper bag at her.

"What's this?" Maggy accepted it rather gingerly. The top was rolled shut, and the bag was heavy for its size.

"Baby, my mission in life is to make *all* your dreams come true," Nick said, taking her by the elbow and steering her toward the back door. "Come on."

31

$\mathcal{A}$s soon as she saw the flock of chickens pecking in the dirt around the barn, Maggy started to laugh. Nick grinned at her, unlatched the metal farm gate that separated the barnyard from the ground surrounding the house, and ushered her through it. The clucking chickens continued on about their business, paying the newcomers no mind.

"You always wanted to feed chickens, so *voilà*, I give you chickens. And, in the bag, chicken feed." Nick made a sweeping gesture at the oblivious flock.

"Whose *are* they?" Still laughing, Maggy made no move to open the bag in her hand. Built of ancient, weathered gray boards, the barn obviously belonged to the farmhouse. Nick had said he and Link had rented a farm, but surely it didn't come complete with livestock? With the best will in the world, she couldn't picture either brother as a farmer. Neither of them had ever had much exposure to animals, except for the few stray cats and dogs that had shown up from time to time around Parkway Place, and Horatio. And Horatio certainly hadn't done much to endear his feathered brethren to Nick.

"They belong to the farmer who rented us this place. He asked if he could keep them here, and we didn't mind. He's got some cows out there in the pasture, too. He sends somebody over to take care of them twice a day. His house is right over that hill."

Nick nodded in the direction of the horizon. As they were in farm country, there were not a lot of trees in sight. A few oaks and maples grew around the house, and a few more were scattered here and there across what was essentially flat pasture land. The fields were a bright, new green with only the occasional tan patch where last winter's grass still held sway. In the process of following Nick's nod, her gaze swept the fields, noting a dozen or so fat black cows chomping contentedly on fresh shoots of grass not far from the barn. Then her gaze passed beyond them, up the gentle incline he referred to as a hill, to where the brightly budding land met the soft blue of the sky. Glancing around, she realized that the farm he had rented was in the center of a bowl of green earth rimmed on all sides by nothing but sky. Except for the house and barn, not another building was in sight.

It made for a delicious feeling of aloneness.

"So go for it," Nick said, nodding at the chickens. He crossed his arms over his chest and leaned back against the gate, prepared to watch.

"Well, I will." Glancing rather uncertainly at the scattered chickens, Maggy unrolled the top of the paper bag.

"Here chicken. Here chicken," she called softly, approaching a fat red hen with a handful of corn. It squawked and ran when she got too close. Maggy, not knowing what else to do, tossed the handful of corn after it. The hen squawked louder as the kernels rained down on her. Then it stopped abruptly and started pecking at the corn that had landed in the dried mud ruts of the farmyard.

"See?" Maggy said proudly to Nick, turning to display her prowess.

He clapped, grinning. Then he pointed behind her. "I think it wants more."

Maggy glanced around to find that the hen was indeed pecking its way toward her—and all its friends were, too. There must have been twenty in all, red ones and white ones and black-and-white-speckled ones and one big black one with a fleshy red comb on its head that Maggy suspected was the rooster. She threw a handful of corn in their midst. With gleeful cackles they descended on the bounty, gobbling it up, and, when it was gone, looking to her for more. Maggy hastily took a step backward as a few of them showed an alarming tendency to peck too close to her feet, and threw another handful of corn.

In this fashion she was backed all the way up against the wall of the barn.

"Help," she called faintly to Nick as she felt the wood at her back. There was only a little corn left, not even enough for a decent handful, and the greedy birds were already gobbling what she had just thrown down and looking to her for more. It occurred to Maggy to wonder what they would do if she didn't have more to give, and that was when she launched her appeal to Nick.

He had moved with her, keeping well clear of the flock of hungry birds, watching her exploits with a wide grin splitting his face.

"What do you want me to do?" He made no move to come to her rescue, just stood there with his arms crossed over his chest and that idiotic grin on his face.

"Call them off." A hint of panic infused her voice as she tossed out the very last of the corn.

"Baby, the only chickens I know anything about come in a cardboard bucket with a picture of the colonel on the front. How do you expect me to call them off? If I were you, I'd run."

Maggy cast him a fulminating look, and then, as the greediest and biggest of the chickens came pecking around her feet, decided that his advice wasn't half bad. Casting the paper bag away—she kind of hoped the chickens might take the flying brown object for a particularly large and luscious kernel of corn—she darted away from the barn wall.

The chickens flew into the air in a squawking, flapping mass of feathered hysteria.

Maggy screamed, threw an arm over her head, and sprinted toward the open barn door. Besieged by flapping fowl, Nick yelped and followed her. He was only half a step behind her as she made it to what she assumed was safety. But two particularly malevolent chickens flapped through the barn door behind them.

It was dark in the barn compared to the glorious brightness of the day outside. Maggy's eyes took a few seconds to adjust, but when they did they immediately focused on the ladder. She reached it in half a second, scrambling up it with the agility of a frightened monkey. Nick was right behind her. As they made it to the safety of the loft, the pursuing chickens landed with indignant squawks on the rungs they had just vacated.

"We're trapped," Maggy said. She was on her hands and knees, peering over the edge.

"Looks that way." Nick was right beside her. They exchanged glances, and he suddenly grinned at her. "Still want to wake up every morning and feed the chickens?"

"So I'm a city girl. Sue me." Maggy sank back on her heels.

"I'd rather screw you." An exaggerated leer accompanied that very bad attempt at a joke.

"Ha, ha." Maggy glanced around the loft. It was large, covering two thirds of the floor space of the barn. Horizontal beams for the drying of tobacco extended across the remaining open space from the floor of the loft to the opposite wall. Several dozen golden-brown bundles of tobacco hung from the beams nearly to the packed-earth floor. In the loft itself the smell of hay was everywhere, earthy and dusty yet pleasant at the same time. Hay in old-fashioned rectangular bales was stacked to the rafters in a step-back fashion beginning about ten feet from where Nick and Maggy sat and continuing on to the rear wall. Loose piles of hay covered most of the wooden floor. Roughhewn beams rose vertically from the floor every ten or so feet to support the peaked metal roof, and narrow bands of sunlight slanted down from roof to floor through numerous hairline cracks where the sheets of metal joined. A veritable city of cobwebs formed a lacy canopy across the corners and just below the peak of the roof. At the opposite end of the loft from the stacked hay was the hay door, complete with pulley. It was open, and light poured in through it in a flood that illuminated what appeared to be a crude but workable artist's retreat. Eyes widening in growing surprise, Maggy identified an easel, a stool, and a small table that seemed, from that distance, to hold supplies.

"Who paints?" Maggy's shocked gaze swung back to Nick. She knew it even before he answered.

"I do," he said, a shade defensively.

"*You* do?" If he'd told her he was a Martian he couldn't have stunned her more. Oh, ever since she had first met him he had always done quick sketches—doodles, she'd considered them—on whatever paper he'd been able to find when the mood struck, but she'd never thought of Nick as a potential artist. He was too blatantly male, and too *street.* "Since when?"

Nick shrugged. "A few years ago. A girl I was seeing made a living doing illustrations for greeting cards. She was always taking art classes. To please her, I went to one. And I got hooked. I don't have a lot of time for it, but I like it. Hey, it keeps me out of trouble." He grinned, but she could tell he was still faintly uncomfortable in case she should think his hobby was less than masculine.

"Are you doing something now? Could I see?"

He nodded, but he needn't have. Maggy was already on her feet and moving toward the easel without waiting for his permission.

His medium was oils, Maggy discovered as she approached. The smell of linseed oil and turpentine was strong as she drew close to the easel, revealing his preference even before she glanced at the table and saw the small metal tubes containing the paints.

"You're very good." A half-finished canvas of the farmhouse nestled amid the surrounding fields rested on the easel. A quick glance out the hay door told Maggy that Nick had painted the view from that vantage point.

"Thank you." He was standing behind her, watching her as she stared at his painting. Maggy threw a quick, nervous smile over her shoulder at him.

"David paints," she said abruptly. As soon as the words left her mouth she wished she hadn't said them. But it was too late. They hung in the air between them, twisting slowly toward earth like dust motes in a ray of sunshine.

"So you said once before." He frowned at her, and Maggy felt her heart sink. She wasn't ready, not yet, not yet . . .

"Does he use oils?"

"Watercolors," Maggy replied in a voice that to her own ears sounded strained.

"Has he had lessons?"

"Lots," Maggy said, nodding. "Lots and lots of lessons. We knew as young as kindergarten age that he had an exceptional talent."

"That's great. At least he and I will have something to talk about now, besides you." Nick slid an arm around Maggy's waist from behind. "Want to see something?"

Maggy nodded, afraid to trust her voice.

Nick reached around her and flicked a tarpaulin off a large flat object that leaned against the wall. Maggy was left staring at a full-length portrait of herself. It was a three-quarter-profile study in which she leaned one pale shoulder against what appeared to be a solid brick wall. Dusky shadows seemed to be closing in around her, and her mouth was unsmiling, the expression in her eyes grave. She was very young, about sixteen, and she was wearing the white tulle-skirted dress she had worn to her junior prom, with a single silver rose in her hair.

"I did it from memory, about six years ago," he said softly, both hands linking around her waist. "That's how I always think of you."

Maggy stood stock-still for a moment longer, her hands moving of their own volition to rest over his, unable to speak, unable to do anything but stare at the portrait.

Then she turned in Nick's hold, wrapping her arms around his neck.

"I love you," she whispered fiercely and went up on tiptoe to kiss his mouth. He forestalled her, his hands flattening on either side of her face and holding it still for his inspection. For a long moment his eyes traveled over her, feature by feature, as if he would commit her face to memory for all time. Finally he met her gaze, and the expression in his eyes stopped her breath.

"You are so Goddamn beautiful," he said softly. Then his arms locked around her waist and back, holding her as if he never meant to let her go, and he kissed her, his lips and tongue alternately caressing and plundering her mouth. Maggy met his ravening hunger with her own desperate need, her arms wound about his neck, her head thrown back against his shoulder. Her knees were suddenly so weak that she was afraid they would no longer support her if he should let her go. Not that there was any danger of that. She could feel his passion building, could feel his hunger for her in the heat and hardness of his body against hers, in the greedy demands of his mouth. She answered that demand with abandon.

At last his mouth left hers to glide hotly across her cheek to her ear. Maggy gasped as he nipped the soft lobe.

"Witch," he murmured huskily, his breath warm against the shell-like structure. "What kind of spell have you cast over me, to keep me wanting you like this over all these years?"

"The same spell you cast on me," Maggy whispered, pressing her lips to the rough warmth of the underside of his jaw. "I think it's called love."

She leaned against him, letting him totally support her weight. One large hand cradled the back of her head as he tilted her so that his mouth could have easy access to the softness of her throat. Maggy closed her eyes as a stray sunbeam glinted in the silvery spiderwebs high overhead, barely conscious of anything but the feel of Nick's hands and mouth and body on her flesh.

His mouth was tracing its way down her neck, nibbling and sucking and licking at the soft column. Finally he reached the warm hollow; his mouth rested there for a moment as if he would count her frenzied pulse. She could feel the hardness of his jaw, the rasp of his unshaven chin, the moist heat of his open mouth as he nuzzled at her throat. Then one hand cupped her breast.

The nipple hardened instantly, butting into his palm through the layers of her sweat shirt and bra. Maggy felt the hardening as an exquisite little pleasure-pain that made her catch her breath. Nick took that importunate bud between his thumb and forefinger, gently pinching it. To Maggy's surprise, the pleasure was so intense that her knees buckled.

Nick went down with her, down onto the hard, hay-strewn floor, half beside her, half on top of her. He kissed her, his hand sliding over the front of her sweat shirt to the hem, then retracing its route against her soft skin. When he discovered her bra, his fingers lightly traced the delicate lace pattern across both breasts before sliding beneath her to fumble at her back. After a few minutes, he lifted his mouth from hers. Maggy's eyes fluttered open to discover the reason for the interruption and found that he was looking down at her with a rueful half smile.

"How the devil does this thing come off?" he asked, giving the elasticized back of her bra a tug.

Maggy sat up, caught the hem of her sweat shirt, and pulled it over her head. Then with fingers that were not quite steady she gripped the tiny plastic buckle between her breasts and pressed the release catch.

"Like this," she whispered as the fastening separated. Lifting the cups away from her breasts, she shrugged out of the straps and dropped the bra to one side.

32

"*Y*ou take my breath away," he said. Maggy felt her insides twist as his gaze feasted on the creamy, strawberry-tipped bounty of her breasts. Nick's eyes darkened, the lids drooping slumberously, as he stared. Dark color washed up to stain his cheekbones. His lips parted as his breath rasped between them. His body was motionless, his muscles taut as a bowstring.

Maggy, watching these signs of his arousal with a growing excitement of her own, felt violent tremors snake out over her skin.

He leaned closer. Maggy's breath stopped as he placed his open mouth against her left breast. The heat and wetness of it was shocking, thrilling. It made her melt inside. She looked down at that wavy black head, at the short, thick fans of his lashes as they rested against the bronze of his cheeks, at the black stubble that was already starting to darken his jaw though it couldn't be long past noon and he had shaved that morning, at the hard, masculine mouth attached to the creamy whiteness of her breast. And she moaned aloud.

Without ever removing his mouth from her breast, he glanced up at her face, and his hands closed over her upper arms to slowly ease her down so that she was lying on her back in the prickly hay.

Maggy's eyes closed helplessly; as she felt him sliding her pants and panties down her legs, she writhed in abject surrender. She wanted him with a fierceness that shocked her.

Once he had her naked, his mouth returned to torment her defenseless nipples; she gasped as his hand stroked down her flesh to delve into her trembling navel with one hard finger, then continued on across the silky flesh of her stomach to cover the triangle of curls between her thighs. Writhing as he touched her, she pushed upward against his warm palm, desperate to end his torture.

"Sweet God in heaven." It was a ragged mutter, accompanied by the complete withdrawal of his hands and mouth. Maggy whimpered a protest, and her lids fluttered up. She discovered that he was standing now, towering above her, his eyes a glittering emerald green as they roamed over her.

As if she were looking down at herself through his eyes, Maggy knew what he must see: a slim, pale-skinned girl, bruised but lovely, utterly naked, the soft white mounds of her breasts topped with rosy peaks already hardened to succulence by his mouth, the gentle curve of her abdomen punctuated by a triangle of auburn curls that wept for him, slim thighs parting in restless longing, pink-tipped nails digging into the bed of prickly hay on which she lay, waiting with shameless eagerness for him to return to her. Her long auburn hair formed a tangled fan around her head. The rich darkness of it contrasted starkly with the warm gold of the hay. Her eyes were a deep, smoldering brown, half closed and slanted like an odalisque's as they watched him; a tawny-pink blush had crept high into her cheekbones, the only sign of modesty remaining to her; her mouth was soft and swollen from his kisses, as temptingly red as the lushest rose.

He started stripping, unbuttoning his shirt with fingers that were less than steady. Maggy watched as he shrugged out of it, letting it fall uncaringly to the floor. Her eyes slid avidly along his broad, bronzed shoulders to where they joined his strong neck, then moved down over his muscled, hair-matted chest. His hands were at his belt, unfastening it, letting it dangle open while he first unbuttoned, then unzipped his jeans. Then he paused for a moment, hands resting negligently on his hips, a slow smile teasing his lips as he took in the fascinated expression on her face.

"Want me to stop?" he asked huskily. Maggy shook her head shamelessly, and something dark and dangerous flared to life in his eyes.

He had to sit down to pull off his boots; he slid out of his jeans and briefs with a single swift movement. Then he was naked, crawling toward her, straddling her waiting body while remaining on his hands and knees.

"Now you're mine," he told her, and the combination of the exultant look in his eyes and the hugeness of his erection made her throat go dry.

His hands gripped her thighs, parting them, and his knees slid between hers. She felt the rasp of his hard, hairy thighs against the softness of her own, felt his turgid flesh burning against the throbbing entrance to her body, and gasped. She reached for him, meaning to guide him into the place where she most needed him to be, but he was already upon her, his big body crushing her into the hard wood beneath the hay as his hands found her breasts and his mouth captured one quivering nipple.

"Now, Nick, please, now," she moaned, her arms clutching his shoulders and her legs twining around his hips in a shameless effort to force the possession she craved.

As if her plea tore the lid off the iron control he'd been exercising over himself, he thrust into her urgently, his hardness impaling her soft flesh. She gasped and moaned, crying out his name. Her fingers burrowed desperately into the thick curls that clustered at his nape.

His arms clamped her to him with a fierce strength that would have frightened her if she had been able to focus on anything but her body's desperate need. His groans mingled with her soft cries as he took her with him to the edge of ecstasy and beyond. Maggy's nails dug into the hard flesh of his back; her body moved with his in a driving dance of passion.

"Yes, oh, yes!" she sobbed when at last he was coming into her with the force and speed of a jackhammer. He groaned an answer, his hands closing over her hipbones as he gave one last, mighty thrust. He buried his face in the sweet-smelling softness of her hair, his body shuddering and throbbing as it spewed its seed deep inside her. Maggy surged against him, holding him tightly, moaning.

Then, with a wonderful melting sensation more pleasurable than anything she had ever known, she found her own release.

Later, a long time later, her equanimity for the most part restored, Maggy tugged the black sweat shirt over her head and, fully dressed again, turned severe eyes on Nick. He was stretched out on his back, naked as the day he was born, on a pile of hay that he described as soft and she insisted was prickly. They had each had a chance to experience what it felt like against their naked backsides, though as Maggy pointed out, *he* had not had a two-hundred-pound man atop him when he did so.

"We *still* didn't use birth control," she wailed.

Nick chewed reflectively on the straw that protruded from his mouth. "I bought some rubbers this morning, but they're in the house. How was I supposed to guess you'd attack me in the barn?"

His eyes slid to her face to see how she would take that, and as she scowled at him he grinned devilishly at her. Recognizing when she was being teased, Maggy refused to give him the satisfaction of snapping at his bait.

"Get dressed," she said. "I'm hungry."

"I'm too tired to move," he answered placidly. "You plumb tuckered me out."

Maggy made a face at him and snatched the straw from his mouth.

"Get dressed," she said again, poking him in the ribs with the pointy-ended straw. When he grabbed at her hand she jumped up, laughing, and retreated toward the ladder.

"Hang on, I'm coming." He got to his feet with a groan and reached for his clothes.

Obediently halting, Maggy watched with unabashed appreciation as he pulled them on piece by piece. He was even sexier naked than he was dressed, she thought, observing the flexing of those broad shoulders and the rippling of the muscles in his sculptured chest and corded arms as he stepped into his briefs. The classic vee of his torso was pure pinup boy. So was the thick, wedge-shaped mat of black hair that covered his chest. Buffy had described him as looking like a divinely sexy thug, Maggy remembered with an inward grin. Eyeing the tough pugilist's face atop the gorgeous linebacker's body, Maggy decided that the description was nothing if not apt.

She watched with appreciation as he zipped up his jeans. His narrow-hipped, long-legged frame was *made* for jeans. And his flannel shirt didn't look half bad on him, either, Maggy decided with a curling grin as he shrugged into it, buttoned it up, and stuffed the tail into his waistband.

In a word, naked or dressed, he was a hunk.

She told him so with a provocative grin just as he was stomping into his boots. Clearly not appreciating the compliment, he grimaced, snatched up a handful of hay, and started purposefully toward her. Maggy shrieked, whirled, and darted for the ladder.

Only to stop short at what awaited them below.

33

$\mathcal{T}$he cows were massed in the barn, milling about with much swishing of tails and stomping of feet. A particularly large one was right at the base of the ladder. As Maggy looked down at the animal, it raised its massive head, met her eyes, and mooed. A clump of hay, dislodged by Maggy's foot, plummeted downward. The cow opened her enormous mouth at the strategic last second and scooped the hay out of the air in mid-fall. Golden strands thrust out from both sides of the velvety black snout as the beast began, very loudly, to munch.

Maggy recoiled.

"What the devil . . . ?" Seeing her reaction, Nick stepped past her, glanced down, and stepped back. From his expression, it was clear that her action needed no further explanation.

"Now what?" Maggy asked.

"Got me." Nick shrugged. He caught her hand, gave a tug, and pulled her into his arms. "I guess we spend the rest of the day up here making whoopee."

The look Maggy shot him would have put a less self-satisfied individual firmly in his place. Nick merely grinned at her, and when she shoved at his shoulders, let her go.

"I'm hungry," she complained. "Go shoo them away or something."

"They're bigger than me. And I think one of them is a bull."

"Nick . . ." Maggy eyed him warningly. She knew when she was being teased.

"I'll get you out of here on one condition: first you have to promise to marry me."

Maggy's breathing stopped. Nick stood not two feet away, one shoulder propped against a roughhewn beam, his arms folded over his chest, his booted feet crossed at the ankle. A slight smile curled around his mouth, and his eyes gleamed at her as he awaited her answer.

"Are you proposing?" she asked, striving for composure though she suddenly felt shattered.

"Sounds like it."

"Do you know, in all the years we've been together, this is the first time you've ever actually asked me to marry you?"

"*Before,* I thought it was understood between us. Apparently I was wrong. I'm not taking any chances this time. So what do you say?" A faint tension overlay the studied calm of his posture. Maggy sensed it, because she knew him so well and because she was feeling a great deal of tension of her own. She wrapped her arms around herself, and gave an unhappy little laugh.

"Nick. Oh, Nick, my heart says yes."

"Your *heart* says yes?" he repeated slowly, raising an eyebrow at her. "Where does that leave the rest of you?"

"The rest of me says whether I like it or not I'm already married."

"I'm not asking you to become a bigamist, Magdalena. I'm asking you to divorce Lyle Forrest and marry me."

There they were, back to the central question she had evaded, both in her own mind and with him, since he had carried her out of Windermere. She was so happy with Nick. They were right for each other. And she loved him, more than anything or anyone else on earth—except David.

At the thought of her son, her heart gave her an especially bitter pang.

She was going to have to tell Nick about David. The prospect was starting to terrify her. Not physically, as Lyle terrified her, but in the deepest reaches of her heart. The question that plagued her was, would Nick still love her when he knew the whole, awful truth about what she had done? She didn't think she could bear it if she lost Nick's love.

Any more than she could bear it if she lost David.

But she didn't have to tell Nick the truth yet. Not yet. This brief time away from harsh reality had been granted her, perhaps even by a penitent Saint Jude, who must be aware, by now, of how he had screwed up all those years ago. It was hers to use as she would. She still had two weeks, maybe even a little longer, of blissful happiness left. She would be a fool to spoil it sooner than was absolutely necessary.

She would face the music when she had to, and not one second before. After twelve years of misery, was such a brief respite too much to ask of life?

So Maggy smiled at Nick, rather tremulously but still a smile, and answered, "The question's about twelve years late, but the answer's yes."

His eyes narrowed. He straightened away from the beam and was in front of her in two lithe strides. His hand came up to cup her chin, tilting her face up to his. He studied her face with sober attention, as if he could see through her flesh and blood and bone to the thoughts inside. The notion scared her. But she did not shrink away, did not by so much as a flicker of an eyelash reveal her inner turmoil. Instead, hoping to distract him, she caught both sides of his flannel collar to pull his face down to hers.

"I'll marry you as soon as I'm free," she promised, going up on tiptoe to press a soft kiss to his hard mouth. It was not a lie, she consoled herself. She meant every word. She would marry him—with great joy—*when* she was free, and *if* he still wanted her.

She would not allow herself to consider that both the *when* and the *if* were very big qualifying words.

He kissed her thoroughly, then let her go.

"I suppose you realize this means you'll have to get rid of the rock," he said.

For a moment Maggy was bewildered. Then she followed his gaze, which was fastened on her hand. The huge diamond that was Lyle's mark of possession glittered even in the muted daylight of the loft. She was so accustomed to its presence that she had forgotten it was there.

"We could always pawn it," she offered with a mischievous glimmer. In the old days pawning things had been a way of life. Usually, but not always, they'd managed to retrieve the hostaged item before it was irretrievably lost.

Nick grinned but shook his head. "Not permanent enough. You might change your mind."

"Oh, you want something permanent?" An idea began to take shape in Maggy's mind. "I'll show you something permanent."

Pulling the ring and its matching wedding band from her finger, she scooped up a handful of hay and entwined the coarse strands through the tiny golden circles. Then she twisted more hay around the jutting stone of her engagement ring to make sure it was thoroughly covered, and took the two steps needed to bring her to the edge of the loft.

"Watch," she said, beckoning. Nick frowned, clearly mystified, but he obediently moved to stand beside her, looking down at the sea of cows below.

"Here, cow, here, cow." When several of them looked up, including—she thought—the one that had snapped up the falling hay earlier, Maggy let the twist of hay containing her rings drop.

Take that, Lyle, she thought with grim satisfaction as she watched the hay's downward trajectory. Then—snap!—a cow caught the prize, rings and all.

"That's permanent," Nick said as the cow began to chew.

"I'm glad to get rid of them." Her hand felt curiously light without the rings that she had scarcely taken off for twelve interminable years. Maggy had never before realized just how much they had weighed her down.

A thought hit her. She looked at Nick with consternation. "You don't suppose swallowing those rings will hurt the cow, do you?"

"Nah." Nick glanced down at the animal in question and then grinned at her. "But you're going to make somebody's day. They're beef cattle, you know. Can you imagine finding a prize like that in your quarter pounder?"

"That's awful!" Maggy said, referring to the cows' eventual fate rather than the prospect of her rings ending up between the halves of a bun.

"That's life. It's a tough world."

Nick took her left hand, and studied the twin bands of pale skin on her ring finger for a moment. Then he carried her hand to his mouth and pressed his lips to the place where the rings had been. Still holding her hand, he lifted his head to meet her eyes over it. "I'll buy you another diamond. Just as big. I promise."

Maggy shook her head. "I don't want one. I don't care about diamonds anymore." She moved toward him, freeing her hand, and wrapped her arms around his waist. Pressing her lips to the vee of bronzed skin just above the open collar of his shirt, she murmured, "I just care about you."

Nick hugged her, rocking her gently back and forth, then tilted up her chin so that he could drop a kiss on her soft lips.

"It's official, then. We're engaged." He grinned suddenly. "Give me twenty-four hours to arrange a hit on your husband, and we'll run off to Indianapolis and get married."

"That's not even funny." Maggy pushed herself out of his arms. "Don't even joke about it. You wouldn't . . . ?" It was a question that she answered herself. "No, you wouldn't."

Nick might murder Lyle with his bare hands in a rage, but he wouldn't hire someone to do the job for him. That was Lyle's style, not Nick's.

Nick laughed. "Trust me, Magdalena, everything's going to work out fine. Now *I'm* hungry. What do you say we go get lunch?"

"But the cows . . ."

"Watch this." He swung down the ladder, stomping his feet noisily against the rungs. To Maggy's surprise, the beasts closest to the ladder moved placidly away, allowing him to reach the ground.

"Come on." He held up his arms to her. With some trepidation she glanced at the large animals jostling each other not two feet behind Nick. But they didn't appear to have attacking him on their minds—in fact, they barely seemed to be aware of his presence—so she turned her back on them and climbed swiftly down.

He lifted her the last few feet to solid ground. Then, catching her hand, he pulled her toward the open door, casually slapping the rumps of the few cows that did not move aside.

"You're *good* at this," Maggy said with some indignation, remembering how she had feared they were stuck in the loft.

"They've trapped me up there before, when I've gone to paint. Every time they see a person go into the loft, they must think it's time to eat. Mr. Clopton—he's the man who feeds them—throws their hay down from up there."

"I see." That explained why they were so eager to devour any dropped hay.

Maggy and Nick were out in the sunshine by this time. The chickens still scratched and pecked around the barnyard. The fat red one, spying Maggy, waddled toward her, making soft clucking noises as if encouraging largesse.

"Sorry, bud, fresh out," Nick told it, and, opening the gate, pulled Maggy through to safety. He closed the gate again, entwined his fingers with hers, and hand in hand they walked to the house.

The next few days were, for Maggy and Nick, as idyllic as any honeymoon. Link, expressing loud disgust with what he termed their sickening billing and cooing, returned to the farmhouse only in time to fall into bed each night, taking himself off again early every morning. Maggy barely saw him, though Nick would roll out of bed early to exchange a few words with his brother before he left. Maggy knew that Link was covering for Nick in some way that had to do with his work, but she didn't worry about it. There was so much else to think about, primarily sex.

She liked sex, she discovered. In fact, she more than liked it: she loved it. For some reason, telling Nick about the unspeakable thing that Lyle and Ham had done to her seemed to have robbed the act of its terrible power. The mental block that she had feared would cripple her for life had crumbled away. With Nick, she was not only unafraid of sex, she was eager for it, and that she attributed directly to the healing power of love.

She was wildly, crazily in love with him. And he with her.

They made love anywhere and everywhere. In bed, on the couch in the living room, on the kitchen floor, in the shower standing up with Nick's back pressed against the wet tile wall and Maggy's legs wrapped around his waist. They made love until Nick was worn out and Maggy had dark circles under her eyes from lack of sleep. They made love until the box of rubbers Nick had bought was empty, and he had to run back to the drugstore for more. They made love until they were both satisfied —temporarily. And then they made love some more.

For Maggy it was a time of revelation. For the first time as an adult, she was exploring her own sexuality. Always before, when Sarah or Buffy or some of the other women in the crowd Maggy ran with moaned about not getting enough sex, saying that they were horny and they'd just die if they didn't do it soon, Maggy had felt nothing but disgust. They could have been speaking a foreign language, for all the comprehension she'd had of what they were talking about.

Now she knew just what kind of itch her friends had been so eager to scratch. It was a delicious, delightful secret that she was ready to share only with Nick.

One night, sitting up in bed wearing a saucy smile and nothing else, she told Nick that he made her horny. Clad only in a towel, fresh out of the shower he had shared to such good purpose with her, he looked at her as if he couldn't believe his ears. Then he roared with laughter, dropped the towel, fell on her willing body, and proceeded to take care of the problem very thoroughly indeed. She only hoped the wildly creaking bedsprings hadn't been audible to Link.

Making love with Nick was a soul-shattering experience every time. Ten-minute quickies on the front seat of the pickup were as rousing in a different way as hours spent exploring each other's body in bed. Maggy had never dreamed she could feel the way he made her feel. He played her like a virtuoso with a prized violin, and she couldn't get enough of it. She had only to look at him, or he at her a certain way, to feel her body start to heat. She craved his kiss, she craved his touch. She craved him.

Why? Oh, he was sexy, of course. Whoever invented the term must have been thinking of Nick. Everything about him, from the midnight waves of his hair to his sleepy green eyes to his wicked smile to his football player's body, made her heart beat faster. Just thinking about him made her go all liquid inside. But the real reason was that she belonged to him, and he to her. They were together again, Nick and Magdalena, Magdalena and Nick.

It started to rain sometime during the week—Maggy was so preoccupied with Nick that she never noticed exactly when—and the weather stayed bad. The rain fell incessantly, until the yard was a muddy quagmire and the barnyard was a veritable river. But since she and Nick spent most of their time in bed, Maggy welcomed the rain. The sound of it hitting the roof and windows was cozy, and the chill that accompanied the rain gave her an excuse to snuggle close to Nick's big, naked body in bed.

Not that she needed an excuse.

On her second Sunday morning at the farm, when Nick rolled out of bed early, she missed him so much that his absence woke her. For a little while she lay there alone, but the bed without him in it was so lonesome that she couldn't bear it. He would be in the kitchen, she knew, sharing a cup of coffee with Link, and she decided to get dressed and join them. She was so far gone in love that Link's teasing didn't even embarrass her any longer. And Link would tease when she came padding down to the kitchen after Nick.

Romeo, Link had taken to calling his brother. It annoyed Nick, but Maggy thought it was kind of cute.

She ran a brush through her hair, pulled on Nick's white terry-cloth robe that was lying across the foot of the bed for that very purpose, and headed downstairs.

It was a dark, gray morning, seeming earlier than the ten o'clock that the alarm clock by the bed had claimed. Rain still fell in a gentle curtain beyond the windows. So much had fallen over the past few days that a smell of dampness permeated the house.

As she had known they would be, Nick and Link were in the kitchen. The light was on. Maggy could see the yellow pool of it on the dark wood of the hall floor as she descended the stairs. She could hear their voices, too.

Link was saying, ". . . Gonna have to move fast. The powers that be ain't happy that you're shacked up here with a woman. The shit's gonna hit the fan when they find out she's Forrest's wife."

"That's too damned bad. She's not going back." Nick's voice was hard.

"I wasn't suggesting that. You know I'm as fond of the baby girl as you are—well, not that fond, but close. But you gotta admit, it makes for a tricky situation. That's why I'm sayin' that we gotta move fast."

Maggy slowed and then stopped altogether a few feet outside the kitchen door, her eyes widening as she listened.

There was a pause before Nick replied. "All right. We've got everything we need. Forrest and the kid have a flight booked home next Saturday. We could hit him at the airport—no, too many people around. We'll hit him the following morning, Sunday, at Windermere." Maggy couldn't see Nick's face, but she recognized the grim smile in his voice as he added, "If we go in around nine o'clock, he'll even be up and dressed. For church."

Link chuckled. "That's damned poetic."

"Isn't it?"

"Nicky—" Link hesitated, and when he continued his voice had a more serious tone to it. "Maybe I should handle this without you. With the way things are between you and Magdalena, it kinda looks like a personal vendetta on your part against Forrest."

"Does it?" Nick spoke almost ruefully. "Maybe it is. My inclination, when we go in there, will be to shoot the son of a bitch right between the eyes."

Maggy gasped, her hand flying to cover her mouth. She couldn't believe what she was hearing.

"That's why—" Link broke off.

"Magdalena, is that you?" Nick's question was sharp. Maggy, shaken, stood rooted to the spot for a second longer. As she heard the scrape of chair legs across the floor, she stiffened her spine, her lips clamped together, and her eyes blazed. Then she marched into the kitchen.

Both men were on their feet, and Nick was in the act of coming around the table to investigate the sound in the hall. When he saw her, he stopped, and started to smile. Until he got a good look at the expression on her face.

"You want to tell me just what the hell you two are talking about in here?" she demanded fiercely.

34

ick and Link exchanged glances.

"There's toast left, and eggs," Nick said soothingly, coming forward to grasp her arm and draw her toward the table. Maggy took it as a measure of his guilt that he didn't reprove her for swearing. "Come on in and sit down."

"I don't give a damn about toast and eggs, and you know it!" Maggy shook off his hand and faced him with suspicion flashing from her eyes. She was sure, or almost sure, that what they had been talking about was arranging—or maybe participating in—a hit on Lyle! Not that Lyle didn't deserve it, and not that Maggy hadn't wished him dead more than once, but she could not conceive of cold-blooded murder, not even of a man she hated as much as she hated Lyle. It was a sin, a mortal sin, for which they would all, herself included if she knew about it and did nothing to stop it, roast in hell. Besides that, what would such an act do to David, and especially on a Sunday morning, when he would be there?

"I want to know what you two were talking about!"

Nick playfully tugged a lock of the long hair that tumbled over the front of her robe. "Nothing that need worry you, querida. Link, pour Magdalena some orange juice, would you?"

"Don't you try to pacify me with orange juice, you—you . . ." Maggy slapped his hand away and took a deep breath. Her furious glare included Link in its angry condemnation. He was obediently pouring orange juice into a glass for her. "Damn it, I don't want any orange juice! Stop that, Link!"

"Okay, okay!" Link set the carton back down on the table and threw up his hands, palms out, in a placating gesture. His gaze slid to his brother, and again they exchanged glances. From Link's slight shrug, clearly he was casting the problem of pacifying her solely onto Nick.

"I heard you say you were planning to hit Lyle next Sunday morning at Windermere. Where I come from, *hit* means murder." Maggy spoke to Nick, her face perfectly white, her hands clenched at her sides. "If that *is* what you're planning, I forbid it, do you hear me? I forbid you to kill Lyle yourself, either of you, or have him killed, or any combination of the two!"

Nick's eyes narrowed. "You're suddenly awfully concerned about Lyle. Remember him, the asshole that knocks you around?"

If there was a sudden twinge of jealousy in his voice, Maggy was too upset to notice.

"It's not Lyle I'm so concerned about, it's you, you fool. If you kill him, your immortal soul will burn forever in hell, and Link's and mine with you," she raged. "And there's David, too. *David* will be at Windermere next Sunday morning at nine o'clock. How could you even dream of killing Lyle with David there?"

For a moment, Nick said nothing. Then, "Magdalena, I've told you before, I don't have the slightest intention of murdering your sick bastard of a husband. So would you please sit the hell down and drink your orange juice?"

Her anger was infecting Nick. Maggy could tell by the deep red color that was rising to stain his cheekbones and the tips of his ears—and the fact that he was swearing at her.

But she was not so easily silenced. She had heard what he and Link were saying with her own ears, and added to the promise he'd made her days ago, the implications were ominous.

"If you're not going to kill him, or have him killed, then what are you going to do? And don't tell me 'nothing.' *I want to know!*"

"Magdalena . . ." Nick began, sounding as if his patience was wearing thin.

"Nicky." There was a warning in Link's voice.

Nick waved a reassuring hand at his brother without ever shifting his gaze from Maggy's face. "You're going to have to trust me on this, baby," he said grimly.

"So you *are* planning to do something to Lyle next Sunday morning at Windermere." Maggy took a deep breath. "You can't! You can't do *anything* to Lyle with David there. No kind of harm, do you understand? And if you tell me to drink my orange juice again before we get this straight, I'm going to dump it over your stubborn, stupid head."

"Oh, yeah?" Nick scowled at her.

"Yeah." She returned him glare for glare.

"Look, guys . . ." Link interjected heavily from the safety of the table. "Chill out, why don't you?"

"Shut up, Link." They spoke in unison without ever glancing his way. Then Nick took a deep, calming breath.

"I give you my word, we won't do anything that will harm your son." The qualified promise just served to alarm Maggy more. They were planning something, and Nick was not going to scrap it despite everything she had just said. And he was not going to tell her what it was, either, which meant that whatever he had in mind had to be something she would dislike. The knowledge was downright scary.

"I'm not worried about you harming David. I'm worried about you traumatizing him. He's eleven years old and he thinks Lyle hung the moon." Tension sharpened her voice.

Nick took in her agitation, and seemed to make a special effort to lighten up. He held up a placating hand.

"All right, querida, we'll be very careful not to *traumatize* your son." The patronizing note Maggy thought she detected in his voice was the last straw. It made her see red.

"*Your* son." The admission came bursting out. It was the last weapon in her arsenal, and she used it in the full knowledge that it could be as devastating to Nick's feelings for her as the atomic bomb was to Japan in World War II. "Haven't you figured it out yet, you moron? If you do anything to Lyle in front of David, you'll be traumatizing *your* son!"

For a moment Nick merely frowned at her, clearly not understanding. Then he seemed to freeze, his eyes widening as her words sank in.

"*What?*"

"Oh, shit," Link muttered from the table and dropped his head into his hands.

Ignoring him, Nick and Maggy locked gazes. After a long, terrible moment in which the truth trembled in the air between them, Nick reached out and grasped Maggy by the elbows, pulling her close. His grip was not hard, and it didn't hurt. But the look in his eyes scared her.

She shouldn't have told him so bluntly, or in the midst of an argument. She had meant to work up to the subject in a roundabout fashion during the next few days, or weeks, or months, whenever the moment seemed right. But circumstances had forced her hand. She had to make him understand how important it was to keep David entirely out of whatever it was they were planning for Lyle. Nick would go to any extreme to protect *her*, but he didn't have the same feeling for David, even though David was her son. He didn't know David, didn't love David. By telling the truth at last, she knew that she would win his ultimate care in anything concerning her boy. Their boy.

"Are you telling me that David is *my* son?" Nick enunciated each word very carefully, as if he were afraid that Maggy might not understand him. "*Our* son? Yours and mine?"

For a moment she stood silent as the rest of the fight drained out of her. Then she nodded.

"He's eleven years old, he looks just like you, not Forrest, and he likes to paint . . ." Nick enumerated these facts slowly, as if to himself. "What's his birth date?"

Maggy told him. She could read the mental calculations he was making as they took place.

"Sweet Mother Mary!" Suddenly Nick's eyes flared, fierce and hot, and he gave her elbows a little shake. "I should have guessed days ago, shouldn't I? Years ago. But it never occurred to me that *you* . . . My God, woman, what have you done?"

"Let me explain . . ." Her temper had cooled with unbelievable speed until now all that was left where it had burned were cold gray ashes of fear.

"What is there to explain? That you were pregnant with my son when you married Lyle Forrest, and that all these years you've never bothered to tell me that I have a son? You knew you were pregnant when you married him, didn't you? Didn't you?" He gave her elbows a harder shake.

Maggy looked up at him. He was looming over her, six feet two inches of solid masculine rage. His green eyes were alive with it, his mouth was grim with it, his linebacker's shoulders were tense with it. The grip on her elbows was hard enough to hurt. Yet she did not physically fear him, because she knew that Nick, even in the extremes of fury, would never harm so much as a hair on her head. And that knowledge almost made her feel worse than anything else.

She had wronged him, grievously.

"Yes! Yes, I knew it." The confession was wrenched out of her.

"You married him deliberately!"

"Yes, I did!"

"Why, Magdalena? For God's sake, why?" It was a roar, the roar of an animal in pain. His grip on her elbows tightened as the deep red color that had always, with Nick, signified utter rage, flooded his entire face.

"Because twelve years ago you were a punk, and a thief, and a thug, and I wanted a better daddy than that for my child!" Beside herself with guilt, she screamed the words at him.

"So you married *Lyle Forrest*?" He said it the way he would have said *Hitler*.

"He was rich! I didn't know him well, and—I thought he was kind! At least David didn't grow up in the projects, and he's always had a roof over his head, and clothes to wear, and plenty to eat!"

"Do you think I wouldn't have provided for you and *my own son*?"

They were in each other's faces, yelling back and forth, his hands tight around her elbows, his body emanating rage as eloquently as his face. Scared of what she'd done to him, to them, and growing angry herself, Maggy stood her ground. All right, so she'd done wrong. With hindsight, that was easy to see. But at the time, she'd meant it for the best. Why couldn't he try to see it from her perspective and understand that at least?

"Oh, you would have provided, all right," she screeched at him. "You would have shoplifted everything we needed. And then maybe you would have sold a little dope, or stolen a car and sold the parts to a chop shop so we'd have some ready cash. And you know where you would have ended up, sooner or later? In prison like your brother! I think he'd been in there about a year when I found out I was pregnant. Just the kind of father I wanted for my baby!"

"You leave my brother out of this!"

"I won't! It's the truth, and you know it! You know how I got pregnant —hell, you were there! Neither one of us thought a lick about birth control, did we? We were in love, and we were kids! When I found out I was knocked up, I got scared. Really, really scared. I was going to tell you, that day you came over with that stupid coat—remember, the one you stole? But when I saw the coat that you had shoplifted because you couldn't afford to buy me one, I knew just what the rest of our lives would be like. We'd get married, and I'd have the baby, and we'd live in the projects for the rest of our lives, scrimping and scraping and doing without, and sometimes the baby wouldn't have enough to eat . . ." Maggy's voice broke, but before the threatened tears could fill her eyes she willed them back and glared at him. "And that was the best-case scenario. The worst case was that you wouldn't be able to make things any better for us any other way, so you'd get mixed up in something illegal like Link did, and they'd haul you off to prison, too, and then there'd be just me and the baby, and what would we do?"

Maggy drew in a deep, ragged breath, and added, "So I decided to get an abortion."

At the look on his face her chin went up. She knew how he felt about that topic, but then, he'd never been in the position in which she had found herself all those years ago. She had been the one who was pregnant, not he.

"Yes, I did," she answered his unspoken accusation defiantly. "I made an appointment and went to the clinic and—and everything. But when they got me up on that table and—I knew this was it, I couldn't do it. I couldn't do it, do you hear? I got off the table and told them *no,* and then I got dressed again and walked out."

Nick's eyes flickered, and his lips parted as if he would interrupt, but Maggy shushed him fiercely. "Just let me finish, would you please?"

When he replied by clamping his mouth into a hard, straight line, she continued: "I got as far as the steps of the abortion clinic when I realized I'd just run out of options. I sank down on the steps and started to cry. I bawled my eyes out, there on those steps, and I prayed, too. Then I heard a car horn honking. I glanced up, and it was a big, fancy car—a Jaguar, I found out later—and the driver was waving to me. It was Lyle. I recognized him from the Harmony Inn. He was one of my best customers. I wiped my eyes on my shirt and went over to the car. He told me to get in, he'd give me a ride home or wherever. So I got in, and he asked what was the matter, and—I told him. I don't know why I did, except that I was so upset, and he was a stranger, and he seemed kind. I told him the whole story, about how I'd run out of the abortion clinic and everything. He'd parked somewhere by this time, and kept patting my hand and saying things like 'there, there' to me when I cried."

Maggy took another deep breath and looked Nick in the eye. "Then, when I stopped talking, he suggested we get married. He said he'd always wanted a child, but there was something wrong with him that prevented him from having children. He said he would marry me and raise my baby as his own if I would promise never to tell anyone that he wasn't the father. He said the baby would have the best of everything, the best care, the best food, the best clothes, the best education. One day the baby would inherit Windermere and everything else he owned. How could I turn that down? I ask you, how could I turn that down?" It was a fierce cry straight from her heart. His lips once again parted as though he would say something, but Maggy forestalled him, rushing on with the story in an effort to get it out, all out, in the open between them at last.

"I found out later—Virginia, Lyle's mother, told me, a long time after David was born—that Lyle had had an accident when he was a little boy. He'd fallen off a jungle gym and his testicles had gotten hung in a crack in the metal framework and were almost ripped off. Virginia said that the doctor who treated him had told her at the time that Lyle would probably be sterile as an adult as a result of the accident, and that knowledge was one of the great tragedies of her life. That was why she was so pleased about David. Not at first, but later, when she'd had time to think about it. Virginia *knows,* you see, that David is not Lyle's biological son. Lyle *is* sterile, he always has been, and he can't—function sexually. Not at all. He can't get it up. That's why, when we were first married and I kept trying to make things—normal—between us, he would get so angry at me. That's why his first two marriages failed. The women weren't from Louisville, and he paid them a lot of money to go away and keep their mouths shut. By the time he offered me marriage, he was over forty, and the one thing he was desperate for that he didn't have was a child." Maggy's voice faltered and softened. "That was my mistake. I didn't realize when I married him that I was giving David over to him as a hostage for life. If I didn't do as he said, if I thought about leaving him or reporting his abuse or getting some kind of help, David was the weapon he used. Sometimes he would threaten to take David away from me, and sometimes he would threaten to take me away from David, meaning have me committed to a mental institution or something. And sometimes, as David grew older, he threatened to tell my son the truth, that he wasn't a Forrest by blood. For a long time that terrified me, because I was afraid David would be messed up for life if that happened. And I was afraid that he would hate me. I don't truly think Lyle would ever tell him the truth, but even if he did, it wouldn't make any real difference to anyone but David. Lyle will never, ever, let David go. And I won't leave David. Because of David, he's had me under his thumb for all these years."

For a moment there was profound silence. Maggy searched Nick's face, hoping against hope for some small sign that he understood why she had done what she had, and what she'd been through. But she searched in vain.

"You let that sick bastard Lyle Forrest bring up my son." For all its quietness, Nick's voice was terrible, and his face was no less so. Maggy despaired. There was no pity for her, no understanding whatsoever, in his hard green eyes.

"I meant it for the best." Her answer sounded lame, even to her own ears.

"You married another man, knowing you were pregnant with my child, hid the fact that I had a son from me for twelve years, and let the boy grow up thinking that that scumbag Lyle Forrest is his dad, and you *meant it for the best?*" Nick's voice rose incredulously on the last words, and he drew in a ragged breath. "I can't believe I ever thought I knew you. The girl I thought I knew was incapable of something like this."

With that he released her elbows as if touching her had become distasteful and turned his back on her, walking out the door. Feeling as if she had been stabbed through the heart, Maggy watched him go, one hand lifting in a futile effort to summon him back. In a choked voice, she said, "Nick . . ."

But he kept walking, his tense back as rejecting as a slap in the face. As he disappeared down the hall she screamed after him, "Don't you judge me, Nick King! Don't you dare presume to judge me!"

The sound of the front door opening and closing a few seconds later was her answer.

"You'd best leave him be for now." Link's face was as unforgiving as Nick's back had been as he brushed by her, heading after his brother. "He ain't gonna be too happy with you for a while. And I can't say that I blame him."

Then Link, too, disappeared down the hall. Seconds later, Maggy heard him leave the house. Moments after that the roar of an engine starting told her that one or both of the brothers was taking the Corvette.

Maggy stood numbly in the center of the kitchen for some little while longer. Then, when it became clear that neither one of them was coming back right away, she walked into the living room, collapsed facedown on the ancient velveteen couch, and wept.

It must have been about four thirty that afternoon when Maggy heard the front door open at last. She had been on tenterhooks for hours, waiting for Nick to come home. After she had cried all the tears she had to cry, she had lain on the couch in abject misery for a while. Then she had got up, put on another of Nick's baggy sweat suits, this one a dark charcoal gray that exactly matched her mood, and waited. While she had waited, she had cleaned the entire house from top to bottom. She was just starting to rearrange the spices in the rack in the kitchen when she heard the front door open.

Wiping her hands on a dish towel, she hurried toward the front door. As she neared her destination, her steps slowed infinitesimally. She loved Nick so much. He was going to have to understand and forgive her. There was no other option she was prepared to accept.

Girding herself for battle, she stepped into the entryway. And stopped dead.

"There you are, Mrs. Forrest," Tipton said politely. "I was afraid I was going to have to search the house. Mr. Forrest sent me to bring you home."

As she gaped at him, Tipton reached into the pocket of his dripping trench coat and produced a small but very serviceable-looking pistol.

35

Because of the rain, it was fully dark by the time they reached Windermere, and Tipton escorted her inside. The house was quiet, the hall deserted. The chandelier was on, lending icy grandeur to the scene as Tipton, holding Maggy's elbow, propelled her toward the back of the house.

Lyle was downstairs, in his office, seated behind his desk in his big green leather chair. He was, as always, immaculately turned out, in an ivory cashmere sweater over a blue button-down shirt and navy slacks. His fair hair gleamed in the light of the green desk lamp that was the room's only illumination. He didn't stand up—he had long since stopped performing that courtesy for his wife—but merely eyed her up and down as Tipton pushed her into the room. His pale blue eyes glowed with barely suppressed excitement.

Maggy felt a frisson of pure fear and in defiance of it lifted her chin and stiffened her spine as she met her husband's gaze.

"How dare you send this—scumball—after me with a gun! He'll be lucky if I don't go straight to the police and swear out a complaint against him for menacing!"

Maggy's angry outburst rolled off the two men like water off an oiled surface.

"There was no trouble, sir." Tipton spoke from behind her without inflection.

"I didn't expect any. Timing is everything, as always. Go upstairs and bring down her luggage, and David's, please. We'll be leaving in fifteen minutes."

"Yes, sir." Tipton vanished, closing the door behind him.

"Leaving?" Maggy's voice was sharp. That Lyle had approved Tipton's use of the gun she had never doubted—frightening and humiliating her in such a way was classic Lyle—but she had thought that the weapon was merely to insure that she went with Tipton without a struggle. Now she began to wonder just what, exactly, was going on. Something was, without a doubt.

"We're going on a nice little trip, darling. To South America. You and David and I."

Maggy's impulse was to scream at him that she wasn't going as far as the backyard, much less South America, with him, but instinct made her cautious.

"To South America? Why?"

"Now, that is for me to know, and you to worry about. And you should worry." Lyle gave a little chuckle that made the hair rise on the back of Maggy's neck. He was high on excitement, tense with it, near to bursting with it. He looked different, somehow, harder, less the gentleman than usual. The idea that he was planning to whisk her and David off to South America, far away from any chance of getting help from anybody they knew, frightened her. Suddenly *Tia* Gloria's message popped into her mind: "Danger is at hand. Beware of harm . . ." All at once Maggy was very much on her guard.

"What about Derby? Have you forgotten about the party Saturday night?" Maggy grasped for the first thing she could think of that might make him think twice about spiriting them out of the country on such short notice. Derby, which would fall on the following Saturday, was a huge event at Windermere, with all of the Forrest clan in their special box at Churchill Downs for the race itself and the blue-blooded socializing that preceded it. Afterward they hosted, at Windermere, the annual Diamonds and Pearls Ball. The tradition dated back twenty-five years. Only the direst of circumstances would force Lyle to miss it.

"Are you implying that I'm getting senile, Maggy? Of course I haven't forgotten about the ball. Mother and Lucy can handle it, in our absence. They're not here, by the way. At my urging, Lucy has taken Mother to New York, to be seen by specialists. And Louella's gone home. We're all alone here in the house tonight, you and David and I—and Tipton. Just in case you should be thinking about making one of your trademark tacky scenes." He smiled at her, that crocodile's smile that had always put the fear of God into her, and came around the desk toward her. To Maggy's relief, he stopped before he reached her and leaned back against the desk, placing his hands flat on its smooth mahogany surface as he surveyed her from head to toe.

"Tell me, darling, have you had a nice little vacation, balling your lover's brains out while I was out of town?"

His tone chilled her blood. Maggy watched him with wary attention and said nothing.

Lyle nodded approvingly. "Smart of you not to deny it. Did you think I wouldn't find out? No, of course you knew I would. I must say, I applaud your taste in men. He's an impressive physical specimen. You don't suppose he'd be willing to put on a little performance for me, do you, if I offered to pay him well? I'd like to watch him getting screwed in the ass." Lyle's eyes wandered over her again. "Did you tell him that he is David's father?"

The question was tossed at her almost casually. As it hit, Maggy drew in her breath and paled. She could feel the color receding from her face. Every warning signal her body possessed went on red alert. For the first time, she realized that Lyle was truly dangerous. What awaited her was not more of the same that she had endured throughout her marriage. It was as if he'd been wearing a mask all those years, a civilized mask that had allowed only glimpses of the monster that he truly was to peek through. Now the monster was out in plain sight, no longer bothering to hide itself. The knowledge with all its implications was terrifying.

"You did." Lyle didn't need a verbal answer. "Well, that might almost be a good thing. It gives me another hold over him—besides you. Were you careful about birth control this time, Maggy? I hope not. I rather fancy giving David a sibling, don't you? Maybe we'll work on it, once we get to where we're going."

Maggy hoped her inner shudder didn't show. "Where *is* David?" she asked, trying to change the subject. Lyle was scaring her. Every bit of a sixth sense she possessed screamed that she was in acute physical danger. Nick had promised that he would keep her safe from Lyle—but where was Nick? Nowhere near enough to intervene. Whatever he and Link had been planning for Lyle would come too late. A whole week too late to help her or David.

"David's here." Lyle smiled at her. "Was your boyfriend very upset when you told him about David? Are you on the outs with him over it?"

"Nick was—understanding." It was a lie, but an innate protectiveness of the man she loved forbade her to reveal just how upset Nick had been. Nick's reaction was a private matter, to be shared with no one who had not witnessed it.

"Was he now?" Lyle chuckled hugely. "I doubt it. I think he was very,

very angry. Your boyfriend is an emotional fool, I saw it twelve years ago when he had the gall to come sniffing around here after you. A bloody romantic emotional fool. I doubt he's gotten any wiser over the last twelve years, certainly not wise enough to appreciate what you've done for his seed by giving the child born of it to me to raise. Come now, Maggy, tell the truth. You told him this morning and he was furious, wasn't he? I know perfectly well that he went stomping out of that farmhouse you two were holed up in and roared off in that gaudy car of his. I've had people watching you for days, you know, waiting for the chance to bring you home where you belong. You weren't expecting that, were you, either of you?" Lyle shook his head at her. "So you told him this morning, and he got mad. Isn't that the way it happened?"

"What if it did?"

"Don't take that tone with me, Maggy my love." The look Lyle turned on her was suddenly ugly, so ugly that Maggy could not control her reflexive shrinking. A satisfied light appeared in his eyes as he saw her cringe. The tension that had infused his body left it again, and he relaxed against the desk.

"All right, so he was a little angry." Maggy made the admission to pacify him.

"I thought so. His kind of people have trouble controlling their emotions. He's poor white trash, you know. He was poor white trash twelve years ago, and he's poor white trash now. It's in his blood. In your blood, too. But I think I've educated it out of David. You know the perennial debate, nature or nurture? With David, I think we've definitely proved the case for nurture, don't you? David's a Forrest through and through, because I've worked hard to make him one. He's my son. *Mine.*"

"I would never dispute that he loves you, Lyle."

"Yes, he does, doesn't he? So you see, I can't be all bad, my darling, can I?" Lyle chuckled again. "What does your boyfriend think he's going to do now that he knows, I wonder—waltz in here and steal my son and my wife out from under my nose? Yes, that's what he thinks, and I know how he thinks he's going to do it. But it's not going to work, because the three of us are going to fly the coop. Tonight."

What was he talking about? There was something going on here, some drama being played out between Lyle and Nick that Maggy was not privy to. It was as if they each knew something about the other that she did not know. . . .

Before she could puzzle at it any longer, a discreet knock sounded on the door. "Suitcases are in the car, Mr. Forrest."

Lyle raised his voice. "Thank you, Tipton. Now, go get David, would you? He's in his room, playing Nintendo, I think. Tell him it's time to go."

"Yes, sir."

Maggy heard Tipton's footsteps receding. Lyle's attention shifted back to her.

"You know, I'm almost glad that your boyfriend knows that he sired David, because it's going to eat at him for the rest of his life. He can't make any legal claim to the boy—did you know that, Maggy? Did you know that since you and I were married when David was born, and since I acknowledge him as my son, in the eyes of the law he *is* my son? No?" Lyle shook his head reprovingly. "You should really check with lawyers before you get into these things, my love."

"What about David's school? You can't just pull him out. There is still a month to go in the semester, and he's just missed two weeks." Again, Maggy was grasping at straws, but panic was clouding her mind so that she could hardly think. In a few minutes, they would be on their way to the airport, where she did not doubt that Lyle had a private jet waiting to whisk them out of the country. She would be completely at his mercy then—and Nick would never find them.

"Don't you worry about my son. I'll always take care of him. No, you should be worried about yourself, right now. I'm giving serious thought to killing you, you know."

Looking at him, at the predatory face and shining blue eyes, Maggy believed it. She was willing to believe anything of Lyle now. It took every bit of willpower she possessed not to glance behind her, at the door. She knew where it was without needing to look. She knew every inch of this house. At the first opportunity she could cut and run—but what about David?

She could not leave David. If she did, she might never see him again. But if she didn't, would she die?

"Yes, I certainly am. David's old enough to be able to cope without a mother, and in a few years you'll be a social embarrassment to him. But on the other hand, he loves you, however misguidedly, and I don't want to cause him unnecessary grief. And that boyfriend of yours seems to be a faithful sort. Perhaps, if he knows that *I* have you, he'll be a little more careful about what steps he takes against me in future. So, on balance, I suppose I'll let you live. For now. But here's the deal: you must do just exactly as I tell you, and pretend to David and the rest of the world that things are hunky-dory between us. If you do, you won't die, and you'll get to act as mother to our boy. But if you do something that makes me think that your presence in this world is more liability than asset, I won't hesitate. You'll suffer a tragic accident, maybe fall off a hideously high cliff, or drown in the surf, or perhaps you'll be struck by a car. I'll work out the details if you put me to the trouble."

Lyle smiled at her, a supremely confident smile with no bravado in it. He had no doubt that he held the upper hand—which, she realized, he did, just as he always had. Maggy felt her composure begin to crumble and fought to keep the utter despair that was filling her from showing.

"Oh, and darling, there's just one other thing: If you do put me to the trouble of arranging an accident, right after you go to your maker I'll make sure David sees this. That way he'll know just what you are, and he won't grieve so much."

Lyle picked up a remote control device from his desk, pointed it toward a console in the corner, and pushed a button. Immediately a wall-size screen descended. He pressed another button, and an image sprang onto the screen, larger than life, in minute resolution and vivid color. An image of herself, dancing almost naked on stage, while "Born to Be Wild" wailed loudly in the background.

Smiling at the stunned expression on her face, Lyle hit the mute button. The grotesque image continued to dance, but without benefit of sound. Maggy watched her teenage self shake her bare behind with every evidence of enjoyment at the audience of drooling men, and felt sick.

"What would David think of his mother if he could see that, do you suppose?" Lyle asked, raising his brows at her. "I have to admit, I was shocked myself. I knew you were a little slut when I married you, but I didn't know you were a professional."

"Where did you get that?" Maggy felt as if she were suffocating.

"From your very charming—aunt, is it? She was, uh, reluctant to surrender it at first, but Tipton was able to persuade her."

Fear clutched Maggy's throat. "If you hurt *Tia* Gloria . . ."

"Yes? What are you going to do about it, my darling wife?"

There was nothing she could do, Maggy knew. Nothing she could do except hate him. And to think she'd had an attack of conscience when she suspected Nick was planning to murder him, she thought with a touch of hysteria. If she had had any kind of weapon within reach at that moment, she would have murdered him herself.

"That's what I thought." When Maggy said nothing, Lyle nodded in satisfaction. Then he stood up and walked back behind the desk, clearly so confident of her that he didn't even feel the need to keep his eyes on her any longer. Opening his desk drawer, he took from it a pistol. The midnight-blue steel of its barrel gleamed dully in the lamplight.

Maggy felt cold terror run up her spine.

"For insurance," Lyle said lightly as he saw where her eyes rested. "But I won't need it, will I, because you're a smart girl. We're going to get in the car with David, and go to the airport like any other happy little family. And we are happy, are we not? So smile, my darling. Smile."

Maggy smiled. As long as Lyle had David, he had her, too, just where he wanted her: under his thumb. She was not going to even try to flee without her son. And he knew it.

He pushed the remote-control button, turning off the video, and ejected the tape, which he slid into his jacket pocket. Then he walked toward her, caught her elbow, and led her toward the door.

"You're going to have to change on the plane," he said disapprovingly as he reached around her to grasp and turn the ornate brass knob. "You look like a bag lady. What're you wearing, *his* clothes? How sweet. How truly sweet."

He pushed her ahead of him out into the hall. Maggy supposed his hold on her arm could be viewed as affectionate by their son, who stood waiting with Tipton in the vast entry hall. The outside door was open, letting in a burst of cool, rain-damp night air, and the Rolls waited at the foot of the steps.

"Hey, Mom, Dad says we're going to Brazil! I don't even have to finish out the school year! Isn't that cool?"

"Cool," Maggy agreed with the best smile she could muster, pulling her arm away from Lyle's grip and walking over to embrace her son. David suffered her hug with fairly good grace, not returning it but not pushing her away. As she looked down at his smiling, innocent face, at the dancing red highlights the chandelier picked up in his wavy hair, she felt her heart clench.

To keep David, she was going to have to give up Nick. Nick, whom she loved more than all the world—except for her son.

Something, she was never afterward sure exactly what—a sound or a sixth sense, maybe—made her glance up. When she did, she froze.

Nick, with Link behind him and what seemed to be a squadron of other men fanned out down the steps beyond Link, stepped through the doorway as calmly as if he owned the house. He was clad in tight jeans and a leather jacket, and raindrops glinted in his black hair. In his hand was a drawn gun.

36

"*D*EA," Nick said, flashing a badge in his left hand. "Don't anybody move."

Nick's pistol was trained on Lyle. His eyes never touched her, but Maggy gaped at him, frozen in place by shock. DEA? Nick? The idea was so bewildering that she could hardly take it in. Could it possibly be true? And even if it were, under what pretext could the DEA raid Windermere? As far as she knew, none of the Forrests had ever used drugs of any type. Which was more than could be said of at least one of the gentlemen who had just taken over the room.

"Hang on a minute," Nick said to the armed men who were now streaming through the doorway behind him. To Link, he growled, "Get the kid out of here."

"Mom!" David was wide-eyed and panicked. Maggy's arms went protectively around his thin shoulders, and then she looked up over David's head to meet Link's eyes. David's uncle's eyes. Link gave a quick nod as if to promise that he'd see to it that David was taken care of.

Maggy leaned down to whisper in David's ear. "It's all right. Go with him. His name's Link. He's a good guy."

David glanced up at her uncertainly and then over at Link. Maggy hugged him again and dropped a quick kiss on his cheek. Then she pushed him toward Link.

"Come on, kid, you ever sat in a police car? I'll even let you work the lights." Link took David's arm and gently but firmly propelled him toward the door.

"I don't care about that. I'm too old," David proclaimed scornfully. With a quick glance back at Maggy, he asked, "What's going on?"

"I'll explain it all to you once we're in the car," Link promised and led him out the door.

Once David was out of sight, Nick nodded, and a quartet of men surrounded Tipton, saying something to him that Maggy couldn't quite decipher, then snapping handcuffs on his wrists and shaking him down. Nick himself, with three other men behind him, came toward Lyle. The two men locked gazes. Nick smiled, a hard, taunting smile.

One of the men accompanying Nick intoned: "Lyle Forrest, you're under arrest. For violating Section . . ."

What he said after that was lost forever for Maggy as a hard arm whipped around her neck without warning, choking her, knocking her off-balance, pulling her back against a whipcord-lean body. She grabbed at the arm for balance and felt the cold muzzle of what she knew instinctively was Lyle's pistol pressed against her temple.

Lyle was using her as a hostage!

"Back off!" Lyle warned in a voice that Maggy scarcely recognized as his. His arm around her neck tightened so that she had to fight to breathe, and her nails sank into the soft cashmere of his sweater as she struggled to stay on her feet. Icy fear shot through her veins as Lyle dug the mouth of the pistol punishingly into her temple. "Back off, or I'll kill her. You know I will, King."

Nick froze, his face going utterly white.

"You heard him, back off!" he barked, holding up a restraining hand to the men who had been in the process of surrounding Lyle and who were now motionless as statues. They obeyed, melting back toward the door.

"Tell them to throw their weapons out the door. You, too."

When Nick was slow to obey, Lyle screamed. "Do it! I mean it! Right now!"

Nick tossed his pistol out the open door, and gestured to the other men to do the same. With obvious reluctance, they obeyed. As if it were her death knell, Maggy heard the ring of metal clanking against stone as the pistols rolled down the steps. There was nothing now to stop Lyle from killing her if he wished—and killing Nick too.

Lyle had her in a choke hold with a pistol to her head. Nick, facing him warily, was unarmed. All that was keeping the two of them alive, Maggy felt, was Lyle's certainty that while he could certainly shoot her and Nick before anyone could stop him, he would just as certainly not escape with his own life. There were too many men, and one or two of them would surely make it to their weapons before he could get away. Maggy prayed that that continued to be enough of a deterrent. She prayed . . ."

"Let her go, Forrest," Nick said.

Lyle gave a short bark of a laugh. "So you can have her? I don't think so."

"So far, we just have drug charges against you. No one's been hurt. You can hire a fancy lawyer and play beat-the-system. With your money, you just might win."

"I might—but I might not. So I'm not prepared to play." Lyle's arm tightened punishingly around Maggy's neck. Nick's eyes flickered down to her face, involuntarily, she thought, and as she looked at him with all the horror she felt in her gaze his jaw turned to granite. That was the only sign of stress he gave before he once again focused on Lyle.

"Let her go. She doesn't have anything to do with this."

"Doesn't she? I think she does. I think she's the whole ball of wax. You never would have started checking into my affairs if it wasn't for the little bitch here." Lyle ground the gun so hard against Maggy's temple that she cried out. Nick's eyes met hers again, and Maggy felt stark terror fill her at what she saw in his gaze. He was terrified, too. Terrified for her.

Lyle saw Nick's fear and chuckled. "Afraid I'm going to blow her brains out right here in front of you, King? I just might, if for no other reason than to teach you a lesson. But if you're smart, if you let me walk out of here, I won't kill her. At least, not tonight."

"Forrest . . ." Nick's voice was hoarse. Maggy was sweating, her heart pounding so hard that she had trouble hearing above the thumping of her own pulse in her ears. She knew Lyle as none of these men, even Nick, did. And she knew that he was capable of any atrocity.

"Call them off," Lyle growled, jerking his head at the men assembled between him and the door. "Tell them to get away from the door. Right now."

"Move back." Nick ordered tensely. The men—there were perhaps a dozen of them—did. Lyle dragged Maggy toward the door.

"Let 'em go," Nick barked to some unseen soul, and Maggy felt Lyle tense. She closed her eyes, praying, then opened them again as Lyle yanked her over the threshold. On the way down the shallow steps she stumbled, only to have Lyle jerk her back onto her feet again with his arm around her neck. Gasping for air, hanging from his arm, she was forced around the waiting Rolls.

"See you in hell, King!" Lyle yelled jubilantly, opening the door and stuffing Maggy into the front seat. He jumped in right behind her and slammed the door shut. He kept the pistol pointed at her head. It took just a second for him to turn the key in the ignition—the keys had been left there by Tipton as was his custom when he brought the car around —and slide the transmission into drive.

Then with a triumphant laugh he stomped on the gas.

"The fools! It was unloaded! It was unloaded, all the time!" Lyle crowed.

Maggy got just a glimpse, in the rearview mirror, of Nick and the whole army of men he'd brought with him spilling out the door as the Rolls gunned down the driveway. Then Lyle's words sank in.

Before she could take any kind of action, the pistol came crashing down on her skull. Maggy cried out, saw stars, and instinctively thrust up a hand to ward off the next blow, which was as furious as the first.

"Prepare to die, bitch," Lyle shrieked. The car careened toward the first turn in the driveway, and all at once Maggy guessed what he was going to do. There were police cars blocking the entrance to the estate —Maggy could see their flashing blue lights from there—so his only way out was death. And he meant to take her with him.

"No!" she screamed as he hit her again. She scrambled for the passenger door, meaning to throw herself from the car. Lyle grabbed the hem of her sweat shirt, hauling her back beside him, his foot stomping down on the gas as the first, most treacherous bend hurtled toward them out of the night.

"Bye, my darling," he crooned and struck her with the gun. Because of her struggles, the blow just glanced off her head instead of rendering her unconscious as she guessed it was meant to do.

She had only seconds left in which to act.

Terror lent her strength and cunning, and paradoxically banished the crippling sensation of fear. She leapt toward him, her nails raking his cheeks, her teeth clamping down over his nose. Lyle screamed, his hand jerking up to ward her off—and then Maggy made a flying dive toward the door.

Her fingers fumbled with the latch, the door swung open, and she launched herself out into the cold, wet night.

Hitting the grassy lawn beside the pavement was as shattering as being slammed into solid cement. Maggy rolled onto her back and lay motionless, the breath knocked from her body, as misty drops of rain fell on her unprotected face.

Seconds later she heard a tremendous crash as the Rolls rammed through the century-old retaining wall. The stones were piled atop one another without mortar, and at the speed the Rolls was going there was no chance the wall could hold it back. Maggy glanced to the side in time to see the car plow through and keep going, its taillights tracing a crazy arc in the night sky as it disappeared over the edge.

What came next was almost an anticlimax: The only sound that heralded the car's landing in the creek three hundred feet below was a muted splash.

"Magdalena! Oh, my God, Magdalena!" Feet pounded down the driveway. Nick was running, running furiously, toward where the Rolls had disappeared. Behind him, the other men were running, too, but Nick was outdistancing them all. The unadulterated fear that drove him was there in his voice as he called her name.

"Magdalena!"

Maggy took a deep, painful breath. "Over here," she gasped, rolling to her stomach and trying, rather unsteadily, to get up on her hands and knees.

"Nick! I'm over here!"

This time he heard her. Maggy was sinking back onto her haunches when he slid to a stop beside her and hunkered down.

"Thank merciful Mary," he breathed, touching her face with a hand that shook. "I thought you were gone."

Then he pulled her into his arms. Maggy wrapped her own arms around his neck, and for a long moment they held each other tightly while the rain spilled over them and soaked the muddy grass in which they crouched and splattered against the driveway just beyond. After a while someone shouted Nick's name, and he raised his head.

"I'm coming," he yelled back, and stood up, lifting Maggy into his arms. Still shaken, she didn't argue as he walked back toward the house with her curled against his chest, past streams of running, shouting men and half a dozen cars that were apparently being moved so that their lights would be in a position to shine out over the place in the wall where the Rolls had gone through. It was a surreal scene of mass confusion. For Maggy, the only thing that was real and solid and safe in it was Nick.

37

$\mathcal{T}$hey did not find Lyle's body. The creek was swollen from two weeks of never-ending rain, and the Rolls was completely submerged when the police got to it. The car's roof and hood were crushed, all the windows including the windshield were shattered, and Lyle was not inside. According to the police, the force of the rushing current must have sucked his body from the car and sent it swirling into the river. It could be anywhere. One day, probably in the summer, it would surface. Floaters always did.

Given the length of that drop, and the condition of the car, they were as certain as it was possible to be without an actual corpse that Lyle was dead.

Privately, John Harden, the chief of police, who was also a longtime friend of the family, told her and Lucy and Ham that what had happened simplified matters considerably. The scandal that would have broken had Lyle not done what he did would have been immense.

The meeting, called at Harden's instigation to explain what was happening, took place on the fourteenth floor of a thirty-story office building downtown, with big glass windows looking out over the city. It was about two o'clock in the afternoon of the day after Lyle's death. Maggy stared out the window as she listened. All she could think of was how ironic it seemed that the sun was finally shining. After almost two weeks of rain, spring was bursting forth in all its splendor.

If Lyle had had his way, she would not have seen this gorgeous day. There was not a doubt in her mind that he had meant to take her with him last night.

Maggy shivered and concentrated on what Harden was saying.

"Seems Mr. Forrest ran one of the biggest marijuana growing operations in the country, believe it or not. We're talking millions of dollars worth of pot a year. Our soil around here's real good for it, you know, and Kentucky Bluegrass—that's what they call the stuff grown in this state—is real popular everywhere right now. Mr. Forrest's magazine apparently has been operating in the red for a long time, and when he inherited it he doesn't seem to have had any other significant source of income. He did what I guess he felt he had to do to repair the family fortunes. You're lucky the way he did it—it was pretty ingenious, I must say. All that marijuana—thousands of acres of it—was planted on National Forest land. Don't look like the federal forfeiture law is gonna apply in this case."

"Because the property was not bought with drug proceeds, and no drug transactions apparently took place on the premises, the deceased's house and surrounding land is not at risk. However, we're still looking into other areas. He had a lot of cash, a lot of investments, vehicles, art collections, jewelry. Some of them may indeed be subject to forfeiture. You'll be notified." The speaker was a clean-cut young man in an immaculate navy suit. Charles Adams was his name, and Chief Harden had introduced him as the DEA agent in charge of the investigation.

"With Mr. Forrest dead, and out of consideration for Mrs. Virginia Forrest's fragile state of health, I think we'll be able to keep it all pretty hush-hush. Isn't that right, Mr. Adams?"

"It looks that way." If Mr. Adams's reply was slightly sour, Maggy was not left to wonder why for long. Link, unfamiliar in a suit and tie, pulled her into a cluttered cubbyhole of an office on her way out of the building. Lucy was not speaking to her, and Maggy was finally able to be as cold as she wished to be to Ham, which made for an uneasy threesome when circumstances such as the police chief's meeting forced them together. Lucy and Ham had gone on ahead, and consequently Maggy was alone when Link appeared out of nowhere and grabbed her arm.

"You hangin' in there all right, baby girl?" Link asked as he shut the door behind them.

"Where's Nick?" Maggy asked the question that had been driving her mad since the night before, when Nick had deposited her safely inside Windermere and disappeared into the rainy night to direct the search for Lyle.

Link shook his head. "Under strict orders to stay away from you, that's where. He's in deep doo-doo with the powers that be. They said he compromised the investigation by getting involved with the subject's

wife—that's you. I warned him they'd think he was on a personal vendetta if he went after Forrest, and they do. They say it's a good thing
Forrest is dead, because Nicky's behavior would weaken the case in
court."

"I can't believe you two really work for the DEA." Maggy sank down
on an aluminum-armed chair and stared up at Link, who was perched
on the corner of a black metal desk.

"Does seem kinda out of character, doesn't it?" Link grinned. "But
we've changed a lot. Nicky was a SEAL, you know."

"A seal?"

"You know, a Navy SEAL. He joined the navy not too long after you
ran off with Forrest, though whether he did it just to get away from it all
or to make something of himself, I don't know. Whatever, they knocked
a lot of discipline into him, made him a SEAL. When he got out—they
wanted him to reenlist but he wouldn't—he wasn't a kid anymore: he'd
grown up. He needed a civilian job, so he hired on as a cop in Cleveland."

"A *cop*? Nick?" Maggy couldn't have been more astonished if Link
had said Nick had walked on the moon. Years ago, they had hated cops,
all three of them, with the fierce animosity of dedicated young lawbreak-
ers.

"Yeah, Nick." Link chuckled. "He couldn't hack it for long, though.
He didn't like arresting people. So he quit and used some money he had
saved up to put a down payment on a nightclub that was on his beat. It
was pretty run-down, with a rough clientele and on the verge of bank-
ruptcy. Nicky thought he could turn it around."

"Now that part he told me," Maggy said dryly.

Link gave her a level look. "Yeah, well, you gotta understand that he
couldn't tell you the *truth*. It was bad enough that he was romancing you
when we were going after your husband. But if he had told you about
the investigation—or even that he was in the DEA—and you had spilled
the beans, it could have really screwed things up, put some people's lives
in danger. We use a lot of snitches, you know. Informants."

"I wouldn't have told." Maggy was indignant.

"I know you wouldn't have, baby girl, and Nicky knew it too. But you
might have acted different, or done or said something that would have
put Forrest on his guard. It was too dicey. Nicky couldn't have done it."

"I understand." If her admission was grudging, it was also the truth.
She did understand, quite a few things. Nick's promise that he would
make everything all right for her, for one, and his obfuscation about how

he earned a living. "So go on. What happened after Nick bought the nightclub?"

"He was just getting it back on its feet when some thugs started pushin' him to launder drug money through it for them. You know Nicky, he don't get pushed easily, and when he said no, things started to happen, like the place catching fire and a waiter getting beat up, things like that. So he went to a cop he knew, and the cop brought in the DEA. The DEA asked Nicky if they could use his place to run a sting. He said yeah, they caught the crooks, and the whole scheme was so successful that they decided to pull it again, in another city. They asked Nicky to set it up for them, offered him a job that paid a lot more than his nightclub was making. So he took it, with conditions. That's how he got me sprung—I was part of the deal he wangled with the DEA. We've stuck together ever since, been responsible for some really big busts. The DEA gets a lot of bang for its bucks, with us." Link grinned. "So they put up with some shit. Usually from me, this time from Nicky."

"What on earth made the DEA start looking into Lyle?"

Link looked suddenly serious. "That was Nicky's doing. A couple of years ago, just about the time when he was getting it into his head to come back and see if he could start things up again with you, Nicky heard through the grapevine that there was a big marijuana operation going down in Kentucky. Guy running it was known in the business by the street name of Colonel Sanders. Our Colonel Sanders was supposed to be a rich son of a bitch, one of the country club set, a blueblood, in it for the fun of it 'cause he didn't need the money. Nicky starts checkin' into this rumor, and the name that comes back at him knocks him out: Lyle Forrest. He can't hardly believe it, but he puts out the word on ol' Lyle. There's all kinds of loose talk about Forrest out there. Pretty soon we were pretty damn sure that Colonel Sanders was none other than our boy. Nicky was in hog heaven over it." Link chuckled, saw that he had Maggy's rapt attention, and continued. "So Nicky went to the big boys, told 'em what he had, and suggested we set something up in Louisville. They were pretty impressed with what we showed 'em and told us to go for it. What they didn't know about was Nicky's personal stake in all this: You. Now that they do know, they don't much like it."

It took Maggy a moment to absorb all this. Then she asked, quietly, "Is he in a lot of trouble?"

Link made a face. "Enough. They'd probably fire him, but they need him to testify in a few other cases. Where his word isn't *tainted*." The mincing way Link said this last made it pretty obvious that he was quoting from a disliked superior.

"Is he still mad at me?" That question was even quieter than the one that preceded it.

Link looked at her, hard. "You'll have to ask him that. All I know is, when we got back to the farm and found you gone, I thought he was gonna have a heart attack. That fella who feeds the cows—Clayton, Clopton, whatever—was there, and he said he saw one of them big, fancy Mercedes leavin' as he drove up. We knew who it was, of course, and came after you lickety-split, calling in the cavalry on the way. The powers that be are mad about that, too. They like to have their raids planned out in advance. They say that if Nicky hadn't gotten involved, if he had let someone else handle this deal from the beginning instead of using a government agency as a weapon of vengeance—I'm quoting there—then Forrest would have been brought to justice and everything would be a lot more clear-cut. *I* think they're mad because they can't seize Windermere. I have to hand it to your hubby, baby girl. He was smart enough not to conduct any kind of drug business on the estate. As far as we can tell, he didn't even use the phone there to call his associates."

"He had a cellular phone. He always preferred to use it," Maggy said, remembering. At the time, she hadn't thought a thing about it. Lyle's constant use of the cellular phone, where every call was billed by the minute, had seemed perfectly normal. So had a lot of things. She had been blind.

"Yeah, well, they're checking records on that now."

"Are you in trouble, too?" Maggy asked.

Link shrugged. "They haven't chewed my ass out yet, if that's what you mean. I think the official line on this is that I can't be held responsible for my little brother."

"Is he at the farm?" She badly wanted to see Nick. Last night, he had held her as if he would never let her go—and then he had disappeared. But Link said he had been ordered to stay away. Knowing that gave her renewed hope. Maybe he was over his anger at her. Maybe he understood and was ready to forgive what she had done.

Link shrugged and slid off the desk. "I really couldn't say. Come on, Magdalena, let me walk you to your car. Before the powers that be see me talkin' to you and come down on *me.*"

Maggy nodded and stood up. She didn't want to get Link in trouble, too. Link took her elbow, and though Maggy insisted there was no need, escorted her down the elevator and out to her car. It was a tan four-door Volvo, one of many cars on the estate, and Maggy had driven herself to the meeting in it. The experience had been enjoyable despite everything, and had given her a glimpse of what life was going to be like without Lyle. At last, after twelve years of always having to do as he wished or suffer the consequences, she was free.

"Thanks, Link. Tell Nick—tell him . . ." Maggy said as Link ceremoniously opened her door for her and ushered her inside.

"Tell him yourself," Link said, grinning, and shut the door. Maggy was so surprised by his answer that she frowned out the window at him. Something large and dark in the seat beside her moved, catching her peripheral vision. She jumped, and her head whipped around as fear clogged her throat.

"You really ought to check out the inside of your car *before* you get in it," Nick said dryly.

"Nick! You scared me to death! What are you doing here? Link said you were in trouble, that they'd told you to stay away from me until this is all over."

"Yeah, well, they did. And I told them that until I actually see Forrest's body, I planned to stick to you like glue. If they didn't like it, they could fire me."

"And did they? Fire you, I mean."

Nick shrugged. "I didn't give them a chance to say. I walked out and headed downstairs just in time to see you and your relatives being ushered into the head local yokel's office. I told Link to keep an eye out for you, and I came out and got in your car. The parking attendant was very helpful in pointing it out, even told me you drove in alone. I tipped him five bucks, which I consider money well spent."

"You don't think Lyle's dead, do you?" A cold frisson of fear ran along Maggy's spine.

"I didn't say that. Everything points to the fact that he's dead. But there's always that chance, that outside chance, that he's not. He tried to kill you, Magdalena. I think he's psychotic. If he's not dead, there's a slight possibility that he may come back to finish the job—or to get the boy."

That last possibility had never occurred to her.

"David . . ." In a sudden panic to reach her son, Maggy started the car, shoved it into gear, and whipped out of the parking space with a squeal of tires. "I sent him to school. I thought he'd be better off sticking to his normal routine. Instead of worrying—and grieving."

"Whoa! Slow down, would you please?" Nick grabbed at the armrest on the passenger side door as her maneuver jerked him forward. "David's covered, all right? Adams isn't stupid, just in love with rules and regulations. With him, everything has to be by the book. But when I pointed out to him that his ass would be on the line if Forrest wasn't dead and did come after the kid, he agreed to put protection on David. There's a man on duty now, at the kid's school."

"You're scaring me."

"I don't mean to. Like I said, the likeliest scenario is that Forrest is dead. If he's not, and he's smart, he's running for cover. And he is smart. One of the smartest assholes I've ever come after."

"Oh, God." Maggy shut her eyes, only to have them fly open again when Nick yelped and jerked the wheel.

"Watch where you're going, would you please?" Considering the fact that they had almost run into one of the concrete pillars that held up the parking garage's four levels, Nick sounded surprisingly calm. "Look, Magdalena, pull over. Let me drive."

Maggy took a deep breath and shook her head. "No. I'm all right. And I like to drive. I haven't driven myself much of anywhere for years."

Nick grimaced, muttering something under his breath. To her he said, "So drive. Just don't kill us, okay?"

"Okay."

Nick was silent as Maggy maneuvered out of the garage, paid the parking fee, and headed down Second Street toward the river.

"Are you hungry?" Nick asked as she turned onto River Road.

Maggy shook her head. Her hands were clenched so tightly around the wheel that her knuckles showed white. From the way she felt, she guessed her face was as pale as her hands. For a little while, a few precious hours, she had felt free. Now, with the notion that Lyle might be alive given credence by Nick, she was afraid again. Desperately afraid.

"Have you eaten?"

Maggy shook her head a second time.

"Then you're hungry. Pull in up here at Kingfish and we'll get a sandwich."

"David gets out of school at three-thirty. He rides home with a friend, but I need to be home no later than three forty-five."

"You will be. Don't worry. There's nothing for you to worry about, understand?" A sudden grin flickered over Nick's face as he glanced at her. "Just consider me your bodyguard, okay? You're not getting out of my sight. I'll keep you safe."

"And David?" Maggy was too worried to reply to that grin.

"And David," Nick echoed, his grin fading. The very way he said their son's name told Maggy that the wound she had inflicted on him had not miraculously healed. She glanced over at him as she pulled into King-fish's parking lot.

"Nick," she began when she had stopped the car, "about David . . ."

"Save it," he said, the words brusque, as he guessed from her tone the subject she meant to address. "Until this situation cools down, I don't think either of us can afford the kind of emotional discussion that we're bound to have if we start talking about David. The last time you got me upset, I walked out on you and Forrest got you back and you nearly died because of it. Right now, I don't want anything happening between us that could affect my judgment again. So let's just keep things kind of impersonal, can we? Until this is over."

Then he opened the door and got out of the car.

38

*W*henever Maggy thought back over the three weeks that followed Lyle's death, events seemed pieced together like a collage, with little bits of memories jumbled on top of each other in no particular order. Most vivid was the sight of *Tia* Gloria's bruised and swollen face when Maggy visited her in the hospital. Tipton had had to hurt her badly to pry from her the reason for Maggy's visit, and to get her to uncover the secret hiding place where the tape was concealed. Though *Tia* Gloria was remarkably upbeat, considering her ordeal—her little group of friends was already gathered around her bed, prophesying a hideous end for the man responsible for the attack—her doctor confirmed that she would be in the hospital for some time. Promising to visit daily, Maggy also agreed to care for Horatio. Nick's first act, as her self-appointed bodyguard, was to move the bird, cage and all, into Maggy's bedroom at Windermere. Nick's expression as he gingerly transported the indignant parrot was one of the few bright spots in those dark days.

Another vivid memory was of the memorial service, a week after the accident, that Virginia insisted be held whether Lyle had been found or not. Everyone who was anyone in the community attended. Business leaders, politicians, society blue bloods, journalists, all turned out to pay their last respects to one of their own. Maggy felt like a complete fraud in her black widow's weeds as people kissed her cheek and murmured their condolences and exclaimed over how very brave she was being under the circumstances. Behind her back, there was other talk: about the ten days she had spent with Nick, including speculation that Lyle's death was actually a suicide fueled by his wife's blatant unfaithfulness. Others were sure that Lyle had been in a rage, again over her unfaithfulness, when the accident had happened, and had therefore taken the curve too fast. Only a few maintained that perhaps he was simply careless and his death was no fault of Maggy's at all. A tiny minority whispered that drugs had been involved, but the consensus was that that was ridiculous. Not Lyle Forrest! He simply wasn't the type.

No matter to what cause it was ascribed, Lyle's death was the talk of the city. It gave an added fillip to the Derby festivities, in which, for the first time in living memory, none of the Forrests took part. Maggy got the sense that a lot of the regret her women friends expressed at Lyle's passing was really over the cancellation of Louisville's social event of the season, the Diamonds and Pearls Ball—and that what they really wanted to ask about was Nick. Most of them were too well-bred to do so, but they certainly ogled him, and her, and the two of them together. Maggy guessed, when they were out of her presence, that what they said about her would have singed her ears if she had heard it. As the self-proclaimed leading authority on Maggy's childhood romance with Nick, Buffy was much in demand at all the many parties of the busy social season. This Maggy heard from another of her friends during the course of a condolence call.

Another piece of the collage was Virginia's sunken, bloodless face. Lyle's mother was grief stricken, and it was a relief when her physician insisted that she get completely away from the scene of her loss. After the memorial service, Sarah took her grandmother to the Drummond home in Texas, for an indefinite visit. Lucy and Ham stayed on in the guesthouse, insisting that they were needed at Windermere until "things" were settled. Maggy assumed they meant the estate's finances. There was no reading of the will, because Lyle was not yet officially declared dead. The lawyers seemed to think that in the absence of a body, an official declaration of death might take years. In any case, everyone knew how things stood. Everything Lyle owned at the time of his death went to David, except for the one-third portion of the estate that the law required should go to Maggy as Lyle's wife. But the DEA investigation complicated matters: How much, if anything, would be confiscated in the end? And the IRS was nosing around. . . . It was a mess, and Maggy was perfectly willing to let the lawyers handle it.

Maggy's most pressing concern was David. The boy cried only once, at the memorial service, and then only when his grandmother broke down. He had occasional nightmares, though he claimed not to remember what they were about when his cries brought Maggy running. Once, after a particularly bad dream, he asked to sleep with her. Maggy knew then that, whatever the dreams were about, they must be scaring him to death. She took him into her bed and held him close, and like that he was able to sleep through the rest of the night. When he was home during the day he stayed physically close to her, as if he was afraid to let her out of his sight. He seemed happiest at school, or at a friend's house. Maggy had to make a determined effort to overcome her morbid fear of letting him go. With a police escort whom Maggy described to her son as a chauffeur hired to replace Tipton, he went to school, played with his friends, did his homework, went to sleep in his own bed. Maggy couldn't do anything about the escort, but otherwise she worked hard to keep things as normal as possible, for David.

During that time Nick was everywhere, shadowing her every footstep. When she attended Lyle's memorial service, he sat discreetly in the rear of the church, but he was there. He was never out of shouting range, even staying in the house at night, in one of the guest rooms. When Lucy remarked that the way Maggy was carrying on with Nick was an open scandal and said that in her opinion it was *sinful* for Maggy to move her lover into Lyle's house when Lyle was scarcely cold, Maggy replied that since it was her house now, she would do as she damn well pleased. Lucy crimsoned but shut up. Apparently the thought that Windermere now belonged to Maggy and David and not to the original Forrests had not, until that moment, sunk in. After that exchange of pleasantries Lucy left the house in a huff and didn't come back. Maggy saw her only at a distance, usually when her sister-in-law was entering or leaving the carriage house. Ham she did not see at all, which suited her just fine. Now that Lyle was gone and there was no one to force her to be polite to him, her inclination was to cut Hamilton Drummond dead. Nick, she was afraid, had harsher aspirations, but for the time being, while Nick was preoccupied with her safety, he seemed prepared to let the matter ride. At least, as long as Ham kept out of his way.

David was not unaware of Nick's presence—that would have been impossible—but Nick did his best to stay out of the way when David was with Maggy. On those occasions, the police officer assigned to David took a break and Nick assumed bodyguard duty for both subjects. He hung back when they were out, or stayed in another room when they were inside, letting mother and son have time alone.

The arrangement did not escape David's notice.

"Why does *he* always have to hang around?" David asked her one afternoon when they were walking the dogs through Windermere's woods with Nick trailing a discreet distance behind.

At David's question, Maggy glanced back at Nick to see if he had heard. Nick was frowning, his hands in the pockets of his jeans, apparently lost in thought as he gazed into the distance. Stray sunbeams slipping through the now-dense canopy overhead gleamed on his black hair. Clad in sneakers, jeans, a white shirt and an orange windbreaker, he looked like the Nick she had loved all her life. He did not look like a DEA agent, or a tough-guy cop.

"He's really very nice, David," she temporized. A woodpecker drummed punctuation from somewhere nearby. A pair of bluejays screamed excitedly at the leaping progress of the dogs. It was mid-May now, and the deciduous trees were in full leaf. Gray-green festoons of moss hung from gnarled gray branches, and the first waxy white blossoms were peeking out through the glossy green foliage of the magnolias. The air was warm and sweet with the fragrance of the flowers that had recently burst into bloom. Overhead, clouds of pink and white dogwood blossoms floated beneath the variegated green of the taller oaks and maples and walnuts. The bright yellow forsythia, the pale pink-and-white azaleas, and the gorgeous deep fuchsia of the peonies provided bright splashes of color across the landscape. Through the trees, Maggy could see the vivid scarlet of the Kentucky Derby hybrids that dominated the rose garden. Periwinkle-blue phlox spilled over the stone wall. Closer at hand, beneath the trees, delicate crimson primroses formed a spreading carpet of color. Windermere in the spring was almost obscenely beautiful, she thought as she drank in the sights and sounds and smells, finding in them nourishment for her reviving spirit.

"He's your boyfriend, isn't he?"

Taken aback, Maggy glanced down at her son and hesitated before replying. "He's a very good friend."

"Dad said you were going to leave us and run away with him."

Maggy caught her breath. "Did he? Well, Dad was wrong. I would never, ever leave you, David. You know that."

"But you would have left Dad."

Maggy sighed. Hiding things from an intelligent eleven-year-old was difficult. Maybe the time had come to tell a cautious version of the truth.

"You know your dad and I didn't always get along."

David snorted. "You mean you fought like cats and dogs."

"Okay." Maggy had to smile. "Sometimes I thought about leaving him. But I never would have left him if it meant leaving you. We're a team, pal. We stick together."

She put her arm around his shoulders, and he didn't pull away. For a while they walked like that, and then David shrugged out from under her arm and glanced up at her again.

"Why do we have to have bodyguards, anyway?"

Maggy looked down at her son in surprise. She had gone to extreme lengths to keep him from realizing exactly why Nick was always trailing them about, and why Bob Jameson, the police officer cum chauffeur, drove him various places. Apparently he hadn't been fooled.

"What makes you think Nick and Bob are bodyguards?" she asked cautiously.

David gave her a look. "Come on, Mom. I know Nick's your boyfriend, but he's a bodyguard too, and so is Bob."

"Okay," Maggy answered, deciding to let the boyfriend matter slide. "You're right. They're with us so much because they want to keep us safe."

"From what? From Dad? But Dad's dead. Isn't he?"

David had always been the smartest kid in the world. Maggy sighed, looked down into her son's questioning eyes, and saw the deep anxiety that lay beneath their surface calm. Again she chose to tell a gentle version of the truth.

"I think so, David. Everybody thinks so. But—they haven't found his body yet, you know, so we can't be one hundred percent positive."

"He was going to kill you, wasn't he?"

Maggy's eyes widened in shock. She had been careful, so careful, to keep that from David. "What makes you think so?"

"I saw him drag you out of the house with a gun to your head." David's voice was dry.

Maggy stared at him. "How on earth did you see that?"

"That guy—Link—and I never made it all the way to the police cars. We took the path instead of following all those curves in the driveway, and just as we started down it I looked back and saw Dad dragging you out of the house. He had you in a headlock, and he looked like he was getting ready to blow your brains out."

"Oh, David." Maggy felt weak. For a moment she couldn't think of anything to say. "I'm sorry you saw that."

"I was scared. I didn't want him to kill you." His confession came in a low voice.

"Oh, David." Maggy stopped walking and pulled him to her, hugging him tightly. "Dad was—a little sick in his head toward the end. He did things that he wouldn't normally do."

"He was weird, on the trip."

"Weird? How?"

"He would wake up cursing in the middle of the night, and sometimes he would laugh for no reason at all. And he kept talking about us all going to Brazil. He said we'd be coffee planters. I didn't want to go to Brazil."

"I thought you said going to Brazil was cool."

"I just said that so as not to make Dad mad. You know what he was like when he was mad."

Maggy rested her head against her son's hair and shut her eyes. She was suddenly, fiercely glad her husband was dead. If he had lived, no telling what kind of psychological damage he would have inflicted on the boy.

"I dream about him, at night. I dream he comes into my room and touches my face. That's what scares me. It's creepy."

"Is that what your nightmares are about?" Maggy pushed him a little away from her so that she could look down into his eyes.

David nodded.

"That is creepy. But it's only a dream, you know. Pretty soon, you won't have it anymore."

"I hope not." He pulled away from her and started walking along the path again. Maggy fell into step beside him. They were at the edge of the woods, almost at the house, and Seamus and Bridey were streaking across the lush green lawn toward their kennel and a drink of water.

"But why do *I* have to have a bodyguard?" David pursued a thought that had obviously been troubling him. "Dad doesn't want to kill *me*. Does he?"

He sounded so frightened suddenly that Maggy caught his hand and gave it a squeeze. "No, of course not. We don't know that Dad wants to do anything to either of us. He's probably in heaven right now, thinking that everybody is making a big fuss over nothing. But just in case he's not, just in case he's here somewhere and thinking about running away to Brazil again, he might want to take you with him. That's why you have a bodyguard. So if Dad's alive and wants to steal you away, he can't do it."

"Oh." David's hand tightened around hers. He looked up at her earnestly. "I don't want to go away with Dad. I want to stay with you."

"I know, baby. You will." Maggy smiled at him over a lump in her throat, and hand in hand they walked out into the sunshine. Someone was hurrying toward them from the house, and Maggy had to shade her eyes with her hand before she recognized Louella. The woman was obviously agitated. Maggy's stomach tightened as she realized something was wrong.

"Mrs. Forrest, you have to come quick! It's loose in the house, and it's got Herd shut in a closet and it won't let him out!"

"What does, Louella?" Maggy asked, mystified.

"Your auntie's bird!"

39

*N*ick followed them inside. There was a faint shadow in his eyes as he watched the willowy, baggy-jeans-and-sweater-clad back of the woman he loved running ahead of him, hand in hand with their son. Two lithe bodies, tall and graceful; two dark auburn heads, the colors identical though one hairstyle was long and flowing and the other was a clipped boy cut; two bright spirits, each with an immutable hold on his heart.

David was his son. Nick's mind was still coming to terms with that, but his heart had accepted the reality of it already. It swelled with pride whenever he looked at the boy. He harbored a touch of sadness, a touch of regret, and more than a touch of residual anger at Magdalena for keeping his son from him all these years, but pride was the uppermost emotion. He looked at the kid and thought his heart would burst.

The irony of it was, the kid didn't even like him. David regarded him with suspicion and as a rival for his mother's attention. Nick feared that it was going to take a while before they even reached the point of being friends. Nick wanted to shout the truth about David's parentage from the rooftops, but instinct warned him that he'd better not.

Maybe someday, when all this was behind them and just the right moment came, David would learn the truth. The thought of what his reaction might be scared Nick. Would he hate both his biological parents for the rest of his life?

Magdalena was laughing when Nick stepped inside the door. The magnificent entry hall was deserted, and her laughter seemed to float down from somewhere overhead. Nick smiled a little as he listened to her laugh. Every day she was becoming more the high-spirited, fun-loving girl he remembered. An abused woman emerging from a cocoon of fear, that was how he thought of the process of rejuvenation that she was undergoing. And he vowed that she would never have reason to be afraid again as long as he lived.

"Where are you?" he called, raising his voice.

"Up here!" The merry answer came from upstairs. "Horatio's let himself out of his cage and chased Herd into a closet! Come up and see!"

"I have better things to do than stand around watching that stupid bird!" he yelled back.

"Coward!"

Damned right, Nick thought with a glinting grin, just as someone, a woman, the housekeeper maybe but not Magdalena, shrieked.

"Look out! Here he comes! Shut the door!" The shout came from Magdalena.

"Look at him go, Mom!"

Nick stopped dead half a dozen strides inside the door as a swoosh of wings and a demented cackle of laughter warned him what was afoot. The blasted bird had taken wing.

The front door was open, providing the winged devil a perfect chance to escape into the great outdoors, but did the bird take it? No, it did not! It came straight for him. Nick ducked, flinging his arms above his head, but to no avail. The damned bird dive-bombed him, swooped up toward the ceiling, and dived again, its claws digging into the cloth of his windbreaker and its wings flapping wildly as it landed. Crouched in anticipation, Nick felt the skin crawl on the back of his neck.

"Bad boy!" it squawked, climbing up his back. "Bad, bad boy!"

If he'd been the little kid he'd once been, he would have shrieked and run. But four pairs of eyes were on him: the housekeeper's, her husband's, Magdalena's, and David's. The quartet was lined up against the upstairs railing, leaning over it, laughing their heads off.

There wasn't much he wouldn't have endured to bring such carefree merriment to Magdalena and the boy.

"I don't think you should have called him a stupid bird," Magdalena managed between giggles.

Nick straightened, cautiously. The bird climbed onto his shoulder and proceeded to nibble his ear while he tried not to visibly wince. Upstairs, the gallery howled.

"Bad boy," the bird crooned, and Nick was thankful that it dropped his ear to bob its head up and down as it spoke.

"Does Horatio *know* you?" David asked between giggles. As far as Nick could recall, those were the first words David had ever addressed to him directly. Nick nodded, felt the beak on his ear again, and froze.

David snickered. Nick grinned sourly as Magdalena recounted the story of how, at about David's age, he had earned the bird's enmity. The whole group of them up there was chortling when she finished.

The bird was still nibbling, despite his shrugging attempts to make it vamoose, and Nick began to wonder just when it was going to turn vicious and take a chunk out of his lobe.

"Magdalena," he said to his tittering beloved. "Do you suppose you could come down here and get this thing off me?"

"But you look so cute. Like a pirate," she said and grinned.

"Magdalena. It's biting my ear."

"What do you think?" she asked David. "Should we go rescue him?"

David was about to answer when his eyes widened. "Oh, look," he cried. "Horatio pooped!"

Magdalena clapped a hand over her mouth. David dissolved into spasms of laughter. The housekeeper and her husband snickered. Nick looked down at the green and white smear on the front of his windbreaker and scowled.

"That's torn it," he said. "You're off there, bird."

"Bad boy! Bad boy!" Horatio screamed, digging in with its claws as Nick tried to shoo the bird off his shoulder with a serious combination of shrugs and waves.

"Hold still! I'll get him!" Still laughing, obviously concerned for the fate of the bird rather than himself, Magdalena came running down the stairs toward him.

"Come up!" she said to the bird when she reached them, holding out her hand. The blasted creature hopped on to her fingers without any hesitation at all, and sat there regarding Nick with baleful orange eyes.

"Stupid bird," Nick muttered, glancing down at his jacket with repugnance.

"Bad boy!" Horatio said with loathing.

"Don't worry, Mr. King, I can clean that off your jacket," the housekeeper said, sounding friendlier than Nick had ever heard her as she came down the stairs with a big grin on her face. Maggy bore Horatio back upstairs, Nick shed his jacket and gave it to Louella, and David and Herd came down the steps toward him.

"Did you really know my mom when she was a little girl?" David asked curiously when he reached the hall.

"I sure did." Nick was cautious, not wanting to say too much, but David suddenly grinned at him.

"I bet it made you mad when all the kids started calling you Junior Birdman."

"It did," Nick said, nodding. "Real mad."

"Did you beat them up?" David sounded almost wistful.

"Some of them. The ones that weren't bigger than me. But your mom was the worst of all, and I couldn't even hit her. She was a girl."

"Yeah," David said. "It's like that at school. The girls are the worst, and there's nothing you can do."

The boy started to walk past, then hesitated, looking back at Nick. "Me and Herd are going digging for night crawlers. You wanna come?"

"I'd like that," Nick said, mentally consigning both his jacket and his plans for the afternoon to the Devil. "I'd like that a lot. Do you have a can?"

"Herd does," David said, pointing to the large tin can in the gardener's hand. Nick fell into step with his son and the silent smiling black man and felt his heart take wing like that stupid bird.

40

*T*hat day marked a turning point in Nick's relationship with David. Maggy felt a warm glow inside her whenever she watched the two of them together. It was obvious that David liked Nick, and she knew, without Nick ever having to tell her, just how the love of her life felt about David. Given the chance, Maggy thought that Nick would prove to be a far better father to him than Lyle would have been. In the twelve years that she and Nick had been apart, she had not been the only one who had matured: Nick, too, had grown up.

David blossomed under Nick's casual approval. Whereas Lyle had expressed pride in David only when David excelled at the things Lyle considered important, Nick was interested in everything David did, even if David didn't do them particularly well. Where Lyle had been fiercely competitive, Nick was laid-back. When David played him in tennis and beat him, Nick grinned while David crowed. And when David took Nick to the Club and discovered that his new pal didn't even know how to play golf, he insisted on taking him around the course there and then for his first "lesson." Maggy, seated in the golf cart watching Nick swing at the ball and hit nothing but air three times in a row, was convulsed. So, too, was David. But Nick was cheerful about what to Lyle would have been a painfully humiliating experience, and pretty soon Maggy joined in the game because she couldn't be any worse than Nick. So the three of them played, and they had a fabulous time sending balls careening all over the place. David's fun was compounded by the fact that he won.

One Saturday Nick drove them out to the farm. Sarah had called the day before to say that Virginia was pining for Windermere, and Lucy, who had about as much tact as a tank, had announced in front of David that she was appropriating Louella and Herd (so that Virginia could have familiar attendants) and flying down to be with her mother during her final days. Maggy had confirmed with her mother-in-law's doctor that Virginia was not in any imminent danger, but still David had been upset. Taking him to the farm had been Nick's idea, to cheer the boy up. And it worked. David was entranced with the animals. He proved far more adept than Maggy at feeding the chickens, and wasn't even particularly afraid of the cows, though Maggy still eyed them askance. Link was there, and Nick made hamburgers for lunch, and the four of them sat around munching companionably as Maggy had once dreamed they would.

After lunch, while Nick stayed inside to talk to Link, Maggy and David wandered back to the barn. He wanted to go up into the loft, so she followed him. They were sitting cross-legged on a bale of hay, chatting about nothing in particular and watching the progress of a spider as it leapt from one rafter to another trailing its silky cord, when Nick joined them.

"You guys about ready to go?" he asked, standing over them.

"Do we have to?" David groaned, stretching out on his back.

"I thought you wanted to catch the four-o'clock movie."

"Oh. Yeah." It was *Terminator II,* and David was thrilled that he was going to be allowed to watch it. They would have to see it on a smaller screen now, some months after its release, because Maggy had refused to let him see it when it first came out. But Nick had persuaded her to grant permission *this one time,* and Maggy thought that David was going to expire of gratitude toward him when she gave in.

"I thought you might show David your paintings first." Her tone was supercasual.

"Oh, yeah?" Nick looked at her sharply. Maggy smiled at him. She knew that he was afraid to push David too far, too fast, but she also knew how badly David felt because his great talent was considered sissy. But if so macho a guy as Nick did it, painting would immediately gain a new legitimacy in David's eyes.

"You *paint?*" David said, incredulous.

"I sure do."

"So do I."

"I know. Your mom told me. She said you're very good." Nick held out his hand to David, and Maggy was thrilled to see her son put his fingers in Nick's with no hesitation at all. Nick pulled him to his feet.

They crossed the loft together while Maggy hung a little behind.

Today, with the hay door closed, the end of the loft where Nick painted was in shadow. But Nick pulled on the rope that swung the hay door open, and suddenly bright sunlight illuminated the easel and table and the stacked, covered paintings.

Nick was still working on the landscape of the farmhouse, Maggy saw as she approached.

The two males were absorbed in talk about palettes and colors and knives and brushes, to which she paid scant attention. Instead, she leaned in the hay door and breathed in the sweet, fresh scent of the farm.

Her gaze turned to her son and his father. She watched them together, Nick's swarthy-skinned face as absorbed as David's paler one as they engaged in their earnest discussion, and the thought that grew inside her mind was, "I'm happy. I am truly, truly happy."

Nick was well on the way to putting what she had done behind him. She knew it without his having to say a word. Though their physical relationship was still on hold, there was a new intimacy between them as they both strove to make the world right again for their son. And now David was growing attached to Nick. Maybe Saint Jude, by way of recompense for his previous misfire, was coming through for her at last.

"Can I look at some of your paintings?" David asked finally.

Nick pulled the canvas away from a couple by way of reply. David commented, Nick replied, and then Nick pulled the canvas off the portrait of Maggy.

"That's my mom," David said after a minute, glancing from the painting to Nick and back.

"It sure is." Only Maggy, who knew him so well, would have divined that Nick was a little nervous about David's reaction.

"She was young." David sounded surprised, as children are always surprised to discover that their parents were once near their own age.

"Sixteen."

"And pretty." David's observation was almost accusing. His eyes darted to Maggy, who smiled at him.

"Yes, she was."

"Were you her boyfriend then?"

"Yep."

"Why didn't you marry her?"

"I wanted to. But she married somebody else before I could."

"My dad."

Nick didn't reply. David was silent for a moment.

"If you'd married my mom then, you'd be my dad, wouldn't you?"

Nick's expression was inscrutable. "I suppose I would."

David stared at him, then made a horrible face. "Man, that would really suck!"

"David!" Maggy cried in consternation, straightening away from the wall. But David was already whirling and running toward the ladder. Nick caught her arm when she would have gone after him.

"Leave it alone."

"I'm sorry," Maggy said, looking up at him.

"Kid's got a right to his opinion." Though he said it lightly, Maggy knew Nick was hurt.

"I'm sorry," she said again, helplessly. "He must have felt he was being disloyal to Lyle. . . ."

The hand on her arm suddenly tightened. "How could you have done it, Magdalena?" Nick burst out, his hazel-green eyes burning as they bored into hers. "How could you have robbed me of my son?"

He dropped her arm and stalked away, leaving Maggy to follow him a few minutes later in miserable silence.

The drive back to Windermere was not a pleasant one. Later, as Maggy supervised David's bath and tucked him in, she was unaccustomedly terse. Finally, when she bent down to give him his good-night kiss and straightened, meaning to leave him, he caught her hand.

"Okay, Mom," he said, sighing. "Spit it out. You're mad at me, I can tell."

"You were extremely rude to Nick today." Her voice was severe.

"I know. I couldn't help it." He hesitated, then burst out: "It just seems—you like him so much better than Dad. You're always smiling when you're with him. And—I like him, too. It doesn't seem fair."

"You hurt Nick's feelings."

"I didn't mean to. But it was like, for a moment, I almost wished he was my dad. Then I thought of Dad, and I felt bad for liking Nick."

There was a pause.

"David," Maggy said quietly, "don't you think, if Dad really loved us, that what he would want most now that he's gone is for us to be happy?"

David pondered that for a minute. "Yeah," he said slowly. "I guess."

"Being with Nick makes me happy. I think it makes you happy, too."

"I guess so." David's admission was grudging.

"Okay." Maggy flicked his nose with her finger. "I forgive you. But in future, be polite to Nick."

David grinned. "Okay."

"Good night."

"Good night, Mom."

Maggy turned out his light and went along to her own room. Horatio was in his cage in the corner, his head tucked under his wing. When she turned on the lamp at her bedside, he untucked himself and glared at her balefully.

"Sorry, Horatio," she murmured and walked into the bathroom to run a bath. She brushed her hair, her teeth, and bathed, then pulled on her nightgown and robe. Perhaps half an hour had passed since she had left David. If she knew anything at all about her son, he would be sound asleep.

Barefoot, she padded along the hall to check on him. For a moment she stood over him in the dark, listening to the rhythmic sounds of his breathing. She had been right: he was asleep.

Then she headed downstairs to confront Nick.

41

*H*e was hurting, and he was *mad.*
Nick used those two facts to justify his inroads into Lyle Forrest's
brandy. He was in the elegant, book-lined room they called the library,
sprawled on a fat burgundy leather couch with his feet in their grungy
white athletic socks propped on what was probably a thousand-dollar
coffee table. He took a drag on his cigarette and flicked his ashes into a
faceted crystal ashtray that looked as though it had never before seen
actual use. An unlit marble fireplace was directly across from where he
sat. Above it was a painting of a pair of glossy-coated thoroughbreds.
The painting was beautifully executed and had obviously cost a mint.
Everything that had belonged to Lyle Forrest had cost a mint. He had to
hand it to the slimy bastard, Nick thought as he swilled down another
shot glass brimming with the aromatic golden liquid and stared moodily
at the painting: everything he possessed had been of the finest. The
finest paintings, furniture, clothes, cars, liquor. The finest woman. The
finest kid.

Only the woman and kid should by rights have belonged to himself.

Nick scowled and poured himself another shot of brandy. The elegant
crystal snifters were near at hand, and despite his upbringing he knew
what they were for. But it gave him a perverse kind of pleasure to pour
the fine brandy into the small shot glass, and chug it down.

Kind of an in-your-eye for ol' Lyle.

He never heard her approach, but when he looked up, Magdalena
was in the doorway frowning at him. He took a drag on his cigarette and
met her gaze with deliberate insolence. She looked as though she was

getting ready to yell at him for something, probably either the booze or the cigarettes.

But for the moment she said nothing, just crossed her arms over her bosom and cocked her head to one side and looked him up and down. He returned the compliment, his eyes sliding over her with almost more appreciation than resentment. She was clad in a quilted satin robe in a color that probably had a fancy name but that he called plain pale green, with a touch of matching green lace peeping out at the wrapped neckline that belonged to the gown beneath. She was barefoot, and her hair was swirled up on top of her head in an artless pile that left long, curling tendrils free to float about her ears, and her face was scrubbed clean of any makeup. Clearly she had just gotten out of the bath. She looked about sixteen, gorgeous, and grumpy. She made his loins ache.

"I want to talk to you," she said at last, apparently having thought better of yelling at him.

"So talk." To annoy her as much as for any other reason, he took a drag on his cigarette and poured himself another brandy.

Magdalena padded across the Oriental rug toward him.

"Are you *drinking*?" she said accusingly when she stood in front of him.

"Does it look like it?" he countered, gulping the brandy.

"Yes."

"Then I must be."

"Are you drunk?" She stood, arms akimbo, eyeing him with suspicion.

"I never get drunk."

"You look drunk. You *smell* drunk."

"Well, I'm not. And it's the brandy that smells, not me."

She appeared unconvinced, and when he poured himself another shot of brandy, she nipped over and grabbed the decanter, placing it back on the shelf out of his reach.

"Give that back," he said, annoyed.

"No way."

"Fine," he said, gulping the tiny amount of liquid in his glass and standing up. "I'll get it myself."

To his surprise, Magdalena was in front of him, shoving him back down onto the couch with her hand in the center of his chest. To his greater surprise, she was able to do it. He must have drunk more than he thought.

"I want to talk to you," she said determinedly, standing over him like a victorious warrior. He rubbed his chest, eyed her, and gave up his intention to try again to retrieve the brandy. If she could push him down, he didn't need any more to drink.

"So talk," he said, and put his cigarette in his mouth.

With an inarticulate cry of rage, Maggy snatched it from between his lips and ground it out in the ashtray.

"Stop it!" she said fiercely. "Just stop it, do you hear me? You are being a total asshole about this, and I have had enough. Do you want me to say I'm sorry? All right, I'm sorry! I *am* sorry about keeping David from you. Sorrier than I can ever begin to say. But I can't take it back. It's done, and I can't take it back. So we have to go on from here. We have to build a family from where we are, and it's not going to work if you stay angry with me over David."

Her chocolate-brown eyes were very big and very passionate, flashing at him as they had a million times in the past. His girl, come back to him. The thought curled around his heart.

"Don't you think I have a right to be mad?" he drawled, using his voice now that he had neither cigarette nor glass as a prop to annoy her.

"All right, yes, you do. But you're going to have to get over it, or you're going to poison what we have. David told me tonight that the reason he said that at the farm was because, just for a minute, he wished you were his dad."

"I *am* his dad. That's the whole point. That's what you took away from me—and from David."

Maggy glared at him for a minute. She looked mad enough to chew nails, and Nick discovered, to his own surprise, that the madder she got the more mellow he felt. He already knew that however she had wronged him, and she had, they were going to move beyond it. It wasn't even a question of his forgiving her. It was a question of their belonging together, of the bond between them being so strong that there was no transgression on either of their parts heinous enough to break it. He would be mad at her for a little while, and then he would get over it and they would go on from there. Hadn't it always been that way, between them?

"You're determined to sulk, aren't you?" she said finally, impaling him with one final glare and then turning away in disgust. "Sulk, then. See if I care."

She was stomping from the room when he got to his feet.

"Magdalena," he said very softly. "Come back here."

"Go to hell," she spat out without looking around.

"Magdalena." There was a suggestion of a laugh in his voice. She stuck her middle finger skyward in a very eloquent nonverbal response, and with a twitch of her satin skirts disappeared from sight.

"Come back here, you little witch," Nick muttered, nettled. He went after her and discovered that he wasn't quite as steady on his feet as he might have wished.

"Magdalena." She was already halfway down the hall and moving away fast. When she ignored him, Nick broke into a trot, and then a run. She must have heard the soft thud of his feet against the Oriental runner, because she gave a quick glance over her shoulder, picked up the trailing skirt of her robe, and dashed for the stairs. She made it almost to the top before he caught her, scooping her up in his arms and taking the remaining steps two at a time. She was soft, warm, surprisingly heavy, and the clean, soapy smell of her could have been the most powerful aphrodisiac in the world if it was judged by the effect it had on him.

"Put me down!"

"Hush," he said. "You'll wake the kid."

Then, to make sure she obeyed, he kissed her. She kept her lips clamped together in silent resistance for just a second or two. Then she surrendered with a little mewling sound that sent shivers down his spine and curled her arms around his neck and kissed him back.

"I love you," he whispered against her mouth as he bore her into her darkened bedroom and nudged the door shut with his shoulder. "Love you, love you, love you."

He laid her on her bed and sank down beside her, and for a very long time neither of them said anything at all.

42

*T*he sudden burst of light woke Maggy. She blinked groggily, needing a moment to orient herself. She was in her own bed, and Nick was snoring beside her . . .

Who had turned on the lamp by her bed?

"Get up, you bitch," a familiar voice growled, and then horror brought Maggy wide awake as her arm was grabbed and she was dragged from her bed by Lyle.

She stared into her husband's pale blue eyes for one hideous instant of recognition before her gaze slid down to the steel-blue pistol in his hand. He was dressed in unfamiliar clothes: dark brown corduroy pants, too loose and too short, and a tan turtleneck. Undistinguished clothes that Lyle would never have chosen for himself. Absurdly, she wondered where he had obtained them.

He made an indecipherable sound, and she looked again at his face: it was working with a terrifying passion that Maggy recognized as hate.

A cold feeling of dread threatened to overwhelm her.

There were three men in the room besides Lyle. Two strangers, and Ham. All armed with guns. Ham. Was he in this, too? The thought was terrifying. She knew better than anyone what kind of brutality Lyle and Ham, working in tandem, were capable of.

One of the strangers had his gun shoved against Nick's ear, and held Nick's arm twisted up behind his back. Nick, his bare back brown against the pale pink sheets that were twisted around his body, lay on his stomach, silent, motionless. His very stillness told Maggy that he was awake and aware. In the cage beside the bed, Horatio ruffled his feathers and muttered to himself, sidling uneasily on his perch, his orange eyes rapidly dilating and shrinking, dilating and shrinking as he surveyed the unaccustomed post-midnight action in the room. His attention caught by the parrot's movements, Lyle glanced quickly around. Then, seeing that the disturbance came from nothing more threatening than a bird, Lyle turned his gaze back to Maggy.

"Thought I was dead, didn't you? You were wrong," Lyle said with gloating satisfaction, his mouth curling in a sneer as his eyes ran over her. There was a tinge of purple in his face now, and his mouth was ugly. "You little whore. I ought to shoot you on the spot."

Only then did Maggy realize she was naked.

"Get her dressed." Ham spoke over his shoulder, his tone that of the man in charge.

They were dragging Nick from the bed as Lyle took her into her dressing room and watched as she dressed. Panties, bra, jeans, sweater, all pulled on under Lyle's glittering gaze. She slid her feet into a pair of rubber-soled espadrilles, then turned to face her husband. He smiled at her, a thin smile that chilled her to her bone marrow.

"Is he good in bed?" Lyle asked. Maggy, unable to hide the fact that she was terrified, didn't reply. Lyle reached over and viciously pinched the tip of her breast. She winced and couldn't hold back a cry.

"Magdalena!" Nick's sharp response was punctuated by the thunk of a blow. Maggy whitened in fear, not needing Lyle's gesture with the pistol to send her hurrying into the other room.

Nick was dressed now, too, in the clothes he had been wearing when he had taken her to bed: jeans, sweatshirt, socks. His hands were cuffed behind his back, and a trickle of blood ran down his forehead where he'd been hit, apparently with a pistol. His gaze locked with hers for one shrieking instant. Maggy knew that he realized as well as she did that what they faced was nothing less than a battle for their lives.

"I didn't think you were dead." Nick said it quite calmly to Lyle. "You jumped out of the car before it went over, didn't you? I started thinking that if Magdalena could do it, you could too. The light was out at that curve, and it was raining and dark as pitch. When you saw you couldn't get away, you had to think fast, didn't you? Good plan, good execution —but you screwed it up by coming back."

Lyle laughed, the sound unpleasant. "I never went away, you fool. I've been here in the house all the time, right under your stupid nose. In the attic mostly, though I've given in to the urge to visit my son once or twice at night. I would have left weeks ago, if *you* hadn't moved in. Can you imagine how I felt, sitting in the attic of my own house, while you were downstairs night after night with *my* wife? I was waiting for you to get careless. I knew it would happen, and tonight it did. I called Ham—he's known where I was, of course—and told him tonight's the night. We're getting out of here, and you and my lovely wife are going to die."

The nightmares, Maggy thought with sickening recognition. David's nightmares, of his father coming back from the dead to touch his face. They hadn't been dreams at all. Her blood curdled at the idea that Lyle had been hiding in the house all this time, watching and waiting, biding his time.

"Where are your shoes?" Ham spoke to Nick as he prodded him out from behind the bed at gunpoint. The two other men, obviously flunkies, kept their pistols trained on Nick, too.

"Downstairs." Nick looked at Ham directly. Even with his hands cuffed behind his back and blood trickling down his forehead, even in his stocking feet with his hair wildly mussed, Nick looked far more dangerous than Ham. Ham, with his compact body and dapper moustache, his bespoke suit and thousand-dollar shoes, was every inch the gentleman confronting a ruffian. Except for the fact that it was Ham who held the gun.

"You're John Y., aren't you? The man who owns Colonel Sanders," Nick said to Ham.

Ham's eyes flickered and sliced to Lyle.

"*I* didn't tell him," Lyle said testily.

"He didn't have to tell me." For a man with three pistols pointed at his head, Nick sounded awfully calm. "I heard weeks ago that there was somebody besides Forrest, somebody bigger. The main man. The dude in charge. They call you John Y. on the street. You put up the money, didn't you? At first, to get him started. And when you saw the kind of bucks that were being generated, you stayed in. Only a handful of people know you're involved."

"Shut up." Ham moved behind Nick and prodded him in the back with the gun. "Get moving. We're going downstairs to get your shoes. It won't do to have the body found without shoes."

Lyle laughed again. Catching Maggy by the arm, he pulled her out of the bedroom in Nick's wake. Maggy felt abject fear as she immediately was reminded of Lyle's strength. As she and Nick were forced along the upper hallway, she was tinglingly aware of the silence all around them—the silence of a huge, empty house.

"Wait a minute. We need to get David." Lyle spoke to Ham as they started along the hall. Ham nodded and pointed, and one of the flunkies broke from the group to enter David's bedroom.

Maggy looked up at her husband. "Please don't let them hurt David." Her voice was unsteady.

Lyle said with smug confidence, "Don't worry, darling. I would never let anyone hurt *my* son. I'm taking him with me to Europe."

"Shut up, Lyle," Ham said tensely.

"What does it matter? They're not going to be around to tell anybody."

"What do you think David is going to think of you when you murder his mother?" Nick asked.

Lyle's lip curled. "I'm not going to do it in front of the boy. As far as he is concerned, Maggy will just disappear. I plan to tell him that she ran off with *you*."

Just as they came even with his room, David emerged. He was clad in Batman pajamas, his hair was rumpled, and his eyes were huge with fear. The flunky gripped his arm.

"Mom . . ." David saw Maggy and headed for her, only to be jerked back. Then he saw Lyle, and his face went perfectly white. "Dad!"

"Hello, David." Lyle sounded as normal as if he'd seen his son over supper only the day before. "Feel like going on a trip?"

David darted a quick, scared glance at Maggy, and then he smiled. For Maggy, that smile was a horrible thing to see, a travesty of David's usual grin that revealed pure fear. "Yeah, sure," he said with a good imitation of enthusiasm.

Even under such awful circumstances, Maggy felt a surge of pride in her boy. He was smart enough, and courageous enough, to play the role that he had to play to survive.

"Let him go," Lyle said to the flunky. Then, to David, "Come here, son."

The flunky looked at Ham, who nodded, and released his grip on David. David was walking toward Lyle when Nick said, in a loud voice, "He's going to shoot us, David. I don't think he should, do you? I think he should shoot *that stupid bird*!"

"Shut up," Lyle snarled, while Maggy looked at Nick, first in horror, then in dawning comprehension. Lyle was just wrapping an arm around David's shoulder when Maggy heard it: the flutter of wings.

"Bad boy!" a raucous voice squawked. "Bad, bad boy!"

Horatio exploded through the door of Maggy's bedroom like a green feather bullet.

"What the hell?" Startled, Lyle and company glanced around, and then, as Horatio flew straight at Nick, every one of the foursome, to a man, ducked.

"Run!" yelled Nick, shoving his shoulder into Ham's side. Ham went sprawling, knocking one of the flunkies off-balance. Nick butted the other with his head; the man went flying back into David's bedroom. Maggy drove her elbow into Lyle's side, wrenched her arm from his grasp, grabbed David's hand, and ran as if the Devil himself was on her heels. Which, in more than just a manner of speaking, he was.

"Bad boy!" shrieked Horatio, flapping toward the ceiling as a gun discharged with an explosion of sound that hurt Maggy's ears. "Bad, bad boy!"

Maggy and David bounded down the stairs with Nick right behind them. Her son fled from Lyle with no hesitation at all, his hand tight in hers, clearly as frantic to escape as she was herself.

"It's only a Goddamn bird!"

"Son of a bitch! Get them!"

Only two strides more, and they would be at the door. Maggy risked a quick glance over her shoulder to see Nick only a step behind, and Lyle, Ham and the others pounding down the stairs. Lyle was in the lead, his long legs eating up the distance, gun in hand and aimed toward them.

"Bad boy!" Horatio cackled, hurtling from the ceiling toward Nick. As he rocketed over the heads of the bad guys, they instinctively ducked again. That gave Maggy the time she needed to wrench open the door.

They were through it, she and David, when another gunshot exploded. Maggy heard the impact of it as it hit somewhere close by with a sound like a hand slapping flesh. Behind them, Nick cursed.

"Are you all right?" She glanced over her shoulder at him to see that he was white faced in the moonlit darkness, but still behind them. With his hands cuffed, running was awkward for him, but he was galloping through the darkness in her wake. David, too, was running as he had never run before in his life. His hand grasped hers tightly, and she prayed that terror continued to give his feet wings. There was no way on earth she was leaving David.

"Go!" Nick hurled the word at her when she faltered to look back at him. "To the cliff! Go, go!"

Nick was behind them as Maggy darted around the corner of the house, pulling David with her, heading across the lawn for the path through the woods that led to the cliff.

"Where'd they go? Damn it, they can't just have disappeared!"

"Spread out! Find them!"

The moon was up, a bright, beautiful moon that Maggy would have loved on any other occasion but tonight wanted to curse. The landscape was bathed in light, the only cover being the black shadows beneath the trees and the lighter shadow thrown into the backyard by the house itself. In this, the wee hours of a Sunday morning, the moon rode high in the western half of the sky. It was in front of the house, accounting for the eerie, elongated shadow in which they ran. But even the shadow didn't afford much cover. Maggy prayed that their pursuers hadn't seen which way they had gone.

"There they are!"

Firecrackers exploded behind them in rapid succession. No, not firecrackers: gunshots. Beyond terror now, Maggy tightened her grip on David's hand and fled.

They were almost to the woods. Branches seemed to stretch out like welcoming arms, beckoning them to safety. Above, the huge rounded tops of the giant oaks and maples were silvered by moonlight. Underfoot the soft turf of the yard suddenly turned to the harder surface of the dirt path as they ducked beneath the sheltering branches.

"To the boat!" Nick gasped behind her. His breathing was labored, and Maggy could only assume that running with his hands fastened behind his back was more exhausting than she would have dreamed.

Ever fleet of foot, Maggy was in the lead, dragging David after her through the murky darkness of the woods. All about them night insects chirred their individual songs, and leaves and supple twigs tugged at their faces and clothes as they passed.

"Ow, Mom, my feet!" David groaned, and she felt him stumble. Only then did she remember that he was barefoot. Of the three of them, only she was wearing shoes. And the path was overgrown with roots, and rocky . . .

"Come *on!*" She jerked David to his feet before he could hit the ground, and kept running. Groaning, he nevertheless managed to stay on his feet, stumbling behind her until he regained his balance. Nick, his breathing audibly labored now, urged him on from behind. Behind them Maggy fancied she could hear the pounding of pursuing feet.

They burst from the woods onto the grassy verge, and Maggy bounded toward the cliff. Like the treetops, the stone of the cliff was silvered by moonlight. Far below, a ladder of silver cellophane stretched across Willow Creek.

"Sit down, push off, and *slide,*" Maggy ordered her son breathlessly, pulling him down beside her as she dropped to a sitting position on the edge of the cliff.

"But, Mom . . ." David, who had never to her knowledge been shown this particular route to the creek, glanced over at her in obvious doubt, his face white, his eyes wide.

"Do it!" Maggy gave him a push and went over after him, her hands skidding in the loose shale. To his credit, David didn't scream, didn't make a sound. Instead he fetched up on the rock ledge only seconds ahead of herself and stood up as she landed.

"Wow!" he exclaimed as Nick slid down almost on his back. The handcuffs were really hampering Nick's mobility, Maggy saw, but there was no time to do anything about it and nothing she could do to free him even if they had the time. She didn't *think* Lyle knew about this way to the creek.

Nick was on his feet, and the three of them stepped out onto the path that snaked down the cliff. Maggy went first, holding David's hand tightly in hers, and Nick brought up the rear. Maggy gave a brief thought to Nick's balance with his hands cuffed behind him, but when she glanced back she saw that he was hugging the cliff face and moving at a steady pace.

It seemed to take forever for them to reach the ground. Maggy was sweating by the time they did, both from physical exertion and from the terror that accompanied fleeing for their lives. Any second she expected to glance back and see Lyle and Ham and their two thugs in hot pursuit.

"Man, that was so *cool,*" David said as he jumped down onto level ground. Maggy, already in the act of dragging him across the road, stopped for a second to stare at him. He grinned at her, the moonlight gleaming on his braces, his eyes alight.

"You are one great kid," she said, gave him a quick, hard hug, and pulled him after her toward the dock.

With David beside her, Maggy was already untying the rope securing *The Lady Dancer* when Nick came up behind them. He was breathing hard, and she spared him a glance of concern as she whipped the rope free.

"Get in the boat," Nick said to David, who nimbly obeyed. Nick followed more awkwardly, and David reached up to steady him as he almost lost his balance stepping in. Nick sank down on a seat. David crouched beside him. Rope in hand, Maggy hopped in and moved to the rear, yanking on the starter for all she was worth.

She gave a sigh of relief as the engine roared to life on the first try.

"Mom," David said in an odd voice as she pointed *The Lady Dancer* toward the center of the creek. "Look at my hand."

He held his hand out toward her, palm out. His fingers were dark in the moonlight instead of pale as they should have been.

"I think it's Nick," he said before Maggy could question him. "I think it's his blood."

43

"**O**h, my God!" Maggy's words were as much a prayer as a gasp.

Nick's expression was inscrutable. "I got hit back there at the house. It's nothing serious."

"Let me see!" Maggy started up from her seat.

"No!" Nick said it fiercely, his eyes gleaming at her from the darkness. "I'm bleeding a little, but I'm not dying. You concentrate on getting us out of here. If you don't . . ."

He broke off, obviously not wanting to state the self-evident conclusion with David listening. Maggy finished the sentence in her own mind. If she didn't, he *would* die. They both would. And maybe David, too.

A sudden report, a sharp pop in the clear night air, caused Maggy to frown.

"Look, Mom," David said, sounding scared again as he pointed. "Look up there!"

On top of the cliff down which they'd just descended stood two figures. Silhouetted against the lighter background behind them, they looked no bigger than fingers at that distance. That they were part of the pursuing party was unmistakable, even before a stray moonbeam glinted off the barrel of a gun. But what worried Maggy was where were the other two?

"Don't worry, we're out of range," Nick said. "They must be crazy mad to try a shot at that distance. But it's good for us. The more noise, the better. Maybe somebody will hear and call the cops."

His speech sounded vaguely slurred, and Maggy gazed at him in concern. How badly was he hurt? If he was dying, he wouldn't tell her, not now.

"They're gone, Mom," David said. Maggy glanced back at the cliff to find that the figures had indeed vanished.

The night was quiet, dark, surprisingly warm. The gurgle of the creek and the drone of the motor were the only sounds. Above them, the sky was obscenely beautiful: a panoply of brilliant stars scattered across a black-velvet ground. The moon was full and yellow and looked as if it had been ordered by some movie's central casting department to provide a touch of romance. Ahead of them, the river flowed serenely past.

As she looked at it, a cold whisper of warning rushed through her mind.

Maggy set herself to getting them out onto the open river with all speed.

The wind was against them. It blew from the north, and their course took them directly into it. *The Lady Dancer* chugged toward the river, seeming to move almost in slow motion.

The mouth of the creek was their most vulnerable point. At only thirty feet wide, with the channel only deep enough in the middle for the boat, the creek was both their route to safety and their Achilles' heel.

If a gunman was there waiting, on that point of land at the mouth of the creek . . .

They made it through and streaked out into the open water. With a quiver of relief, Maggy felt the swell of the river catch the boat, tugging it vainly downstream. What she had feared most had not come to pass.

With River Road running the entire length of the Kentucky bank, Maggy dared not try to make a landfall on that side. It was very possible that Lyle, Ham, and the flunkies, together or in any combination, were already cruising along River Road, hoping they would do just that. Perhaps they were even watching *The Lady Dancer*'s progress across the river at that very moment. But even if they were, there was nothing they could do. No matter how fast they drove, Lyle and his cohorts could not make it all the way downtown, across the bridge, and over to the Indiana side before *The Lady Dancer* reached the floating service station that was Maggy's immediate destination. The station itself would be closed, but there was a pay phone. She didn't have a quarter on her at the moment, but it didn't matter: Calls to 911 were free.

They were perhaps halfway there when she suddenly discerned the shadowy gray shape of a large boat, like *The Lady Dancer* running without lights, sliding toward them through the water on a course that would eventually intercept their own. At that distance it was impossible to identify it positively, impossible to make out distinguishing features, but Maggy knew, as surely as if the wind whispered its name, what the boat was.

"The *Iris,*" she said bleakly, staring at the dark hull that was closing fast. It was between them and the Kentucky shore. There was no going back. Giving up all thought of getting to the phone, she cut the rudder hard to starboard. They would have to land on the closest parcel of Indiana land they could reach and run for it.

Could Nick run? He had to. It was their only hope.

At least the *Iris* needed deeper water to dock than did *The Lady Dancer.* Maggy realized that she needed to go in somewhere shallow, beaching the boat. Lyle would have to break out the *Iris*'s dinghy to follow, which would take time.

Neither Nick nor David said anything. Maggy wasn't sure that they realized the true extent of the danger they were in. The *Iris,* in a straight race, could overtake *The Lady Dancer* easily. Would their lead be enough to keep them safe?

Another wave caught *The Lady Dancer* and sent it scudding forward. For a moment it seemed as if they were flying through the water. Maggy leaned forward, trying to urge the little boat on with her own body's motion. She was way beyond terror now, beyond anything except a fierce determination to save her boy and the man she loved.

She would not let Lyle win.

Six-Mile Island loomed just ahead. The prospect of making landfall there was briefly tempting, but immediately a tiny voice inside her cautioned no. If she did, they would be trapped like rats.

But she could use the island as cover, maybe hide behind it as she raced for land. Yanking the rudder hard to port, she sent the little boat scooting around the tip of the island. The island's dense foliage blocked the *Iris* from view.

"They can't catch us now, Mom!" David exclaimed excitedly. Then, glancing back, his mouth drooped, and he added, "Can they?"

The *Iris* had seen her maneuver and was following, full speed ahead. Maggy didn't have the heart to answer David's question. The knowledge was there, dragging down his face just as it dragged down her heart.

Grimly, Nick and David stared over Maggy's shoulder as the fast-closing yacht came on. Maggy concentrated every atom of her being on getting as much speed from *The Lady Dancer* as she could. They were almost there. . . . Scanning Indiana's rocky shoreline, she searched for a place to beach. Behind her, she could hear the pulsing of the *Iris*'s powerful engine. Another ten minutes and they would reach land.

They weren't going to make it. Maggy already knew it even before she saw the huge dark bulk of the *Iris* looming alongside. Terror caused her to grit her teeth, made her palms sweat. David, staring up at the yacht too, was white faced, whimpering. Nick was pale, his jaw grim, his eyes dark and dangerous. But wounded as he was, and handcuffed, there was nothing he could do.

The *Iris* pulled in front of them, cutting off their access to the shore. Maggy cursed and pushed the tiller over. They would run the other way, run all night if necessary.

A powerful light was suddenly turned on *The Lady Dancer*, pinioning the three of them in its strong beam.

"Cut the engine! Cut the engine or we'll shoot the boy," a voice crackled at them from over a bullhorn.

Maggy froze. *The Lady Dancer* was racing at top speed, but the *Iris* was staying with them easily, keeping them pinioned in the blinding light. From the sound of the engine, she knew that Lyle had cut back the power: the yacht's full speed was no longer needed, now that it was through playing catch-up. Glancing wildly around, Maggy saw that there was no escape. The *Iris* had her cut off from land, and could easily outrace her on the open river.

The question was, would Lyle really shoot David? She didn't think so, but it also occurred to her, from what Nick had said, that it was possible that Lyle was no longer the man in charge. Ham would shoot David if it served his purpose, she had no doubt.

The Lady Dancer churned through the choppy water, straining for the safety it was never going to reach.

"This is your last chance to cut the engine before we start shooting. If you make me, I'll kill the kid, Maggy. I mean it." Distorted as the voice was by the bullhorn, Maggy recognized it: Ham's.

"Cut the engine," Nick said grimly. Maggy stared at him for a long, helpless minute. Then she did as he said.

"Good girl." The voice came at her over the bullhorn again. The bright light shone relentlessly down. Shading her eyes, she looked up at the looming bulk of the *Iris*, idling now in the water beside them. A shot rang out, exploding in the quiet night. Maggy jumped, covering her head, while Nick threw himself, handcuffs and all, atop David.

In the ringing aftermath, Maggy glanced fearfully over at the slumped figures of her two males, her stomach churning with fear. Dear God, had one or both of them been shot?

Before she could even call their names, Ham spoke over the bullhorn again, terrifyingly cheerful.

"Don't worry, we just shot your engine. I don't have time to play cat and mouse on the river all night. Come aboard! The kid first, then you, Maggy. Then King."

Maggy glanced again at the dark deck above her head, able now to make out the shadowy figures despite the light glaring in her face: Ham with the bullhorn, Lyle beside him, another man—a flunky, Maggy presumed—beside Lyle. But not, Maggy thought, one of the same flunkies that had been in the house. This one was broader, stockier.

David was struggling into a sitting position in the bottom of the boat. Tears spilled from his eyes. His mouth worked. Nick lay curled around him, his eyes closed, unmoving. Maggy scrambled across to them even as a ladder lowered, and the flunky swung down to take possession of *The Lady Dancer.*

As the man's weight rocked the boat, Maggy hugged her son, whispering frantically in his ear, "Go to Dad. Stay by him. He'll see that you're all right."

"Mom . . ." David wrapped his arms around her waist, clinging, weeping openly. The flunky loomed over them.

"I love you," she whispered. She couldn't help it: her eyes filled, and tears spilled down her cheeks. Stark terror claimed her as Maggy realized that this might be the last time in this life she would ever hold her son.

"Come on, kid." The flunky pulled David away from her, set him on the ladder. David climbed slowly up, was grabbed from above and hauled aboard the *Iris.*

Maggy shut her eyes and said a brief, fierce prayer for his safety. For *their* safety, all three of them. Saint Jude, Saint Jude . . .

"Mrs. Forrest." The flunky sounded ridiculously respectful as he reached down, caught her arm, hauled her to her feet. She glanced up into a pockmarked, flat-featured face. His eyes were a deeper blue than Lyle's, and didn't look unkind.

His pistol prodded her in the side. "You gotta climb the ladder now," he said.

Maggy glanced down at Nick. He still lay motionless on the floor of the boat, his body curled into a ball, his eyes closed. Had he fainted? Or . . .

"He's been shot," she said to the man, dashing the tears from her eyes with both hands. "He can't climb."

"Shit." The flunky glanced down at Nick, then squatted beside him, feeling behind Nick's ear for a pulse. "He ain't dead."

He stood up again, feet spaced wide apart to keep his balance in the rocking boat, and pointed his pistol at Maggy.

"Get up the ladder," he said.

With a last, backward glance at Nick, Maggy climbed.

"King's unconscious," the flunky called up to Ham as hands grabbed Maggy and hauled her onto the *Iris*'s deck.

"Carry him up."

"Shit," came the reply, and Maggy caught just a glimpse of the man struggling to hoist Nick in a fireman's lift before Lyle reached out and dragged her close to his side.

David was on his other side, standing in the circle of Lyle's arm. The boy glanced at his mother, and then up at Lyle.

"Please don't kill Mom," he begged in a quavery voice.

Maggy's heart broke. Terror had already frozen it, and now that pathetic little plea from her son shattered it into a billion tiny pieces. Tears welled in her eyes again as she looked first at David, then at Lyle.

"I won't," he said, smiling that crocodile's smile at Maggy even as he gave David's shoulders a squeeze designed to be reassuring. "Go on down to the cabin now, David. I'll be in in a little while."

"Mom . . ." David's eyes were dark with terror as they met hers. Clearly he was no more convinced by Lyle's promise than Maggy was. But he couldn't save her. The question was, could she save him?

"Go on," she said sternly, nodding in the direction of the cabin. Head hanging, footsteps dragging, David obeyed. Maggy bit her lip as she watched him go. Whatever happened, David would be better out of the way. Out of the line of fire.

"Scuttle the little boat."

Nick was dumped on the deck on his side and lay there, motionless. The flunky went back down the ladder to carry out Ham's order, while Lyle, dragging Maggy by the hand, moved aft to poke at Nick with a booted foot.

"I hope he comes to in time to know who it is who's blowing his brains out."

The flunky reappeared, stepping onto the deck. Ham glanced at him, and he nodded. Then Ham turned to Lyle.

"Get us out of here."

"Aye, aye," Lyle said, grinning.

Releasing Maggy's hand, Lyle moved toward the controls, and seconds later the *Iris* was under way again. Maggy braced herself against the forward movement, gripping the metal rail beside her for support.

Ham had his pistol trained on Maggy. Almost at her feet, the flunky crouched over Nick.

"Where's the kid?" Ham asked, frowning.

"I sent him down to the cabin." Lyle spoke over his shoulder. He was in his element, the wind whipping his fair hair back away from his face, his expression relaxed. Lyle liked nothing better than being at the wheel of his yacht, and it was obvious that he was enjoying himself hugely.

"Get him!" Ham's order to the flunky reverberated like a shot. Maggy stood transfixed as the man obediently headed into the cabin after David.

"I don't want my boy watching while we blow these two away," Lyle objected, frowning.

"You are the stupidest . . ." Ham spoke through his teeth.

"The little shit was on the radio!" The flunky reappeared in the cabin doorway, hauling David after him with a fist hooked in the neck of his pajamas. David looked scared to death, but also oddly triumphant. Maggy's blood ran cold.

"Fuck!" Ham exploded, kicking the wooden rim of the deck, his face apoplectic as he turned on Lyle. "You stupid son of a bitch! You sent the kid to a cabin *where there's a radio?*"

"It's a CB. I can't believe . . ." Lyle glanced at David in a way that boded no good for him. "Did you raise anybody, son?"

The question was deceptively gentle. Still in the grip of the flunky, David shook his head.

"You see? No harm done," Lyle said to Ham, relaxing again.

"No harm done?" Ham was visibly livid. *"No harm done?* You're obsessed, you dumb shit. You're obsessed with a fucking kid who's not even yours, and you're going to drag us all down because of it! Well, not me. Not me! Do you hear, you stupid son of a bitch? *Not me!"*

Ham was standing beside Lyle by that time, practically yelling in his face. Without warning, his arm flashed up, and there was a deafening report. Maggy watched, thunderstruck, as Lyle was lifted off his feet and flung backward as if by an invisible giant hand. He hit the deck with a thud and lay flat on his back, motionless, face pale in the moonlight, eyes wide and staring, a tiny black hole in his forehead the only visible mark of harm. Beneath his head a dark liquid pool began to spread. . . .

Blood.

Ham had shot Lyle in the head. Even as Maggy registered it, David broke away from the flunky and ran to her side.

"Mom!"

"Don't look, David," she said, holding him close, pushing his face into her sweater.

Maggy caught her breath in horror as Ham turned his pistol on them. . . .

Nick exploded with a roar, coming up off the deck with his feet beneath him and launching himself at Ham. The sheer force of his body knocked the smaller man down. Ham's pistol flew from his hand and landed close to Maggy's feet.

Even as the flunky was running to Ham's rescue, Maggy wrenched herself away from David and scrambled for the pistol. She scooped it up and bounded forward, shoved the nozzle into the flunky's nape and pulled the trigger.

The gun bucked in her hand. The boom deafened her. Blood and matter splattered over the struggling figures like pulp from an exploding watermelon. The flunky crumpled to the deck. Maggy leaped over his fallen body and took a precious few seconds to gauge the relative positions of the men on the deck.

Ham was on top, his hands around Nick's throat. Nick, his face already purpling from lack of oxygen, was trying to heave Ham off him with great upward lunges of his body.

Maggy jammed the mouth of the pistol into Ham's spine.

"Ham," she said and meant it. "Let go, or die."

Ham froze. Then, after a long moment, his hands lifted from around Nick's neck.

"Maggy," he began uneasily, glancing at her over his shoulder.

"Back away from him, Magdalena." Nick was panting. "Back away from him, but keep the pistol on him. If he so much as looks at you funny, blow him to hell."

Maggy obediently backed away, both hands on the pistol now, holding it steady. Her feet were braced apart to keep her balance as the boat continued to surge forward with no one at the wheel. Her finger stayed curled around the trigger. Her eyes never left Ham as he got slowly to his feet and turned around, facing her. The deck beneath her feet was slippery with blood, Lyle's and the other man's.

All she had to do was squeeze just a little tighter on the trigger, and Ham's blood would wash the deck, too.

Staring at him over the motionless bodies, she remembered the night he had raped her in excruciating detail. She saw that he remembered it too. He licked his lips, and his eyes were wide with fear.

All she had to do was squeeze. . . .

A bright light caught her in its beam.

"Coast Guard!" came a stern voice. "Everybody freeze!"

Maggy glanced around to see a large white boat bearing down on them. The light shone directly into her face because the *Iris* and the Coast Guard vessel were approximately the same height.

"Magdalena!" Another voice came over the loudspeaker. "I see you and the kid, but where's Nicky?"

It was Link.

"Cavalry to the rescue," Nick said dryly, struggling to his feet. Ham, apparently realizing that the game was over, seemed to slump.

"Yo, little brother!" Link greeted Nick. Seconds later an armed, uniformed Coast Guardsman leaped onto the *Iris*'s deck.

Maggy lowered the pistol and glanced around for David. He came running, wrapping his arms around her waist.

They were safe.

Epilogue

*T*hree days later, Maggy rode with her son up the elevator that would take them to Nick's sixth-floor hospital room. It was around four o'clock in the afternoon, a Wednesday, and she had just picked him up from school. He had a wrapped present that he had made for Nick that day in school in his hands. Maggy had no idea what it was, and he would only shake his head when she asked.

Everyone said, and she agreed, that he had come through the horror remarkably well. He had already started the process of mourning for the father he had loved when Lyle had first "died" weeks before. Sunday night's tragic violence had not taken his father from him again: the man who had died on the deck of the *Iris* was not the man he had loved.

Maggy had tried to explain how Lyle's mind had grown ill; she told David it had to have been ill for him to have committed, and planned to commit, the crimes he had. But she didn't really understand herself, so she gave it up and called in a professional counselor to talk with David. After one session, the counselor pronounced David a "remarkably resilient child." He suggested that David continue to visit him regularly for a while, but the counselor did not expect that he would have any problems. David seemed to adapt well to changing circumstances, he said.

She had told David the truth about his parentage. He had heard Ham's remark about Lyle's being obsessed with "a kid who's not even yours" as well as everybody else on the boat that night had.

"Was what Uncle Ham said true? Wasn't Dad my father?" David had asked her on the way home from the police station, where they had all been taken to give statements about the events of the night.

Exhausted, drained, and worried about Nick, who had been conveyed straight to a hospital for surgery to remove the bullet that had lodged just beneath his right shoulder blade, Maggy had listened to the question and felt her stomach clench.

She had hesitated, her eyes troubled as they met his. Poor child, he looked as wiped out as she felt. His auburn hair stood up all over his head, his face was pale, and faint dark circles lodged beneath his eyes. He was still wearing the Batman pajamas under a blanket a kind policeman had given him to wrap around himself, and his feet were bare.

If nothing else, last night had proved that her precious boy was no longer entirely a child. He had asked, and he deserved the truth.

"No, Dad wasn't your father. Not your biological father, anyway."

He absorbed that. "But you're my mother. My real—I mean, biological—mother." His glance at her was just a little anxious.

Maggy nodded, emotion clogging her throat. He needed only to look in a mirror to be assured of that.

"Nick's my biological father, isn't he?"

Maggy's eyes widened on her son's face. Sometimes his perceptive abilities floored her.

"It didn't take a genius to figure it out," David said calmly, correctly interpreting her expression. "He is, isn't he?"

"David . . ." Maggy began, then answered simply, "yes."

"Does he know?"

"Yes. Yes, he knows."

"I thought so. He's been looking at me kind of weird, when he thought I didn't see."

"He loves you," Maggy said helplessly. She was not prepared for this, had not had time to think out what she needed to say. Somehow she had to help her son understand . . .

"It's okay, Mom," David said, patting her hand. "I don't mind. You made a mistake when you were young, and all that."

"You," Maggy said fiercely, wrapping her arms around him and holding him close, "were never a mistake. Never."

She had told Nick that David knew, of course, the very same day. But neither David nor Nick had addressed the matter to the other directly. Of course, hospital visits tended to be short and rather artificial, anyway. Nick would be released on Friday, and then they would all of them just have to take it from there.

But with no prompting from her, David had brought Nick a present. Maggy took that as a positive sign.

As soon as they stepped off the elevator, Maggy heard Link's booming voice. David heard it too and pleased her by quickening his step. He liked Link.

"Here's the *real* hero," Link proclaimed as David walked into the room. "We were already on the river when his Mayday came over the radio, but we had no idea where to look."

Maggy watched David beam with pride as she smiled a greeting at Link and *Tia* Gloria, who had been released from the same hospital only two days before and now was back as a visitor, bearing a big bouquet of daffodils for the invalid. Crossing to Nick, Maggy dropped a casual kiss on his bristly cheek and turned to look at Link.

"What I want to know is, why were you on the river in the first place? How could you have known that anything was going on?"

Tia Gloria said, "That was my doing. That night, I kept getting a bad feeling every time I thought about you. It was so strong that I tried to call you at Windermere at two o'clock in the morning. The phone rang and rang, but no one answered. I knew you were supposed to be there, with David and Nick. I *knew* something was wrong. So I got a message to Link."

Link picked up where she left off. "I drove over to Windermere, found the doors open, the lights on, and the house empty. I jumped back in my car and drove down to the dock and saw that Magdalena's little boat was gone. I knew you must be on the river somewhere. So I called the Coast Guard, and they picked me up. We were just starting the search when David's Mayday came through."

"I have one question," Maggy said, eyes twinkling as she looked at *Tia* Gloria. "Are you telling us that you sent, and Link received, a *psychic* message?"

"My dear," *Tia* Gloria responded, looking down her nose at Maggy, "when the matter is truly urgent, I use the telephone."

Everybody laughed. Then Link clapped Nick on the knee and said, "Gotta go, little brother. Some of us have to work for a living, you know."

"Tell Adams I'll be back—in a month or so," Nick said with a grin.

"I'll tell him." Link departed with a wave and an answering grin.

"I have to go too," *Tia* Gloria said, having deposited her flowers on a sunny window sill. "If you don't object, my dear, I think I'll run over to Windermere later this afternoon and collect Horatio. He must be badly stressed from all the excitement. He'll start to lose feathers, you know."

"Magdalena doesn't object at all," Nick replied for her in a fervent tone that made Maggy and David glance at each other and grin.

When *Tia* Gloria had left, David looked rather shyly at Nick. Nick smiled at him.

"What's that?" he asked, indicating the parcel in David's hand.

"I brought you a present," David said and held it out to him.

David moved closer to the bed as Nick unwrapped the gift with due care. Maggy watched his face, and Nick's.

When the paper came off, there was a silence so profound that Maggy glanced down to see just what kind of gift David had made. It was a pencil sketch of David, Maggy, and Nick standing arm in arm on the front porch of the farmhouse. They were smiling, obviously happy, obviously a family.

"Thank you, David," Nick said softly, and the look in his eyes as he smiled at his son brought a lump to Maggy's throat. Briefly she remembered David's hopeful painting of her and himself and Lyle in the rose garden. The pictures were strikingly similar in type: the happy family, the pastoral setting, the spilling sunshine.

The primary difference was that Maggy could make the wish expressed in this one come true.

She closed her eyes against the tears that suddenly threatened, and sent a tiny prayer winging skyward:

Thank you, Saint Jude.